# CLEANSED BY FIRE

## LAURIE ROCKENBECK

# CLEANSED BY FIRE

## LAURIE ROCKENBECK

BANE & BODKIN PRESS

REDMOND, WA

Copyright © 2018 by Laurie Rockenbeck

All rights reserved.

Published by Bane and Bodkin Press
Redmond, WA

No part of this book may be reproduced in any form or by any electronic or mechanical means, including information storage and retrieval systems, without written permission from the author, except for the use of brief quotations in a book review.

*This is a work of fiction. Any resemblance to persons living or dead is entirely coincidental.*

Cover Design by Mariah Sinclair

Ebook ISBN:  978-1-947234-15-4

Paperback ISBN: 978-1-947234-16-1

There is a myth that homeless youth have done something wrong, that they didn't want to follow the rules at home. That is not the case. They are strong and resilient. It is amazing they can get out of bed considering what they have gone through.

— Jocelyn Helland

**1**

———

Karen Hunter was doing her best to fight boredom-induced sleep. Then the guy she'd been following for the last week launched into a temper tantrum.

She couldn't hear anything from across the street, even with the window of her car rolled down. There was a silent-film sensibility to the scene as Thad Wagner kicked the living-room coffee table onto its side, scattering books and toys across the mauve plush carpet. He took aim at a fluffy purple bunny and kicked it out of the room. As he swung around, he stepped squarely onto one of the Lego blocks he'd knocked off the table.

Grabbing his foot with one hand, he hopped over to the sofa, which he missed by inches, and slid down its side to land hard on his ass. His movements were so overblown and dramatic that Karen could imagine the organ soundtrack that would play over it. The only thing that would make it popcorn-worthy would be a thick handlebar mustache and a subtitle card: Thad gets bad news.

This was the most emotion Thad had shown since Karen had started this whole shit-show of a gig. Even when he was playing with his kids, his face was a mask of animatronic-level happiness. Everything about him was fake. Smarmy. Nothing about his woodenness was illegal or worthy of siccing Child Protective Services on him. The mind-games, the hidden anger, the creepy stalker-like bullshit that Bernice, his ex-wife and Karen's client, had to put up with—that was much more difficult to prove.

Karen dropped her binoculars on the front passenger seat and peeled her sweat-soaked back from the vinyl of her ancient Honda. She needed to be closer to find out what he was so upset about, and she wanted to get it on record if only to remind herself that this was really happening.

The neighborhood was empty even though it was barely eight-thirty in the evening. Running across the street would draw attention, so Karen feigned nonchalance as she walked. As far as she could tell, there was no one outside, but there was always one busybody in every neighborhood —watching, listening, paying attention. Meddling.

Karen cut across the lawn and dropped to her haunches behind a large rhododendron, making sure she wasn't visible from the street. Twilight had fallen into a monochromatic blue-gray. Thad turned on the interior lights, which gave her a slight visual advantage.

She settled in, kneeling and leaning against the cool wooden shakes under the living room window. It was hot enough that Thad had opened the windows to let in the evening air. Karen lifted her phone so her camera could act as a periscope. Then she hit RECORD.

Surreptitious video recording was illegal. While she'd

spent her entire past career as a dominatrix living and working in the shade, this was the first time she'd broken the law so blatantly as a private investigator. *Why hadn't she chosen to become a nurse or a teacher instead?* For some reason, the only careers that called to her were ones that thrived in murky waters.

She watched as Thad got back on his feet and made a call. "Mm–hmm. I'll hold, sure." His jaw worked with the effort to be pleasant.

Thad paced back and forth in the living room, his phone pressed between his ear and shoulder, hair still wet from a recent shower. He righted the coffee table and picked up everything he'd knocked over.

For each of the last six nights, Thad had put the kids to bed, taken a shower, and gone out for the evening once a babysitter arrived. So far, he'd rotated his evenings between a strip club, a sketchy massage parlor, and a porn shop—the kind with questionable viewing booths and glory-holes hidden in their inky interiors. No need to follow him in for the details. No judgment from her about what he was doing inside.

Hiring a sitter and going out wasn't the problem here. What single parent didn't want to escape? Once a week, maybe, but he'd been out every night Karen had been tailing him. That indicated obsession.

She guessed, based on t-shirt and jeans, that he was heading to the strip club. When he had gone to the massage parlor and porn shop, he'd worn sweats. Karen followed him on her camera as he circled the living room. It was a long thirty seconds before the phone conversation picked up again.

"I already told you, I need a substitute here, ASAP." Thad stopped in the middle of the room, his back to the window. He straightened and put one hand on his hip. "No… no… that's not acceptable. I have to get to work. You can't drop me like this."

Karen couldn't make out what the person on the other end of the phone was saying. Thad's voice was layered in condescension and anger.

"What the fuck?" He spun to face the window. Karen sucked in her breath, praying he couldn't see her phone. If she was lucky, the glare from the window was reflecting enough that he couldn't see much outside. His eyebrows formed a dark V on his forehead, and his lips crushed together. "You're supposed to give me a day's warning so I can get a substitute here. Canceling like this last-minute is ridiculous. Can't you send anyone?"

Karen was finally seeing the angry Thad that Bernice had described time and time again. The Mr. Hyde to his public Dr. Jekyll. Thad had such a nice-guy halo floating over him, capturing this was almost too good to be true.

"Once again. Must I remind you that you are contractually bound to give me more than ten minutes' notice?" He ran a hand through his hair as he spun toward the stairs. "Hold on."

Tiny bare feet appeared at the top of the stairs. Chubby legs disappeared under a ruffled blue princess nightgown.

Thad held the phone to his chest and hissed, "Get the fuck back to bed."

*Whoa.* Karen had not expected him to talk like that to his little girl.

"Daddy, I'm thirsty." Her voice was sweet, plaintive.

*Poor little thing.*

"Get some water from the bathroom, and get back to your room. Now."

The tiny feet whirled around, making the cotton fabric of her gown swirl around her ankles as she raced away.

Thad spun away from the stairs, his jaw bulging and his face red. "I pay you people good money to be here. Are you going to pay me lost wages? Huh? What if I lose my job because you don't show up?" He stood still, listening, his hand on his hips. "That's not even enough to cover half of it. Give me a week free. Yes. I'm totally serious."

The dude had some nerve lying like that. He didn't have an evening job. The agency must know Thad was a litigation attorney. Though, given how poorly he'd done with the receptionist, Karen wondered how he'd ever won an argument at trial. Cheeky asshole for sure. Dude totally needed a good whipping. Karen stopped herself. That was her previous profession.

Thad strode over to the window, and Karen ducked down, heart racing. She dared not move, even though her little screen showed nothing except his belt buckle now. If he looked down now, she was done for.

"Seriously? You'd rather lose me as a client? Really? Well, fuck you."

He threw his phone hard against the sofa. It bounced off and onto the ground. He kicked the sofa and paced around the room.

Convincing anyone that the mellow and suave Thad Wagner was abusive and unstable had proven nearly impossible. He only showed that side of himself in the privacy of his home. In the whole week of following him around, this was the first sign of it.

Bernice had been right. Thad Wagner had a very nasty side to him. She had it on record. Unfortunately, she'd obtained it illegally. She couldn't show it to anyone, and it couldn't be used in a custody trial. If she could find out the name of the babysitting agency he was working with, maybe she could get them to testify about his anger.

Thad tiptoed up the stairs. If he wasn't going anywhere, Karen could probably head home for the evening. She retraced her steps back to her car and settled in for the drive back across the lake. She was passing his house when the front door opened and Thad strode to his car. She parked again up the street, then knelt on her seat backwards and peered through the rear window. What the hell was he up to? The kids were asleep upstairs. Would he really leave them home alone, without anyone to watch over them?

He stood in his driveway, hand poised above the car door handle as he looked up at the second-story windows—the children's bedrooms. He made a face and headed back toward the front door. Then stopped and went back to his car. This time, he climbed in and zoomed away.

*Fuck no. Don't do it… Don't leave your kids alone… You don't leave kids home alone. Ever.*

What kind of guy would do that? Every other night, he'd waited for the sitter before leaving, so this was different. Was his impulsive behavior so out of control that he couldn't skip a single night out? The guilty expression on his face was enough for her to know that he wasn't going out for milk.

This should've been good news for Bernice, but at what

price? Two children were home alone—a thirsty little girl and a sleeping tyke. She waited until after Thad's taillights had disappeared before moving her car into a space directly in front of the house. Her instincts as a mom had kicked in. She had to stay close.

She rolled the window down to let the air in. She made a note in her official notebook to keep track of the time. It had been five minutes since he left. He was usually gone about two hours.

She texted Bernice to let her know Thad had left the kids home alone. Bernice didn't answer right away, so Karen settled in with a book. The kids were asleep. What could happen?

KAREN SHIFTED and wiggled in her seat to bring back some sensation in her legs. Surveillance could bite her in the ass, almost literally. She was never taking another job that required her to sit in her car for more than an hour, even if she was getting caught up on her reading. She checked her watch. Again. How could it only have been half an hour since Thad had taken off?

As an ex-dominatrix, Karen didn't judge people about their kinks or desires, but going out every night while leaving your kids home with a sitter? She felt fine judging them on how they treated their kids. She would be as annoyed about his leaving the kids even if he was bowling or watching a movie. Why have kids if you were going to leave them home alone? Sure, their being asleep by the time he left was no excuse. None whatsoever. *Scuzzbag.*

Thad Wagner didn't come across as a bad father. Not overtly, anyway. Emotional abuse wasn't something visible from a distance like this. He kept them clothed, fed, and physically safe. Child Protective Services had a low bar for what constituted child safety, and he'd certainly exceeded it.

Karen's client was Thad's ex-wife, Bernice Wagner, a high-powered attorney who was a friend, and the only reason she was on this gig.

Bernice hadn't managed to get a nanny-cam into her old house for a really good close-up of what was going on inside. Karen was unwilling to sneak inside with one. Breaking and entering was still breaking and entering, even if a licensed private investigator does it. It had been a huge disappointment to learn that most of the fun things that a P.I. did on television were actually illegal. Karen had lived skirting the law most of her life already. Sneaking a video she didn't plan on sharing with anyone was one thing. Breaking and entering to install an illegal video cam was a whole other level.

Bernice was convinced she'd lost the drawn-out custody battle because the judge didn't like strong women, let alone strong female attorneys. He had given Thad full custody. Bernice wound up with weekends twice a month and had vowed to get her kids back. The re-trial was coming up, and his leaving the kids home alone was exactly what they had needed to prove he wasn't the perfect father everyone made him out to be.

Sophie texted her, asking her to call, and Karen welcomed the diversion. Talking would help keep her awake.

Sophie picked up right away. "Mom? When are you getting home? Dad's here, but he's grumpy."

*Grumpy* was family code for *depressed*. She and her kids had developed an elaborate system for talking about him while he was in the room.

"Sorry, sweetie, I'm gonna be super-late again. Is he okay grumpy or bad grumpy?" Karen appreciated her ex's willingness to stay over when she was working late, but it was hard on her kids when he was at the bottom of one of his depressive cycles.

"I guess you could say okay. He's being boring. Watching a fishing show on Netflix."

"Is there something specific you wanted?"

"I want to go to the beauty school on Capitol Hill tomorrow and get my hair done."

The word choice was another clue to her daughter's clever mind. "Done? Cut? Dyed? What do you mean 'done'?"

"Ugh. Mom. Why can't you say yes to things without going through all the semantic variations?"

Sophie had such lovely, long dark hair that Karen didn't want her to mess with it. Not that the girl would listen to her advice about it. "I don't really care much what you do to your hair. It grows back. Make sure you consider everything coming up in the next couple of months before doing anything drastic."

"Like what?"

"I don't know… if you're going to shave one side off and color the other side rainbow, you should think how it might affect your school activities. Speech and debate? Orchestra? Don't they have dress codes?"

"You really think I would shave off my hair?"

"You weren't specific. When are you going?"

"All day, probably. I can have Dad drop me for the bus on his way in to work if you need to sleep in. He will stay the whole night if I ask him to."

"Not that he needs to be there with you."

"Tell him that."

Karen could hear the eye-roll in Sophie's voice. As much as Robbie annoyed Sophie, she adored her father with a girlish charm she no longer had for Karen. Karen tapped the speaker setting to on and flipped to the Find My Friends app on her phone. Sophie was at home, where she was supposed to be.

"Who you going with?"

"Friends."

*Of course.* The nebulous answer had become Sophie's favorite and pushing back against it was like shoving into a brick wall. Besides, she was probably going with Jamie and some of the other kids they were hanging with these days. Jamie's parents, who lived in the neighborhood, had kicked him out of the house in the spring. He'd found a band of other homeless youth to hang out with.

Karen begged him to come live with them every time she saw him. She'd made up a bedroom in the basement and told him it was his. He had always refused the offer. Sophie jumped in to help him as much as possible. Karen's experience as a homeless teen, apparently, didn't count when it came to Jamie's experience.

Whenever Karen reminded Sophie about those years, Sophie rolled her eyes and talked back. *"Mom, that was, like twenty years ago and in Montana. This is now. Seattle. Totally diff."*

Karen didn't like it even after she and Sophie had negotiated a détente. Sophie could hang out with Jamie as long as she checked in with Karen and left her phone on so Karen could track her whereabouts via GPS. It was way better to pretend to be cool to remain close than to push either teen away.

"Fine. Friends. Whatever. Regular rules apply, is all."

Sophie paused. "Of course, Mom. Regular rules. Phone is charging now."

Karen hung up and settled back into her seat. The night was going by awfully slowly. She had another hour and a half before Thad was likely to show back home, if not more. And Bernice had yet to respond to her text. She'd wait a little longer before calling CPS.

***

THE BLARING screech of a fire alarm made Karen jump in her seat. Her arm hit the steering wheel, sending a jabbing pain up to her shoulder. Sound traveled in weird ways, and she couldn't immediately tell where it was coming from. Blinking away her drowsy malaise, she jumped out of the car and homed in on the house.

*The kids.* Bernice's kids were home alone in Thad's house. And smoke was billowing out of the front window where she'd hidden only an hour before. She dialed 911 as she sprinted toward the door. "House fire at 876 West Spinasse Street," she said. "I'm on the outside, I know there are two kids alone on the inside."

The response came quickly: "We're dispatching fire and police to your location. Do not enter the building."

Karen pressed her forehead against the glass of the front door. Lorelei stood, hands clamped to her ears, in the doorway to the kitchen. The bottom edge of her princess nightie fluttered in the breeze from the window.

Karen rang the doorbell. The alarm blared so loudly there was no way the little girl could hear it. Karen ran to the open window and pushed. The interior lock kept her from opening it more than a couple of inches, barely enough for air and smoke to escape.

"Lorelei," Karen yelled, "I'm a friend of your mom's. Come open the door."

Flickering light from beyond indicated something flaming away on the stove top. Smoke rolled along the ceiling like thick, angry storm clouds. Lorelei continued to ignore Karen in favor of the fireworks in the kitchen.

Where were the neighbors? Lights were on all round, but people weren't coming outside to investigate.

Karen listened for sirens. How long did it take for the alarm to get from dispatch until firefighters were out the door? The glass on the front door was too high up for her to break and reach around to open the lock. She raced back to her car, emptied her tool bag onto the back seat, and grabbed her lock-pick kit. She thrust her picks into the lock.

"Hey, what's going on?" a woman's voice asked.

Karen glanced over her shoulder. An older woman in a blue track suit stood at the edge of the driveway, hand on her throat. "There's a fire inside," Karen said. "The kids are inside alone. I'm picking the lock to get in."

"I've called 911." The woman held up a phone in her gnarled fingers.

"I did, too. I gotta get them out of the smoke. The fire

department might take too long." Karen turned back to the lock, grateful that Thad hadn't flicked the dead bolt.

The neighbor approached and hovered behind Karen as she worked. *Great, an audience.*

"Are you picking the lock? With real lock picks? Isn't that illegal?"

*Not only an audience but a talkative one.* "Bernice is a friend." That was all the explanation Karen could give at the moment. She had to get the door open.

"Oh. Well, you know, I have a key. I'll go get it."

"That would be awesome," Karen said. By the time the woman got back, Karen would probably be inside, and, if not, the key would be useful.

She closed her eyes and imagined the tumblers moving out of the way as she held them up with the pick and worked them one, by one. She opened it in less than a minute.

Karen ran into the kitchen, the neighbor close on her heels. There was a fire in a pot on the stove. Clouds of smoke roiled out of it. The flames from the gas range licked around the pot. Karen shut off the burner and slammed a lid over the flames. Then she turned the fan on high to start clearing out the smoke.

"Who are you?" Lorelei asked, blinking and coming out of her trance.

"A friend of your mom's," Karen said. "We need to get out of here, sweetie."

Tears streaked Lorelei's face. "I was making pepmint coco like Daddy does. The pepmint spilled. I didn't know what to do."

On the counter next to the stove was a bottle of milk, a

container of Cadbury's hot chocolate, and a bottle of peppermint schnapps. The booze was open and half empty. Lorelei must have watched her father put it in hot chocolate before.

Karen dropped to her knees in front of the little girl. "It's okay. We need to get you outside and away from the smoke. Let's get your brother, all right?"

"He's in bed."

"No I'm not." Jason, the little boy, stood in the doorway to the living room wearing his footed Bugs Bunny pajamas.

The neighbor lady had returned and followed Karen inside. She held out her hands to Jason.

He grinned and launched himself into her arms. "Gracie!"

"Let's all get outside and away from the smoke and let the firefighters figure out what's going on." Karen held out her hand to Lorelei and led them outside. She helped Lorelei onto the hood of her car. Jason resisted leaving the other woman's arms and leaned in even closer against her. The sirens announced the fire trucks were close.

"I'm Grace Witherspoon," the older lady said, offering her hand around the cuddling child.

"I'm Karen Hunter." She fished out a card and handed it to Grace. "Have you ever noticed Thad leaving the kids home alone like this before?"

Grace's eyes widened and her attention shifted to the empty driveway. "Oh, dear. I can't say that I have, but I don't really pay much attention. Thad made it clear my services were no longer required." She casually stroked the back of Jason's head. He sighed and leaned into her shoulder.

"I take it you sat with them a lot?" Karen asked.

"Nanny. Until the divorce," she said. "I say hello when they're outside when I can. Thad prevents any other interaction."

Jason sniffled into her neck as his thumb disappeared into his mouth.

"Have there been any unusual interactions between him and the kids?" Karen asked, hoping for an additional witness on Bernice's behalf.

Grace eyed the children and shook her head almost imperceptibly. "Perhaps you can call me and we can chat after this is all cleared up. When the kids are out of earshot."

"No, of course, you're right. We can talk tomorrow," Karen said. "Can you keep an eye on them while I call Bernice?"

Grace sat next to Lorelei on the hood and put her free arm around the girl's shoulders. Lorelei leaned into her side with as much comfort as Jason showed with the woman. Karen moved herself far enough away that the kids couldn't hear her and dialed Bernice. She picked up on the first ring.

"I'll be over there as soon as I can. Probably another ten or so," Bernice said, after Karen filled her in. "I started over as soon as I got your text."

"That was a while ago, what took so long?"

"I was busy. I called CPS already. Go ahead and tell the police you've called me, and I'll be there soon. They can't get anyone from CPS over there any faster than I can get there at this point."

Karen clicked off the call and turned to the elderly neighbor.

"Grace, I want to go inside and get a photo of the mess in the kitchen," Karen said, stinging from her earlier insensitivity earlier. Talking about the dad in front of the kids was not cool. The last thing they needed was for the toddler version of any smack-talk to get back to him and his attorney.

Grace nodded and smiled knowingly.

The kitchen was still smoky, but Karen could breathe easily enough. She took several quick snaps, highlighting the booze on the counter. Leaving it where the kids could get at it and then abandoning them for whatever reason was not going to impress any judge.

Karen returned to the Grace and the kids. Jason finally pulled away from Grace, stood on the hood of the car, and waved at the firetrucks as they pulled up.

Karen met the firemen at the edge of the driveway and pointed them in the right direction. A team went in with a handheld extinguisher. Karen leaned against the hood of the car and waited for the cops to show up.

Lorelei tapped her on the shoulder. "How do you know Momma?"

"We're friends. We've known each other for a long time. Since before you were born."

"Are you a lawyer, too?"

"Nope. I'm what they call a private investigator."

**2**

———

KAREN WOKE TO THE LAST GURGLING WHEEZE OF THE coffeemaker pushing the last few drops into the carafe. The smoky smell of cooking bacon layered in with the rich earthiness of coffee drew her to the kitchen.

"What time did you get in?" Robbie turned the bacon in the frying pan.

"Late. After two a.m. Wrote up my report and then crashed." Karen poured herself coffee and settled into a stool at the counter. The newspaper was open to the front page.

POLICE DRAGGING FEET ON YOUTH KILLINGS screamed at her in all-caps. Below the headline was a photo of Court Pearson standing in front of a tent, shielding a crime scene from view. This was the same photo they'd used a couple days ago when the body of a sixth teenager had been found. Court held his hands up, fingers spread wide in a "not now" gesture. The sunlight ringed his head in a halo effect, making his light brown hair appear almost white.

Karen touched Court's photo, pretending she was working a wrinkle out of the paper as she ran her fingertip along the side of his strong, square jaw. She had met him on one of the worst days of her life—the day she found her favorite client hanging dead in her studio. The week that followed had been a whirlwind of accusations, discovery, and trauma.

In the end, Court had saved her life and that of her kids, which thrust him into white-knight status. A guy being a cop was usually a deal-breaker for her. Her impulsive urge to kiss him was, thankfully, neatly rebuffed. The reality was, he had no desire to be with a pro-domme any more than she had to be with a cop. And yet? That one kiss was nothing short of amazing.

Their worlds would never mesh. Then or now. Private investigators were marginally above sex workers in the most-loathed professions by cops. While her former profession skirted the law in one direction, her new one did it in another. She made a mental note to remove the video of Thad Wagner from her phone. After the debacle of the previous night, it wouldn't be needed and it was a liability to her now.

She skimmed the article which excoriated the local police for not finding the serial killer who had begun leaving young bodies in local dog parks in the area after the new year. Nearly eight months had gone by since the first had been found, and now the count was six dead.

Newspaper headlines dubbed him the "Dog Park Killer," but the reports were skimpy on details. The photos of all the victims were lined up in a row at the bottom of the article. Six boys aged fourteen to twenty.

Karen had a sudden urge to hug her son close. At thirteen, Brian was not much of a snuggle-bunny any more. She could count on a good hug from him when no one was around to witness it. He was thousands of miles away at summer camp. At least he was safe from all of this. The photographs of the boys in the newspapers were hauntingly similar to his latest school picture—happy, smiling, innocent looking young men who had no way of knowing what was in their future.

The article finished with the now-familiar boilerplate about the lead detective on the case, Court Pearson. The short paragraph reminded readers this was the same officer who was hospitalized for two months after being gravely injured in a major methamphetamine bust in downtown Seattle. That, and he was SPD's only transmale homicide detective.

Robbie waved a plate of eggs, bacon, and hash browns under her nose. "Earth to Karen..." Her ex-husband's voice took on a sing-song quality.

Karen shoved the paper to the side to make room for the plate. "Thanks. I guess I'm a bit dazed from last night."

"You know, Sophie would be okay being home alone in the evenings. Not that I mind spending time with her. Or mind being here. I hate my apartment." Robbie piled food on his plate and joined her at the counter.

"Is Sophie in Seattle already?" Karen glanced again at the paper next to her. All the victims were young men. And homeless. Karen tamped down the helicopter mom that threatened to whir into life. Sophie was a girl. She had a home.

"I took her to Redmond to catch a bus a while ago. Came back to make sure you were okay."

"You know," Karen said, "there's no real reason for you to stay the night unless you want to."

"Maybe we should move away from here." He nodded toward the vast woods beyond the back yard. The greenbelt was a wonderland for kids in the neighborhood, but it had been a source of vulnerability for them the previous year when Karen's stalker invaded their home, shot their dog, and threatened to kill her and the kids.

"I seriously doubt I'll have another crazy like that in my life any time soon—if ever. There are too many good memories in those woods. Besides, switching schools? Not gonna make our kids go through that." She shoved a forkful of crisp potato into her mouth. Robbie was a hell of a good cook. "The kids are fine. I really appreciate you being so willing to hang with her all these extra days this week."

He gave a little laugh and leaned in closer so he could drop his voice. "I snuck into her room before starting breakfast. She's all young and innocent when she's sleeping. So vulnerable."

Karen put her hand on his and squeezed.

"You know," Robbie continued, "you don't have to work. I can give you more money each month."

Karen couldn't imagine not working. She'd put aside most of the money she had made as a professional dominatrix for Sophie's and Brian's college funds. What they didn't spend would go into her retirement account. And while she still had significant savings she could draw upon, Karen still needed to earn something to pay daily expenses. Living off her ex was not something she would do.

"I know. I appreciate your willingness to support us. And I appreciate everything you do. But…" Karen left the rest unsaid. There was no reason to rub in the fact that she couldn't count on him, not when he disappeared into clouds of depression for months at a time. He worked eight months of the year, making oodles of money before crashing into the depths of wherever he went right along with the sun from October to February. The painful truth was he should move south during the winter months to avoid the seasonal depressions. They were like clockwork, and yet, his excuse was he wanted to be near his kids. Near her.

Karen cleared her throat and her head of the circular problems that had plagued them for fifteen years. "But … I'll tell you one thing. I am never taking another surveillance job again. Hated every second of it."

"Don't say never. You know how that ends up."

She laughed. When she was in her teens, she was never going to have kids, she was never going to have a house in the suburbs, she was never going to have a car. The list of things she was never going to do and had ended up doing was long. She had few regrets.

The doorbell rang, bright and cheery. She waved Robbie back onto the kitchen stool next to hers. Her baggy sweats and rumpled t-shirt were decent enough for anyone this time of morning.

She raised herself on tiptoes and peered through the glass top of her front door. Maria Wells stood on her stoop. Her eyes were closed as if in prayer and she clutched a rolled-up newspaper to her chest. Karen pulled herself away from the glass.

This was interesting. Maria had led an ugly campaign against Karen for months after the local media had filled their little cul-de-sac with their vans and sensationalistic coverage. After trying to rally her neighbors to force Karen to move, Maria had given up when the majority made it clear they did not care about Karen's "sordid lifestyle." They had known her for fifteen years as Sophie's and Brian's mother, and the woman who made the best peanut-butter pie on the planet—or at least in their neighborhood.

Maria had retreated into her own private hell of a home. They hadn't spoken for months. There was only one reason she would be at Karen's doorstep—her son Jamie. Karen took a deep breath and opened the door.

Maria swung around and met Karen's eyes for the first time in months. Maria swayed in front of her, the look of anger and judgment she'd been sporting for months replaced by something Karen had seen so many times on her clients. Need. Longing. Helplessness.

"Karen," she said, her voice an echo of her usual braying alto. "Thank you for opening the door to me. You have every right to ignore me after what I've done to you."

New wrinkles and dramatic weight loss gave Maria a gaunt, unhealthy appearance. Her once-lustrous black hair, usually kept neatly tied into a bun, hung lank and dull around her face. Karen stifled her initial response to reach out and hug her. Why be kind to this woman who'd inflicted so much misery? "What do you want, Maria?"

Maria half-laughed and half-sobbed. She covered her

mouth with the back of her hand. "I deserve all your anger. I know I do. Can I come inside? Please?"

Karen spread her arm across the doorway to block Maria's entry. "Why? Why would you think you would be welcome in my home? After all that you've done to us."

Maria's hands twisted around the newspaper. "Because I know you care about Jamie."

*Jamie.* Sophie's best friend since they were toddlers. "I do. Do *you*?"

"You're a private investigator now, right?"

"News travels, eh?" Karen had only told one other person in the neighborhood about her new career.

Maria cast a glance behind her. "Please let me in. Don't you have an office where we can talk?"

"You don't want anyone in the neighborhood to see you fraternizing with the enemy?"

Now that kids were being killed, the woman was finally worried about the son she'd kicked out months before? A real threat sometimes brought people to their senses. Maria drew in a shuddering breath. She was barely keeping it together.

"Please, Karen. I need your help."

Karen considered the other woman a moment longer before relenting. If this were her own kid they were talking about, she'd probably fall apart, too. Of course, she'd never consider kicking either of her kids to the curb. She stepped aside to make room for the other woman to pass. "Come on down."

"I like what you've done in here, Karen," Maria said as Karen opened the door to her basement office. "It's so modern."

"I don't generally meet people here," Karen said. "Most of my clients are attorneys. This space is for me. To keep my work separate and to give me a place where I can be alone to do it."

Her workplace was nothing like one of those high-rise offices used by fancy television PIs. Karen had initially thrown it together to meet the inspection for a database company only law enforcement, journalists, and private investigators had access to. A serious guy in a suit had come to her house, asked her a dozen questions, and verified she had a shredder and a lock on the door before she could even log on to the site.

On her teal metal desk was a simple computer with three monitors, all white.  Under the window, a trim cupboard hid her printer and supplies from view. Book-shelves and a locking file cabinet filled one wall. The room radiated calmness.

Karen pointed to the grey nubuck chair across from her desk as she lowered herself in its ergonomic big brother. "Have a seat. Why are you here?"

Maria lowered herself gingerly onto the edge of the chair and spread the newspaper she was carrying open to the latest headline. Karen ran her palms along the front page from four days before. It was old news, and this morn-ing's update was fresh in her mind.

"You believe Jamie is in danger?" she asked.

Maria clasped her hands in front of her and held them

to her chest. "I think he is the next victim. I think the killer already has him."

"Why?" Karen asked. "What makes you so certain?"

"Because. I haven't heard from him since Friday."

As far as Karen knew, Jamie hadn't had any contact with his parents since they tossed him out on the street in March. "You mean you've been talking to him all along?"

"Well, I haven't really spoken to him since... since he left. He's come home a few times, snuck into the house to get a few things. He leaves me notes to let me know what he's taken. And, well, he texts me every once in a while. And I text him daily. I have to delete them from my phone so Mitch doesn't see them. I also track him through my Starbucks account. And... I've seen him a few times when he's here with Sophie."

Karen kept her face still. How could Maria keep her distance, knowing her son was so close? Karen hosted a sleepover for a few street kids every Wednesday night, including Jamie. He had refused to come live with her, but he had agreed to stay overnight once a week as a compromise. When he asked to bring friends, she shrugged aside her initial reservations about having strangers in her home. They were all teens. She could handle a bunch of teens. So far, everyone Jamie brought with him had appreciated a night in a real home.

"You haven't come over even though you knew he was here."

"I wouldn't have been welcome."

"You've been watching?"

"I use binoculars."

"You've been watching my house?"

Maria closed her eyes and nodded. "I know you've been keeping Jamie here, safe for one night every week. The occasional text is not something I can count on. I put money into the Starbucks account for him each week. I also put money on his ORCA card. He hasn't used either since Friday. And he rides the bus every single day."

"I didn't know you were keeping such close tabs on him."

"I do all I can do without Mitch knowing. I have to help Jamie where I can, but Mitch would be furious if he knew how much I've been doing."

Karen loathed Maria's husband on any number of levels. She put up with him the way neighbors put up with each other for general peacekeeping efforts. He had railed at Jamie and Maria in public, calling them names and ordering them around. Karen could imagine what he might be like behind closed doors when no one was watching.

"And you put up with that?"

Maria stiffened. "I can only do so much. You don't understand what it's like for me. You have your own life. Your own career. Your own money. Mitch loves Jamie. He really does. And yet, he won't *accept* Jamie until he's cured."

"Cured? You mean, no longer gay?"

"Well… yes. We've offered to take him to a place that will help him. There's a place up in Shoreline that he refuses to go to."

"Places like that do more harm than good."

"That hardly matters at the moment." Maria fell back into her chair and scrubbed at her face with her hands, pushing them together into a prayer position in front of her heart. "Karen, I want you to find my son and save him from this maniac." She smoothed the newspaper flat and slammed her palm down on top of the headline.

What was the likelihood that Jamie was in real danger? Karen had last seen him on Wednesday as usual, but she didn't keep tabs on him daily.

"You honestly think Jamie is with the Dog Park Killer?"

"He uses his Starbucks card and ORCA pass every day. He hasn't used either since Friday. He usually buys something. A drink, a sandwich. *Something.* And he always goes somewhere on the bus." She spread her fingers out wide to emphasis how clear a point she was making. "There's been *nothing* at all since Friday."

"What did the police say when you called to file a missing-persons report?"

Maria's lips tightened. "They took a report. They added it to the pile, I guess. They promised to investigate, but what is one boy to them?"

"Did you tell them you kicked him out months ago, or that he was missing as of Friday?"

"Just since Friday. We knew he was okay for sure until then."

*Really? How okay can anyone be while living on the street?* Karen held back the snark, as getting into it with Maria wouldn't solve anything.

"I ask him to stay with us, you know, every time he's here. He refuses. He appreciates the weekly shower, meal, laundry. He says that living in a pack is safer for them all."

Maria nodded as if it made sense for her son to put himself at risk for others. "Has he ever asked about us? About me?"

Karen didn't need to rub salt into the woman's wounds.

Jamie hated his father with a passion. He'd been less vitriolic about his mother. "He doesn't hate you, Maria. If anything, he sees you as weak and under Mitch's control."

"He's right. It's time for me to do the right thing, Karen. I need you to find my son before he's murdered. Once I have him back safe and sound, I'm never letting him go again."

"Well, honestly? I think you are overreacting," Karen said. "Jamie has gone silent for a couple days at a time before this. It's not unusual for him to drop off the grid or go with friends on road trips for music gigs. A couple of weeks ago, he lost his phone charger. It's way more likely he went off with friends or his phone died than he's been kidnapped by a serial killer."

Karen never pressed Jamie hard for the details of his occasional disappearances. She was afraid of the answers he might give. She wondered who was being weak. If she'd pushed him a little harder on how he spent his time, she might have a fast and easy answer for Maria.

"As a matter of fact," Karen said, "Sophie mentioned he was heading down to Portland for a gig with his trio. That was Friday or Saturday night? He's probably still down there crashed on someone's sofa."

Maria shook her head vigorously. "No. No. You're wrong. I *know*. In my heart." She spread her fingers wide over her chest. "Something is wrong. My heart aches, Karen. Maybe it's mother's intuition. I don't know. It's there and it's strong. You have to believe me. I never felt this the whole time he has been gone."

Karen didn't *have* to believe anything, especially a woman riddled with guilt. Jamie was probably safe in Portland. And yet… there were undeniable similarities between the victims and Jamie. They were all young males. Homeless. Blond. Elfin. Of course that could be said of hundreds of kids.

Likely Jamie was off with friends as planned. Karen bet he would show up the following night with a group of strays as usual. Reading too many startling and scary headlines could make anyone assume the worst.

There was a huge conflict of interest inherent in this case, too. Jamie was her daughter's best friend. They'd been playmates since they were babies, and Karen loved Jamie as if he were her own. Almost. She would never understand parents who thought it was okay to kick their kids out unless they were being destructive to others in the home. Even then, she'd find a way to help them, not just leave them on the streets to fend for themselves.

"Why come to me? It wasn't that long ago you were trying to get the homeowner's association to get us kicked out of the neighborhood."

Maria bowed her head and focused on her clasped hands in her lap. "I am sorry, Karen. I shouldn't have treated you like that. It was wrong." Her voice quavered as she spoke. After a long moment, she lifted her head. Her eyes shimmered with tears. "Please accept my apology for judging you so harshly. I need help."

If Karen saw auras, Maria's would be streaming with whatever color stood for pain and earnestness. Why wasn't the obligatory "no worries" slipping from her lips? Holding a grudge against the other woman wouldn't get her anywhere, but Karen wasn't quite ready to forgive her.

Tracing a teen would be a completely different task from

tracing an adult. She'd start with the Starbucks and ORCA cards. At least the bus system kept track of each bus he took. There wasn't much else to start with, and Karen had never done a skip trace on a kid before. All the tools she knew about wouldn't be very useful finding someone without a credit, job, or rental history.

She'd have to call her P.I. mentor, Maggie, and pick her brain about how to proceed. It always helped to talk through the process with the more experienced P.I.

"Do you have a budget for this?" she asked. "If I decide I can't handle this, or if I run into snags, I'll want to pass you off to someone more experienced or hire some help."

Maria slumped down further into her seat. She shook her head and sucked in her lips. "I've been scrimping cash from our grocery budget and putting it onto a credit card Mitch doesn't know about to pay for the Starbucks and ORCA card. There's barely enough to cover that. Or to pay you either. If you'd let me pay over time or something…"

Karen couldn't say yes to Maria right away. A small streak of sadism that had carried her as a dominatrix wanted the other woman to squirm at her mercy for a while. "I'll let you know tomorrow what I am willing to do. Frankly, I think he'll show up here tomorrow night as usual."

"Please, Karen. I'm begging you to start now. Before it's too late."

"What have you done to find him so far?"

"I didn't think driving around town would make any sense. I asked the youth pastor at our church to let me know if he showed up at our shelter in Seattle."

"Maria. There are hundreds of kids on the street in

Seattle right now. Maybe thousands, I don't really know how many. The last victim was found on Friday. Four days ago. The last one was six weeks before that."

Was it true that serial killers increased their frequency as time went on? The captions under photos of the six victims gave their names, the dates and where they were found. The first victim was found was late last year.

"Everything points to a significant break between the deaths."

"The police have said nothing about how long he's keeping them before he kills them." Maria dropped an accusing index finger on the paper.

"Exactly my point. It could be hours. It could be weeks. In any case, that means we still have time, Maria. Jamie's been gone for four *days*. We don't even know that he's actually missing. He's gone offline several times since you kicked him out."

Statistics suggested that Jamie was somewhere safe, not in the clutches of a serial killer. Statistics would also suggest that Thad Wagner's kids should have been safe for two hours alone in their house, too.

**3**

———

As soon Maria was out of her house, Karen texted Jamie. With any luck, he'd check in with her soon and settle any questions about where he might be. Prove he was safe. The last time he'd gone to Portland, he'd stayed with friends in a crappy little flophouse without electricity. His phone went uncharged the whole time, and she'd worried about him for days.

The previous weekend, she'd been so wrapped up in following Bernice's scuzzball of an ex around that she hadn't even given Jamie a thought. Maybe she had become too complacent about his circumstances. It wasn't unusual for a week to pass by without seeing him. She didn't want to buy into Maria's paranoia, but the similarities between the victims and Jamie's overall appearance were too many to ignore.

Robbie handed her a fresh cup of coffee as she returned to the kitchen.

"What did Maria want?"

Normal confidentiality rules did not apply in this case. If Maria or Jamie were complete strangers, Karen would have been obliged to keep mum. Her family was too close to Jamie for her to not tell them about what was going on. Besides, Sophie would be her first prime source for information on Jamie. They were best friends.

Karen stepped up next to Robbie at the double sink to rinse and dry while he washed the remaining breakfast dishes. She filled him in on Maria's theory as they worked.

"To go from kicking your kid out for being gay to suddenly worrying about him being in the clutches of a serial killer…" Robbie made air circles with his finger near his temple and whistled.

"I'm not sure how worried to be. I should have insisted he stay with us. And yet, he has gone silent for a few days at a time before."

"You don't *really* think there's any chance he's been taken by a serial killer, do you? Like you said, they found the latest victim a couple of days ago. Hasn't it been every six weeks?" Robbie rinsed his hands. "Besides, things like this don't happen to people you know."

She leaned against the sink. "Really? After all we've been through this last year?"

"That was *totally* different. Besides, having something freaky happen once means it's not likely to happen a second time, right?"

"You really think that?" Every time Robbie mentioned Berkeley Drummond's death and the subsequent attack on her and Brian, the hair on her arms and along her neck prickled.

Robbie wiped the sink clean with a sponge as she rinsed the last dish. "Nah, I guess not, but there are so many kids out there. The chances this guy would pick Jamie out of all of them? It's gotta be super low."

Karen wanted Robbie to be right. "I'm choosing to believe he's in Portland with friends."

"I'm a big fan of statistics. In this case, the odds are certainly in his favor," Robbie said. "They have to be."

"Jamie's being in Portland over the weekend would totally explain his lack of contact."

"How are you gonna work this while following the dweeb around?"

Following Thad Wagner was another weird case she'd felt okay discussing with Robbie. Years ago, she and Robbie used hang out a lot with Bernice and Thad. They lived in the same neighborhood, shared meals, hiked together during the summers, and skied together during the winters.

Shortly after Sophie was born, Karen and Robbie moved to Redmond from their little bungalow in Seattle. Time and distance, plus the rapid changes children brought to their schedule, created a natural distance between the couples. Both Bernice and Thad were lawyers focused on their careers with no time for kids. Bernice put off having kids for as long as possible.

Bernice's career took her on a different trajectory than Thad's, and they eventually split. Karen and Bernice remained close friends, and Bernice handled Karen's legal work. When Karen switched careers, Bernice was there to help her along.

Robbie had been asleep when Karen had gotten home the previous night so he wasn't up on the latest. She filled him in, and added, "It could not have worked out better for Bernice. CPS showed and handed the kids straight over to her. He returned to find his street lined with police cars and firetrucks and his kids cuddling their mom."

"Seriously? He is not the guy I used to know." Robbie leaned against the counter, arms crossed over his chest. "They were always heading for divorce. But leaving his kids home alone like that? Who does that?"

"I know, right?" Karen hooked the frying pan she'd dried on the ceiling rack. She filled a glass with water and focused on the back yard. Aspen was asleep on her side under the shade of a tree. Poor dog had a permanent limp after being shot.

The swing set they'd installed when Sophie was three was faded and unused. Piles of pine needles and broken branches from a recent storm nearly covered its base. It was time to pass the set on to someone with younger kids. Kids who still spent time playing in their own back yards.

Robbie nudged her with his upper arm. "Aspen's slowing down, isn't she?"

"Yup. And, the yard needs work."

"I'll come back in the evening, when it cools down. Mow. Do some weeding. If you want."

"That would be nice," Karen said turning to face him. "You're an awesome ex, you know that, right?"

"I do." Robbie kissed her on the lips. A light, friendly peck. "So you'd only be on one case at a time? That seems sensible to me."

"Well... I still have a backlog of background checks to run for Bernice. The regular work she hired me for. And I won't be doing this to help Maria."

Robbie glared at her over the top rim of his glasses. "You aren't going to let a petty grudge get in your way, are you?"

"Petty? You call what she did to me petty?"

He held his hands up, palms open. "Well, yeah. In the scheme of life. It's not like her efforts to oust you from the neighborhood worked."

"You notice how many block parties we've been invited to since then?"

"I notice that you always refer to Berkeley's murder as 'the event' and 'that thing' and 'since then' without mentioning his name. You don't talk about him or his murder or about what happened directly."

"Do you always have to bring that up?"

"You don't like talking about important things. Painful things. And that was before a nut job tried to kill you and our children." He wrapped his arms around her and pulled her tight against him. "I gotta get out of here before we end up in a new screaming match. I'm glad you're safe and Bernice's kids are safe. I bet Jamie is down in Portland busking and eating his weight in elaborate donuts."

She hugged him back, breathing in his familiar scent and breaking it off before it became too long and intimate. Managing their unique ex-but-friends-with-benefits relationship got trickier every day. The physical chemistry between them was as hot as ever, and if they stayed connected too long, they ended up in bed out of habit.

"I'm gonna go back to my place for the next week or so, excepting for the yard work I promised," he said. "Call me if you need anything else. 'Kay?"

Brian was safely ensconced in a sleepaway camp for

another week, so having Robbie around was hardly necessary for the kids' sake.

"Sophie can manage on her own if I go anywhere. Besides, I might take her with me. She's been hanging out with a lot of those kids all summer."

Robbie stiffened as he withdrew. "I don't want you dragging her into this. What if there is some connection here between Jamie and that serial killer? You can't put Sophie in harm's way."

"There's no way I'll let any harm come to her. You should know that."

Robbie sighed and held his hands up in surrender. "Whatever. Karen, you do what you do. I'm telling you now that there'll be hell to pay if anything happens to Sophie."

"You were right," Karen said. "This is a good time for you to leave." She swept her arm out toward the front door, unwilling to meet his eyes.

---

"You haven't said a word about my hair," Sophie said as she laid two plates and silverware on the dining table.

Karen tossed the salad with oil and vinegar. "Honestly? It's going to take time to get used to it. It's so different."

"But do you *like* it?"

Karen hadn't said anything because she was so taken aback. The bright blue turquoise would clash with Sophie's school colors—green and gold. She didn't want to tamp down the obvious sparkle in Sophie's eyes when she sashayed into the house, spun around, and displayed her new colors.

"It's very fresh and hip. And, honestly, the shorter cut and layers really look good on you. I'm just a little shocked by the brightness of it all." And maybe a little jealous. Karen's hair was a dark auburn that turned disastrous colors if she ever attempted anything with it. When she was in her twenties, she tried to bleach and die it much like Sophie had done. Instead of Sophie's glorious peacock, Karen had ended up with a garish orange-green. It had taken her months of conditioning and treatment to get it back to her natural color.

"I keep catching myself in the mirror and stopping. Is it too over the top?"

"It's remarkable, yes. But I've seen brighter. A Mohawk, on the other hand—that I might have a hard time with. Okay?"

"Okay. Thanks, Mom." Sophie surprised her with a warm hug. "I'll be back in a couple." She disappeared down the hall toward her bedroom.

After spending an hour on the phone with Maggie, her P.I. mentor, Karen developed a working plan on how to handle the case and Maria Wells as a client. Maggie promised to be on call to help with sticky situations. And with interviews or computer searches.

Conflict-of-interest didn't really matter in this case—as long as Karen could manage her emotions and remain unbiased when she uncovered dirt she didn't want to know about, Maggie said. But Karen decided she wouldn't accept money from Maria, or enter into an official contract with her.

The deep love for Jamie was driving her desire to find

him—not to help Maria. It might come down to semantics, but it mattered to her.

She, of all people, should have known that any time on the street would put him in a vulnerable position, even if not in the hands of a bona-fide serial killer. The niggling worry that Maria could possibly be right about that was definitely part of it, too. If Maria was right, Karen's inaction would make her culpable if anything did happen to him. Maybe not in the eyes of the law, but Karen would never forgive herself if Jamie ended up dead. His refusal to talk about his issues reminded her a bit too much of herself.

Though she trusted her daughter, she bet that Jamie and Sophie were protecting her in their teenage way. Jamie was close to others in greater need than he was, and was out there helping them. If he left the street, his friends would be left vulnerable. That was the story they'd told her, anyway. They lived in a pack, fending off threats to their small group as a unit.

She and Sophie argued about her hanging out with Jamie and his other street friends. Karen understood Sophie's desire to help Jamie, but Karen insisted that Sophie not give them cash or many details about herself. Because Sophie and Jamie had been nearly inseparable since toddlers, it was reasonable to assume they'd remain friends even with Jamie living on the street. During the school year, that had been minimal. Once the summer had kicked in, Sophie had spent more and more time with Jamie in the city and with their new group.

Karen new better than to overtly try to thwart the friendships Sophie was forming. Rather, she chose to hang back and watch as Sophie navigated her own way through the complex relationships. As summer was drawing near its end, school activities were already pulling Sophie back from her time in Seattle.

Sophie would come home each Wednesday evening with Jamie, and they would bring along a couple of street kids for a meal, a hot shower, and a place to stay. Over the last couple months, the cast changed, but there were a number of repeat visitors. Karen managed to get on friendly enough terms with them, though they weren't exactly chatty with her.

Karen leaned against the counter, studying her daughter for a full minute before Sophie noticed. "Mom? You've got that *I'm thinking* look on your face."

"Well, yeah. So, Jamie's mom has it in her head that he is in real danger."

Sophie stopped folding the napkin in her hands. "Wait. What? You talked to Mrs. Wells?"

"She's convinced the Dog Park Killer has kidnapped him. That Jamie is his next victim."

Sophie's eyes bugged out and her jaw dropped open. She laughed. "No way, Mom. Not Jamie. He's not stupid enough to go off with a stranger. That's just Mrs. W feeling guilty."

"She knows he's been staying with us once a week."

"Does she know you reported them to CPS in February?"

Karen called CPS when she learned the Wells had kicked Jamie out of their house and turned them in for abandonment. The CPS investigation declared Jamie a runaway based on his parents' story. They did not interview Karen or try to contact Jamie as far as she was aware.

"We didn't talk about that. She thanked me for having him here. Apparently, she's been keeping his Starbucks and ORCA cards filled."

"His apps, Mom. Not his cards. No one uses cards anymore."

"Whatever. She's been tracking him by his purchases at Starbucks and his bus trips."

"He said he was getting food, but didn't tell me it was from his mom," Sophie said. "You know, the app only shows her what he buys. It doesn't show her that he's giving half or more away."

Karen's heart clenched. Jamie had always been a generous little boy. She carried the lasagna-for-two over to the table.

"When was the last time you heard from him? I tried texting him today, but he hasn't gotten back to me."

"Uhmmmm… like last week?" Sophie frowned and bent over her phone. "He was here Wednesday, was heading over to the Harbor House on Thursday for open-mic night. He usually spends Fridays in Green Lake at the recording studio. And… he had definite plans for Portland on the weekend."

"Last time he went to Portland, he ended up with a dead phone."

"He said he was going down with Mullet and Sage. Sage was gonna drive, and her car is like, totally disgusting."

"Weren't you going to the beauty school with Jamie today?"

Sophie poked at her lasagna. "We're kinda growing apart, Mom. It's hard. You know. With all his new peeps."

"You're feeling left out?" Karen asked.

"It's not like I have all that much in common with most of them." She waved her hands around her head, encompassing the food, the room, the house—everything—in the gesture.

"I texted Jamie this morning. He hasn't responded."

"I did too, but only because we made plans last week to get our hair dyed. He never showed."

"You say he was going to Portland with Sage and Mullet? Did you see either of them today?"

"No. Maybe they're all still down there?" Sophie said. "Jamie is awful about keeping his phone charged."

"I don't suppose you can text Sage and Mullet? Maybe they're all still together down there. That would make this a whole lot easier."

"Sure. I'll text a few people he hangs with. Find out what they know."

Dinner with the two of them was a nice change of pace. Karen had worked more evenings this summer as a P.I. than she had as a domme. For way less money, too. Brian was the jokester in the family, always bringing up quirky topics and making them laugh. She missed him even though he was entering those prickly teenage years.

"We got a postcard from Brian today. He's having a good time," Karen said, hoping a change of topic from Jamie would lighten her mood.

"Is it wrong that I don't miss him?" Sophie stabbed at some lettuce. "It's been awesome being here alone with you, or Dad. Where is he anyway?"

"My surveillance gig is finished, so he went to his apartment for a few days. Needed some downtime, I guess." Karen tiptoed around anything negative about Robbie. Sophie was at a stage where any slight to her dad was blown out of proportion. "He might be around in the evenings to do yard work, though."

They ate in silence for a while, each absorbed in their own thoughts.

"We watched *The Godfather* last night. What a disgusting movie," Sophie said after a while.

"You glad your dad's not a mob boss?"

Sophie rolled her eyes again. Karen bit back her own mom's warning about them getting stuck. If that ever happened, surely Sophie would be the first.

"So, what about Jamie, anyway? I mean, he's probably in Portland. I haven't heard from him either. That is weird."

"Are you worried?"

"I know you don't like Mrs. Wells, but it must have taken a lot for her to come over here. After the way she treated you and all."

"I suppose. The last few months have been hard on her physically, and it shows."

"Mom, what would I have to do for you to want to kick me out?" Sophie asked.

Karen shoved a big bite of lasagna into her mouth to buy some time. There was nothing she wouldn't help her daughter through. "I suppose if you became a gang member and were doing a lot of illegal things. Drugs. Killing people. I'd still probably try to get you help. Get you out of it."

Sophie sprinkled more parmesan cheese on her lasagna.

"I'm never going gangbanger. But, what if I tried some marijuana? Like a couple of times, maybe?"

Karen felt the world slip from under her feet, even though she was seated. The way Sophie asked—it was the way she always asked about things she had already done. There was this slight hesitance to her words, a tilt of the head as she tested the water.

"I wouldn't kick you out for that. I'd definitely be concerned," she said. "Your brain is still developing until you're twenty-five, and studies show trying drugs or alcohol before your brain is all done cooking can make addiction a lot easier."

"You smoke it."

"*Occasionally.* But this is Washington. And it's totally legal for people over twenty-one."

"Do you like it?"

"Only when I'm in the mood for it."

"So you didn't get addicted to it the first time you tried it, did you?"

"No, but I was in college and eighteen years old, too."

"You *just* said twenty-five is when your brain is all adult, so you tried it before your brain was ready and you didn't get addicted."

"Maybe I shouldn't have allowed you to join the speech and debate team," Karen said as she stood to clear the table. "Will you be okay with time alone at home this week while I look for Jamie?"

"I'm glad you're going to do it, Mom. I mean, I know working for Mrs. Wells is kinda sucky, but you have to help if Jamie really is missing."

"I have to admit, some part of me was chortling with

glee as Maria asked me for help. After all she put me—put us—through."

"It's not like *that* worked."

Sometimes Sophie sounded exactly like her dad. "She threw aside fifteen years of friendship."

"You lied to her for years. She felt betrayed. You lied to all of us."

"I never lied."

"Not outright." Then, in a voice mimicking Karen's, she said, "Lies by omission are still lies."

Karen bit back a smile. Sometimes Sophie was exactly like her, too. "I did it to protect my family, my clients."

"Well, yeah, see how well that worked out in the end?"

Karen was tired of this argument. Tired of Sophie and Robbie defending Maria Wells, of all people. She shoved the remains of food off her plate into the garbage disposal.

"You know it's your fault Jamie was kicked out, right?"

Karen spun around to face Sophie. "What?"

"Yeah, the night he was kicked out? He was defending you to his parents."

Karen fell back against the counter. "Defending *me?* How?"

"Yeah. You," Sophie said. "His parents were arguing about what to do about you, and Jamie got up in their faces about you being all cool and alternative, and they should mind their own business." She leaned across the counter, palms flat against the granite surface. "Then, they started in on some sort of *everything is so perverted and insane* rants against everything sexual. He told them if you were disgusting and perverted for being a dominatrix, then what was he? He told them he was done hiding being gay. That's when his dad lost it. Told him to not come back until he was *over being gay*."

Karen's mouth went dry. "I didn't know."

"Yeah, well, Jamie didn't want you to blame yourself for it."

The thing was, Karen didn't blame herself. That kind of logic was all too adolescent. The gradual loss of her closest friend must be devastating for Sophie, and she was striking out at the safest person around—her mother. Sure, Karen felt bad for Jamie, for having such close-minded and close-hearted parents, but she didn't blame herself for them kicking him out. Her heart ached for Jamie. And Sophie.

"Oh. Oh… Poor Jamie."

"You need to make sure he's okay." Sophie checked her phone. "By the way, no one has texted me back."

Karen went around the counter to gather Sophie into her arms. Her daughter would sometimes allow hugs in private. "He's probably still in Portland or on the road."

Sophie shrugged Karen off and opened the phone app that let her keep tabs on friends. The app showed dots somewhere around people's locations, via GPS. "Well, I can tell you, he's not showing up here either."

Karen studied the screen. At least two dozen little dots were clustered together in several parts of Seattle with a half dozen blinking in what were probably their family homes nearby. She and Sophie showed up right on top of each other.

"Neither are Mullet and Sage. He's probably with them, Mom."

"Yeah, *probably*. I'm pretty sure finding Jamie won't be

that hard. He'll appear back on the grid once his phone is charged again."

"I get that you hate Mrs. W, Mom…."

"I don't hate her. It's more complicated than that. I will refuse to take any money from her. I'll find Jamie for you. For me. For him. For free."

## 4

_______

Karen checked the Wells driveway for Mitch's car before calling Maria. It wouldn't do to have him around when they talked. He wasn't home yet, and it was already eight o'clock.

"A couple of things," Karen said. "I need your username and passwords for both your Starbucks and ORCA cards. I want to be able to delve into the information on my own and keep tabs on any activity."

Maria handed over the information without question. "Thank you again, Karen. I appreciate you calling when Mitch isn't home."

"Where is he, anyway? Isn't it kind of late for him to be out?"

"He's bowling," Maria said. "There's a church league he goes to after work on Mondays. Call me before he gets home, please?"

Bowling? That must be a new thing. Maybe it was Mitch's way of coping with kicking Jamie out.

Next, Karen called Bernice to check in. Karen used to pay Bernice for her legal advice when she was working as a pro-domme. Now, Bernice paid her to do investigation work. Wrapping up the surveillance on Thad would make it easier to focus on finding Jamie.

"Also, Grace called me to tell me that she'd be happy to testify. She was on a long vacation during the last hearing. As if it would have mattered." Bernice paused. "I have a couple of new cases that are perfect for you. Can you swing by sometime tomorrow?"

"I'll see if I can fit you in. I have a new case, and I'm not sure how much time it's going to take." Karen didn't want to overload herself, but she wasn't going to skip out on paying work.

"Hmm. Okay. I'll email you the new backgrounds I need, and then you can give me a heads-up when you're on your way over. The one isn't imminent. More of an in-person kind of thing. A long-term investigation. I am glad you're getting work on your own."

Bernice mostly asked Karen to perform background checks for professional sex workers of one sort or another. Bernice's life revolved around legalizing the sex industry and fighting against slave trafficking. Her clients were primarily women, but she helped men when it fit her agenda.

The money as a P.I. wasn't quite as good as being a domme, but the work was relaxing in a way that domming wasn't. As a domme, she was always in character when she was with her clients. It was exhausting work mentally, and sometimes physically.

Once off the phone with Bernice, Karen jumped into the initial work on finding Jamie. After an hour on social media, she couldn't find anything from Jamie since Friday. There was a selfie of him with Mullet and Sage on Friday morning, on Sage's Instagram account. The restaurant behind them in the photo was in the U-District. The caption read: *This hot trio is Portland Bound!!!!! See you tonight!!!!!!!!* It would have been helpful if she'd added where they were performing.

She pored through Sage and Mullet's accounts. There wasn't much from them over the weekend. Sage posted a photo of the two of them with a donut at a famous Portland shop on Saturday morning and one of them all gothed-out for a late-night party the same evening. The caption on the first read *need the carbs after last night's show.* The one on the second read *done performing, ready to celebrate.* Given that most of Sage's photos were of her and Mullet cheek-to-cheek, it only proved the two of them had gone to Portland, not that they were alone. Nothing from either of them since the goth photo.

Jamie's ORCA card was tapped three times Friday, the last at a stop in the U-District for a bus heading toward Green Lake. His Starbucks account showed him spending money at a shop north of Green Lake shortly after noon, about half an hour after his last ORCA tap.

Nothing after that. No ORCA taps, no Starbucks usage, no friends tagging him on Instagram, no personal posts, no mentions of him anywhere.

He could have left his phone somewhere. The battery could be dead. Or he could be ignoring it. He wasn't like those kids who posted everything on Instagram or Snapchat. He went days with zero social media, so the dearth of information wasn't out of character.

The next thing Maggie had suggested was for Karen to contact Missing Persons at the Seattle Police Department to let them know she was working the case. Since Maria had filed an official report, they would have some paper on him. It was unlikely that the police knew anything more than she did, but it wouldn't hurt to make her connection official. It was always a good idea to have positive contacts on the police force.

With her long history of avoiding law enforcement, this was the major sticking point for Karen's P.I. career. She did everything she could to avoid taking jobs that made contact with the police necessary. She knew only one person at SPD, and she didn't want to call him.

She turned back to her computer and googled Court's name. A number of photos popped up onto the screen. He'd been featured in a dozen or so articles after he'd been injured during a police raid three months ago. One article focused on the heroics of his partner, Ivy Langston, while most focused on Court's injuries and the bust itself. If it weren't for Ivy, Court would certainly be dead.

When he returned to work after a month in the hospital, there were several articles about Seattle Police Department's only transgender homicide detective. It had taken her by surprise because she had no idea Court was trans until she read about it in the paper.

She'd never met a trans cop before she'd met Court. And every other single trans person she knew had a very high distrust of law enforcement—even more so than she did. She couldn't imagine the trans community embracing him. Or the police community, for that matter. They were usually at such odds with each other, she doubted he could be fully part of either one. And yet, he came across as a well-adjusted guy passing totally as cisgendered.

Even after she had kissed him, she hadn't picked up that he was trans. She considered herself to be pretty savvy when it came to sexuality and gender issues, so she'd read and re-read the article about a dozen times before it sank in. There was nothing feminine about this man. Absolutely nothing. He was tall, muscular, and had a pretty deep voice. His five o'clock shadow was a little spare more because he was blonde than anything else.

The one kiss they'd shared had been brief but near perfect. She didn't really care what might be between his legs. As if it mattered, anyway. He had made it perfectly clear he wasn't interested in a relationship with a professional dominatrix. Cops and sex workers didn't mix. Neither did cops and private investigators. That was pretty much it.

Court was the only cop she knew by name. Well, other than his partner, Ivy Langston—but Ivy was icy and suspicious. Plus, Ivy was a woman, and Karen didn't get along with other women in general. Other than Bernice, Karen didn't have many close female friends.

Calling Court out of the blue would be awkward. He was the lead detective in a major case, and didn't have time for something like a missing teen. Karen hoped he would be willing to introduce her to someone in Missing Persons because he was a generally good cop.

It was almost ten o'clock at night. Karen hesitated only for a moment before hitting the call button. She held her breath as it rang.

"Pearson." His voice was crisp, businesslike. Maybe he'd deleted her number from his contact list and didn't know

who was calling. There were people talking in the background. The lack of clinking glasses or dishes told her he
was probably at work, not at a bar or on a date.

"Hi, Court, I mean, Detective Pearson, this is Karen
Hunter." He didn't say anything, so she plowed on into the
silence. "I was hoping you could help me out with
something."

"Hold on a sec…" The phone rustled as if he'd shoved
it against his chest. It was a few seconds before he came
back on. "What's up?"

"Remember how I told you I was getting my P.I.
license?"

"Sure. You mentioned it at the Indigo Girls concert."

Karen had run into Court and some friends at the
concert in June. As soon as Karen said hello, his date laid
claim to him with "all mine" body language that couldn't
have been more clear than if she'd been wearing one of
those shirts emblazoned with Mine and a giant arrow across
the front.

Court did not seem like a man who would do well with
the clingy type. He was still healing from the injuries that
had landed him on the front page and in the hospital earlier
in the spring. The scar on his face was a bright pink.

In the photo in the newspaper in front of her now,
Court's scar had healed into a fine silver line. She traced it
absently with her finger.

"I'm working on a missing-person case, and I wasn't
sure who to talk to at SPD. I was hoping you'd be willing to
introduce me to someone directly."

"Adult or juvie?"

"He's fifteen. The mom is convinced he has been taken by the Dog Park killer."

His weary sigh came through with startling clarity. "What makes her think that?"

"I'm sure you're getting tons of calls from parents of missing kids."

"You have no idea. Fill me in."

He listened without interrupting as Karen went through everything she'd already done. When she was finished she let out a huge breath of air. "What do you think?"

"If he told your daughter he was going to Portland, then he is most likely in Portland, like you said. However, we *are* prioritizing missing teens at the moment because of the killings."

"You mean you're working missing-persons in tandem with the murder investigations?"

"Something like that."

"What are the chances Jamie's in real danger?"

"Given what you told me, your kid is probably down in Portland. And, you know, living on the street by itself is inherently dangerous."

Karen twitched at the less than comforting dichotomous answer. "How many calls have you gotten from moms worried about their kids?"

He laughed. Not a funny laugh, but a worn-out one. "It's amazing how many parents suddenly get worried about the kids they've kicked out."

"What do you tell them?"

"Same thing I'm about to tell you." He paused his tone shifted into the one he used for press conferences. "There are almost a thousand kids on Seattle streets right now. The odds are your kiddo is just out of touch."

"Court, that's the total street population. All the victims are male, though." And blond. Karen smoothed down the lower fold of the newspaper still on her desk. The photos of the boys were mostly school head shots and awkward smiles. "Court, all these kids? They are one type, aren't they?"

"That's usually the case," Court said.

"Jamie's slender. Fine-featured. Blond. Wears plaid. He looks a lot like the boys in the newspaper."

The silence that followed was as disconcerting as if they were on a first date and she'd blurted out something terribly awkward.

"What else can you tell me about him?"

"His parents kicked him out when he came out to them. He busks. Like I said, he plays guitar in a trio that was going to Portland on Friday."

"I'll get you connected to the right people. Do you have a recent photo you can text me?" His voice was tight. The tone had changed from weary to slightly charged.

"Court, what is it you're not saying?"

They were interrupted by a crashing noise on his end. "Shit. I need to go. Send me that recent photo. Let's check in tomorrow." And he was gone.

Karen texted Court the photo of Jamie with Mullet and Sage from Friday morning. Instead of stewing over the conversation, she worked on a timeline. She started with Jamie's last known purchase at Starbucks and worked backward from there, interweaving the ORCA usage.

She put the time stamp from every purchase and bus trip from the last three weeks on her whiteboard. She added in other activities she knew about—Thursday open-mic nights at one shelter, his recording sessions on Fridays, various busking spots and times. The one thing he used Instagram for was posting his performance schedules.

Jamie was always at Karen's house on Wednesdays from about four in the afternoon until Thursday morning around ten. She mapped out the shelters he frequented—and the days she knew he stayed there.

She didn't know much about his Friday recording gig. Jamie only spoke of it shyly, as if saying too much about it might jinx it. There was a bus stop opposite the Starbucks where he always bought lunch on the same day. The studio must be in Green Lake.

Jamie frequented so many places, Karen got confused trying to track it all in her head. She found an old map of Seattle and attached it to her cork board. She made little Post-it flags of each location and pinned them on the map. She switched things up and color-coded the little Post-it notes by the day of the week, and a more coherent story emerged.

There were only two nights a week Karen was certain of where he would be—Wednesdays at her house, and Thursdays at a shelter called Harbor House. He spent the other five nights a week at other shelters and on the street with his mini-tribe.

She grabbed a few more photos of Jamie off his Instagram page and put together a collage. She made a missing-person flyer with the photos and her contact information, and sent it off to the local print shop to make a hundred copies. They would be ready in the morning. She could pick them up on her way into Seattle and staple them to posts around town. She really didn't like that Jamie hadn't returned her or Sophie's texts all day long.

Karen's phone alarm dinged with her bedtime reminder. She turned off her computer and went upstairs. She spent several minutes hovering in Sophie's doorway meditating on the comforting rhythm of her sleeping daughter's breath.

## 5

—————

Mom?" Are you awake yet?"

Karen rolled onto her back. "Yeah. What time is it?"

"It's eight thirty. I'm walking over to school."

"Wait, what's going on?" Karen sat up, vaguely remembering Sophie saying something about needing to be there most of the day.

Sophie stood in the doorway, her new do shiny and straight, clashing wonderfully with the green and gold of her volleyball team jersey. "I'm volunteering for that new program with all the freshmen. You know, where they take all the newbies around the building for tours so they don't get lost when school starts."

"Right. I'll be going into Seattle today. I'm going to follow Jamie's general path around. Put up some flyers. Ask people questions."

Jamie spent the majority of his waking hours roaming around and busking, so it made sense he'd be out there working. The mapping exercise from the evening before neatly outlined Jamie's routine. Lots of busking spots were negotiated by half-day increments, and he was often in the same general area each day of the week.

"Any chance you heard from him? Or Mullet? Sage?"

Sophie crossed her arms over her chest. "No. Not from any of them. I'll try again, and I'll ask other people at school. He's kept in touch with a few of us."

"I've got a decent idea of where he tends to hang out, and I've met a lot of his group over the summer," Karen said. "I'm hoping they'll talk to me."

"Yeah, Mom, about that? Don't pull the P.I. thing, okay? You need to be my mom helping me look for Jamie. P.I. is too cop-like, right? I gotta run so I won't be late." Sophie blew her a kiss and left. "Text me progress."

It was going to be a long day of walking around. Karen got out of bed and dressed in the most non-threatening jeans and t-shirt she could find. And comfortable walking shoes. She eyed her three pairs of stilettos with a tiny pang of remorse. A thin layer of dust around the thin points underscored how little used they were. At least as a domme she dressed up for work.

Jamie and Sophie chose people to bring home for their sleepovers by a mysterious process Karen didn't understand. Some kids she saw only once while others she saw every other week.

At first, Karen refused Sophie's request to bring other kids home, allowing only Jamie to spend the night. As the summer kicked in, Sophie's argument to help other kids out wore Karen down. After a couple of weeks of nothing bad coming from Sophie's visits to Seattle, and Sophie's relentless appeals, they made a deal.

Sophie wasn't allowed to spend all her free time in Seattle. While Karen wanted Sophie to stay in her room with the door locked, Sophie adamantly refused to separate herself from the group sleeping on the floor of the basement—as if the other kids didn't sense the wall of separation between them. On her part, Sophie agreed to not give people money outright or buy them things other than the occasional sandwich or drink.

Living on the street required a certain degree of street smarts. Every street youth knew manipulative tricks to get things from people. Karen coached Sophie so she wouldn't fall for them all with her sweet and tender heart.

Karen's internet search confirmed what she already knew from her Wednesday-night interactions with Jamie and his friends. The places where street kids slept that correlated with Jamie's bus usage were Capitol Hill, the U-District, Westlake, and Pioneer Square, in that order.

Once known for being the gay part of town, Capitol Hill had, in the last five years or so, transitioned into Portlandia-style hipsterdom. Two youth shelters a few blocks apart served slightly different youth demographics. Harbor House was funded by a liberal ecumenical group. Rainbow Landing was a grant and donations-funded LGBTQ-centered shelter.

The U-District—the local abbreviation for the University District—was where Jamie spent a lot of time busking. There were a couple of shelters in the area, but Karen couldn't recall Jamie mentioning either of them. Sleeping in the rough in the U-District was made relatively safe by the sheer number of kids who piled into the same storefront.

Westlake Center encompassed a couple downtown

blocks of stores and shopping complexes. It was a convenient place to hang out and served as a major hub for buses and light rail. It wasn't too far from popular tourist spots and was a pretty safe place to be in the daytime. Groups of kids could be seen moving around the center like flocks of birds being shooed from unwelcome perches by security guards.

Pioneer Square was rarely on Jamie's circuit. He'd been there a few times, but there was no pattern to his visits that Karen could find. The youth shelter in the area was run by the Wells' church—one of those mega-churches with thousands of members and a dozen linked congregations around the Puget Sound. It was possible Jamie went there as a way to contact Maria, but Karen doubted that. Mitch was an elder in the church and word would get back to him.

Homeless shelters served different populations. Some served only young adults. Rarely did a shelter serve kids and older adults. The vast majority of street kids, Karen learned, had become homeless the day they turned eighteen. Some parents couldn't wait to get rid of their "problems."

These homeless young adults were able to sign themselves into a shelter. Kids under eighteen were actually the minority, as it was illegal for parents to abandon their non-adult children. Police returned juveniles to their homes as quickly as possible or brought them to detention centers.

Regardless, most shelters required an adult's permission for a minor to stay in the shelter overnight. Because of this, the most vulnerable younger teens were out on the street because they often didn't want their parents to know where they were. It made no sense to Karen. Maria Wells was likely the one giving permission for Jamie to stay in any shelter. Mitch certainly wouldn't be.

She had stopped at Midori in Redmond to buy a bag of baked goods after picking the flyers up at the print shop. She liked the idea of offering kids something to eat while she talked to them. Not a bribe so much as a meal. If the sugar got someone talking, Karen wouldn't complain.

Karen left her car in an all-day lot a couple blocks from Cal Anderson Park, a large city-block-sized park in the central part of the Capitol Hill neighborhood. Since Jamie appeared to spend more time here than anywhere else, she figured it was a good place to start.

The morning was already getting warm by ten, and the kids would be out of the shelters for the day. She walked past the basketball court and toward the steps near the reflecting pool where a group of six kids were already hanging out for the day. The steps were in a convenient bit of shade.

She recognized one girl from the Wednesday-night sleepovers. Tink was hardly five feet tall and weighed maybe ninety pounds. Her waif-like face was made even more so by enormous green eyes that were artfully lined in swirls of makeup. Her bleached-blond hair stuck out from under her knit cap in pink-tipped spikes.

The girl did a double take when Karen waved, and separated herself from her group as Karen approached.

"Tink, right?" Karen asked as she reached out her free hand. Tink was the girl's street name. She'd come with Jamie to spend the night at her house a couple of times earlier in the summer.

The girl nodded and shook it, a little wrinkle of a smile lighting up her face. "You're Sophie's mom, right?"

"Yep." Sophie was totally right about playing the concerned-mom angle. "So, I'm hoping you can help me. Sophie and I haven't heard from Ja—I mean, Strings—in a few days. We're kind of worried. Have you seen him?"

Tink's nose wrinkled and she pursed her lips to one side. "You know? I haven't? You know, seen him, like, for a week? Prolly longer. Last I saw him? He was busking down at Westlake."

"Would you mind introducing me to your friends? I'd like to ask if anyone else has seen him?"

Tink tilted her head toward the group that was pretending to ignore them and nodded, waving Karen to follow her over. "This is Sophie's mom. Anyone know where Strings is?"

They exchanged glances, no one willing to jump in. Karen couldn't read whatever secret signals were passing between them. It was like a weird psychic connection between them—she felt a vibe she couldn't quite read.

Tink clapped her hands in their faces. "Come on, people. Not that hard, ya know? She's good. You all know Strings."

Karen handed Tink the bag of pastries to pass around. "I got these for you all to snack on."

Tink sucked in her lower lip as she peeked into the bag. She suddenly appeared five years younger and that much more vulnerable. Tink pulled out a smaller bag with a little almond cake inside before handing the bag to the person closest to her.

A boy who was a full head taller than Karen rubbed at

his nose with the back of his hand and jerked his head upward. "I ain't seen Strings since last mic night? Right? He was jammin' with Sage and Mullet. Ripping some nice shit, ya know?"

Karen didn't ask how the group collective came to this conclusion, but the others nodded in unison as he spoke.

"They're good together."

"Totally dope."

Sage and Mullet had been in her home twice over the summer. Each time, the trio had jammed in her basement until late in the evening on music Karen couldn't relate to. Even so, the quality of their work was there.

One by one, the kids selected a pastry and retreated to sit on the stone steps to eat them. Karen gave the remains to Tink to eat later or pass out to others as she saw fit.

One of the girls came closer and bit into her croissant before speaking. "I saw Strings Friday morning. He stayed at Harbor House with some of us Thursday night after open mic. Him and Sage and Mullet did a practice set for their gig in Portland. He was heading up to Jolly's place Friday and meetin' up with Sage and Mullet later."

She spoke around a mouthful of the flaky pastry so it came out garbled. She pushed up her thick plastic glasses with the back of a finger. Someone needed to tell that kid to not talk with her mouth full. It took effort to understand her as her words were wrapped around the food.

Who calls himself *Jolly*? The name gave Karen the creeps. Images of a balding man with suspenders, uneven teeth, and white cheeky jowls came to mind. "Is that the guy who runs the recording studio?"

The two girls nodded.

"Do you know which studio it is? What it's called? You'd be surprised at how many studios there are near Green Lake." Her search had pulled up twenty studios in the general area, though only a handful were within easy walking distance of the Starbucks that Jamie frequented. Any lead to keep her from visiting every one of them would be helpful.

The girl shrugged. "I don't play an instrument, so I never went. Besides, I'm a girl. He prefers boys, if you know what I mean."

Karen wasn't quite sure how to take that. "So, this Jolly guy likes young guys? Like Strings? In an inappropriate way?"

The girl shrugged. "Could be a rumor."

Karen turned to Tink. "Do you know the name of the studio or anyway for me to find him?"

Tink tilted her head to the side. "Like she said, Jolly tends to work with guys."

"Anyone else have any ideas about where Strings might be? If he's with Mullet and Sage, where they might be?"

A few shrugs.

"Ain't seen none of them for days," Tink said. "And, it is kinda weird."

Karen ripped off a piece of paper from the pastry bag and wrote her number on it and handed it to Tink. "Call me if you hear anything, will you? And, you know where I live. It's Wednesday, pizza will be there by seven."

She might be opening her door to way more kids than she was used to with that particular invitation. If there was any chance anyone who showed up tonight could help find Jamie, it would be worth it.

Tink took the paper and studied it before folding it into a tiny square and squirreling it away into one of many zippered pockets lining her pants. "Thanks."

A scruffy kid wiped the crumbs off his fingers and stood up as she thanked everyone for their help. "Yo. I bet the three of them was taken by them cleaners." He spat the last word out.

"Cleaners?" Something vague tried to make its way through to her.

The other kids rolled their eyes and hooted with laughter. "Dreamy, you got that name for a reason, dude."

Dreamy frowned at the others. "Y'all need to get real. People are disappearing, and so is all their gear." He turned back to Karen. "Cleaners. *You know.* Those people who come through and steal all our stuff, destroy our shit, you know. They's *cleaning* us up. Grabbing us and shifting us out of town."

It hit Karen then. *Of course!* Dreamy was talking about the latest of Seattle's homeless fiascos. The city hired professionals on a regular basis to go into areas where homeless people set up tents to clean them up. Technically, the company was paid to "pick up trash"—which, in this case, included tents, clothing, pieces of furniture, basically anything kept in these encampments, trash or not. They tended to go in while their owners were off getting food and left things unguarded.

"Did you see Strings get taken?"

"Nah. Not directly. But, whenever them cleaners see a kid, though, they take 'em."

"You've seen that happen?"

"Yeah."

"When? Where?"

His shoulders moved up and down, sending a wave of unwashed teen stink with it. "These people in hazmat suits come in with giant black bags and fill them up with our stuff. Toss them in trucks. Throwing away people's shit."

"Did they take anything of yours?"

"Yeah. My tent and pack. And they took Dog, Spike and Gem away."

"Dog, Spike and Gem are friends of yours?"

"Yeah. They ganged up on 'em. The cleaners called someone, and they come and took 'em."

"Were they wearing uniforms? The people who took them?"

Dreamy wiped his nose with the back of his hand and sniffed in loudly. "Maybe. I don't know for sure."

"How old were Dog, Spike and Gem?"

"Fifteen? Fourteen? Not sure. They's young."

If the city's cleanup crew found "runaways" in an encampment, they would have called CPS. Most likely, the three had been taken to juvenile detention until their parents either claimed them or abandoned them. It was likely the kids were tossed into the foster system. Jamie was not officially part of the system even though he was out on the street. CPS had believed the Wells' story that Jamie had run away, not that they had tossed him out, and never opened a case against them.

"How old are you, Dreamy?"

"Don't matter, does it?"

Karen guessed fifteen, *maybe*. She held out her hands, fingers spread wide. "Don't worry, I'm not calling anyone. Do you know anything about Jolly?"

Dreamy shrugged. "Heard about him. Never met him."

"And do you know Strings?"

"Sure." Dreamy lifted his arms into air-guitar position and waggled his right hand to demonstrate, his left moving up and down the invisible fret board with a wildness that would have produced a cacophony of nothing on a real guitar.

"He's good, isn't he?"

"That boy could make it big, if he got heard by the right people, ya know?" Dreamy shook his head in admiration.

"What do you want to do, Dreamy?"

"When I was a kid, I wanted to be a fireman. Now? I don't know. I want to get out of here, maybe get a real job. Tired of *working*. Ya know?"

Karen's heart clenched. Poor kid. So he was too young to get a job, but he was "working"—code for survival sex, earning money through sexual favors because you have no choice. "Where are your parents?"

"Momma died last year. Pops, he don't like it when I'm around. Says I remind him of her too much."

"Can you go home?"

"I do. Once a week or so. Wash up. Steal some clothes. I sneak in when Pops is gone or outta it."

There wasn't much she could do for all these kids. Feeding them and listening was about it. "You want some ice cream? Molly Moon's just opened." The line out the door already wrapped around the corner.

**6**

———

Over ice cream, Dreamy had given her an insider's perspective of the two shelters on Capitol Hill. Teens used both, but he personally preferred Harbor House because the food was better and the beds had a little more space between them. He used Rainbow Landing as a second choice and moved onto the U-District if both of those were full. He hated sleeping on the street because there was always some rando kicking him in the middle of the night. He ended up outside with a cluster of other kids about once a week.

Karen walked the couple of blocks from the ice cream shop to Harbor House, stopping to staple her flyers to light poles as she went. She covered over concert posters rather than the lost-people or lost-animal flyers. There were too many of both of those.

Harbor House was originally built by a great Seattle family during the prosperous gold-rush years, when Seattle was the staging area for miners heading off to make their fortunes in Alaska.

The wide wraparound porch was a welcome shady spot. Eight teens lounged in plastic chairs that were at odds with the grandeur of the house. Two leaned intently over a chess board, chins propped on hands. One read a magazine, while the rest were absorbed in their phones. Two wooden swings held by enormous hooks that had been painted over so many times they were losing their shape creaked as they swayed back and forth under the weight of more kids.

The shelters were required to collect legal names. Additionally, for minors, they required adult or guardian permission to stay there. Karen hoped the shelter workers on her list would help her by checking their rosters. She didn't have the authority the police department did and couldn't get a warrant to force the issue. She'd have to rely on her powers of persuasion. If there were a man involved, she could pull some other tricks out of her sleeve.

Jamie typically stayed at Harbor House on Thursday nights. Its open-mic night gave him the chance to perform for an audience, and Jamie rarely missed it. He often practiced for it Wednesday nights at her house. There was no doubt that Jamie would do well on a professional stage someday.

His unique voice went hard rock or classic folk equally well. His guitar playing had improved in quality the last few months—one of the few positives to busking for several hours a day.

She climbed the wide steps to the front door of Harbor House. The period stained glass was a mixture of blurry and colored geometric elements, very much Frank Lloyd

Wright, but on a Victorian house. They would let a lot of light into the house without losing privacy.

A handwritten sign describing the lottery rules for the shelter's thirty beds was laminated and taped next to the bell. Karen tried the door and was slightly surprised when it opened. A woman sat at the desk in the foyer. The woman's mouse-brown hair was cut in a conservative bob. A bright stripe of purple dye from her center part on one side softened the overall severity of the style.

"Oh, hello." She stood, straightened her skirt, and leaned forward with her hand out in greeting, a welcome smile on her lips. "Can I help you?"

Karen introduced herself and handed the woman one of her cards. With teens, she would introduce herself as Sophie's mom, and Strings's friend. With adults, she would pull out the pro-card and not mention her personal connection to Jamie at all.

"I'm a private investigator," she said. "Jamie Wells' mother has hired me to find him." She handed the woman one of the flyers and introduced herself.

"I'm Donna. Donna Richards." The woman took the paper with one hand and examined it, her eyes growing wide and full of concern. "Oh, dear. Oh, my gracious sakes alive. This boy is missing? He goes by Strings, you know. I see him here all the time. Didn't get in every night, of course, they never do, there are so many of them, you know."

"Do you work here every day?"

"Me? No, I'm only a volunteer. I'm usually in once or twice a week. More during the summer when people are off on vacation."

"What about last Thursday? Were you here? Did you see him?"

"Thursday? Why of course. I love open-mic night. It's so much fun to watch them all. You'd be surprised at the talent."

"Can you check if he actually spent the night on Thursday?"

Donna sucked her lips in, considering the request. "You know, actually? I was here. I remember him playing a song with a couple of the other regulars—Sage and Mullet. I'm certain he stayed the night."

"Can you tell me what adult gave permission for him to stay?"

"His mom. She's the one who I speak to." Donna glanced down the hallway and pulled out a thick binder from a drawer in the desk. She put it on the desk at an angle, close to her chest. "I'm not supposed to share this information. But, given this is to help find him… Let's see… Yes. Here he is." She ran her finger under a handwritten note on the form. "Maria Wells. His mother. She hired you, right?"

*Exactly as she had figured.* Maria Wells' actions in support of her son were in the right direction at least. Even if she was too weak to keep Mitch from throwing Jamie out, she was helping in small ways.

"Has Jamie been back since Friday morning? For a meal? Anything?"

"I haven't seen him. But then again, I'm not here in the mornings unless I'm filling in for someone." Donna flipped through a couple of pages and shut the binder. "He hasn't spent the night since Thursday. We don't require names or sign-ins for meals, so I can't tell you if he dropped in for food. We can feed a lot more people than we can house for the night." She slipped the binder back into the drawer. "Does that help at all?"

"I really appreciate you looking, Donna. I'm still trying to get a sense of his usual schedule. Do you know the kids he usually hangs out with?"

Donna sucked her lower lip in between her teeth and chewed on it. "Well, he usually performed with the same two kids I already told you about."

"Mullet and Sage?"

"Yeah, those are their street names."

"I don't suppose you happen to know their legal names?"

"Not off the top of my head. I only remember Jamie's because I talk to his mom almost once a week."

"Any chance you have their cell numbers or other contact info?" Karen nodded to the drawer with the binder. "Last we know, Jamie was heading to Portland with Mullet and Sage to play at some sort of music gig."

Donna clasped her hands on top of the closed binder. "I'm not sure I should. Giving you information for Strings is fine, but I don't think I should for the others."

Karen shrugged as if it wasn't a big deal. "Is there anything you can tell me about them? Generally speaking?"

Donna visibly relaxed. "Well, they're both older than Jamie. Mullet is twenty-two and Sage is older, almost aging out. They hooked into him as soon as they heard him play guitar. They're old enough to sign themselves in, so I've never talked to their parents."

"In what way do you mean, hooked into him?"

"As soon as he played, they were all over him. You know. Sage plays bass and sings, and Mullet sings and plays guitar, but nothing so good as Jamie. Together they make a pretty decent trio. They've been busking all over the place ever since."

"Do they earn enough with busking?"

"Probably. I hope so." Donna's face shifted. "I know a lot of these kids end up resorting to survival mode. The ones with real skills sometimes escape that. And Jamie and those other two? They have talent."

*Survival mode* sounded a lot less messy and a lot less dangerous than *survival sex.* While it was possible to live on the street and not resort to selling one's body, it was hard. Karen had managed it for two years herself, a lifetime ago now. She knocked on the wood of the desk. "Jamie has been lucky that way."

"I'm so pleased to hear his mother has hired you. He's a very lucky boy. Some kids don't have anyone to care about them."

"So, Mullet and Sage. Have you seen either of them since Friday?"

Donna shook her head. "I haven't been here since Thursday evening. I wouldn't be here on Wednesday normally, either. Filling in for people on summer vacation means I'm here a lot more often than usual."

"How often do you normally volunteer here?"

Donna's lips twitched into a half smile. "Usually, I try to come in twice a week. More lately, you know how it is. I can never do enough."

"You know Jamie well then?"

"Oh, not well. I mean, I saw him here now and again. I

like to work on Thursday night because I get to watch the kids perform."

"I've heard that some of the kids have been doing some recording work with some guy named Jolly. You know him?"

Donna pulled a face and leaned forward. "All I know is he pays these kids some ridiculous low amount of money and sends them on their way. I overheard a couple of the boys talking, and it sounds like he might be some sort of pervert."

"What did you hear?" Karen asked in her most gossip-inducing lilt.

"Well, you know, not much really. Whispers and rumors. One boy mentioned that this Jolly person offered some money for more than his guitar playing."

"What did you do with that information?"

"I called the police, of course," she said, straightening up. "Little good it did. I have no idea whether they ever checked him out. They thanked me for the report, but I doubt they did anything about it."

"Anything else about Jolly?"

"I've never met the man, so I really can't say."

"I heard his studio is over in Green Lake. Any idea what part?"

"I live in Green Lake. I'd hate to think there's someone like that around me. But you know, I have seen several kids who play at open-mic night hanging out at the bus stop nearby."

"Which one would that be?" Karen asked, opening up her map app so Donna could point it out to her. The bus stop was directly across from the Starbucks Jamie used every Friday.

"Do you drive by there regularly?"

"I live around the corner. I have seen kids busking at the Starbucks or waiting for the bus, sure. Lots of times."

"Well, I imagine Jolly must be within walking distance of that particular stop. That narrows my search down a lot."

"I do wish you all the best of luck. Is there anything else? While I am a volunteer, I do have work to do."

"If you think of anything else, please give me a call, will you?"

Donna examined the card briefly and slipped it into the top desk drawer.

"Why do you volunteer here?" Karen asked. "As opposed to a pet shelter or a food bank."

Donna's hand grasped at a small gold cross pendant and moved it back and forth on the delicate gold chain. "It's complicated, Mrs. Hunter."

Her suddenly chilled tone of voice made it clear that was all Karen would get from her—a clear line drawn. Karen liked people with boundaries.

7

Karen emerged from Harbor House into the blinding heat of late afternoon. She hadn't noticed the peek-a-boo view of Puget Sound from the porch on her way in. It was too far away to make out anything but the largest of ships on the bright bit of reflective water. The white peaks of the Olympic Mountain range beyond Puget Sound sparkled in the distance.

As soon as the kids were out of high school, she'd find an apartment in Belltown, high up where she could look at that view all day long. Sitting on a balcony somewhere, drinking iced tea and reading a book with that in the background, would make an ideal retirement.

It took her a few minutes to find the next closest shelter on her phone's map app. Connectivity around here should have been better than this. She got better reception in downtown Redmond. Her parking time was up, so she moved her car to a space in the shade directly across from Rainbow Landing. Years of living in the area had made

Karen suspicious of the sun. Most people spent eight months of the year complaining about the gray slow drip, only to turn around and bitch about the bright sun the other four.

Rainbow Landing was much more hippie-dippy than Harbor House. The giant free-form rainbow painted across the front with drips of color flowing from one to the next like a giant melting popsicle bordered on childish graffiti with just enough charm to pull it off. The words Rainbow Landing painted in slightly uneven white letters across the whole rainbow was the crowning crafty touch.

The bright orange front door was wedged open with a thick triangle of wood. It took a moment for her to adjust her eyes to the darkness inside. A sign on a table directed youth to sign in and leave their number. Like Harbor House, this shelter would draw a lottery for their fifty beds. There was no one sitting at the desk checking IDs or verifying birthdates.

Karen ran her finger down the list of names already signed in for the day to see if Strings, Sage, or Mullet showed up anywhere. They weren't, at least not by their street names. Interestingly, these kids put their phone numbers next to legal and street names alike. Text notifications would let them know they had a bed for the night. She snapped a shot of the list. The pages underneath were blank. Surely Sage and Mullet would have signed in here and left their number at some point. The house was smaller than Harbor House, yet it claimed fifty beds to Harbor House's thirty.

A cool voice startled Karen. "Can I help you?"

A tall, slender man in his early thirties bustled out of the door to the right of the entry. He shifted demeanor when he saw her. "Oh, hello. I thought you might be one of our young clients. What can I do for you?" A casual weariness infused his voice. He wore a name tag pinned to his rumpled oxford that said Adin.

Karen introduced herself as a private investigator and showed him the photo of Jamie.

"I'm Adin Sanchez." He opened his hands so the fingers were splayed wide and crossed them over his chest when he saw the photo. He drew in a shocked breath. "Strings? Oh. Dear. Oh dear me. You say he's missing?"

"When was the last time you saw him?"

Adin leaned in closer and dropped his voice to a strangled whisper. "Oh my. Oh my. I hope he hasn't been taken."

"Taken?" Karen asked.

"You know." He bobbed his head meaningfully with exaggerated widened eyes. "Taken. As in *taken*."

He sure jumped to that conclusion fast. Adin was hiding something, but what? His whole demeanor wreaked of submissive gay male. The air of anxiety that swirled around him put her on edge.

"He's missing, yes. Why would you immediately conclude he'd been kidnapped?"

"He's a boy. He's missing. Why *wouldn't* I make that connection? Am I the only one who knows that there is a killer taking young gay men and doing God knows what to them? Of course the police don't care. If it were rich white businessmen showing up dead in dog parks, they'd have caught this killer months ago."

"You honestly believe the cops don't care? Haven't they been all over this place?" Karen assumed shelters

would have been the first place the cops would have inves-
tigated.

"Yes, but it's all a show," Adin said. "They are just
pretending to care. They show up every time they find a
body. When it's too late to help. They flash a picture around
and ask a few questions. Would it be too much to ask that
they stop the actual killings? All the cops care about is if
they got the right identification, and they leave. They aren't
interested in justice for these babies."

Karen didn't interrupt Adin's rant. He needed to vent.
Everyone was tired of seeing children being murdered. His
big round eyes shimmered with tears.

"I take it you knew the other victims?" she asked.

He put both hands to his face and sucked at his lips.
"Not all of them as well as I knew Jamie. They all stayed
here at some point or another. One boy was here a couple
of times. Wagyu. He was so sweet." His shoulders shuddered as he breathed in hard. "Oh lord. Lordy, lordy, lord.
Please not Strings. Such musical talent gone to waste."

"When was the last time you saw him, Adin?"

Adin bounced on his tiptoes. "He's not a regular here. I
mean, not regular-regular. Just now and again. He usually
shows up on taco night."

"When's that?"

"Every other Tuesday. Last one was this week. Don't
think he was here, though. So, that would make it over two
weeks ago."

"Did you notice him hanging out with any kids in
particular?"

"He hung out with Sage and Mullet a lot. He was going
to Portland with them this last weekend," he said. His eyes

widened and he waved his hand around in the air. "Oh, maybe he's still with them. Maybe they're all still down there…"

"Any chance you know where they were supposed to play? What clubs they were going to?"

"I'm really not sure of any of their names. I think one was near the university down there? Shimmering Wings? Golden Beetle? I'm sorry. I wasn't paying attention to that kind of detail."

"Have you seen Mullet or Sage since Friday?"

"I haven't. I would have asked them how their trip went if I had seen them, and I didn't do that. Hey, let me take a peek at our books. Let you know if any of the three have been in at all."

He waved Karen toward the dark abyss from which he had emerged. The office he led her into was a great deal lighter. The desk was strewn with papers heaped in a way that made Karen's fingers itch to straighten them.

"Let's see… Ah. Here we go." Adin flipped through a thick black binder. "I can't let you see this, of course, but I can confirm that none of them have been in this week. Last I saw Strings signed in was two weeks ago for taco night— just as I suspected." He closed the book and put it on top of a particularly precarious stack of papers and folders.

"Oh. Did he actually stay here?"

"Yes…"

"And his mother gave him permission to stay here?" Once again, Karen was shocked by this rule. How did kids fleeing a dangerous situation ever stay in a shelter?

"Of course. You know, it's not like any of them to not at least drop by for a whole week. The weather being nice could explain that. I understand a good number of kids have found some hiding places to camp out in various parks. No need for their parents to call in, it's pretty warm and all that."

"They're not all freaked out about staying in parks, considering what's happening?"

"We do what we can to educate. Ask kids to go home if they can. We've put together a flyer to help remind them of ways to be safe."

Adin stepped back from his desk and eyed the layers of papers with a practiced eye. "Ah, here it is." He pulled out an inch-thick stack of green papers without knocking anything else over.

Karen read through the list of standard precautions. *Don't go anywhere alone. Stay in groups of two or more! Don't accept rides from strangers. Check in with friends regularly.* She folded the paper and shoved it in her pocket.

"Some of the kids I spoke to earlier today were talking about this Seattle Clean Streets Movement. *Cleaners.* You know anything about that?"

Adin sighed and shook her head. "Only that the kids are un-informed and scared of something that's not really happening."

"Are you saying these cleanings aren't happening?"

"The part the kids are talking about, the kids being taken away? Yeah, it's happening, but the kids aren't being shoved into ovens or anything. These days, it might be safer for them to be taken into juvie, or sent home."

"The cleaners, though. I only know what I've read in the papers. Have you seen them grab kids?"

Adin shook his head. "Nah. It's nasty, and if they see

someone underage, they do have to report it. They're not supposed to engage with people beyond that. They call CPS, and the CPS folks handle it. Usually, the kids go to detention until parents claim them. Or they go into foster."

"So, is there any chance you know a guy the kids call Jolly?"

"Jolly? Kids who play music talk about him. From what I can tell, he's recording them and using their music. Background beeps and whistles. Something about video games, maybe? Sorry, I don't know much else."

"Can you give me Sage or Mullet's phone number?"

Adin shook his head. "That's stretching the rules."

"And you never stretch the rules?"

"I break rules when it helps a child. Giving you, a total stranger, their contact information could bring them harm. So no."

"Notice any weirdos hanging around?"

Adin's chin skin tripled as he pulled his head back in an exaggerated show of surprise. "Define weirdo? Take a look around you."

"Right." The shelter was within a block of one of the city's largest parks, where you could score any kind or combination of drugs and sex. And they were on Capitol Hill, long known as Seattle's counterculture neighborhood. "Anyone hanging around that shouldn't be? Perverts? Pedos?"

Adin recoiled at her bluntness. "Ms. Hunter, I assure you that we are very safe around here. The kids we serve are very safe. We protect them here."

He was ruffled. Defensive. She'd hit a nerve then.

Maybe the pervs were attracted to this place for the plethora of gay youth it served.

"I'm trying to find out if someone from the shelter might have seen Strings since Friday. The last time *anyone* has seen him. Anyone who hangs out with the kids? Takes them to lunch? Offers to buy them food or clothing?"

Adin blinked a couple of times, and his jaw dropped open for a second. He cupped one arm at the elbow as he fanned his face with the other.

"Adin?" Karen asked, drawing out the second syllable in a long question.

"You know what, Ms. Hunter? It's time for you to go. Staff needs to get ready for this evening."

Karen picked up a brochure from the information table in the front hall and made a note to check out all the staff online. The shelters required staff and volunteers to have background checks. And the police must have checked out everyone connected to all the local shelters. She doubted the police would open their files for her. Besides, if they'd found anything incriminating on someone at a shelter they would have made an arrest or something.

Karen went for a long walk around the perimeter of the park to clear her head. She had slept in her car for only three weeks between welcome couches. She'd managed the car time by showering at the school gym before classes. Luckily, friends were kind and Karen couch-surfed for two years while she finished high school. Shelters hardly existed back in the eighties, and there certainly were none in Bozeman, Montana.

Her first college dorm room had been her first experience of having a place all to herself. No roommates meant no one going through her belongings. Having a reliable bed available was like winning the lottery.

Karen meandered in and out of the little restaurants and coffee shops up and down Capitol Hill, leaving flyers everywhere that would let her. She put one on every post she passed. Each thump of the staple gun against wood chipped at her resolve to ignore the thought that Jamie might be with a killer.

## 8

_______________

As Karen was about to head home for the day, she got a text from Court saying that there was a detective from the missing-teens task force who wanted to interview her. A shiver ran down her back. While she was getting more comfortable talking to Court, other cops still made her antsy. All this would be a huge non-issue soon anyway. She would have a good laugh with Jamie when he showed up at her house for dinner as usual in a couple hours.

Karen took the light rail downtown and walked the last few blocks to the police station. The last time she'd ridden up the elevator, she'd been a suspect in the murder of her favorite client, Berkeley Drummond.

Now, she was voluntarily visiting the man who had accused her of killing Berkeley, though Court had never been as convinced of her guilt as his partner had been. Ivy Langston had treated Karen like she was a different level of humanity.

As Karen stepped out onto the fifth floor, she scanned

the room. Court Pearson stood up, his arms up overhead in a stretch. A scar ran along the left side of his face, not quite hugging his hairline. It was a fine silver now, maybe invisible in poor light. When she'd seen him a couple months before, it was pinker. Fresher.

She approached with a calm dignity, as though she was wandering in to a place she totally belonged. A sudden case of imposter syndrome flooded through her. She tossed on the old mantle of professional domme—an aloof, commanding presence. She was suddenly someone who belonged and didn't give a rat's ass about what others thought of her. She was a licensed P.I. now, damn it, and she had every right to be there.

Court put his hand on Ivy's shoulder. "Thanks. When you're done with that, can you see if the tox report on Mason Helms is back yet?"

Karen shuddered. Mason Helms was the most recent of the victims. "Tox report? Were these kids being drugged?"

Court spun around to face her, obviously unaware she was there. "Tox reports are part of the regular routine in homicide investigations." His jaw was a little more square than she remembered. Was it from clenching his teeth, or was he feeding her a line?

"Sorry. I overheard you. It's all pretty interesting."

"Yeah. Hey, I need to grab that report for you. I'll be right back." He spun away and left her at the entrance to Ivy's cubicle.

"How's it going, Detective Langston?"

"You know, I never really apologized for accusing you of murder. I was sure you were guilty for a while there." Ivy stood and held out her hand. "I hope you'll accept my apology now."

Karen was not expecting that. She smiled and took Ivy's hand. "Thanks for saying that, Detective Langston. I appreciate it."

"So, pro-dominatrix to private investigator? You're not trying very hard to be likable to cops, are you?"

"It's my personal goal in life to choose careers that piss you all off."

Ivy laughed. "You do seem attracted to careers that skirt the law."

Karen leaned to the side so she could get the best view of Court as he walked away. "It must be hard to work with someone who is so..." She fanned herself with her fingers.

Ivy followed her gaze. "Court? Really?"

"He's pretty irresistible. I would get distracted being around him all the time..." It was more than his classic good looks. He was smooth? Confident? Manly? *Ding. Ding. Ding.* All of the above.

"Yeah, well, you get used to him. Besides, he's not my type, if you know what I mean." Ivy's eyes grew wide with emphasis.

*Yes*, Karen did know what she meant. She stopped herself from rolling her eyes at Ivy. There was no reason to alienate a possible ally. "Well, he would be mine if he weren't a cop. Now that? *Dating a cop? That* is a complete deal breaker."

Court appeared then, waving a slim file at Karen.

"Here's the MP report on your boy." He flipped it open, pausing, his eyes narrowing on Ivy and Karen. "Anyway, there's not a huge amount going on here. We've got the report. A photo. We put a BOLO out on him, technically for his own safety."

"They won't arrest him, will they?"

"Probably take him into custody, hand him over to CPS. Since he's only sixteen, they'd process him as a runaway, most likely. Since his parents reported him, they'd try to reunify right away." Court lifted a couple pages up and skimmed some more. "Yeah, well, the parents reported that there was an argument and he was told to come back later. Since he didn't come back, they declared him a runaway."

"That's how they spun their 'don't come back until you're no longer gay' eviction," Karen said, not even trying to keep the acid tone out of her voice.

Court shook his head and let out a tired sigh. "Not that they mentioned that to CPS. They couldn't admit to kicking him out, now could they?"

"I know for a fact his father said he was only welcome back after he stopped being gay. So the come-back-later thing?" Karen's heart was pounding in her chest like she'd run a mile sprint in record time. *How could they lie like that? It was so brazen.*

Court made a note in the file. "Sucks."

"I should have insisted he live with us. I tried. But he refused."

"So, maybe he *is* more of a runaway since he refused to stay in a safe environment when offered."

"Right. CPS is overworked and overloaded. I'm sure it's not getting any better."

Karen filled him in on the rest of her day. "There's something weird about Rainbow Landing. I can't quite put a finger on it."

"It's ramshackle. All the victims stayed there at some point. Every one of them. But, I can tell you, all the victims stayed at Harbor House, too. There are several other things they had in common I can't disclose."

"You don't think Adin has anything to do with it?"

"The guy who runs Rainbow Landing?" Court paused. "We checked him out early on. I get the sense he's a drama queen, not a killer."

That fit with her impression, too. "Maybe it's the place. Both shelters are within walking distance of Cal Anderson, but this one is a magnet for LGBTQ youth."

"Yeah, the whole area is changing, but there's a still a pretty strong gay element to it. Plus there are people working the streets all the time… drugs, sex, you can find it there."

"I am still hoping he's in Portland or somewhere between here and Portland," Karen said. "This will all be moot when he shows up at my house tonight for his regular sleepover."

"The State Patrol is part of the BOLO. If their car is broken down on the interstate, they'll be the ones to find them."

"So, you said there was someone in Missing Persons who wanted to interview me?"

"As I said on the phone," Court said, "this special task force is taking a keen interest in all current missing-youth cases. Especially males."

"I can be of help. I'll be spending quite a bit of time on the streets and in the shelters. Maybe I can see the other cases? I have a pretty good memory for faces."

Court tilted his head to one side, his gray eyes narrowing

as he studied her. It must have only been a few seconds, but it felt way longer.

"Let's me take you over there and introduce you."

<br>

"I'm heading back in," Ivy said as she passed Karen and Court. "See you around, Karen."

Ivy slipped into a room. The door swung open wide enough for Karen get a glimpse of a huge smart screen outlined in orange on the far wall and several tables ringing the room. Boxes marked EVIDENCE were neatly organized on top of the tables. Karen was pretty sure that was the room where everything was happening.

About six people were inside the room going through the boxes. "FBI? I thought cops didn't like the FBI getting involved."

"Au contraire. We *love* the FBI getting involved." Court grabbed at her elbow to urge her past the door. "You don't want to see all that. Trust me."

"That the incident room?"

"You watch too much television."

"You know, being a P.I. is nothing like I thought it was going to be."

"Were you hoping to be a female Magnum?"

"Okay, maybe not that. I spent most of last week sitting in my car following an asshole dad around to porn shops and strip clubs."

"Yeah, that's the lot of most P.I.s I know. Classy work. At least the job you're on now is maybe going to help someone, right?"

Karen didn't need anyone trying to justify her career. It wasn't like he really knew what her life was like. "I saved two kids from a house fire on Monday night. I get plenty of opportunity to help people."

The corner of Court's mouth twitched a little. "I'd like to hear about that sometime."

He opened another door onto a room with five desks in it. The tangle of wires hanging off the back of monitors on each desk were a mess. The room had been cobbled together in a hurry and felt temporary at best.

Court introduced her to Denzel Cook, a younger man with a thick shadow of stubble on his face.

"Thanks for coming in, Ms. Hunter." Denzel stood up halfway and held out his hand, palm up, over the chair next to his desk. Karen sank into the chair, crossing her legs comfortably.

"I'll leave you to it," Court said, leaving the file on Jamie with Denzel. He put a hand on Karen's shoulder and squeezed. She tried to get a read on the gesture, but he turned away and left before she could see his face.

Denzel's eyes were streaked with red, and he blinked at his screen to focus on it. "Let's see. We're still linking paper and computers on this." He opened a fresh yellow pad and spent half an hour grilling her on Jamie and her investigation.

"He's already got a **BOLO** out on him. If a cop finds him, they'll snag him and take him to Juvie. That's about all we can do," he concluded.

"I'll be coming across a lot of kids on the street," Karen said. "I can let you know if I see any others who have been reported missing. Not that I can memorize every one of their faces."

"That would be awesome. Truly." He stood up and pointed to a desk in the corner. "You can work over there. I'll bring the books over to you."

Karen's heart swelled as she flipped through the pages, happy to recognize a couple of kids already. Tink's parents had reported her missing four weeks ago, even though she'd been living on the street much longer. Her real name was Shawna Cleary. Shawna's photo showed her with long brown hair, but her features hadn't changed.

"I saw Shawna this morning. Her street name is Tink. She helped me talk to a group of kids, including this guy," Karen said flipping to another page. "I didn't talk to him directly, but he was enjoying a chocolate croissant when I left." Those were the only two she recognized from the morning.

"This morning? Where?"

Karen told him about her earlier trip to Cal Anderson Park. She fanned the pages in the binder. "I'm not sure I can memorize all of their names, but I have a lot of their faces in my head. I'll let you know if I see anyone."

"We appreciate the extra eyes out there."

"The people at the shelter are pretty good at recognizing kids, too. You might run this book by them."

"Yeah. The shelter people are likely to talk to you before they talk to us," Denzel said. "Most of the kids they serve are actively hiding from authorities, and they don't want to be seen as colluding with the enemy."

The detective made notes on the files of the two kids Karen had seen. The fact that there were only about a hundred kids in their investigation files made her queasy. Only a hundred kids with families who cared enough to call the police. Denzel shook her hand and set her loose.

She wanted to thank Court for his help, but he wasn't at his desk. Ivy wasn't at hers, either. They were probably both in the incident room. With all that enticing evidence. There weren't many people in the squad room. Karen edged away from Court's desk until she was at the door.

She opened it without knocking and stepped inside. The guys she guessed were FBI agents stood in a semi-circle behind Court and Ivy. They faced a smart board as Ivy clicked through various slides. Each was outlined in a different color, and it wasn't until they'd scrolled through it a couple of times that Karen realized they were in order of the rainbow colors, like in that kid's song. *Red, Orange, Yellow, Green and Blue, Indigo and Violet, too.*

There were boxes labeled with names she recognized from news reports on color coded tables, also in the order of the rainbow. The board was far enough away that she couldn't make out faces on any of the photos, but she could make out the shape of a naked body on the ground, tied with ropes into a fetal position.

The image of Berkeley hanging dead in her studio, the smell of his body, the surreal nature of it all, suddenly overwhelmed her. The ropes he'd been bound in were purple, and the knot-work done in neat Shibari bondage. These were boys, hardly men at all, tied up to make them as small a package as possible.

The air around her was extremely hot all of a sudden, as if it had been completely sucked out of the space until breathing was nearly impossible. A strong whiff of patchouli, cloying and musky made her gag and cough.

"What are you doing in here?" Court came directly at her, and spun her toward the door.

Karen couldn't find the air to breathe. She was sweating. And shaking. As she turned to face Court, his face shifted and everything around him was turning into shadows. All of a sudden, his face was inches from hers.

"Shit. Come over here."

He guided her out of the room and to the chair at his desk. He placed a hand on her neck. "Drop your head to your knees and breathe."

Court dropped to his haunches, keeping a hand on her shoulder the whole time. It took a couple of minutes to be able to breathe freely again. She lifted her head and saw more concern than annoyance on Court's face. "I'm sorry. I don't know what happened."

"What did you see in there?"

The way he asked it wasn't accusatory, but more like he wanted to help her figure it out. "It was the ropes."

He tilted his head to the side. "Drummond?"

"*My* ropes." He had been meticulously bound in rope she had bought specifically for him. To please him. Not to kill him.

"These aren't the same."

"I know. I don't understand why I got all…" She waved a hand around as she flailed for the words to describe what was happening inside. She shook her head, defeated.

"Let's get outside, into some fresh air. Can you walk okay?"

He used an arm to support her down the escalator and

all the way onto the sidewalk. He couldn't wait to get rid of her, could he?

"Where's your car?"

"Over by Rainbow Landing. I took the light rail over."

"Do you want a ride back?"

"No. Don't worry about me. I'm fine. I'm so embarrassed."

"What you saw in there would make a lot of people throw up."

"I'm not generally the queasy type."

"Stay focused on your kid and, keep me updated, okay?"

"I will."

Court ran his fingers through his hair. It was longer than she'd ever seen it, not that she'd seen him that many times. He usually kept it close-cropped like most police.

"I'm sorry. I should have knocked. I wanted to thank you for helping me out. Introducing me to Denzel. He's really nice."

He gave her a half-smile. He knew she was stretching the truth. She had wanted to see what was inside the room. She couldn't un-see it now. She would be haunted by these fresh images of children cut down in their prime. Images of Jamie's body, all gory and tangled with ropes and gaping gashes, flitted through her mind.

"I won't lie," Court said. "Jamie fits the victim profile. Young. Gay. Homeless. The good news is this guy is taking his time between victims. It's been less than a week since his last was found, so we have time. And the odds are still with you that your kid is okay."

She hugged herself and stood back up onto the curb next to him. "What is happening to them, Court? The press hasn't mentioned the knife wounds or the ropes. Those gashes were knife wounds, right?"

"We don't tell them everything." He put a hand on her shoulders. His grip was firm and warm. "And I'm trusting you to keep what you saw up there to yourself."

"Like what happened with me last year?" Someone had leaked photos of Drummond's body and doxxed Karen's private information to the public during the investigation into his death. The leak originated somewhere in the Seattle Police Department, and yet, no one had ever been held accountable for it.

Court colored. "I can't tell you how sorry I am about all that. I'm really, really, sorry. I don't see any way to make it up to you. If there is a way, I would totally do it."

"It's not like it was your fault, right?"

There was a long uncomfortable silence. Karen stared at a piece of trash on the ground and breathed in to calm herself. "You're the one who let me loose in the police station."

"You were supposed to leave directly from Missing Persons."

"I missed that message somehow." Karen didn't move away. The warmth of his fingers against her skin was comforting.

"Right. Stay focused on Jamie. Straying from that isn't going to help anyone. Besides, it could be dangerous." He squeezed her shoulders gently before letting go.

"There's a part of you that believes Jamie could be with the killer, isn't there?" she asked.

"Let the cops do the cop work. Look for your kid, not for a killer. It's not your job." Court's smile vanished. "Keep me updated on anything you learn. Text anytime. I'm here twenty hours a day."

In spite of the heat of the late afternoon hovering over the city, a cold chill traipsed up her spine and left the fine hairs on her arms and back of neck rigid. The fact that Court took everything she'd told him about Jamie seriously was way more disconcerting than comforting.

"I'll text you later, after Jamie shows up at my house," Karen said, feigning a lightness that wasn't there. The denial was rote, and she walked slowly toward the light rail station. She could tell herself that Jamie was safe, that he would be waiting at her house with Sophie, but, deep down, she knew Jamie was in trouble.

## 9

WHILE ON THE TRAIN BACK TO CAPITOL HILL, KAREN texted Sophie to let her know she was heading home and had ordered delivery of four pizzas and a big salad from Zeek's. The "duplicated past orders" feature on their website made ordering a breeze.

The change in Cal Anderson Park from the morning to now was marked. In the morning, the park was crowded with homeless teens and moms with strollers. Now, as dinner and evening approached, the greens were covered in picnic blankets. Couples lounged against each other and families sat in circles with plates balanced on their knees.

Karen passed out flyers and asked people if they'd seen Jamie as she meandered through the park and back toward Rainbow House. Many recognized him and commented on his music. But nobody had new information.

Even though the car was in the shade, the steering wheel was too hot to touch. She started the car, cranked up the air, and checked her email.

A white minivan pulled into the loading space in front of the shelter. Karen rolled down her window and turned off her car. Adin Sanchez scurried out of the shelter and approached the van. The driver smiled and rolled down his window. Adin put both hands on the car door and leaned in. Karen could only see Adin's profile, and she was too far away to hear what they were saying, but their frowny faces and broad hand gestures made it obvious they were arguing about something.

Vans in general gave her the creeps, and the guy who was driving it put Karen on edge. Maybe it was his perfect hair, gelled into place. Or maybe it was the button-down shirt and tie that remained fixed even in ninety-degree weather. The van was immaculately clean. Karen snapped a quick picture of the plates as Adin stepped away and it sped off.

Adin beelined back toward the shelter. Karen scrambled out of her car and raced to intercept him, catching up with him at a side door. A couple of the kids in line waiting to get through the front door gave them the once-over.

Adin pulled at the door. Karen shouldered herself against it, shutting it again.

"You're looking guilty about something, Adin. What's up with the creeper in the minivan?"

He cast a furtive glance down the street in the direction the van had gone and slumped his shoulders. "It's none of your business."

"You were arguing. Why was he so angry?"

Adin heaved a huge sigh. His eyes were huge round shimmering pools, ready to overflow onto his pasty white cheeks. She got the sense he was good at turning the waterworks on and off at will. *Fool me once, buddy…* Any ounce of pity she might have felt for him evaporated. Court had called him a drama queen for a reason.

"We don't have enough beds here. Mr. P… *he* takes four or five kids home a couple nights a week. They would be on the street otherwise."

"How does he select who he helps? Surely he can't house everyone that doesn't fit here."

"We send him the younger ones. We're not allowed to house anyone under eighteen without parental permission. Sometimes these kids are afraid of letting their parents know where they are, and it's too, too awful to know they'll be out on the street."

"So you send them off in a minivan with a stranger? Without documenting them or getting parental permission?"

Adin shook his head vigorously. "It's not like that. We've done a background check on him as a regular volunteer. He offered to take some home one night after a boy broke down out front crying. He was working the kitchen, and he told me about his house. I did an inspection and everything. It's a nice house, and he has two rooms with bunk beds. He can take six kids in. Six!"

"It's not legal." Was his discomfort about helping kids where he wasn't supposed to? "You ever see Strings go off with him?"

"No. Not that I recall. But, I don't keep track because…" His long fingers fluttered up and around his head and away in a gesture that mimicked a butterfly or moth.

"Any chance he's exploiting them?"

Adin shook his head. "No. Of that, I'm certain. He's doing this to atone for his sins. You see, his son was murdered while living on the streets. And he feels guilty. He lives a couple of blocks away from here. Takes in kids to make amends."

"His son was murdered?" Karen asked.

"Yes. For being gay. It happens more than you hear about."

"When was this?" There were way too many stories like this one. "Had he kicked his kid out for being gay?"

"Isn't that the truth for most of these babies?"

"So, this guy? His kid died and now he's doing penance or something to make up for it?"

"Yes. He only had one son, and he was gutted by the murder." Adin put his hand up to his throat and tugged at his collar. "I need to get inside. I'm not allowed to facilitate third-party spaces, and I could get in huge trouble if anyone finds out about this."

"Does this guy have a name?"

Adin shook his head vigorously. "You need to leave now, Ms. Hunter."

"How about the police? Have you told them this guy is taking kids to his house?"

Adin's jaw dropped open and his hand flew to his mouth. Karen took that as another no-comment. A tiny part of her rejoiced in snagging a new lead that Court probably didn't have.

She released the door and Adin yanked it open. A moment later it closed with a decisive bang, leaving Karen alone on the side porch. As she passed the kids standing in line, she tried to memorize their faces and compare them to the photos she'd seen back at the station. Where were the hundred kids in the book? And if the twenty or so lined up outside the shelter weren't in the Missing-Persons reports, why not?

She got back to her car and turned the air on high again. While she waited for the car to cool, she called Maggie. Karen didn't have quick access to DMV records. Maggie, however, had contacts that would bypass the wait.

"No problem," Maggie said after Karen gave her the plate information. "I'm guessing my guy can't get to it until tomorrow. He's probably already left for the day."

"I'm heading home anyway," Karen said. "I'm bushed. You never mentioned how tiring it can be to chase leads all day."

There was something totally creepy about the guy picking up kids in a minivan. Maybe he wasn't a serial killer. Maybe he was a pervert preying on kids in a different way.

**10**

---

When Karen arrived home, it was to a house full of laughter. Acorn, Bean, Poe, Tink, Velma and Sophie crowded around the open pizza boxes on the table. Tonight, there were no complete strangers at her table. All the kids had been here at least once before.

"Hi, Mrs. H," Tink said brightly. "Thanks for having us again. Pizza is awesome."

"You're welcome," Karen said, trying to hide her rising panic when it sank in that Jamie wasn't there. She loaded up a plate with salad and a slice of pizza, and retreated to the kitchen to let the kids talk more freely. She relied on the out-of-sight-out-of-mind theory for spying on them.

She nibbled at her pizza and sucked down small swallows of a beer. At first, Karen had insisted the kids Sophie brought home on Wednesdays give her their "real names." It took her a month to fully understand that some of them used their street names because their given names were hurtful and painful reminders of their past. When they separated from their parents, they wanted it to be as complete as possible.

Their adults had messed up in one way or another, and the last thing Karen wanted was to be seen in the same light as their parents—an adult, sure, but not a hateful one. It was a tricky balance at times. She wasn't a friend, either. She sometimes wondered if Sophie used a street name or what it might be. She hadn't asked because she was not sure she wanted to know or put Sophie into the awkward position of having to lie to her.

Karen leaned against the counter in the kitchen, far enough away from the table that they might forget she was there, but close enough that she could hear them. As usual, once Karen was out of sight, the kids opened right up.

"I really hoped Strings would show up tonight," Sophie said.

"Dude went to Portland." Bean's reedy tenor was muffled around a bite of pizza.

"That's what everyone is saying, but he usually texts me back no matter where he is," Sophie said.

"Maybe he decided to stay down there," Poe said. "The busking at the market is really good."

"Isn't that only on the weekends?" Velma asked.

"I don't know. He was with Mullet and Sage, and, like, they haven't been around either," Poe said. "They're all probably still down there and are too selfish to check in."

"He's been here every week that I've been here," Acorn said. Acorn preferred the pronoun "they" rather than "he" or "she." The kid was the most androgynous of this whole street family. They shifted between neckties paired with flouncy skirts and a lacy scarf over a t-shirt and jeans. The tiny braided knots crowning their head were three inches longer than since she'd last seen them. They went the next step beyond wearing gender-specific clothing to a unique blend of mystification.

In spite of Karen's liberal tendencies, the use of the word "they" for a single person tripped her up. She continued to work at it although she would sometimes get confused about how many people she was talking about or to. When Sophie said that "they are coming over," it no longer necessarily meant multiple friends.

Jamie showed for the sleepovers every Wednesday except for one since he'd been kicked out. Even then, he texted ahead so she wouldn't buy extra food. As if he needed to worry about her having leftovers.

"I've texted them all," Sophie said. "Multiple times. Jamie? Sage? Mullet? And none of them have answered."

"Like any of them are reliable," Poe said. "Phones probably got stolen or somethin'."

"It's weird," Sophie said.

"At least," Bean said, "with all three of them gone, it's not likely Strings is, you know, off with that Dog Park dude."

Karen peered around the corner. Of course they were all following this disaster.

"Dude, why did you go there?" Velma asked, tossing her pizza onto her plate. "That whole thing is so sick."

"Isn't it where we all go whenever someone new goes missing?" Tink asked. "You know, at some, like, deep level we have to be thinking it. Not that any of us want it to be true."

"Did you know any of the others?" Velma asked.

"Shit. Others?" Acorn said. "You gotta not talk about Strings like that."

"But did you?" Velma asked again.

The others fell silent for a moment. Poe's already pale face lost what little color it had. He picked at his fingernails. "I liked JoJo. A lot. Wagyu? Him too. Fuck. I knew them all."

Tink sighed. "I knew Stain and JoJo. They were both awesome. Stain was like, Mr. Speedy on the guitar. Maybe not as good as Strings. They were all good."

"I guess I'm safe," Velma said. "But all you twinks are, like, open prey, dudes."

"I'm not a twink," Poe said, straightening up. He pulled his shoulders back and flexed his arm. "I'm going straight for bear." He rubbed at the scraggly growth on his chin. He had a long way to go.

Velma threw a napkin at him. "Yeah, right. Keep telling yourself that."

Acorn laughed. "Poe is going to be hot someday. When he's all grown up."

Poe wrapped his arms around himself and slumped back into his chair. "I bet it's that pervert Jolly."

Sophie's eyes widened and she shook her head. "That's like, way, way, too obvious. Everyone knows about him, so the police would have figured him out by now." There was something in Sophie's tone when she spoke about Jolly that niggled at Karen.

"Do the police know about him? Really? 'Cause I was there yesterday recording some licks for him," Acorn said. "He didn't act any different than usual."

"That's because you're like, so black he doesn't bother you," Beans said.

"He better not," Acorn said, laughing. "This might be the only thing in my entire life that is good about being midnight. Fucking Jolly only likes young white twinks on the side. He likes my music and *that is all* he likes about me."

Karen grabbed a second beer out of the fridge and slammed down half of it. It was cold, and fizzy and felt nice going down her throat. Jolly. She was going to hunt down this guy and figure him out.

Robbie came into the kitchen and grabbed a beer out of the fridge. They clinked their bottles gently and tipped them at each other.

"I thought you were hiding at your place," Karen said.

"I got bored. And lonely."

She nodded toward Sophie. "I sometimes wonder where she came from." Her personality was unlike that of either of her parents. Easygoing. Friendly. Happy.

"She's her own person," Robbie said.

"I need to ask these guys some things about Jamie. She's going to hate me for it."

"She'll get over it."

Karen took another swig of her beer and another bite of pepperoni before approaching the table. They probably expected her to grab another slice and disappear again. Instead, she dropped into the empty chair at the table. The one Jamie would normally sit in.

"So, I'm really worried about Strings," she said. "I'm sure you all are, too. Anything you can tell me about him might be helpful, even if it makes him look bad. I'm going to help find him, and make sure he's okay."

The kids all exchanged glances with each other, except Sophie. She had dropped her head and was closely examining her pizza.

Karen spent ten minutes chatting with them in general about Strings. The songs he usually played, where he busked. They confirmed what she already knew about his schedule. She was building a picture of him that was both comforting and concerning. He was friendly to all, but no one was as close to him as Sophie was. If she didn't know where he was, no one would. He skittered from group to group, generally making himself friendly and useful from moment to moment—a social butterfly liked by everyone.

"Things have changed a lot since I was homeless," Karen said. "That was a long time ago, and I can't pretend to know what it's like for you all these days." Sophie gave Karen a small smile of encouragement. "I know things can get… rough out there. Anyone know if Strings used drugs?"

"No way." A chorus of denials filled the room. "No… no… not Strings…"

She held up her hands. "Okay, Okay. Fine. I'll assume he's not lying in a flophouse out of his mind on meth or whatever it is people are doing these days. Do any of you know if Strings was *working* at all?"

Poe shifted in his seat and stuck his hands under his thighs. The rest found great interest in their pizza.

"Hey, no judgment here. This is all about helping Jamie."

Silence.

"Okay, so maybe something easier. If you could all ask everyone you know to help find him. Take flyers around town. Ask about Mullet and Sage, too. If they're all partying down in Portland, we need to know." Karen waved a stack of flyers at them. "Take some in the morning before you leave, okay?"

The awkwardness that descended after she asked about Jamie working the street disappeared as she gave them some tasks that might actually help finding him.

"All right, then," she said. "One last thing. If you see any of the three, text or call me immediately and let me know where. My number is on the flyer, okay?"

Everyone nodded their heads. "Tink, I need a word with you in private."

Tink followed Karen down the hall. Karen lowered her voice so the others wouldn't overhear. "Tink, I was at the missing-persons desk today. They have a special task force in place. Your parents filed a report last week placing you as a runaway."

"They noticed I was gone, huh?"

"They'd welcome you back. Would you like me to take you home tomorrow morning? I could go with you to be a buffer."

Tink stepped back, hands up. "No! There's no way I'm going back there. Ever. Okay? They may want me, but I sure as hell don't want them."

If a kid ran away, usually something on the parental end was messed up. "You can get emancipation so you're not on the runaway grind," Karen said. "We could get you into proper foster care if you want. If something bad is going on at home."

Tink shook her head, strong and firm. "No. Thanks, but no. Like I said, Ms. H, I am fine the way I am. Okay?"

Pushing Tink any harder would achieve nothing. "Okay, okay. If you change your mind, I'm here to help. Got it?"

"I've been in foster," Tink said. "At least, you know, I know my mom loves me, even if she's a shit mom. Fosters? They are in it for the money. Love isn't part of the deal. I can't go back there. You have to promise me you're not going to tell anyone I'm here." Her eyes darted toward the front door as if she were ready to run for it.

Karen had blundered into another mistake by telling Denzel about seeing Tink earlier in the day. "I won't let anyone know you are here, okay? But I did tell the detective running missing persons that I saw you at the park this morning. You might want to keep your head down when you're there next."

Karen returned to the kitchen and leaned against Robbie, seeking physical warmth and strength. "Well, that wasn't a complete bust," she said.

"Teens are not known for being open to adults," he said around his mouthful of food.

"I suspect she has some sort of abuse going on at home. Stepdad. Something."

"Any proof?"

"Nope. And that's why I'll keep my promise to not tell the cops where she is."

"Still breaking the law a little bit at a time, eh?" he asked, teasing.

"Some habits are hard to break." She kissed Robbie on the cheek. "I'm going down to my office to do some research. I have to find this Jolly guy they were talking about."

**11**

———

AS SOON AS THE KIDS WERE SITUATED IN THE BASEMENT, Karen went into her office and let Court know that Jamie was a no-show.

She texted Denzel Cook a note that she had offered Shawna a ride home. She didn't tell him that the teen was still in her house for fear he might send someone to collect her. He sent back a sad face and a thanks, telling her he'd let her parents know that she was sighted and safe sometime today.

Karen could now claim two contacts in the police department and not feel squigged by either one of them. Not that anyone else was keeping score. She wasn't ready to count Ivy as a safe cop. The way Ivy had said "he's not my kind of guy, if you know what I mean" felt like a subtle invitation for Karen to diss Court. She wasn't joining in on that game. Not with Ivy.

After an hour of eye-straining searching, she figured out that Jolly was actually Marcus Jolly, the thirty-five-year-old owner of Green Lake Studios. Not a very inspiring name, but easy enough to find on Google Maps.

The photo of Jolly on his website showed him to every bit as smarmy as she had imagined. There was something about his dimples and boyish face that reminded her of a young Tom Cruise doing some *Risky Business*, but with a layer of gel in his hair that would give Tom Hiddleston's Loki a run for his money. She knew men like this.

Karen did a thorough background check on him. Nothing popped up as particularly unusual. The website was misleading. It was crammed with modern and artsy shots to make the studio look like a major concern. The profile she'd built on her own painted a slightly different picture.

He owned a moderately sized condo not far from his studio. The only vehicle registered under his name was a used BMW, and there were none listed under his business. Jolly moved from place to place, switching states every couple of years following bankruptcy filings each time. Either he was a crappy businessman, or he was doing something illegal.

All of his businesses were linked to the music industry. His Colorado company description from 2012 listed his primary occupation as agent. Maybe he saw Jamie as his ticket to the top after so many failed attempts.

Jolly's website linked to a number of other studios and recording artists. There were half a dozen samples of music tracks on the site. All of them sounded pretty good to her, but she was no musician. There were no names of the musicians who'd made his samples anywhere.

None of the teens he was paying were given any credit.

He earned the majority of his money from larger studios by producing individual tracks for projects. She was listening to them when Sophie popped her head into her office.

"Mom, where'd you get that song?"

Karen clicked on the play button again. "Do you recognize this?" She turned the volume up to maximum. A plaintive guitar solo filled the room.

"That's a song Jamie is working on. The one he's all excited about."

"Is it his own music? Or is it from another group?"

"His own. He's always making things up like that. It's sad, isn't it?"

"Did you ever meet this Jolly guy?"

Sophie stared at the floor.

"Sophie?" Karen used her mommy tone, almost singing the last syllable and drawing it out.

Sophie chewed at her lower lip and sighed a long one before answering. "I think Jolly was paying people extra for other stuff."

"Stuff?"

"You know." Sophie focused on the corner of the room. "Besides music."

"Ahhh… Sophie, honey, was Jolly paying kids to have sex with him?" Karen had always believed talking openly about sexual things would make it easier, but teens would be teens.

Sophie avoided eye contact. "Yeah. I think so. I don't know the details, but Jolly liked people showing up alone for their sessions. And Jamie said something once…"

"Like?" Karen prompted.

"Jamie said he'd sorted it out, but not *what* exactly.

Something sexual, but I never got the details. The thing was, Jolly really wanted Jamie's music. And so, Jamie was all, like, music only. And Jolly never bugged him again."

"Other kids who might not be as talented? Jolly required sexual favors from them?"

Sophie finally met Karen's eyes again. "It's really hard to know what's a rumor and what's real. There *was* real music going on there. Lots of it. And he paid kids for it."

Engaging in survival sex might have made things easier for Karen when she was living in the street. She'd barely been able to scrape by on her two part-time jobs until she swung a nice scholarship at the University of Washington. Her Lifetime channel movie-of-the-week sob story of a life moved the right people enough to fund her way through school.

"Honey, you know I'm not the judge-y type."

"You are when it comes to me."

"I don't want you to have to resort to dangerous tactics to stay alive and fed."

"If Jamie were taking money for… things like that, would you still let him stay here?"

Karen stood up and put her arms around Sophie. "Of course. He's always welcome here."

"It's hard to know what you'd think. You come down hard on me when I get a B in school, and I'm not out there, doing, you know, whatever."

"You're my daughter. I have high expectations. You know I was a professional sex worker for years; I'm the last person to be mad at someone for selling their body for food."

Sophie hugged her back for a long, glorious moment.

Karen relished it. These clingy hugs were few and far between, and she imagined they'd shrivel up all together for a few years. Her mother hadn't lived long enough for her to experience the promised reunion between mother and daughter.

"If you ever end up out on the streets, it will mean something major has gone wrong between us. Like, I'm thinking a refusal to deal with a major drug addiction. Or I'm dead," Karen said. "Actually, your dad would have to be dead, too."

Sophie laughed, but Karen wasn't joking.

"Sophie, you know I wouldn't ask if it weren't important. I need you to give me Sage and Mullet's numbers. I can't have you waiting on texts from them. I need to call them until they answer."

"Mom, that's like… breaking a trust. I can't do that."

"We're talking about Jamie. It is possible he is in some very real danger. Sage and Mullet are our best clues to piecing together this timeline." Karen pointed to the cork board and whiteboard on the wall.

Sophie approached it as if she hadn't seen it before. "Wow. This is detailed, Mom. It's like something on CSI." She pulled her phone out of her pocket and held it against her chest for a moment before handing it over. "Don't tell them how you got their numbers, okay?"

"I'll make something up if it ever comes to that."

Karen copied the numbers down, kicking herself for not demanding them earlier as a place to start. Sophie shifted out of her arms before Karen could hug her again. Sophie gave her an apologetic smile as she left to rejoin the others in front of the movie they'd chosen.

As soon as Sophie's door was closed behind her, she dialed Sage's number. No answer. She left a detailed message. She repeated the same with Mullet's number. She'd try again in the morning.

Before she started in on the venues where Sage and Mullet were supposed to play, Karen went through her notes and added each new person to a sticky note on her cork board. She assumed the police were checking out the staff and volunteers at the shelters. She decided to focus on whether Jamie was with Mullet and Sage. If he was down in Portland hanging with friends, her relief would be about equal to her annoyance at his not answering her texts. At least that would mean he was safe.

Karen moved on to Adin's nebulous description about golden beetles and shimmering scarabs. After a half hour of poking around, she found six small-scale clubs that would host trios like Jamie's. One of these was The Screaming Scarab. The banner visuals included a golden scarab beetle flying across the screen and spinning around before landing on its feet in the middle of the banner. *Score one for Adin.*

The shows for that evening and forward were the only thing listed on the site. The past weekend had already been wiped clean. Luckily, the venue was open and the contact information clearly linked on the website. The manager told Karen they'd had an amateur night Friday night with a dozen groups performing. She texted him a photo of Jamie, Mullet and Sage as soon as she hung up. He didn't respond right away so she called four other clubs and got four solid dead ends.

The manager from The Screaming Scarab called back

as she hung up with the last club on her list. It was a good thing she'd included Sage and Mullet's photo with Jamie's.

"Yeah, there was just the two of them. Not the boy in the middle with the big smile. Just the redhead and the dorky-looking guy with the eighties hair."

"They had been booked as a trio originally?"

"I try not to get involved with all the drama, but those two had a screaming fight backstage. Almost kicked them out because of it."

"What were they fighting about?"

"I bet they were fighting about the kid in the middle. Yeah. So anyways, Red says, *It isn't fair to play it without him, it's his song.* And her boyfriend says, *Fuck him. He never showed. He doesn't have a say in it.* Girl goes quiet and says something I can't hear. Then the boy gets all pouty and says, *And, yeah, well, fuck him anyway.*"

**12**

---

KAREN SAT IN HER CAR FACING THE FRONT OF HARBOR House as she tried calling Sage and Mullet for the gazillionth time. After leaving yet another set of messages, she locked up her car and found the bus stop Jamie used most often to get to Green Lake. It wasn't Friday, but she followed the route as well as she could to duplicate his last known day.

The closest bus stop to Jolly's studio was right across the street from the Starbucks that Jamie used regularly on Fridays. She'd stop in there later to leave flyers and ask questions.

As she walked to the studio, she called Maggie to check in and update her on her progress, or lack of it.

"Did you do a criminal check on Marcus Jolly?" Maggie asked.

"Not a thorough one. He didn't have anything pop up right away."

"Tell you what, I'll do a more thorough one this afternoon, if you don't mind me butting in on your process," Maggie said.

"Mind? Hell, I don't accept free help from you. I appreciate it. Please keep track of your database expenses and I'll reimburse you."

"Your client's not paying, is she?" Maggie asked.

"No, she's not, but you shouldn't take a hit for me."

"It's a slow week. I'll do a deeper search on Jolly. He's only been here for two years. That's what I don't like."

"He moved around a lot and always after a bankruptcy," Karen said.

"Frequent moves can signify any number of things. Sounds like he could just be crap at business. And I'll be in that neighborhood on another case. You want me to give his condo the once-over?"

Some of the weight of the case lifted off Karen's shoulders at the offer. "Would you? That would be incredible. We could meet up for coffee later if you want and talk about it."

"I don't know if I'll have time for that. I'll text or email you with anything interesting."

The photo on the Green Lake Studios website was a masterpiece in Photoshop and wide-angle lenses. Jolly could argue artistic license over outright misrepresentation, but barely.

According to her search the previous evening, the building was three years old. There were shops on the ground floor and offices above. A glass door from the sidewalk opened directly onto a set of stairs leading up to the office space on the second floor.

A placard with the list of businesses was near the front door. It was an eclectic blend. A couple of non-profit organizations, a psychotherapy office, and two attorneys filled out the space. Green Lake Studios took up half of the building—a substantial bit of real estate.

The doors to the offices were made of frosted glass with a simple gold number next to them on the wall. The locks were old-school-keypad deadbolts with a separate key slot and simple pull-down knobs.

The door opened onto a small reception area decorated to impress. To the left of the door was a counter height L-shaped reception desk. Standing at the desk was a woman in leopard-skin leggings, a black crop top and golden stilettos that matched her six-inch-diameter hoop earrings.

Her long nails, also shiny gold, clicked against the keyboard for a few seconds before she turned her face toward Karen. Her mouth curved into a smile, but her eyes remained locked on the screen in front of her.

"Sign in. It'll be ten or fifteen." Her New York accent was emphasized by a grating nasal tone. She tapped a clipboard on the desk, still without looking away from her monitor.

Karen shut the door behind her and examined the clipboard in front of her. The sign-in sheet asked for a name, time, and instrument. That was it. Nine people had signed in ahead of her that morning already, but the waiting room was entirely empty. Either they were already gone or were in the back working. The other names on the list were a mixture of full names and street names and a variety of instruments—not all were guitar players.

"Is Jolly in?" Karen asked.

The receptionist dropped her chin and peered at Karen over her oversized cat-eye glasses, making eye contact for the first time. "Yeah. Oh, hey. You ain't here to play, though, are ya?"

"No. I just want to talk to him."

"Sign in, anyway. Wait your turn. Talk, play, his time's all the same." She shrugged and turned back to the computer.

"But there's no one else here," Karen said. She couldn't hear any music coming from behind the door leading from the reception room.

"Name on the paper, have a seat. He'll be ready when he's ready."

Karen put her name down and lifted the sheet to see if the previous days' sign-ins were there, but it was blank.

After several minutes, an inner door near the reception desk opened and Jolly called her name. In person, Jolly was more real, less polished than the photo on his website. He was almost model-perfect—tanned, tall, toned, bright white smile. His Dockers and tucked-in dress shirt open at the collar were pretty standard for Seattle business casual.

"Are you Marcus Jolly?" she asked as he waved her in.

"You didn't state your instrument on the sign-in sheet."

"I don't have one. I'm a private investigator. I need to ask you some questions about a kid who plays for you."

Jolly tossed the receptionist an icy look. Her eyes were glued to her monitor, but she raised a hand with her middle finger up in salute.

He sighed and motioned for her to follow him. "You have any idea how many kids I work with here?"

"Nope. Why don't you tell me?"

Jolly led her down the short hall to a room piled high with electronic equipment. He waved her to a seat and sat down in front of a large console. "Look, lady, I already talked to the cops. I don't have nothing to do with those dead kids."

Even though he put up a good front, Jolly came across as a con artist from New Jersey in person. If the cops had already been here to talk to him, she must be doing something right. What else tied Jolly to the dead boys?

"I'm here about Jamie Wells."

Genuine concern crossed his face. "Jamie? Why? Is he okay?"

"If I knew that, I wouldn't be here. When did you last see him?"

Jolly shrugged. "Friday. He comes every week for about three hours, we work on a bunch of tracks and he leaves. You wanna see him again? Come back tomorrow. He never misses a session."

"What happens during one of your sessions with him?"

Jolly spread out his hands and spun to face the huge console behind him. "Let me show you."

He tapped at some buttons and guitar music filled the room. It was an annoying, repetitive melody. "So, Jamie is an awesome guitar player. Seriously talented. Hendrix talented."

"You mean *Jimi* Hendrix?"

"You got it." He pointed a finger at her. "You know your music, don't you? Yeah, anyway. This track doesn't show his talent. I need this drivel you're hearing for a video game I'm workin' on. That's the bread and butter of my business. I write scores for games, get musicians to come in and play the individual parts for me, and put them together. It's fuckin' boring. Not music. But it pays the bills."

He tapped another button and the room was filled with a much more complicated song. Way better than the guitar had been by itself. He tapped again and another layer was added. He did this several times until the complete sound-track made sense.

"So, they don't have to play this all at the same time, you record each bit separately and put them together?"

"Exactly. I could never get them all in the same room at once. So friggin' unreliable. Jamie though? He's my golden boy. He comes every week at the same time. Solid worker."

"You know him as Jamie, not Strings?" Karen asked.

"Yeah. Jamie. What a great kid. Terrific. Just terrific. He's comfortable with me, I guess. No need to hide behind his street identity." Jolly sat back, lacing his fingers together over his stomach and shaking his head.

His bright smile and easy going manner came across as alpha-male, but her creepy-guy-dar was dinging at full bore. In spite of his overt solicitousness, Jolly had a wall built up around him.

He was holding back while merely pretending he was being open and forthcoming. His smile was a bit too bright and easy. He gushed information without really saying anything.

"Anything unusual happen when you saw him last?"

Jolly's lip twitched a little. "Not really. Just the same old, same old. He came in, we worked, he left. Just like usual."

"Did he say where he was going next?"

"It's not like we're buddies."

"How much did you pay him?"

Jolly's mouth tightened. "I pay twenty bucks an hour." He leaned forward and dropped his voice. "But, hey, ya know, I pay these kids in cash. As a favor to them. They don't have bank accounts, and they need the cash."

"You're telling me that you do it for their convenience, and not to save tons of money? How many teens working for you know musician union-scale rates are way more than what you pay them?" Karen was guessing, but she was sure as hell union rates would be more than twenty bucks an hour.

Jolly pursed his lips as a faint flush worked its way up his neck and cheeks. "I'm helping them. They're getting experience and pay. And, it's not illegal for me to hire independent contractors. None of them is union."

"You said Jamie is one of the best. And your sole motivation is to help these kids out with a little extra cash. For playing music."

Jolly stood up. "Is there anything else?"

"Can you play me the song that Jamie wrote? The one he's been working on?"

His eyes narrowed on Karen. He angled his head away from her to the side. "Who told you about that?"

"His best friend." No need to mention that his best friend was her daughter.

He sighed and twisted a few dials and punched some keys. Music flooded the room. Jolly dropped back into the chair and closed his eyes. The tiny lines on his face disappeared and he lapsed into something like a trance.

The music was pleasing. Beautiful, even. As was the voice. A female voice. Clear, sweet. The words were familiar, too. The last time she'd heard them was when Jamie played it at her house. He was doing the singing. The ballad was beautiful and as good as anything she'd heard on the radio.

"Wow. Who's the singer?"

Jolly shrugged. "Some girl that came with him a couple weeks ago. We laid down her track, but Jamie wanted to add another layer with the guitar last week."

A second guitar would account for why it sounded different than when she'd heard it before. That and the female voice. It could be Sage singing. *Had Jamie somehow gotten into the middle of that relationship?*

"What are your plans for this?"

Jolly wouldn't meet her eyes. "I told Jamie he needed some more songs. So that he could put out a whole album. But he wanted to put this up on YouTube." Jolly ran his hands through his hair. "Fuckin' *YouTube?* That's like giving your soul away."

"You wanted him to sell it. Or, more accurately, you wanted to sell it *for* him, didn't you? So you could take the majority of the profits for yourself and give him some measly percentage?"

Jolly's mouth tightened. "It ain't like that. I plan on doin' right by him. Make him into something big. He can be, you know?"

"What about the girl? What were you going to give her?"

"I don't even know who she is, okay? She came in and sang. Said she was doing it for Jamie. She wouldn't even take the twenty I offered her."

A tiny frisson of energy trilled up Karen's spine. "She wouldn't get any compensation? Even if this song went to the top of the charts?"

"She's well-fed and taken care of. Not a street kid, you know? Jamie knows who she is, and I'd find a way to include something for her when that song hits it. It totally can with a little more work."

"And what did Jamie think of this plan of yours?"

"We aren't done with it yet. He's booked for tomorrow to do the last edits. If he's around." Jolly held up his hands. "If what you say is true, he's missing? Really missing?" His shoulders drooped.

"Where was Jamie going after he left you on Friday?"

"Like, I said, I have no idea. He didn't talk much while he was here. Focused on the work. It's like he went to another world when he played. A real musician."

That was all well and good, but Karen wondered if Jolly had other plans for the song. "Did you argue with Jamie about what you were planning to do? Did he figure out you were going to make money off of him?"

Jolly shook his head violently. "No. Nothing like that. We didn't argue about nothin'. I just wanted him to wait until the song was really good. As it is, it's very close. He's young, though, and he doesn't understand the industry. He just wanted it out there. So people could hear him. He has no patience."

Karen tilted her head to the side. "I want a copy of his song. Can you email it to me?" She handed him a card.

He examined the card. "Sure. Sure. I'll send it to you. Look, I like Jamie. He's a good kid, you know? Talented. I swear, I wasn't going to rip him off. If he shows up again, I'll make sure he gets a fair shake. I promise."

"And you don't have other ways of exploiting these kids?" she asked.

Jolly's face set into a hard-edged mask. "Time for you to

leave." He rose and flung the door open, pointing her way out.

"There are rumors."

"Every gay man is attacked by rumors. Evil, awful things. I am not into children."

Karen stood, not surprised by the angry denial. The tiny niggle about the female vocalist blossomed into a new possibility, one she didn't really want to consider. She opened her phone to a photo of Sophie. "Is this the girl who sang for Jamie's song in that recording?"

Jolly pinched his lips in annoyance and looked at the photo. His eyes widened in surprise. "Hey, yeah. That's her."

## 13

______

Karen walked back to the Starbucks that Jamie frequented as her emotions shifted through a staggering range. Sophie had outright lied to her about never having met Jolly before. Why? And what else had she lied about? Karen had been so proud of her relationship with her daughter as being based on an amazing openness. Was she completely delusional?

She would have a long chat with Sophie at home. For now, she would focus on her task.

After leaving another round of messages for Mullet and Sage, she went inside, the rich coffee aroma calming her. She ordered a quadruple-shot caramel macchiato. She found a seat at a table in the corner with her back to the wall, and made notes about her conversation with Jolly.

Jolly came across sort of sleazy without being a total scumbag. If she had met him on the street, would she have found him creepy? Or was she influenced by knowing he was using the kids to save money? Was the fact he was obviously gay part of the issue? Were he and Jamie involved physically? She didn't think so, but it was impossible to know for sure.

Karen had purposefully ignored all thoughts regarding Jamie's sexual partners as they bubbled into her consciousness. People say kids don't like to think about their parents having sex, but she had an equally difficult time contemplating her kids or their friends having sex.

Jamie was on the twink end of the gay spectrum. That said nothing about the kind of men he might be attracted to, though. She tried to remember anyone he'd mentioned specifically and couldn't.

A few weeks ago, Poe had watched Jamie with big puppy-dog eyes when Jamie played the ballad for all of them after dinner. Then again, so had Sophie. It was hard not to become mesmerized when Jamie performed. Poe was as gay as they came, so it made sense that he'd crush on Jamie. Jamie hadn't obviously been interested in Poe. He was harder to read than most. Maybe he was better at hiding things than she gave him credit for.

Karen drew a map of Jolly's studio as she remembered it. Obviously, she hadn't seen the whole place. Did he have room there to hide indiscretions? What about the receptionist? There was obviously no love lost between the two, but why would he keep on someone who would flip him off in the open like that? Wouldn't she pick up on it if he were abusing any of these kids? Most likely, she was profiting from whatever was going on. The game industry fueled its own small economy in the area.

What if Jamie was off with a boyfriend or an older man for the weekend? Or turned to survival sex? A several-day gig wasn't unheard of. Men traveling into Seattle could keep him in a hotel with room service for days. Jamie would get paid in money and food, plus have a bed and shower.

How the hell did hoping Jamie was off on a sex gig begin sounding like the better option? Karen leaned back in her chair as she sipped at the last half of her drink. Jamie had been in this store on a weekly basis for months. This was a standalone shop without a drive-thru. All the traffic coming in was foot traffic, and a lot of it was walk-by—there were only three small parking spaces attached to the shop. Street parking was at a premium.

A girl in twin braids and a floral print that only someone in their twenties could wear was the manager. She acknowledged more than half the people coming in by name and knew their orders. It was impressive. Karen sometimes couldn't remember what she had ordered by the time she got to the pick-up line. She'd make a pathetic waitress of any kind.

She made a list of questions to ask the staff, and waited until there was no one in line before approaching them. She handed the manager a flyer and asked if they could post it in the store. "Any chance you recognize him?"

"Sure," Boss Lady smiled. "That's Strings. He's here about once a week."

"What's his order?" Karen asked, sure the woman would have it down.

"Why're you asking?"

"I was hired to find him." It was a subtle shift in demeanor, but an invisible cold wall slid between them. Karen held up a hand, hoping to ward off the negativity. "I need to make sure he's safe. The last anyone ever heard from him was when he was here on Friday."

The woman's eyes narrowed even further. While Karen had meant to be reassuring, what she said must have come across as accusatory. Her name tag was hidden under her crossed arms, so Karen couldn't make inroads by using her name.

Karen tried again. "I was hired to find him—that's it. To make sure he's safe and tell him he's got a place to live. I'm not going to be dragging him anywhere without his consent. He's got people who love him who are freaking out that he's gone dark. That's all."

The other woman remained silent for an uncomfortably long time. Karen wasn't used to being the one made to wait, the one being scrutinized.

The manager finally shrugged and let out a sigh. "There's not a lot I can tell you. He came in, got his usual."

She pointed at a guy leaning against the outside window with her chin. "That's where all the musicians play. It's next to an outlet. He'd play for half an hour or so and get some change. Half the time, he'd bring some in for the tip jar."

"Do you have a regular crowd in here at the same time of day each day?"

"Sometimes. There are plenty of people who come by every day, timing varies, but that time of day can be crazy busy. People need their post-lunch pick-me-ups."

"Do you recall Strings talking to anyone in particular?"

Just then a group of eight young guys came in. Karen retreated to a table to give them space. They were all in their late twenties, and wearing t-shirts and shorts. Their footwear was split between Keens and Birkenstocks. Their matching lanyards with photo ID for a gaming company in the area made their geekdom more than a little obvious. They hardly needed their Doctor Who t-shirts to make it more clear.

They got their drinks to go, most of them ponying up to the counter and ordering their "usual, please."

The interactions with the staff made her jealous of the fact she didn't have a place to go to like this herself, a place that knew her order. She'd have to remedy that. Get out of the house more. Karen swallowed the last bits of her drink, relishing the sweet goo that had settled at the bottom.

She spent another hour watching customers come and go and interviewing the staff in fits and starts as they became available. All of them knew Jamie as Strings, but none of them remembered anything unusual about the previous Friday. He was often there until late afternoon, playing out front for money. No one could remember when he left that particular day or if he'd busked outside.

No one knew which way he went as he left, no one saw him at the bus stop across the street. A few weren't even sure he'd been there on Friday even though it was clear he had been.

"Karen, right?"

It was the woman from the front desk at Harbor House.

"Yeah, that's right," Karen said. "Donna Richards?"

Donna had mentioned that she lived around the corner from here, but there was something odd about her showing up right that moment. Donna slid into the seat across from Karen, wrapped her fingers around her cup and leaned forward. "Have you had any luck finding Jamie?"

"Not yet."

"Man. I feel for his family. Are they out of their mind with worry?"

"It's troubling. I keep reminding them Jamie's gone off the grid for longer than this before. What are you doing here?"

Donna tilted her head to the side. "As I said yesterday, I live around the corner. I'm here almost every day."

"Did you ever run into Jamie?"

Donna bounced her head from side to side. "Him and a bunch of other kids from the shelter." She pointed to the bus stop across the street. "They busk here for a while and then catch the bus back to Harbor House."

"Did you see him last Friday?"

"Hard to say. I see him often enough that I'm not sure about this week or the one before."

"Have you ever met Marcus Jolly?" Karen asked.

Donna shook her head. "No. I haven't had a need to. As I told you yesterday, there're those rumors floating around. I've heard whispered talk, but the kids aren't necessarily free-wheeling in their conversation around us adults. I've heard he's handsome, in a gay sort of way."

Karen couldn't have put it better herself. "Yeah. He's pretty tan and chiseled. Almost a surfer boy."

Donna laughed and shook her head. "Ah. You know, I'd probably be attracted to him. Half the men I've ever fallen for have ended up being gay."

Karen had always fallen for straight guys—*alpha* straight guys. Even when she was working as a professional dominatrix, she was personally attracted to men who could hold their own in bed. That made it a lot easier to not be attracted to her clients.

Court Pearson came across as alpha, but his lack of melanin was an unusual choice for her. She tended to be drawn toward dark-haired men. There was something about his gray eyes that made her quiver. And that fresh scar on his forehead was a magnet.

A lot of women were attracted to gay men. It was sort of a running joke among her few female friends. Karen suspected that a lot of women simply felt safe around them because they could be friends with a gay man in a way they couldn't with a straight man. There was always an underlying sexual question with straight men. She wasn't sure what it meant about Donna, though.

She glanced over at a new wave of geek guys entering the shop. Crumpled shorts, t-shirts and sandals were not exactly attractive on anyone. Their general appearance wouldn't be completely fixed with a simple change of clothes, though. The Queer Eye team could get a season out of the guys in this shop alone.

Donna followed her gaze. "And, yeah. It's ironic isn't it? They probably rake in top dollar as computer geeks, but as a whole, they are not terribly attractive, are they? I mean, look at their clothes. Not a one of them cares. Maybe they make enough money that appearance means nothing to them. I find something innately attractive about a man who takes time to dress and care for himself."

"I agree," Karen said, forcing herself to pay attention to Donna and not the group of men. There were a couple of hot guys in the group, regardless of their clothing. A couple made her feel a bit like a cougar on the prowl. Not a one was in her age bracket. Her ex dressed much like these guys did—Seattle Tech. It had never bothered her. Men were pretty much the same once they were naked.

"Back in the day, I had a lot of male friends," Donna continued, "People thought I had a lot of boyfriends. But so many were actually gay, and I had no idea. They used me as their beard, as they say."

"Did you stay friends once you realized they were gay?"

Donna's shoulders tensed, and her face colored. "Not usually. I found it a betrayal. I was falling in love and they weren't. Besides, that was a long time ago. I'm done with all that. Life is much simpler for me as a single woman."

Karen would lose her if she continued this line of questioning.

"Have you heard anything about Jamie? From other kids at the shelter?"

"No. But, you know, I'm not always listening in. That defeats the trust I'm trying to build with them."

*Even though you've heard whispers…*

Karen checked the time. "The next bus is coming soon. I want to get over to the shelter to do some more interviews as people start showing up."

They got rid of their cups and walked up the sidewalk toward the bus stop. Donna paused, placing a hand on Karen's arm. She let her breath out in a long slow hiss before dropping her voice low. "I know I shouldn't be admitting to this, but… I want you to know. I drove Jamie over to the shelter a couple of times. Not just him. Other kids, too."

"From here?"

"Yeah. Well, it's…" Donna sucked in both lips and closed her eyes. Her hand grasped at the cross that dangled from a thin gold chain around her neck. She was either praying or sorting through what she was going to say.

Karen gave her time. It reminded her of a submissive gathering strength to continue. Karen stuck her hands in her pockets to stanch the sudden urge to reach out and trace a finger along the other woman's brow.

Donna finally opened her eyes, nodded, and straightened her shoulders. "We're not supposed to transport the kids at the shelter. It's a liability thing, and I could probably get in trouble. I couldn't just drive past them standing at the bus stop and not offer them a lift knowing we were going to the same place."

"Them?"

"Yeah. Well, if I see someone I know, usually busking at the Starbucks when I get my afternoon latte... I'll offer them a ride. It's not really a big deal. Jamie didn't want a ride on Friday."

"Wait. You were here, you saw Jamie here on Friday?" She had said she couldn't remember.

"Yes. I know I told you otherwise. I was worried that if I told you, I'd get in trouble for the driving thing. But... It's more important for you to know that I did see him here on Friday afternoon. Please, please, don't tell the shelter staff about me driving the kids. They'd fire me if they found out."

"So you offered him a ride. What did he say?"

"He told me he was heading down to Portland for the weekend and his friends were on their way to pick him up."

"So, they were going to pick him up here?"

"That's what he told me."

"Wait, so you don't drive by the bus stop and pick them up?"

"What?"

"You said you didn't like driving by them and leaving them."

"Well, yeah. That, or if, like I said, they're busking out front, I offer them a ride. We walk back to my place and take my car."

"You aren't worried about letting them know where you live?" Karen had let Sophie bring in dozens of strangers over the summer. None of them had made her feel unsafe, but it was always a consideration.

"No. They all know me, and I know them, right? I mean…" She put her hand to her mouth. "I honestly don't think any of them would hurt me. Do you?"

Karen didn't want to scare the other woman with all the things that could go wrong. The most likely scenario was that they might steal something, not hurt her physically.

"Nah. So, did Jamie say anything about when these friends were picking him up?"

Donna considered the question before shaking her head. "No. I assumed it was going to be soon."

"My bus is coming. You have my card, right?"

"You know, this is silly. I'm heading to the shelter. Why don't I give you a lift over?"

"You're volunteering again tonight?"

"I try to never miss open-mic night. I love hearing the kids perform."

## 14

She linked her arm through Karen's and guided her away from the stop. "My house is only a short walk away, and we can take my car. The bus takes twice as long."

Karen let herself be led away. Donna hadn't lied about her house being around the corner. The house was only a three-minute walk from the coffee shop. Karen and Robbie had lived only a few blocks away when they were first married. The houses were a mix of early twentieth-century Craftsman homes and post-war monstrosities. The latter were slowly being replaced by modern feats of architecture; the former were being lovingly restored.

Donna's house was one of the smaller bungalows with a full porch, complete with a swing. Miniature azaleas lined both sides of the path leading up to the porch. The heat of the summer had dried up the blossoms, and they hung dry and limp on the greenery. Karen automatically pinched one off as she followed Donna up the path.

"Come on in for a moment, why don't you? I need to

grab my keys. The car is in the carport behind the house." She held the door open.

The entry was simple and delineated by a half wall wrapped in dark wood that matched the molding around the entire ceiling of the front room. The wallpaper was a rich green with an art-nouveau flower pattern on it. Karen and Robbie had always wanted to do up their old house like this, but they couldn't afford it at the time.

"This is gorgeous. Did you do the restoration?"

"Me? Oh, no. I'm useless at anything requiring a hammer. The last owner was one of those people that buys houses and lives in them while restoring them. He moved three houses down to start the process all over again when I bought this."

Karen followed Donna into the immaculate living room. A single photo on the mantle gave Karen a glimpse into the other woman's life. It was of a very young Donna with a baby perched on her lap. A much older man stood awkwardly behind them, a limp hand on Donna's shoulder.

"You look so young," Karen said.

"I was only fifteen when I had Blake. My husband was a much older man." Donna ran a finger along the frame and flicked away a bit of accumulated dust. "They're both… gone now."

"Oh, I'm sorry," Karen said.

"You go through what you go through…"

The room shifted a little, became suddenly claustrophobic. Karen didn't know what to say. It would be horrible to be a widow, but losing a child? There were no other photos on the mantle. No wedding pictures, nothing to indicate other family members.

Donna directed Karen toward the kitchen. The pile of things on the retro-diner-style table put Karen at ease. While Karen worked hard to keep her house clean, she had stacks of books everywhere and her pile of mail was a paper avalanche waiting to happen.

Donna patted her pants and frowned. "Actually, I need to change. I'll be back faster than a hot knife in butter," she said with a pronounced Southern twang, and tittered nervously. "Sometimes my past just slips out."

Several piles of sorted mail were stacked neatly on the kitchen table. Magazines in one, catalogues in another, envelopes another. She poked through the magazines and accidentally sent them spilling off the table, along with several other items on the table. Karen quickly picked up the odd assortment of household items: sponges, water filter, latex gloves, night light, hummingbird feeder, a package of cat flea collars, and a package of cleaning brushes. The kinds of things Karen would normally pick up at Target or the grocery store.

She hastily put things back, hoping they weren't too out of order and took a deep breath. She didn't want Donna to think she was nosy.

In the center of the table was an old-fashioned cruet set. Karen had seen these things in antique shops before, but this was the first time she'd seen one in use. Oil, vinegar, mustard, salt and pepper, something white she guessed as sugar, another tall jar with little peppers floating in a liquid, and something dark and thick. Karen picked up the latter, lifted the lid and sniffed. Sweet, cinnamon and cloves. She closed her eyes, and sniffed again.

"It's chutney," Donna said.

Karen flushed. "Sorry, I've never seen one of these being used before. I've seen them empty in shops, you know? I always wondered what all the jars were for."

"My momma used to say you could always tell someone's upbringing by the quality of their table set." Donna spun the tray around slowly, tapping the other mystery bottle. "This is peppa sauce—vinegar and hot peppers. I use it on braised greens."

"That would be delicious."

"Here I use kale, because that's what you get in the store. Back home, we'd have used collards stewed in ham until it was almost slimy. I've grown to like kale in spite of its trendy nature."

"I am not a huge kale fan, it's too bitter," Karen said. "I'm an asparagus and broccoli girl."

"You're missing out. I can guarantee you, kale is a thousand times better with the peppa sauce."

"I'll have to try it sometime."

A small pet door Karen hadn't noticed popped open as a fluffy cat jumped onto the chair next to hers.

"Oh, Marley, you are not supposed to be on the furniture." Donna scooped the cat into her arms, pet her and dropped her to the floor.

The cat shook herself and rubbed herself against Karen's legs, doing that figure eight thing cats do. Karen scratched behind the cat's ears, her thick rumble of appreciation as loud as a Harley. The cat rolled onto her back, tummy side up, inviting Karen in for more attention.

**15**

———

As MUCH AS KAREN WANTED TO ASK DONNA ABOUT HER dead husband and child, she decided to not push it. Maybe she'd open up over time.

As they drove, Donna pointed out a couple of the local places that kids had talked about. A coffee shop here, a sandwich shop there, all places where various kids could count on discounted or even free food from other customers or the owners. The teens' vulnerability touched people into giving in a way that adult homeless people didn't.

"You know a lot about what these kids do when they're not at the shelter," Karen said.

"I see them. That's all. Most people put on this weird filter that lets them walk or drive right on by as if they didn't exist. It's self-preservation, really."

"You mean people choose not to see them so they can ignore them?"

"Yeah. You see people with their hands out all the time, but you don't even smile or say hello, right? Another stranger, maybe someone dressed all nice, walks by and smiles, and you smile back. That's why busking works so well for some of these kids. People fool themselves into believing they're busking after school. Making some extra cash from their hobby."

They were at a red light, and Donna pointed to the corner opposite them. "See that kid there? He's clean. He looks like he was walking home from school and whipped his violin out for a couple bucks on a lark. Nothing about him looks homeless. He goes by Strad, like the violin, and he comes to Harbor House every chance he can."

It was pretty sound logic. He appeared a little undernourished, but the point Donna was making was still valid. "And people feel guilty if they stop to listen and don't drop in some change in return. No one feels guilty about walking by some old dude with a cup." People were dropping coins into his open music case before moving on.

Karen rolled down the window to listen.

"Oh, I love that song," Donna said. "How does he do that with one instrument? It sounds like a whole orchestra."

"He's got an amp, and that thing at his foot is a looper," Karen said. "Jamie has a similar setup for his guitar. The thing I don't get is how they carry all that equipment around while living on the street."

"Luggage carts. That's one reason they like having time at the shelter. They can stash their belongings under a bed for the night."

The violinist launched into a cover for "Bohemian Rhapsody" as the light turned green. They spent the rest of the drive singing it and laughing.

Donna found parking a couple of blocks away from

Harbor House and they walked through the park together. Half a dozen teens greeted Donna by name and waved. It was clear she was well liked by the kids she served. Karen could see Donna maybe becoming a friend over time.

Her phone buzzed with a text from Bernice as they climbed out of Donna's car. She let Donna go ahead so she could find out if there was anything new going on with Bernice's kids and Thad.

"I'm calling about something else," she said.

"Did the judge grant you custody?"

"Official hearing is set for three months from now. Thanks to you, I have my kids full-time, for now anyway. DSHS frowns upon people leaving kids home alone like that. So, all's good there. I'm hoping you could drop by this afternoon?"

"I told you I'd call you when I had a minute. I'm not sure how much more I can take on right now. I'm working a case that's keeping me pretty busy."

"I know, I know. But, I've got something kind of unique that came up—it involves a journalist who's getting in pretty deep in some undercover work she's doing for a story. She's here for the next hour or so, any chance you can get over here? You'll like her."

"I'm on Cap Hill, so I'm not too far away. I have an hour or two before I need to be anywhere, so… yeah. I suppose I could come over. What do you need me for?"

"More research. Honestly, she's in over her head. She pissed off a friend last year and wants to make up for her screwups by doing an important top-notch investigative story."

"And you want me? Why?"

"I'll explain when you get here. It's complicated. Plus, I have some files to hand over to you. Paper only, you know?"

"It'll take me twenty to get there," Karen said.

"Yay. So head on over. Hey, how're those other background checks coming?"

"Not. I was planning on running a couple tonight and some tomorrow. I'll head over now."

As she clicked off from Bernice her phone rang again. It was Sage.

Karen almost dropped the phone in her haste to answer it. The connection was pretty bad, and it sounded as though Sage was in a convertible going a hundred miles an hour. The traffic noise was loud and Sage kept cutting in and out.

"Do you know where Strings is?" Karen asked.

"Strings… Friday… we… Portland… Seattle soon."

"I'm sorry. I didn't catch that."

"…open mic… tonight…" Sage said and then her phone went dead.

At least those last words made sense. Karen was definitely coming back once the shelter had opened for dinner.

She caught the light rail from the station at the north end of Cal Anderson downtown and hoofed it over to Bernice's office.

BERNICE WAGNER WORKED for a high-end firm in downtown Seattle. Karen had visited her a number of times over the years. At the start, Bernice was a budding trial attorney. The rampant chauvinism in the courtroom drove her nearly insane, so she switched her focus and left the courtroom to the men in her office. It was more than a little ironic that the very thing that drove her out of trial work would make her more successful.

Bernice's personal secretary waved her on into the inner office. She was focused on the person sitting across from her, and her fingers were interlinked and resting in the middle of her desk. She wore her reserved poker face, the one she used when she was listening carefully.

Karen coughed loudly so they'd stop talking and she wouldn't hear anything she wasn't supposed to.

Bernice waved her in. "Karen, I want you to meet Camille Poulin, a freelance reporter and writer. She's hired me to protect her and her work should the need arise."

Camille was familiar to Karen, but she couldn't put her finger on where she'd met her before. That happened a lot these days. People she'd met in her old life were popping up all over, though it was rare anyone admitted to knowing her as a professional domme.

Her stomach tightened as Camille laid out the premise. The story she was working on involved a lot of men in the area who were involved in an underage sex slave ring. There had been a bust in Bellevue a few months back. The newspapers got things wrong, called the girls prostitutes and gave the guys a free pass. There wasn't much different in the local reporting. Headlines screamed prostitute ring rather than sex slavery.

Camille was working on the larger issues. She had jumped on Bernice's bandwagon to educate the public about the difference. She wanted to expose the men who went after kids, help shut down what she could, and bring sex-worker rights into a modern discussion.

"I'm down with the program," Karen said. "All you need from me is background checks on guys?"

Camille and Bernice exchanged a look that told her it was more complicated than a couple of internet searches.

"Out with it," Karen said. "Come on, Bernice. I know there's more to this."

"Before you say no, let me explain," Bernice said.

Karen held up her hands. "I'm not saying no. What are you leaving out?"

"I want you to follow Camille and keep her safe. Maybe follow some of the johns around a bit if necessary."

"Fuck no," Karen said. "Are you kidding me? One, I am not a bodyguard. Two, I don't have a gun license. And I have no plans on getting one. Being an armed P.I. takes on way more risk than I want to deal with. Three, following your…" Karen paused. While she could tell Robbie about their friend's crazy divorce drama, revealing it to a reporter was another story. "Three, following someone for another case around for ten days taught me I hate surveillance. With a passion. Times ten."

"Oh, now you're being melodramatic. What do you suggest for protection then? I thought P.I.s did that too. My last guy did." Bernice leveled her gaze at Karen, challenging her.

"I'm not your last guy. I do know people who do security," Karen said. "It's a different kind of gig. I can give you names for all of this. You don't need me."

"But I want you," Bernice said. "You are in a unique position to understand what we are trying to achieve here."

"It's not like Camille is in a great position to go undercover," Karen said. "What's going to be her story? I mean … sorry, Camille, but most of the johns are men."

"I have friends. I'll be playing a wife who's providing bed toys for her husband," Camille said.

"I got that a lot as a domme. I don't see it working for this. I mean, a woman providing kids for her husband? That's a stretch."

Bernice leaned back in her chair. "You would think, but, the reality is…"

"And this friend of yours? How does he get involved without tipping them off? He's not going to…"

"God no. He'll find some excuse to keep anything from happening," Camille said. "He's a cop. He can't really do anything to help with this project right at the moment. He's busy at work, and this would be a side gig if I can talk him into it. It's a long term project."

Karen's alarm bells were ringing loud and clear on this one. She stood up. "If? If you can talk him into it? You're kidding, right?"

Camille held out a thumb drive. "Here's what I've got already. This is a long-term thing. I want to do it right. It's going to be six months. Maybe a year. If I put up a fake ad online for a fourteen-year-old hottie, I'll get fifty thousand hits in a couple hours. Did you know that? Even when I use a photo of an actual kid who looks twelve. Thousands of hits right away. From men who all want a piece of that kid."

Karen dropped into her seat. "That's so many. You can't even make a drop in the bucket." Nothing about this project made sense to her. It was insane.

"It's about changing attitudes, the system as a whole. We

have to expose this. A lot of the guys actually aren't pedophiles, they're buying a story. Some honestly believe the girls are happy eager adults acting a part. There are people making money off these girls."

"It's not about prostitution. It's about separating prostitution and honest sex-work from slavery, Karen." Bernice's eyes shone as she broke into her favorite topic.

"You're preaching to the choir," Karen said. "Believe me when I say this. I am with you on the cause. I don't see this as a remote computer-search kind of gig. I am not the person for this."

THE PORCH OF HARBOR HOUSE WAS OVERFLOWING WITH people when Karen returned. A line from inside the dining room wound its way around the outside and wrapped around the porch. Since she wasn't there to eat, she hung out on the porch and showed Jamie's picture to everyone waiting in line.

Again, more than half the people she talked to knew who he was and hadn't seen him. There was no sign of Sage or Mullet.

She hung around outside until everyone was inside and eating dinner before going in. Wayne Tomlinson, the staff member who had given her a tour the day before, waved at her from a corner and headed her way.

"Any word?" he asked.

"None." She scanned the crowd. "I don't see Sage or Mullet. Are they here?"

"Not that I'm aware of, but they often don't show up until the last chance to get dinner. There's no line now, you see?" He tipped his head in the direction of the food-service counter.

"I'll hang out over there, in case they come in." Karen found a free seat at the edge of a table and made small talk with people. Finally, Sage waltzed into the room with a guitar on her back and went straight to the end of the line. Mullet followed her in shortly. He set his guitar case on the floor against a wall before getting his food.

Karen waited until both of them were seated and slipped into an empty seat at their table.

"Long time no see," Karen said.

"Ms. H, damn fine to see you again," Mullet said with a slow giddiness to his words.

Karen leaned in a little closer. Sure enough, his pupils were dilated.

Sage rolled her eyes. "Never mind him, Ms. H. I got your messages once we were on the road, and then the noise made that call impossible. Sorry for the hang-up. What's all this about Jamie?"

"Did he meet up with you on Friday to go down to Portland?"

"That fucker," Mullet said. "He never showed. We texted. We called. We waited two hours for him. We almost missed our gig."

"Calm down, Mullybaby. I wasn't sure if I heard your message right, Ms. H. Has he actually gone missing?"

"His last known interaction was at the Starbucks near Jolly's studio. Weren't you supposed to pick him up there?"

"No. Well, we had originally planned to pick him up near there, at the Starbucks a couple blocks away, but then we decided to have him meet us where we store our electronics. A friend of mine has a bit of garage space he lets us use."

"And where was this?"

"Columbia City," Sage said. "We'd originally planned to pick up Jamie, then head down there on our way to Portland. Then my friend said he had to be to work early, so we agreed to pick up everything before he went to work."

Mullet bounced his head in a generally affirmative motion. There was enough sideways motion to it Karen wasn't entirely sure he wasn't listening to music in his head. "The drive back up to Green Lake would have sucked, so we asked Jamie to hitch a ride down to Columbia City. Or take the bus."

"He confirmed he would do that?"

"Yeah. He texted back he'd be down there soon. Then we didn't hear from him again," Sage said. "We thought he'd bailed on us for some stupid-ass reason. Now that I think about it, it makes no sense. Jamie was psyched about the trip."

Mullet shoveled more food into his mouth. "Whatever. We were fine without him before, we'll be fine without him again."

Sage elbowed him. "Even if we don't perform with him, he's our friend, baby. We need to be worried if we haven't heard from him. Not mad."

Karen's heart tightened as she digested what this all meant. The last time anyone had seen Jamie was Friday. Donna had seen him at the Starbucks and that was that.

Wayne waited until everyone was seated with a plate of food before getting up to MC the open-mic night.

"Are you playing?" Karen asked.

Sage picked at the remnants on her plate. "Yeah, I suppose, eh?" She cast a morose glance at Mullet. "Not feelin' the jam today. We can't stop just because we don't know where Jamie is."

Mullet examined a piece of lettuce on his fork with the kind of awe only pot could induce for lettuce. "This shit is amazing," he said, closing his mouth around his fork. "So good."

Sage put a hand on his shoulder and shook him. "Dude, you need to clear up if we're going to sing together tonight."

"Sure. Sure," Mullet said. "The show must go on. Don't you know it."

They took their trays to the kitchen and opened up their guitar cases to get ready. Donna came and sat next to Karen. There were four other acts before Wayne called Sage and Mullet up.

The first act was a guy with his guitar covering "Mr. Tambourine Man." Maybe it was the fluffy pile of curly hair, or the narrow face, or, maybe it was the nasal twang to his voice. Whatever it was, the kid nailed Bob Dylan full on. Karen tuned it out best she could, but the song got to her anyway.

Karen must have been around five years old when her mother and father had the first fight she could remember. The details had faded into a dream-like fuzziness over the years, and she'd never really understood what it was about. They had yelled. He had left. Their family drifted into a pattern of him coming home for a time before disappearing, with his time home less and less while his time away grew and grew. Eventually, he left and never came back. Karen had typed his name into the fancy P.I. database she used once. She'd stared at it for a long while before deleting it. What good would it do for her to know if he was dead or alive? He had left them. Left her.

The song ended and Karen was left with the same empty hunger she always had when her father crossed her mind. The room was filled with people who had lived through similar abandonments, and yet they smiled and clapped and carried on with their lives.

Next up, a young woman performed a spoken poem. The pain and anger that had thrust her from her home fueled her words and brought tears to more than half the audience. Either the poem was a repeat or the people who weren't crying had hearts of stone. Karen wiped hers away with an extra napkin someone had left on the table.

Sage spoke into the mic before starting their song. "This piece was written by someone we all here know and love. Strings. Sweet boy, wherever you are, we're all thinking of you. Come back home so we can sing together again. And, y'all need to know, Mrs. H, over there?"

She pointed directly at Karen and sixty heads swung around to look at her. She stood up and held the flyers overhead and sat back down again, perfectly happy to let Sage do all the talking.

"A lot of you know her and Sophie, and how they really help and love us. So, like, if you have seen Strings since Friday? Or if you have any idea if he's off on a gig or a job or anything. Please. Please. Let her know, Okay?"

She nodded to Mullet and he lit into the song Karen had heard at Jolly's. It wasn't quite as deftly performed as the studio version where Jamie had laid down both guitar tracks at Jolly's. Sage sang the same part that Sophie had.

Talking to Sophie about her lying about being at Jolly's was going to be rough. As far as Karen knew, Sophie had never been so cagey about anything. And if Sophie was also pretending to be Maria Wells to approve his stay at shelters…

Karen lost herself in the music for a while. If she was so wrong about her own daughter, what else had she been wrong about?

Sage and Mullet were really good. By the time they were done, half a dozen kids were openly weeping. Everyone jumped up to give them a standing ovation. Teens were often dramatic, but the atmosphere of the gathering had developed into a hearty moroseness. These kids were living with a real fear over their heads. No one near her brought up the Dog Park Killer, but the specter of it took up an invisible space among them.

Karen emerged from the shelter into the warm summer twilight. If she left the city now, she could get home and spend a bit of time with Sophie and finish the online background checks she'd promised Bernice.

It would take a special kind of mom energy to confront Sophie about Jolly. Sophie had probably lied to cover up the fact she'd been at the studio, though why she would do that was puzzling. Would Karen have given Sophie permission to record a song if asked? She would like to think she would have said yes, but now? After meeting Jolly, she didn't want her daughter anywhere near him.

"G'night, Mrs. H," Sage said.

Karen hadn't even noticed the pair had followed her out of the shelter. "Aren't you staying for the night?"

"Nah. My parents are out of town and asked me to dog-sit," Sage said. "We can't live together long-term, that's for sure. They have no idea I live on the street when I'm not there. It's easier on them that way."

If Karen weren't so practiced in hiding her surprise in almost any situation, her jaw would have hit the floor. "They don't know you're homeless?"

"I'm twenty-five, Mrs. H. They'd feel like failures if they knew I couldn't make it all on my own. They're off on a vacation, so I get three weeks in my old room. Those two gigs in Portland, and our Saturday busking, got me to what I need for my part of the first and last on an apartment. There're six of us getting together to share it. It'll be crammed. And it will still be better than being out on the street."

"Sweet," Karen said. Did all youth think their parents were so fragile? Was that why Sophie had lied to her about knowing Jolly? Sophie thought she would break?

"Come on Mullet." She tugged at him. "Penelope needs a walk soon."

The moroseness that had floated around Sage at the dinner table clung to Mullet as much as the sweet smell of weed. "I like Strings, Mrs. H. I do. I hope you can find him." They walked off hand in hand.

Karen was about to climb in her car when her phone buzzed with two texts simultaneously. One was from the manager at one of the venues in Portland she'd chatted with the previous night, confirming that they'd never seen Jamie on the weekend. She sent him a quick thanks, even though it wasn't news or helpful. The second text was from Maggie to check her email for a full background on the owner of the minivan.

17

YOU WANT SOME DINNER, MOM?" SOPHIE ASKED, POINTING to the congealing plate of something stir-fried. "It's not half as bad as it looks."

Karen doubted this, as both Robbie and Sophie had quite a bit left on each of their plates. Robbie held up a particularly jellied bit of broccoli. "We put in too much cornstarch."

"Thanks, but … I'll go take care of the dog while you two finish up," Karen said, grabbing a beer from the fridge. There was no way she was going to bring up Jolly with Robbie around.

Robbie must have gone through earlier in the day because she only found the one fresh pile. Karen kicked the lid on the poop can closed and walked to the gate at the back of her yard knowing that she wasn't likely to step in any nasty surprises. The gate had a lock on it, a security measure she'd only added a few months ago when that crazy whack-job had come after her through this very gate.

She stood on her tiptoes and stared over the fence into the dark gray of the dwindling twilight. No one was on the trail behind her house. The neighborhood was eerily quiet.

Karen turned her back to the fence and leaned on it as she faced her house. Robbie appeared at the downstairs door in silhouette, hands on hips. She took a swig of her beer, willing him to make the first move.

He crossed the lawn and leaned against the fence next to her. Sophie was finishing up the dinner dishes, oblivious to them watching. Sophie's head rocked side to side in the rhythm to some song being piped directly into her via her bright purple earbuds.

"What is she listening to?" Robbie asked.

"My Walkman was practically glued to my head when I was her age," Karen said. "Some things never change."

"Yeah, but you were stuck with whatever tapes you had. Or crappy radio. She's got Spotify and a never-ending array of choices."

"I still have mine." Karen had only kept four tapes because she could only carry so much on her back. They were tucked away in a box under her bed with other mementos that had gotten her through the toughest times in her life. "Do you think a tape from back then would still work? Or would the tape have gotten brittle and broken up?"

"I don't know. I tossed all mine years ago. About to do the same with CDs. I've been playing all my music out of the cloud for a while now."

"I can't tell what she's listening to. Her head is bopping around and she's smiling. And she's doing dishes, so I'm not going to complain," Karen said.

Robbie leaned in close and kissed her shoulder. "We did a couple of things right, didn't we?"

She nudged him back. "We did."

"Can I spend the night?"

Karen kept her eyes on Sophie. "I'm not interested in sex tonight. You can stay in your own room if you want."

"Never hurts to ask. I get the sense you have something going on and need your space. I'll hit the road." He kissed her on the cheek and left.

Karen called to Aspen. The old lab hobbled over and leaned heavily into her leg. She absently slipped her hand between the dog's collar and her fur. Aspen's fur where the collar hung was worn down a bit, and she always appreciated a little love there.

Sophie was finishing the dish-drying as Karen entered the kitchen. She wrapped her arms around her daughter, who stiffened and then relented into a full hug. Karen wasn't ready to confront Sophie about her lies around Jolly and the music. What if there was more to it than Karen suspected? Things she didn't really want to know?

"Mom?"

"I'm getting nostalgic, is all. What are you listening to?"

Sophie pulled her phone out of her bra and held it so Karen could read the playlist.

"You like ABBA and Queen?"

The list was titled 'upbeat pick-up songs.' The music was all pretty fast-paced happy songs for picking up around the house, not picking up dates. Karen recognized about two-thirds of the songs on the list.

"Why are you surprised?" Sophie asked.

"Oh, my god… this is hilarious." Karen grabbed Sophie

by the wrist and pulled her toward the hallway. "I have something to show you."

Sophie resisted at first. "Really, Mom? You're so weird sometimes."

"Trust me, Sophie. You'll appreciate this," she said, practically dragging Sophie the rest of the way to her bedroom. Karen dropped to her knees in front of her bed and pulled on the handle of the wooden box. She shifted to sit cross-legged.

This would be the perfect opportunity to share a partial truth with Sophie and to get her talking about Jolly and Jamie. If Karen gave Sophie something, surely Sophie would give back.

Karen patted the space next to her on the floor. "Sit. There's a lot about my past I never told you. You're old enough to know, but Brian's a little young yet. I would like to share it with you, but I'd also like you to talk to me or your dad about it."

Sophie adopted the same cross-legged position Karen had taken. "I have always wondered what's in this box."

Sophie had probably snooped under Karen's bed before. Karen had seven locked boxes in the house, but this one contained everything from her life before Seattle. All twenty-four by eighteen by ten inches of it. She spun the lock's dial, slid the lock off, and lifted the lid.

A slightly musty Montana-y smell wafted up from the contents. A t-shirt from the 1984 Olympics lay neatly folded on top. She set it in the lid of the box and moved a couple of inner boxes around.

She set a bundle of letters neatly wrapped in ribbon to the pile and tapped it. "These are the letters from my dad.

Everything he wrote to my mom while he was in Vietnam. The ones he sent me after he left. Everything until he disappeared completely."

Sophie reached for them, but Karen put her hand on top of hers. "I'm not sure I'm ready for you to read them. I'd like to go through them one more time before you do."

Sophie withdrew her hand and peered into the bottom of the box. At the bottom was the Walkman with a bunch of cassette tapes neatly ensconced in an Adidas box. The whole collection was right out of the eighties. She held up the Walkman. "Ever see one of these before?"

Sophie rolled her eyes. "Of course. It's a disc player, right?"

Karen laughed, although she was pretty sure Sophie wasn't joking. "This thing kept me sane. What I wanted to share was my tapes." She scanned the small handwriting on the labels and found the one she was looking for. "See?"

"Oh wow. 'Dancing Queen'… 'Don't Stop Me Now'… 'Fat Bottomed Girls'… 'Beat It'… 'Girls Just Want to Have Fun'…"

"See what I mean? A lot of overlap."

Sophie continued to examine the tape. "I haven't heard of half of these, though. Like 'Psycho Killer'? 'Burning Down the House'? Really? Are these actually your favorite songs?"

"Not exactly."

Sophie turned the cassette over, and poked her finger in one of the reels. "Wow. These are weird. Does it still work?"

"We'll need fresh batteries to test it."

She popped the battery storage open. A mass of dried green battery corrosion exploded onto her lap.

"Eww." Sophie fell back onto her hands. "What the heck is that?"

"Old batteries… I'm betting this thing won't work at all." She pushed a finger at the mass of metal. Nothing gave easily. She might have to take it somewhere if she wanted to use it.

"Do we have another cassette player?"

"Nope. That's it. Unless your dad's old boom box is working. It might still be out in the garage." Karen's shoulders sagged a bit. Now that the tapes were in her hand she wanted to hear them again. To hear Lisa's voice again.

Sophie turned the tape over. "The last song is 'You're My Best Friend'. Did someone make you this tape?"

Karen put her arm over Sophie's shoulders. "Yeah. Actually. Your Aunt Lisa made that for me."

Sophie slowly turned toward Karen. "I have an Aunt Lisa?"

"You *would* have, but she died a long time ago. Before you were born. So you never met her."

"How come you've never even mentioned her before?"

Karen closed her eyes, a sudden flush of emotions making it hard for her to answer right away. "It's hard to talk about her. She was my older sister, but she also was more than that. She took care of me more than anyone else. More than Mom or Dad."

"What happened to her?"

Karen picked up another tape and tightened a spool with a fingernail. "She died. I was thirteen. Everything fell apart after that."

It was another three years before her mom worked herself up into actually committing suicide and left Karen alone in their rented rambler on the outskirts of Bozeman. It took six months of missed rent payments before the landlord evicted her. She fit what belongings she could into her mom's ancient Pinto and drove to a friend's house. The next day, she stood, helpless, on the sidewalk as the landlord moved everything left in the house into a gigantic trash container.

Sophie tapped her knee. "Mom? Yoohoo? You held onto this all this time?"

"Yeah. Well, Lisa didn't leave much behind." She poked at the Walkman again. It was too bad that the thing was so corroded. It must be possible to get a cassette player somewhere.

"Let's order a new player while we're thinking about it."

"We can copy the playlists and download the songs to my phone."

"It's not quite the same as listening to the tape. There are pauses… and she… Lisa recorded some things about what she liked about the songs in between. Bits of advice for me. Why she picked the song and what she wanted me to get out of it."

Sophie considered this and nodded slowly. "I get it. It was a lot of work to put one of these together. Different than clicking and adding to a list."

"Yeah. It is. Was. When you made one of these, you had to play the whole song in order to record it over to cassette."

"That sounds boring."

"It was a labor of love, kiddo. Besides, what's boring about listening to your favorite music?"

"What if you made a mistake?"

"You rewound the tape and re-recorded it until you got

it right. If you messed up on what you said, you had to fix it. Recording over the song is pretty easy."

"Did you make any?"

"None that I kept," Karen said. "I tell you what, I'll get a new player and we'll listen to these sometime soon." She put everything but the Walkman and tapes back into the box and locked it up again.

"Mom?" Sophie asked. "You never talk about your dad. Or your mom. Or this aunt I've never heard of," Sophie said. "Why not?"

"Your dad would say I'm not good about talking about painful things."

"Is that why you shared the mix tapes? Because it doesn't hurt?"

"Not the same way. Lisa didn't choose to leave me behind. She got taken. The overlap between your play list and this? It's like you were channeling her."

"Channeling? That sounds kind of woo-woo, Mom."

"Yeah, well, sometimes things are like that."

"You know I saw the combination on the lock?"

"I trust you."

## 18

<hr>

As they returned to the kitchen, Karen jumped into the topic that weighed most heavily on her mind. "I met Jolly today. Is there anything you've heard about him you haven't told me?"

"Like what?" Sophie's whole body tensed up a notch or two.

Was it the fact Karen was already suspicious, knowing Sophie had lied, or was that Sophie had closed part of herself off from her? The subtle difference was there for sure. As soon as Karen mentioned Jolly, Sophie was on alert and on edge.

"Jamie had a scheduled session at Jolly's studio on Friday. As far as I can tell, he took the bus to Green Lake, spent his time with Jolly, and then hit Starbucks. After that? *Nothing*. And, as I already told you, he never met up with Sage and Mullet as planned."

Sophie gnawed at a corner of her lower lip. "People

either love or hate Jolly. From what I hear, anyway. But they take his money. Mostly."

Karen rummaged in the freezer for some ice cream, giving Sophie some time to formulate a more-thorough answer. She put the chocolate-chip cookie-dough container on the counter and waggled her eyebrows at Sophie. "One scoop or two?"

"Bribery. Even if I don't have anything of value to offer?"

Sophie slid into one of the bar stools at the kitchen counter and cupped her chin in her hands. "Lots of the kids who busk have been over to Jolly's studio. He pays them decent money in quick cash."

Karen scooped ice cream into two bowls as she waited for Sophie to give her more. She shoved one bowl across to Sophie, who stabbed at the scoop with her spoon. She waited until she was done with her slow, deliberate bite before asking, "How much did he pay Jamie, do you know?"

"Not sure how much. It was always in cash. Jamie was excited because that song he was working on was going to be more... like he'd get credit for it somehow? Some contract or deal thing? I was never really sure what he meant. I guess until recently, he'd play something on the guitar and he'd get cash for playing it one time. This? It was something bigger, more like, he'd get credit and royalties."

"Jolly was going to represent him, like as an agent?"

"Maybe. He told Jamie he'd make him a big star."

"Well, that would be awesome for Jamie."

"Yeah."

Enough skirting the issue. "Sage and Mullet did a version at open-mic tonight. And, I heard the recorded version earlier at Jolly's today. The version at Jolly's studio? The vocals on it were amazing. That girl could go far with a voice like that."

*Come on Sophie. Fess up, baby girl.* Why wouldn't she come clean now?

Sophie's shoulders slumped. She shoved her spoon deep into the ice cream and pushed the bowl away. "You know. Why didn't you come out and ask me if you knew already? Why toy with me like that?"

"Why didn't you tell me that was you when I asked about him last night?" Karen asked.

Sophie crossed her arms and hunched back, deep in her chair. "I didn't want you to know I've been going into Seattle a lot more than I told you."

"As in how much more?"

"Mom. There's nothing to do during the summer. I can only spend so much time reading and hanging out around here. Jamie's my best friend. I went in to hang with him. That's all."

"How often?" Karen asked using a warning tone she reserved for serious situations with her kids.

Sophie straightened, but refused to meet Karen's eyes. "A couple times a week. Sometimes more, sometimes less."

"And how many times did you go with Jamie to Jolly's studio?"

"Three times. We worked on that song the whole time. Jolly is super gay, but he's not creepy. Not to me. Or Jamie."

Karen reached across the counter and grabbed Sophie's hands. "You're supposed to tell me when you're going out."

"Would you have let me go if I asked?"

"It's kind of late for that kind of speculation." Karen

met her daughter's eyes. "Now, I need you to tell me anything, anything at all, that will help us find Jamie."

"Like what? Mom, don't you think if I knew something I would have told you already?"

"There are things you know that you might not recognize as important. Tell me everything you know about Jolly." There was something more sinister about the man. Could he be holding Jamie somewhere?

"There's not much. He'll come down to the Ave and scout for talent, hand out his card to people, and tell them to come to his studio to record for some money."

"Boys and girls?"

"Yeah?"

"Have you heard any rumors about him?"

Sophie pressed her palms against her cheeks and closed her eyes. "I think he pays some kids… you know… like for oral? Blow jobs? I'm not really sure. I've heard some vague talk, is all. And people talk about his… you know… being small. So, maybe they've seen it?"

People? What people would Sophie be talking to that would have any reason to talk about Marcus Jolly's dick? Talk was, of course, no proof of anything. Karen would need to ask Court if he could share anything on Jolly. Maybe they'd already cleared him.

"Sophie, if you have any other ideas, other connections Jamie has that you know about, this is the time to share them. He never went to Portland. So something happened to him in Green Lake."

Sophie finally brought her eyes up to meet Karen's. They shimmered brightly and threatened to overflow with tears. "You swear you won't hate him. Or me?"

Karen wanted to pull her daughter into her arms, tell her everything would be fine, but she was no longer sure of anything. Karen had always assumed she and Sophie had a close, no-secrets kind of relationship. Learning she was wrong about that colored everything Sophie said now. But Karen would love her kid no matter what she'd gotten into.

"I promise. No matter what." Karen held her hand up over her heart and blew her daughter a kiss, the sign they used to each other when they made a solemn vow.

Sophie's face crumpled and the tears that merely threatened now flowed down her cheeks. She squeezed her eyes shut and breathed in deeply to regain control. "Okay. He was doing these party things. To make money."

*Party things* could only mean one thing.

"Do you know how they work?" Karen asked, trying to keep her voice calm.

"Yes," Sophie said. "Someone would text him with an address. He'd go to the place on the text and get picked up."

"Along with other kids?"

"I guess?" Sophie wiped at her face. "I was never around when he went to them. He only told me about it after that last time he was gone for a while. They take all their stuff, and they don't get it back until they're done with the party, so he didn't have his phone."

"You think that's why he's gone dark now? He's at one of these parties and they have his phone?"

"I don't know, Mom. It could be. Right? I mean, he could have gone thinking it would be a one-day thing, and then they kept him?"

Or he was sold off to someone as a sex slave. The majority of victims in this country were African-American or Native American girls, but it did happen to vulnerable white kids, too.

A party wouldn't necessarily explain this extended absence. Karen's heart blossomed in her chest for Sophie. *Poor kid.* And poor Jamie, if the best Karen was hoping for him now was being a teen sex slave.

"Do you know who organizes these parties?" Karen asked.

"He wouldn't give me details. He was ashamed of all of it. Wouldn't want anyone knowing about it. Not you. Not his mom."

"Any idea how often he does them?"

"Once a month, maybe? Do you remember that time in June, when he was gone for a week? He was taken down to a spa somewhere on the coast. Near Seaside. They kept him there the whole time."

Karen's gut twisted. "A whole week?"

"He got a lot of money for it, but he told the people who do it he only wanted one-night parties after that."

"So do you think they lied and might have taken him somewhere like that again?"

"I hope so," Sophie said, falling into giant hiccupping sobs. "Where else can he be, Mom?"

"Do you know anyone else who might know? Another kid who went with him to these parties?"

Sophie mopped at her face with her shirt. "I don't know. Maybe? There was this girl who I met once. She might know."

"You'd recognize her?"

"Yeah." Sophie gave a little laugh. "Definitely."

"Any idea where she hangs out during the day?"

"Westlake? Pioneer Square, sometimes. I don't have her calendar on my phone, you know?"

Karen was getting valuable information here. She would normally shut Sophie down with that tone. She'd let it slide this time. "Okay, kiddo. You're coming with me tomorrow. We're going to find that girl and ask her some questions."

**19**

———

Karen sent Sophie off to bed and headed down to her office to do some research and catch up on her work for Bernice. Maggie's email briefed her on her visit to Marcus Jolly's condo and a detailed background check on the guy in the van.

Jolly's condo was more a townhouse with two other identical units on either side. Maggie had knocked on his door and gotten no response. The neighbor reported that he was very quiet and never brought anyone around. He didn't party, and they liked him well enough.

Maggie's take on it was that Jolly couldn't hide much from his nosy neighbors. All the parking was on the street, and there were no basements or attics. Maggie said she had looked in through the windows where she could, but didn't see anything unusual inside.

Maggie also included a full background check and a "known-associates graph" for the guy in the van. The lines linking people across their history was fascinating.

The van belonged to Garland Parker. He and his wife, Morena, divorced after their son was murdered in a gruesome beating. Maggie included links to a dozen articles about the death and the subsequent investigation that led to nothing. No arrests. Garland moved to Capitol Hill, leaving the house in Green Lake to his ex. *Green Lake, again.*

The newspaper articles reported that Garland and Morena Parker were devout Christians who were pictured on their knees next to their son, who was smothered by tubes and machines. The quote underneath stated that the Parkers were praying for Carmen's full recovery. "But," Garland said, "God has served his judgement, however harsh, on our son's life. If he dies, it is because God wishes to send a message to all the homosexuals."

The news source was an offbeat Christian paper. Karen read the entire article, more disgusted with each sentence. The Parkers not only prayed for his full recovery, they also had their minister perform a formal re-baptismal ceremony while Carmen was in a coma to ensure his path to heaven.

Carmen died eight years ago. The Parkers divorced two months later.

Morena's only employment history was a year-long stint as a secretary at a law office in Seattle. She met Garland Parker while working there and moved on to be a housewife. After Carmen's death, she remained officially unemployed and spent her time volunteering at her church. Her mortgage was paid and Garland sent monthly support payments.

She added Garland and Morena's homes to her map. Morena lived less than two blocks from Donna Richards and was only three blocks away from the Starbucks where

Jamie was last seen. Garland was an attorney with an office in Green Lake—*again.*

Garland's office was within a block of the Starbucks, Donna Richards' house, and Marcus Jolly's office and condo. Karen pushed the pin into her board and stared at it. All of these places were so close together, it was uncanny. Maggie had already been by Jolly's house and found it an unlikely place for anything nefarious. Karen would make her way over there if she needed to, but something about his studio drew her like a magnet.

Not every high-powered attorney was in a fancy building in the main part of downtown, particularly those that didn't represent a lot of criminal cases. Parker's website was slick and filled with typical fear-filled rhetoric. He spent his time hunting down insurance-liability maximums. Parker was an old-school ambulance chaser with a fresh face.

Could Garland be picking up kids after they saw Marcus Jolly? Everyone was so close together in Green Lake it could not be a coincidence. By being so visible at Rainbow Landing, with Adin's over-blessing, had Parker made himself a "clearly safe" adult and, therefore, likely to be trusted?

Karen shivered as the full implication of what she was doing hit her. This whole thing had blossomed from a missing-persons case into something much bigger and way more terrifying.

Karen sat hard on her desk, accepting the fact that she was, indeed, looking for the Dog Park Killer. If she could find him, she would find Jamie. The painful reality of it almost took her breath away. Court had told her to concentrate on finding Jamie, and this is where it led her.

Garland Parker was definitely someone she needed to talk to. She'd be sure to visit him the next day, maybe after she and Sophie had finished canvassing Westlake Center.

Shoving aside Jamie's case for a while, she spent half an hour doing background checks for Bernice. It was amazing how much information you could get about someone through their email address or phone number. She red-flagged one guy after finding multiple sexual-assault arrests. The rest were milquetoast businessmen willing to pay top dollar for spankings and humiliation. Life as a domme was easy and carefree in comparison to what she was going through now. And, honestly, there were aspects of it that fed her needs. Accepting that a significant part of her truly enjoyed the power and control had been key to being a successful domme.

She wrote her reports and sent them on to Bernice to forward to her clients. Her eyes were tired and she turned off her computer. She stretched and switched off the light just as Court texted, asking if it was too late to talk. It was about one-thirty in the morning.

Intrigued, she dialed his number. "What's up?"

"How are you doing?" he said. "You saw some pretty nasty shit today."

*I compartmentalize everything and have refused to think much about it* was not the right response.

"I'm doing okay, considering. Hey, I'm chasing down some leads on my guy. Any chance you can tell me what you know about a few people?"

Court didn't answer right away. "It's kind of late. I was more concerned about your personal reaction to what you saw. You were pretty shaken up."

"You're the one who texted me. Don't you sleep, Detective?"

"Not very much lately. This case is whipping my butt."

Karen laughed at his choice of words. "I didn't think that was your kind of thing."

"It's…" He paused and laughed. "Very funny. If you don't want to talk about what you saw, I can try to answer a couple of questions. What do you have?"

"Marcus Jolly?"

"He's creepy and weird. Skeevy labor practices, trolls kids busking the street, probably not our killer, though. Can't share the deets on why."

"Right. He pays kids twenty bucks when pros make a couple hundred. Rumors are he pays kids for oral sex, you hear anything about that?"

"Rumors. Nothing more. Let me know if you can get any one of those kids to talk openly about it, though. Anyone who will testify, you know? They are friggin tight-lipped."

"Will do. What about Garland Parker?"

"Uhm. You got me on that one," Court said, his voice perking up. "What's the connection?"

Karen dished. No reason not to tell a cop about a guy picking up kids in a mini-van. "So, does this mean I gave you a new lead?" she asked.

"Fucking Adin. He is so over the top about being helpful and cooperative, yet he tells us nothing about this little friend of his."

"Parker's office is super-close to Jolly's studio. The kids who go there usually take the bus to the stop across from the Starbucks. They'd have to walk right by Parker's office to get to the stop. You think Parker could be snagging them off the street as they're heading to the bus?"

"That would be hard to pull off in broad daylight. That's a pretty populated part of town."

"It's weird they're so close together," Karen said. "Add in Donna Richards and Morena Garland, and it's like a party over there."

"Donna Richards?" Court asked. "A volunteer at one of the shelters, right?"

"Yeah. At Harbor House. You've probably seen her at the front desk. She's been really nice. Checked the logs for me. I kind of like her."

"Oh, right. The blonde with the Southern accent," Court said. "I can't get a fix on her. You like her? Really?"

"I do, yeah. She's really into her volunteer work. I don't know exactly what happened. I'm guessing her son was killed young. There's only one photo of her with him, and he's not much more than a baby in it."

"You were inside her house?"

"I told you. She lives near the Starbucks where Jamie last bought something. She offered me a lift over to the shelter and we walked over to get her car."

"Going inside strangers' homes is risky."

"Thanks for being worried about me."

"Yeah, well, you should be aware you're stepping into some scary water here."

"You told me that statistics were on my side. That Jamie was probably safe." Karen lowered her voice so she didn't come across as whiny. So that the fear about the alternatives didn't show.

"He probably is, but there's no excuse for following people into their houses, regardless."

They both fell silent.

"Anyone else?" Court asked. "Or are we done?"

"That's about it," she said.

"Thanks for the lead on Parker. It's pretty exciting to have a new name to throw into the mix."

She was chuffed over bringing Court a solid lead. She didn't mention her plans to visit Parker the next day. Maybe her feminine wiles could get more information out of him than Court could.

"One more thing, Court? My daughter says there is a group of people who are picking up teens for parties. It sounds like Jamie has been going off with them pretty regularly."

"Parties?" Court asked.

"Seriously?"

"Oh. Gotcha. That would be good news, if he were at an extended party, Karen. There's hope yet."

"Isn't that trafficking youth?"

"Yeah. It's a huge problem. And, you know, I'll bring this up at the joint squad meeting tomorrow. The problem is, we shut down one ring, and another takes over."

"What is wrong with people?"

"Sick fucks who like kids? They're all over the place. Like a fucking plague."

"You swear a lot, Detective," she said, trying to lighten the mood.

"I have a lot to swear about."

"I suppose you do. I've told you everything I've got for now."

"Too bad you didn't become a cop when you were younger. You woulda made a good detective. Solid work."

"I am. A *private* one," she said, letting down her guard. "Never could be a cop, though. Too much bad history there."

"Was that always the case?"

"Pretty much since I was sixteen and a cop cracked my window to wake me up. I was sleeping in my car at the time, and he made me move it at two in the morning. Scared the hell out of me."

"Power-cops drive me nuts. They get off on being able to wield their badge around."

"My relationship with cops went downhill from there."

"Your offer last fall seemed pretty genuine to me."

"You'd saved my life. Brian's life," she said. "I was grateful. You were my white knight."

"Ah. Were, huh? Well, a guy can hope."

Karen felt the warmth of a blush move up her neck and into her face. "Sure." She made her voice as noncommittal as possible. She was wishing she'd never kissed him. Everything about him was complicated.

"So, anyway. Thanks for the info. I'll be checking out both the Parkers tomorrow. I want to go back to Jolly's, too. Their proximity to each other is unnerving."

The idea that Jolly was up to something more nefarious than tax evasion made her turn her computer back on. If Jolly were grabbing kids to torture and kill, would he be doing it at his office? Or his home? Even with a receptionist in the front room? The soundproofing in the studios would blunt any screams. She shivered at the notion.

Karen found the blueprint for Jolly's studio in the online archives for the planning department. God bless bureaucracy! Now all she needed to do was find a way to compare the actual studio space to the blueprint.

## 20

———

KAREN CHECKED HERSELF OUT IN THE MIRROR. DRESSING UP in her daughter's clothes as a way to fit in on the street was a huge mistake.

Sophie tilted her head sideways at Karen's reflection in the mirror. "Mom, there's nothing we can do. You are just too old."

"Thanks, kiddo. I told you I should go simply as your mom helping you look for a friend. This is ridiculous."

The shortened top highlighted the silver lines stretching across her tummy—battle scars from her two pregnancies. She wasn't terribly self-conscious about them, but she didn't want to draw attention to them either. The shirt, emblazoned with a bright pink set of lips, screamed *teenager*.

Karen tugged the t-shirt off her body and slipped on one of her own. The cling was as tight and the overall effect was more "young adult" than the sparkling lips.

"I might do better if I go alone," Sophie said.

"No way are you going to do this alone, young lady." Karen pulled the mom voice out and laid it on thick.

They argued for another few seconds as Karen fought to get her socks on under her jeans. She was never going to be a woman who dressed in clothes meant for teenagers any more than she was going to be a sun-wizened-country-club-wife with multiple rings on knobby, spotted and wrinkled hands, wearing separates from Chico's.

Karen left her Fluevogs on the shelf and sighed as she slipped on the cheap, scuffed pair of no-brand loafers she'd been wearing off and on for ten years. They were only ten bucks at the thrift shop and as comfortable as anything else she owned.

This was yet another thing she missed about being a domme. She enjoyed the level of detail she'd used with each of her clients, and she dressed the part. As a mom and P.I., her clothing had taken a decided turn toward the mundane.

The 545 bus went straight from Redmond into down-town Seattle with about twenty stops along the way. They were at Westlake Center in forty minutes, and went straight to the Starbucks outside the mall.

A series of round planters with cement borders had been built as outdoor seating for people. A ridiculous city ordinance making it illegal to sit outside in Seattle rendered them useless. Okay, you could sit outside if you had a chair or bench, but stairs, steps, sidewalks, and, apparently, large planters with twelve-inch lips on them were out of bounds.

It was pretty routine to see people sitting on the planters as they scarfed their lunches or snacks. Every once in a while, a cop would wander by and wave people off, but that usually only happened if there was an obviously homeless person in the mix. If you sat alone and were dressed well, you could get away with a good half hour or more before the cops got involved. God forbid you put a backpack down next to where you were sitting.

"Okay, Mom, don't be a dork."

"Hey, I'm never a dork."

Sophie gave Karen a withering look. She waved her hands at a group of kids hovering near a planter, and was more than comfortable approaching the small band. It was disconcerting on a number of levels for Karen to watch her daughter navigate this foreign landscape with such ease.

How many guys cruising by were creeper adults hoping to find some young kid to suck them off for cash? Karen didn't know what kind of money these kids could make with survival sex. Only ten bucks? Was it fifty? More?

Karen had gone into her career as a pro-domme knowing the legal risks, the mental challenges, choosing them, choosing to delve into the psychological aspects, and using what she'd learned to make a lot of money. She'd learned something about herself from every client she worked with. Sometimes what she learned surprised her.

Kids on the street weren't free to choose. Their position gave them zero bargaining power, and they probably ended up grateful for whatever the john of the day threw at them as he zipped up.

Karen chose her career because grad school would have cost thousands of dollars she didn't have. She'd originally intended to save up for a master's degree so she could be a family and marriage therapist. Turns out, she was doing pretty much the same kind of work making three times the money without the expense of grad school. She dumped the savings for her grad school into an educational savings account for her kids so they could study whatever they wanted. Thanks to Berkeley Drummond's generous bequest, they could go to any school in the country, private or public without racking up student debt.

Karen hung back behind Sophie, giving her daughter the chance to approach the group and then introduce herself and wave in "my mom."

Sophie didn't seem to know anyone in this particular circle, but she was able to dip her head and shoulders in some indistinguishable body language Karen couldn't interpret to allow her into their circle. She was better dressed, but still basically one of them.

Sophie unrolled one of the flyers. "He's my bestie, you know? I miss him. We're really worried."

A girl with green hair and blonde roots piped up. "Strings? Sure. He plays guitar and sings sad songs when he busks. Sometimes he plays over by the park there." She gestured over to the small set of play structures. "There's some benches and, like, he plays cute little Raffi tunes when kids're around. You know, cutesy kiddy shit."

A lanky androgynous teen with stringy hair leaned in closer to the flyer. "Oh, is that him? Man, he's the dude that plays a bunch of those songs from when we were kids. 'Baby Beluga'? 'Oats and Beans'? You know. It's pretty cute the way the little kids think he's like a rock star, ya know?"

The girl punched the stringy-haired kid in the shoulder. "'Oats and Peas'. Not 'Oats and Beans'. Get it right."

"Oats and beans and barley. That's how the song goes."

The girl rolled her eyes and started singing a song Sophie demanded for three weeks straight when she was four years old. The derailment lightened the mood as others chimed in with their renditions.

Finally, the stringy-haired kid held up their hands and waved the all-knowing Wikipedia page in their faces. "We're all wrong."

Once the matter was cleared up, Karen jumped back in with her agenda. "Now that we know Strings was a fan of Raffi, everyone, when was the last time you saw him?"

The girl tilted her head to the side, shaking it slowly. "I don't know. I mean, days are kinda confusing. Know what I'm sayin'?"

They spent another hour moving from group to group at Westlake, stopping to grab sandwiches from a local sub shop to hand out as they canvassed the area. Most everyone they spoke to was happy to pass the flyers on and promised to let Karen or the police know if they saw Jamie. Karen did her best to ignore the obvious lies inherent in the promises.

The adults they talked to were almost entirely unaware of Jamie's presence unless they were buskers. There were some incomprehensible rules about who played on what corner and during what time. Jamie played at the park at Westlake on Tuesday mornings and then at a spot near the bronze pig in Pike Place Market in the afternoon.

At the market, Friday mornings were never as busy as the weekend, and the late-summer heat was keeping the massive throngs away. Instead of the usual hustle and bustle, the crowds today were manageable and made it easier for some to talk. Karen and Sophie handed flyers to all the vendors who would give them a minute. She loved the colorful stalls, the myriad arts and crafts filling the spaces. Painters, ceramicists, musicians, and other artisans intermingled with the butchers, florists, and greengrocers. The warm scent of fried dough blended with briny seafood and fresh fruit.

As they were leaving the market, a voice called out. "Sophie, Ms. H. Hey."

Karen caught Poe's shaggy head and raised arm out of the corner of her eye. "What are you doing down here?" he asked.

"Looking for Strings," Sophie said.

"Oh, right. Anything?"

"Nope," Sophie said. "What are you doing down here?"

He lifted a bag with floppy heads of carrots peeking out. "Shopping."

"Groceries?" Karen asked. "Do you have a camp somewhere?"

Poe colored. "Actually, my mom invited me for dinner."

"And you're cooking?" Karen asked.

"Nah. Ma told me what to get. Gave me money." He shrugged. "I think she's worried about me with all that's happening, you know? Might be okay with me being home again."

Sophie bounced on her toes. "That would be awesome, Poe. Wouldn't it?"

Poe shrugged and looked down at his feet. "I guess." Sophie put a reassuring hand on his shoulder. "I better be off," Poe said, lifting the bag.

"Let me know how it goes," Sophie said. "And, like, if you need a beard or something, let me know."

Poe eyes were calm and bright. Karen wasn't sure she'd ever seen him this relaxed. "Thank you, Sophie. I appreciate that. More than you know."

Karen waited until Poe was out of sight before turning to Sophie. "Did you just offer to be his beard? Seriously?"

"Hey, if all he needs is to pretend he's straight so he has a roof over his head, I'm willing to fake being a girlfriend."

"Even to Poe? He's a little… obvious. And, a little odd, don't you think?" Poe was quiet. He didn't smile a whole lot, either. There was something weird about that kid, for sure.

"He's definitely got a dark streak; his nick isn't for nothing. But, yeah, Mom, a parent who desperately hopes their kid suddenly straightens out will believe anything."

Karen wasn't sure she liked the ease at which Sophie came to the *parents will believe anything* conclusion. She'd believed Sophie about never being to Jolly's and she'd believed her about Jamie not working the streets. Were there more landmines out there waiting for her to blunder into?

They were about to catch a train to Capitol Hill when Sophie's arm shot out and grabbed Karen's arm, stopping them short. "Mom, you see the girl with the rainbow hair? Over by the kiosk?"

Karen followed Sophie's gaze. "Yeah, she's hard to miss."

"That's her. That's Ozzie, the girl who helps Jamie get into the parties."

"Hi, Ozzie, you have a sec? Remember me? Sophie? Jamie's friend."

Ozzie raised an eyebrow at Karen. "Who's this?"

"My mom. We're trying to find Strings. Haven't seen him in more than a week." People milled all around them, passing the small trio without so much as a glance.

"Tell me about it," Ozzie said. "That boy is off my list. He didn't show Monday night like he promised."

Sophie glanced at Karen. "You mean he didn't make it to your… erm…"

Ozzie rolled her eyes. "Girl, we call it a party." She stepped back to give Sophie an appraising glance and shook her head. Her eyes narrowed on Karen, then. "But you? You def know what I'm talkin' about, doncha?"

"Probably more than Sophie does. You were expecting him Monday, but he didn't show and didn't call or text you?"

"Nope. And that means he's off my list."

"So you said. I take it that's unusual for him?"

Ozzie tilted her head to the side. Her spiked, colored hair made the gesture seem birdlike and speculative. "Now that you mention it, yeah. He's a regular guy, and he always lets me know when he can't be there."

"When was the last time you saw Strings?" Karen asked.

Ozzie shrugged. "Couple weeks."

"And who organizes your parties?"

"You think I'd tell you that?"

Karen held out her hands, palms up. "Strings is like a second son to me. I want to make sure he's safe. Do you think he's with one of your parties somewhere, anywhere?"

Ozzie shook her head. "Nah. The party was small last night. Ain't been no other big party for a while."

"And who calls the parties? Organizes them?"

Ozzie pursed her lips. "Some lady."

"So, this lady takes you to parties?" Ozzie nodded. "Was the pay pretty good?"

"Yeah, really good. And the parties ain't too bad, you know, considerin'. The guys were all clean, anyway."

"Were they straight?"

"They want it young. They're all, like, my dad's age. I don't think they care whether they're fucking a boy or girl half the time. So long as it's young and tight."

"Are you from the area?"

"Yeah. I actually saw this guy I used to know at a party recently. Lives in my neighborhood. His daughter and I rode the same bus. He didn't even recognize me. I stayed clear, anyway. Didn't want someone I know getting all up in my business, you know?"

Karen didn't want Ozzie to lose focus. "Hey, why don't you come home with us for the evening. Get a nice shower, have a hot meal, sleep on the sofa."

"Right. That's exactly what I'm not doing right now. Going off with someone I don't know."

"Fair enough. Anything strange going on with these parties?"

"Well..." Ozzie considered her words. "The lady who runs everything? She came by a couple nights ago and she was, like, all in a snit. She said the party for that evening was canceled. She gave us each ten bucks because she felt bad we weren't getting work. But, the canceling thing pissed her off, ya know? She drove off cursing in Chinese."

"Chinese? How did you know she was speaking Chinese?"

"You don't have to know a language to know when someone's cussing in it." Ozzie hit one palm against her forehead. "Forget that last bit."

"So this lady who organizes the parties is Chinese?"

Ozzie rubbed at her face with her hands and breathed out hard, her shoulders slumping in defeat. "I don't know her name. We call her Mama Gong. That's it."

"And do you think her being angry the other night had anything to do with Strings?"

"I don't know, maybe. I don't speak Chinese."

Karen's throat tightened as something occurred to her. "When was the last time Strings went with you to one of these parties?"

"Two weeks ago. We went to a hotel in Bellevue. Big party. Good food. Catered from some new highfalutin apartments near Lincoln Square. Strings was supposed to meet up here with us Monday night, but he wasn't here. Wouldn't've mattered none since it got canceled."

"Did she mention when there might be another party?"

"No. She said she'd text. But she hasn't."

"Did you know where Strings might be coming from, before Monday?"

The girl shook her head.

"Did you work with him other places or only at the parties?"

"Just at parties."

Karen wanted to cry. She wanted to cry for all these kids who should have homes. For these babies who did what they needed to survive. For Jamie, who she should have insisted stay with her.

She had been fooling herself. She had allowed herself to believe Jamie's constant reassurances that he was surviving on busking. He'd never told her his mother was putting money on his Starbucks and ORCA cards, and he'd lied about the fact he was selling himself to old farts in business suits. What else had he lied about? Was he doing it to protect her? Why?

"What?" Karen roused herself from her private guilt trip. "What did you just say?"

Ozzie repeated herself. "I think he went with us to kinda protect us."

"Was Strings the only boy who went?"

"There were a few regular boys. Three or four others." The girl paused and blinked a couple of times. She brought a hand to her lips. "I've seen most of them around the last few days. One I haven't seen in… weeks? I guess I don't really think much about who's around and who isn't. Could be they went home, you know?"

A cold chill inched its way up Karen's spine. The fine hair on her neck and arms prickled into upright little fronds. "Do you know which one?"

"He went by Wagyu." Ozzie shook her head as if clearing it. "People come and go. They stay for a while, you get close, and then, sometimes they go home. Or… you know… they go away."

Karen let that sink in. *They go away.* "You don't know Wagyu's real name?"

"No."

Karen found the photos of the victims stored in her phone. "Do you know any of these boys?"

Ozzie swiped through the six-packs. The photos were a blend of school pics and mugshots. She paused over one. "I think…Yeah. This is Wagyu."

She swiped again. "This is Goober. Oh, and this one's JoJo."

Karen made notes on the photos. "All of these boys went with you to parties?" A new wave of nausea rolled over her. Three of the six victims worked for Mama Gong. "Any chance you'd be willing to talk to the police about any of this?"

Ozzie stepped back with her hands out in front of her. "Hell no. I am not talking to no police about nothing."

"Wagyu's real name was Jordan King. Does that sound familiar to you?"

"No. Should it?"

"Yeah. He was killed in July."

Ozzie teared up. "I didn't know."

"Goober? He was killed in May. And Jojo was the second victim in February. Now, will you be willing to talk to the police?"

"What could they learn from me? Not like they'd listen to me anyhow." Ozzie wiped at her eyes with the palms of her hands and sniffled loudly.

Karen switched tack. "Can you reach Mama Gong?"

"She texts us, we don't text her. She blocks her number from us."

Karen didn't think relaying a request through this girl was a very good idea, anyway. "Any chance you have a picture of her?"

"Nope."

"What's she look like?"

"She's Chinese. Older. Nice looking. Clean. She dresses like my mom."

Karen figured that described at least ten thousand people in the Seattle area. "Any chance you could connect me with her?"

The girl took the card Karen was holding out to her, but she was shaking her head. "I need the work she gets me."

"Three of the six Dog Park Killer victims worked for Mama Gong. What if Strings is next?"

The girl slipped the card in her pocket and shrugged without conviction.

"We're heading over to Rainbow Landing, you can come with us if you want."

The girl's eyes narrowed and she shook her head vehemently. "No way. I stay away from that place."

"Why?"

"The pervs are like flies around that shithole."

"Pervs?"

"Look, I don't mind going to parties where Mama Gong has organized things. The guys there are pretty much straight-up wanting a couple things. Predictable. Boring, even. Guys in cars? There's no telling what they're gonna do to you."

"You think men circle the shelter, hoping to pick up people?"

"I don't think it. I *know* it. Sit in the park and count the passes some cars make, circling around us like hungry sharks. Some kids go right up to them and hop inside. Not me. No way."

"Thanks for helping us out," Karen said. She handed the girl twenty bucks. "It's not a lot, but maybe it'll get you a couple of meals."

The girl held it between two fingers and saluted her. "Saves me one blow job today, thanks." She spun on her heel and walked away.

## 21

———

KAREN SENT SOPHIE HOME ON THE BUS AND HEADED BACK to Green Lake. There was too much going on there for it to be a complete coincidence. There were too many people with intertwined connections to the homeless youth and the shelters—Garland Parker's office, the Parker home, Jolly's studio, the bus stop, the Starbucks, Donna's house. It was all too much.

She would go back to Jolly's studio first. If she could get him to give her a whole tour of the studio, then she might be able to figure out if he was hiding anything. Or anyone.

The bus dropped her off at the now-familiar stop. She didn't see anyone she recognized inside the Starbucks or out front busking, so she walked back to Jolly's studio.

She wrote down all the businesses that shared a hallway. It was possible that the boys left Jolly's office and were yanked into one of these. Or were lured with some entice-ment. Proximity and opportunity could be the only link between Jolly and the victims.

She quietly pushed open the door to the studio. Jolly and his receptionist stood side-by-side, peering into her monitor behind the desk. His face was mottled with red.

Jolly eyed Karen like she was a giant spider on the wall. "You again? What do you want this time?"

"I came back because that girl who sang on Strings's song? She's my daughter."

She held up the photo of Sophie as a reminder. Jolly's face lost all color. He was practically gray. His eyes darted around the room, and he motioned her back to a different studio than before. The door to that one was shut, and she couldn't hear a sound coming from inside.

"What do you want? She wouldn't take pay from me," he said.

"Do you agree she has a possible career in music?"

"Well, yeah. She's raw, but she's got it," Jolly said. Some of his color was coming back.

"If she sings for you again, you will pay her professional union rates as a contractor. If you produce an album, she will receive royalties on sales."

Jolly nodded along, sweat beading along his forehead. "Look, I swear, I'm just trying to find that hit, you know? I wouldn't screw over anyone who made me money. I just have to keep my overhead down."

"By paying kids a tenth of what they're giving you."

"They're down on their luck. They don't have bank accounts, how would they even cash a check? Cash works for them."

"You keep telling yourself that, Jolly. It makes you feel good about yourself."

"Man, you gotta listen to me. If this thing with Jamie

pans out, he will have a contract. I sent it out to some people last week. And I've gotten nibbles. Legit nibbles."

"Nibbles are nothing, and you know it."

Jolly huffed with annoyance. "Is that everything? I've got a session to deal with."

"Not everything. I'd like a tour of this entire studio so I can see the scope of your actual operations."

"What, now?"

"Yes. Now."

He rolled his eyes and his head as if this were the biggest inconvenience on the planet. "Sure. Sure, I can manage that. Come on."

He opened each door off the hallway. Different spaces were used for different sizes of groups and different sounds. On the one side of the hallway were two larger studios, each split into a walled-off sound room and a control room. On the other side of the hallway were four doors.

The first three were similar studios, but half the size of the larger ones. The space closest to the door housed elaborate sound control panels and fancy looking recording equipment. A glassed-off wall behind served as the actual recording space. Each was filled with mikes, music stands, and stools.

The final door he swung open just enough for her to see inside while barring her entry. "This is my office. I'm the only one who goes inside …"

The desk was neatly arranged with a traditional in-and-out box, a pile of papers in the middle and some photo frames. She couldn't see who was in them because they faced away from the door. The desk, a chair and a few filing cabinets filled the space. Where the glass would have been for the recording space was a solid wall with a floor-to-ceiling bookshelf against one corner. The rest of the wall was bare. If her calculations were correct, then there was a space behind the wall there.

"Oh, another thing," she said as casually as she could. "What else can you tell me about these kids?" She held out her phone and scrolled through the photos of the victims. "They all spent time with you, didn't they?"

"Yeah. They did," he said, his tone angry and beleaguered. "You know, the police have been here, I answered their questions already. I don't have anything to do with their deaths. I swear. It's some freaky coincidence that they all played for me. They swabbed my DNA. I'm not the guy."

"What instruments did they play?"

He blinked and shook his head as if the question made no sense. "All of them played guitar. Electric guitar. Why?"

"I'm trying to find as many connections between them. Were they all the same brand?"

Jolly closed his eyes. "Nah. Let's see. Pipes, Stain, and Goober had Gibsons. Jojo had a Fender. Wagyu had something like Arbol? Not sure of the name. Pretty sure it's a one-off from down in Mexico. Rapster and Strings both had Distorted Branches. Man, those are beauties."

He looked at her. "What could their guitars have to do with this?"

"It's possible the killer has pawned or sold them."

"Oh. Right. Well, then, those Distorted Branch guitars are memorable. So is the Arbol. Must be why the police asked the same question."

Karen relaxed a little. Spending the day on the phone

talking to pawn shops and scouring the internet for guitars up for sale could take a lot of time. Chances were Court's team was already delving into that angle.

"Thank you, Mr. Jolly. Again, here's my card. If you can think of anything else they might have in common, I'd appreciate a call."

Jolly slipped the card into his shirt pocket. "You know they were all gay, right?"

"Everyone pretty much knows that." Karen paused. Poking the bear sometimes gets interesting reactions, so she took aim and poked. "You know there is a rumor about you, don't you? That you pay kids for more than their music."

Jolly drew back as his face colored brightly through his tan. His jaw tightened. "It's time for you to go."

He grabbed her elbow and led her firmly to the front door. "And we won't be needing your daughter's voice for anything. Ever. I've got other girls that can do better than her any day. And to think I was trying to help you."

*Bingo.* She had hit a nerve. She wouldn't let Sophie anywhere near him again, anyway. Sophie wasn't interested in a career in music.

Karen saluted the receptionist as Jolly shoved her through the waiting room. "Get a good look, Sharon. This woman is not allowed back in here."

"Yes, sir, Mr. Jolly." Sharon appeared nonplussed, as if Jolly were constantly kicking people out.

As she left the building, Karen walked around the outside of the building. It was perfectly rectangular, so there must be a hidden space behind his office. Karen counted the windows on the outside of the building. Those that lined up with the office and the other studios were filled in with something black. It was probably some kind of rigid sound-proofing. The window behind the reception area sported an exterior fire ladder. It was the only space in Jolly's part of the building with glass.

A parking lot behind the building held twelve spaces. A generic parking-for-tenants sign was posted on the wall above the spaces. Karen found Jolly's BMW and peeked inside. The seats were empty and clean. The exterior gleamed as though it had been through a carwash recently. There wasn't even a cup in the cup holder. Immaculate.

She finished her circumnavigation of the building, noting the lack of exterior security cameras in the parking lot or facing the building. Would someone like Jolly want extra security for all the sound equipment? Or was he more concerned about the comings and goings to his office?

Karen walked back to Starbucks and ordered a mocha so she could regroup. The coffee shop was the center of a tangled web. It was across the street from the bus stop, and where all the victims had busked at one time or another, and where Jamie had last been seen—at least digitally. It was a ten-minute easy walk from the Starbucks to Jolly's studio.

Karen closed her eyes and pictured Jolly's studio. Each individual studio had a door separating the control booth from the sound stage. Each door was in the same position for each room. In the case of the office, the bookshelf was standing right in front of where the door should have been.

The bookshelf was a door. It would be a perfect place to hide someone.

AFTER SHE'D FINISHED her coffee, Karen walked to Garland Parker's office, staying in the shade of the trees as much as possible. The day had warmed up under a fierce August sun.

One of her gifts was reading people. She got it right most of the time. The only time she missed was when she was with someone close to her. Like Sophie. And Jamie. But strangers? They were like books.

Parker's office was in a blocky postwar house converted into a duplex. One side housed Parker's office. Heavy waves of lavender incense wafted from an open window from the massage therapist housed in the other side.

The door to Parker's office was a solid piece of wood that stuck until she pushed her shoulder into it. If it was this heavy in the dry summer heat, she bet it would be almost impossible to budge come fall.

A small woman with Bettie Page style bangs sat behind the desk. The rest of her hair was pulled back away from her head and her long face reminded Karen of the Wicked Witch from *The Wizard of Oz*. The woman tore her attention away from the computer and greeted Karen with a smile that was startling in its sweetness.

"Can I help you?" she asked in a surprisingly soft and sweet voice. A plate on the desk gave the woman's name: Dorothy Hamilton.

Karen held out her card. "I'm here to speak to Mr. Parker."

"I'm afraid we're full up on investigators, but I'll add it to our Rolodex in case someone can't come through." Dorothy took the card and reached for a metal box on her desk.

"Oh, no. I'm here on a case, and I need to speak to Mr. Parker about it."

Dorothy blinked a couple of times and filed the card into the Rolodex anyway. "Well, you'll have to make an appointment. Mr. Garland is in court the rest of the day."

"I'm sorry to hear that. I was hoping talk to him about his work over at Rainbow Landing."

Dorothy raised her penciled brows in unison. "Oh?"

Karen tossed the woman her most comforting-mom smile. "I'm working a missing-persons case. A kid who's not checked in with any of his friends for a week now. I was wondering if Jamie ever attended one of Mr. Parker's overnight parties."

Dorothy drew back, her neck folding into creased lines that would have been several chins if she were fat. "Well. They are not *parties*. Of that I can assure you. Mr. Parker is very devoted to his work with the youth and helping them transform."

The word sent tingles along Karen's spine. *Transform. Into what? And how?* "I'm sorry. I didn't mean to imply anything inappropriate. I wasn't sure what to call his… erm… gatherings. What does he do with them after he gets them to his house?"

"He gives them each a bed. Access to a shower. He wants to give them a home for the night, where they can relax and feel loved." Dorothy slid the small gold cross dangling at her neck back and forth along the chain. "Garland is an exceptional cook. One of his gifts to them is home-cooked food. The shelters give them enough to get by on, but it's not exactly restaurant quality."

"Oh, I get it," Karen said. "I'm not sure I get how providing all that would transform them, though."

"He's a loving, kind man. The boys he takes home have very little love from their fathers. He's showing them how a real relationship could work."

"Are you ever there with the kids?"

"No. But, I order all of the supplies and clothing for him. He also gives them fresh socks, underwear, pants. Whatever they need at the moment."

"He's doing all this out of the goodness of his heart?"

Dorothy dropped her necklace and covered her heart with crossed hands. "He cares deeply about them. After what happened to Carmen, he completely fell apart."

Parker's breakdown wasn't mentioned in the news articles. "I can well imagine. I read about that in the papers. What a difficult time. Were you working for him back then?"

Dorothy nodded. "He and Morena reacted quite differently. She dug her heels in, and Garland broke apart. He was in a facility for three months, healing, trying to piece things together. He came out of it a better man, if you ask me."

"Was he different to work for after that?"

"Yes. Frankly, before he was a much crueler man. After he returned to work, he'd found a much more, erm, *true Christian* nature."

The description made Karen's stomach twist. She was sick of Christians constantly bickering over what Jesus might have said or done or what he would do in the modern world. The term *true Christian* could have as many meanings as there were Christians.

"Much more true? What do you mean?" Karen asked.

"Well. He has… let's say, a softer and kinder heart. He took a lot of blame for throwing Carmen out. And now, well, he's trying to make up for it. He personally treats everyone better than before. He drops a couple of dollars when he passes a busker. He hands out food cards, like Subway, Starbucks, that kind of thing, to homeless people. He's haunted by kids on the street and still sees Carmen in each of them. Do you see?"

"So, before this big change, you worked for him when he was, as you said, crueler?"

Dorothy sighed. "Maybe cruel was the wrong word to use. Self-righteous might be better. He believed God was on his side on all things, so he ignored those less fortunate than he was."

"Was his breakdown over Carmen because he kicked Carmen out of the house for being gay?"

Dorothy shifted her gaze to a photo on her desk. "Carmen wasn't exactly gay, though that's what the papers said. Carmen came out that he was female, not male. And he liked women. She? She liked women? Oh, my. I'm really not good with all the terminology. I guess, nowadays, Carmen was a she who liked women, so technically, she was a lesbian? Honestly, it's hard for me to keep track, and I only knew Carmen as a teenage boy. It all makes me a little dizzy."

"Sexuality and gender are complicated subjects," Karen said. At least Dorothy was trying to make sense of it best she could.

Dorothy breathed out heavily. "The point is, being gay,

or lesbian, was abhorrent to both the Parkers. Denying your biology? That was a whole different level of evil to them."

"You don't sound horrified by it."

"I have a niece… erm… nephew, who has been going through this, and I am committed to loving them no matter what," Dorothy said. "As far as working for Garland goes, it's so much better for me. I needed this job so badly, I put up with the nasty. I was close to quitting because Garland's temper escalated when Carmen lived on the street. Then, when Carmen was beaten up? I watched Garland fall apart with guilt and his loss of faith."

"And now, you and he are an item?" Karen asked, making a guess.

"What makes you ask that?" Dorothy's eyes widened and her face flushed bright.

"You switched from calling him Mr. Parker to Garland."

Dorothy didn't answer for a moment. "I found him in his office after he tried to commit suicide. Called an ambulance. Sat by his side and held his hand until they found a place to help him. Kept things running here. We are close. Not an item."

"Ah, so he doesn't reciprocate your feelings?"

Dorothy shook her head, a wistful half-smile on her lips. "He's too focused on helping these kids. Maybe he will heal enough from all this and he'll see me here, waiting for him."

**22**

———

THE WALK FROM GARLAND PARKER'S OFFICE TO MORENA Parker's home was less than five minutes. The adorable Craftsman bungalow was much like Donna Richards' home, which was two blocks away. Garland Parker must have moved to Capitol Hill after his divorce to be near the youth shelters, because giving up this awesome commute was insane otherwise.

One of the best parts about Karen's job now was that her daily commute averaged out to sixteen stairs. Except when she was running all over town chasing down endless leads or sitting in her car bored out of her mind.

Karen opened the cheery white picket fence and walked up the rosebush-lined walkway. Their heady scent perfumed the air in delicious rose waves. The welcome mat in front of the door said, May Christ be with you, with a huge cross forming across the T in Christ and the other words looping around it in cursive script.

Karen knocked and waited. A white woman in her late

fifties opened the door a couple of inches. Her gray hair was cut in an orderly bob. It was about all she could make out through the chain lock across the door.

"Can I help you?"

From what she knew about Morena Parker, Karen didn't think asking about a missing gay boy would get her very far.

"I'm a private investigator," she said smiling brightly. "Do you have few minutes to spare?"

"Is it about the burglaries in the neighborhood?"

"Anything you can tell me would be very helpful," Karen said, picking up on the pretense happily. It wasn't an active lie.

"Well, come in. Come in. I've not been a victim, of course, but so many people have." She closed the door to unlock it and opened it wide. "When we moved here, the neighborhood was crime-free. Now?" She tsked and shook her head.

Morena Parker wore a simple cotton shirt buttoned up to her neck. A large bulky wooden cross hung around her neck. It was easily seven inches tall. She waved Karen over to an armchair near the fireplace as she lowered herself onto the sofa across from it.

Above the mantle was a painting of Carmen. Karen was pretty sure that was who it was, anyway. He was painted as an angel with fluffy white wings sprouting off his back, a halo over his head, and his fingers clasped around a crude wooden cross. Clouds and streaming sun strokes radiated outward from him. Karen stared at it with an odd fascination. *Kick out your son, he dies, and then you immortalize him as an angel?*

"What can I do for you, miss…?"

Karen ripped her eyes from the beatified portrait. "Hunter. My name is Karen Hunter." She slid a card across the coffee table, right next to the only other thing on it—a large-print version of the Bible.

Karen asked Morena a number of questions about the neighborhood, wandering all over the place so that there was no obvious direction to her questioning. When Morena mentioned she lived alone Karen asked, "I take it you're a widow then?"

"Oh, no. I'm actually divorced. Of course, I never expected to get a divorce, but sometimes the Lord seems fit to give us tests."

"I'm sorry, I didn't mean to pry," Karen said. "I assumed…"

"My husband and I parted soon after my son died." She mentioned her son's death as casually as if she'd forgotten to buy milk at the grocery store. Morena pointed up toward the angel on the wall. "He's in heaven with our Heavenly Father now. My sweet angel."

"Oh, I'm so sorry. That must have been horrible. Losing a child?"

Morena smiled. She actually smiled. "Oh, don't be. My son is in heaven now, I'm certain of that one. God erased his sins before he died through re-baptism."

"I don't understand."

"The Lord gives us tests, Ms. Hunter. And he had tested my son's poor soul mightily. However, I do believe my son's final days were given over to God and prayer. He lived for forty days after he was beaten. It's a magical number, you know."

Karen nodded politely as the woman testified. She was appalled and fascinated at the same time.

"Yes. He had been gone from our home for forty days. He returned to us for forty days before he went to God. I'm certain our prayers over him cleansed his soul before returning him."

"Forty days?" Karen asked.

"Yes. All traces of his abomination were cleansed from his soul while in the hospital."

"His… abomination?" Karen asked.

"Why he… You see? That's the beauty of it all. It doesn't matter now, does it? God forgives all of those who righteously ask for it. I am certain my son entered His heavenly arms clean and pure." She gazed at the portrait, eyes filling with tears.

Karen remained silent. What the hell could she say to that? "Why are you telling me all this? I mean, it's all kind of personal."

"I'm called to testify, Miss Hunter. When people, especially non-believers like yourself…" She held up her hand and shook her head. "I can tell by looking at you that you do not believe in the Lord our Savior Jesus Christ. I can only hope that my testifying to you might sway you toward our Lord, even if only an inch at a time."

"I'm curious, what is it about me that makes you think I'm not a Christian?"

Morena lifted a single eyebrow. "Your clothing. It's slutty. I can see your cleavage. Your demeanor—very casual and insolent. Your smell."

"My smell?" Karen asked. She had showered that

morning. Put on a light mist of Black Opium. She sniffed herself. "Perfume is a sin?"

"Anything interfering with the Lord's natural gifts is an abomination."

"Like cutting or dyeing your hair?"

Morena stiffened. "That's taking it to an extreme."

"I don't see the difference," Karen said. "If you're not supposed to interfere, where do you draw the line?"

"God shows the way," Morena said. "Cleanliness is next to godliness. Being well-kempt and tidy is a far cry from being a siren trying to lure men to you with crass attractions."

"I see," Karen said, not seeing anything. But continuing a discussion in bat-shit crazy theology wouldn't help her find Jamie. "It's probably best if we stick to other topics. Have you seen anyone unusual in the neighborhood lately? Sitting in cars, walking around?"

"Not that I can recall. There're always *those people* at Starbucks. I never go there anymore because they sit outside playing their foul music, tainting the atmosphere. I wouldn't be surprised if that's their headquarters."

"*Those people?*"

Morena sat forward, her eyes blazing. "Deviants. Abominations. Demons. They are not children of God. I can't stand being near them. But I pray for them. I pray for their wasting, immortal souls every day."

*Sure you do, lady.*

Maybe showing Morena the photos of the dead kids would get a reaction. "I have some photos to show you. Maybe you can tell me if you ever saw these kids around here?"

Karen swiped through the phone slowly so Morena could see each photo of the boys. Her eyes narrowed on the screen and she sucked in air, hissing sharply. "Who are you really? Why are you showing me all these photos? These are all those dead boys." Morena stood up, placing her hands defensively on her hips.

"I take it you recognize them?" Karen asked, rising to be on equal footing with the other woman.

"Of course I do. I read the papers. You're not here about the burglaries, are you? What's this all about?"

Karen held out one of the flyers with Jamie's photos. "I'm a private investigator. His mother hired me to find him. He's been gone a week."

Morena didn't even look at the paper. "Never saw him."

"You didn't even look," Karen said holding it up higher, in Morena's face.

Morena ripped the paper out of Karen's hand, crumpled it into a small ball, and tossed it on the coffee table. "Find God. Find God soon—before you go to Hell along with the rest of them. Cleansing by the fires of hell will be all that is left for your immortal soul. Now get out of my house." Morena strode to the door and thrust it open, her free arm pointing the way out.

Karen flattened the flyer and tucked the edge underneath the Bible. "My contact information is on the flyer if you see Jamie." She smiled with her sweetest kiss-my-ass smile as she swept past Morena Parker and out into the bright hot day.

Morena Parker's wild-eyed rhetoric was what she considered to be scary-Christian crazy. The kind of people who spoke in tongues and threatened violence in a way she didn't think most Christians believed. Karen was still shaking from the experience by the time she found herself in front of Donna Richards' house. She opened the little picket fence and knocked on Donna's door.

"Karen, what has you in the neighborhood now? Come in, come on in. I was cooking up some dinner."

She waved Karen into the kitchen. A huge pot of chili bubbled on the stove.

"Looks like you're cooking for the shelter."

"Oh, yes. Well, I learned long ago that cooking for myself is not rewarding on a daily basis. I make a huge mess of something and then I freeze it into individual meals. It's the only way I cook anymore."

"I keep meaning to join one of those cook-for-a-whole-month clubs where people get together and make a month's worth of dinners."

"I never heard of that, but it sounds like a great idea." Donna kicked a door shut near the fridge with her toe and turned toward the pot on the stove, stirring the contents with a large wooden spoon.

"Do you have a basement?" Karen asked.

"Only one of a dozen in the neighborhood. It's nice and cool down there during the summer, but not if I leave the door open all day long."

"Are you going to the shelter tonight?" Karen asked.

"Oh, no. I've spent enough time there this week. I'm happy to be a homebody for the weekend." She opened the fridge and pulled out a glass pitcher of lemonade and poured two glasses. "I probably won't be back until next Thursday for open-mic night."

"Ah. I can see why it appeals to you. I really enjoyed it last night. "

Donna put the glasses on the table, pulled a seat out for Karen, and sat in the one opposite. Karen settled in and took a sip of the lemonade. It was cool and tangy, just what she needed.

"So, do you know a neighbor of yours a couple blocks over? Her name is Morena Garland."

"Hmmmm… Morena Garland?  Pretty sure I know who you're talking about. Gigantic wooden cross hanging around her neck?"

"That would be her," Karen said.

"She's taken her views to a whole new level."

"In what way?"

"Well, she's a fire-and-brimstone, God-is-vengeful kind of believer. She runs around the neighborhood handing out flyers about events at her church."

"Creepy in a scary-creepy way? Or more of a ridiculous-creepy way?"

Donna tilted her head to the side. "Do you know her history? Her son was murdered. Beaten to death for being gay. Horrific."

"You think that sent her over the rails?"

"Wouldn't it you? Losing a child is a test no parent should have to bear."

"It breaks families up. Parents blame each other. Play the what-if game. They often end up getting a divorce. It's a tragedy that doesn't stop with the child's death."

Donna grasped her lemonade with both hands. "I

should be grateful I didn't have to endure a divorce. My husband died when Blake was very young. By the time I lost Blake, I was already on my own."

"Talking about them keeps their memory alive. Next best thing to immortality."

Donna let out a breathy half-laugh. "Yeah. Well, it was a mixed bag for me. I was young. Got pregnant. Got married. That's what you do where I'm from. I probably would have divorced him eventually—he was a mean old bastard, really, but he died before it came to that."

Him. He. Donna never used her husband's name. He must have been difficult, and he was way older than Donna.

Karen waited for more while Donna focused on the rim of her glass. After nearly a minute of silence, Donna suddenly blinked, startled, and wide-eyed. She focused intently on Karen, and the hairs on Karen's arms lifted and prickled.

"I'm sorry. I sometimes go back to the accident and get lost in it."

"Accident?" Karen tried to shake the creepy sensation that still danced along her skin.

Donna sighed and waved a hand in the air. "I don't talk about it much. It usually makes people uncomfortable, and I can't abide being pitied."

Karen could relate to this. After the people in her neighborhood learned she was a dominatrix, everything changed. Men looked at her with more lascivious open longing. Women had always been jealous and wary of her, and now they added disdain and disgust to the mix.

"I kind of get it."

"Do you?" Donna examined her carefully for a minute.

"My husband was driving when we were hit by a semi that ran a red light. We were spun around and around into a construction site, and my husband was decapitated by the windshield of our car. His head landed on my lap. Blake was in the seat between us."

Donna's voice had dropped to a whisper. Karen swallowed and leaned forward to hear the rest. She couldn't back out now. Donna's eyes had lost their focus and she was off in another world of her own, maybe remembering the scene in more vivid detail.

"He looked up at me, eyes wide open and pleading. He knew his head was no longer attached to his body. I'll never forget the way his eyes talked to me like that. Blake was young. You'd think he wouldn't remember it. Still, he never was the same after that." Donna's accent had shifted, become more Southern and twangy.

Karen didn't have a response to this. What did you say to someone who's been through that kind of trauma? Poor woman. Poor little boy.

The cat she'd met the other day walked lazily into the room and jumped on Karen's lap. Karen shifted her legs to provide a flat surface. After the cat settled into a furball on her lap, Karen slid her hand under her purple collar, scratching at the spot where her dog loved the most attention.

Donna shook herself and downed the last of her lemonade. "Well," she said, her voice brightening a bit, "I don't dwell on it too much these days. But that's when everything in my life changed. I got out of Dodge, so to speak. I was no longer 'the preacher's wife,' I was 'that poor woman.' I couldn't abide that."

Karen took in a sudden breath. She'd gone straight to "that poor woman." She did her best to hide it. "You went through something horrible, but when people saw you, their contemplation of something so horrific happening to them were reflected as pity. *It's horrible, but better you than me.*"

"Well, there you are. I do believe you understand."

Karen reached out and covered Donna's free hand, squeezing it gently. "And then, after your husband died, you lost Blake, too?"

Donna stiffened and pulled her hand away. "Children are so much more dear than husbands. I can't go there right now."

Was what happened to her son worse than what happened to her husband? Or was it that the pain of losing one's child is worse than that of losing a spouse? The only picture on the mantle showed Blake as a young boy. Life lost so young was so much harder to accept. "It must be painful to think about. I'm willing to listen whenever you want to talk about it."

"Thank you, Karen. I'll keep that in mind." Donna sipped at her tea. "Do you think Morena Parker has something to do with these Dog Park killings?"

"Do you?"

"I've always wondered about her. The idea she'd actually *hurt* someone is pretty far-fetched. Then again, she does live close to where they catch the bus. And the Starbucks where they busk."

"As do you."

Donna's eyes widened and she laughed. "Oh, my, I guess I do, don't I? And, I also volunteer at the shelter where every one of those poor dear boys stayed at least once." She paused, her face suddenly serious. "That's actually a lot in common. More so than Morena Parker. Oh, dear, me."

*It was a lot in common. And there are no coincidences. Now who was paranoid?* And yet, Karen could not laugh with the other woman.

Donna fanned herself with a hand. "I shouldn't laugh at any of this, but it's all so horrible I can't do much else. We'll all be much safer once that sordid business is all done with."

"Morena seems too small," Karen said. "I mean, they end up way far away from here, way out in various parks. She'd need a car and then the ability to carry them."

"Oh. True. I am certain I cannot lift any of those boys, and I am a good five inches taller than she is."

"Unless she has a partner," Karen said. What about the crueler version of Mr. Parker? Maybe his latest devotion to the cause was all a lie to get his hands on their victims? "Did you know Garland Parker as well?"

"Only by reputation. Godly man. Not as wild-eyed-fundamentalist as his wife. Why?"

"Huh. I was thinking maybe Garland and Morena were working together. Garland's law office is on the same route as the bus the kids use to get over here. Her house is nearby."

"Well, isn't it always some old white guy in the end?" Donna asked.

## 23

Karen left Donna's house a good deal calmer but still with her mind in a whirl. She caught a bus over to Capitol Hill still trying to get over the bizarre interaction with Morena Parker. As soon as Morena saw the photos of the victims, she had exploded with rage.

Karen had concentrated on the victims' faces in order to memorize them. How would someone put it together that fast if they hadn't known the victims? Was it possible Morena had a terrific facial memory? Or did she have more intimate knowledge of the victims as part of a team of killers?

Garland Parker's house was close to Rainbow Landing. Maybe he was home from court for the day and she could talk to him. She walked from the park, past Harbor House and then Rainbow Landing, to Parker's house. It took about three minutes. Why use a van to transport kids this far? He could have walked them over, or invited them to come on their own once they knew where he lived.

There was no driveway or garage for the house out front, and the van wasn't evident anywhere along the street. The only light inside appeared to come from a dull yellow glow coming through the frosted glass of a basement window.

Karen made sure the street was empty and that she wasn't being watched before opening Parker's mailbox. She paused, considering the crime she was about to commit. Going through Parker's mail was one way of figuring him out. If she got caught she could lose her license. But, if there was anything in his mail that could help her find Jamie, then it would be worth it, wouldn't it?

Karen walked up and down the street a few times, trying to gauge the neighborhood. No one was out at the moment. It was very unlikely anyone would see her. Opening someone's mailbox was illegal, but she wasn't going to steal anything. She would take a quick look and put everything back.

Inside were the usual assortment of fliers, three bills, three fishing magazines, two hunting magazines, and two professional law magazines. The assortment gave her the impression Garland Parker was an alpha male. She kept looking over her shoulder to see if anyone was watching, her heart beating harder with each moment.

She put the mail back in, carefully. The last thing she needed was to get on the wrong side of an attorney in this town. Seattle was a big city, and the legal community was a bunch of hens in a small hen house. Everyone knew each other and their unwritten blacklist was something she wanted to stay clear of. Maybe Bernice could give her inside information on the man.

Karen knocked on the door, not expecting an answer. She put her forehead against the glass part of the door and cupped her hands around her eyes to block out light. The inside was *Architectural Digest* perfection—clean, organized, and professionally decorated.

With all those hunting magazines, she half expected there to be gun racks adorning the walls. Maybe the magazines were more a fantasy fix than reality. Or he was a responsible gun owner who kept them hidden and not on display, especially since he had teens in his home a lot of the time.

Either way, the space screamed *man*. The light fixtures were modern stainless steel and glass. The artwork was modern, filled with blotchy primary colors. Only a few throw pillows and rugs softened the surfaces.

Karen scanned for security cameras. She couldn't pick the massive deadbolt on the front door in daylight without getting caught. There was still no one obviously around. An occasional car glided by, but no one seemed to pay her any attention. She casually slipped around to the side of the house. The wooden gate latch to the back yard was easy to open: a rotting cord was draped over the top like an invitation.

Luckily, there was a regular door instead of a sliding-glass door at the back of the house. She knocked again in case Parker was home and hadn't heard her earlier knock. The window on the back of the door gave her a glimpse into the kitchen, which was as equally clean and organized as the front of the house. No piles of mail scattered on the table or counter. Dishes cleared up. Not even a mug on the counter.

She pulled out her picks and weighed the circumstances. What if this guy was the Dog Park Killer and Jamie was tied up in his basement? She could save him here and now and no one would care that she used her picks to get in. And this would all be over for everyone. If he wasn't, then no harm done—unless she got caught. Karen would do a quick search of the house to figure him out. Maybe he was the grand philanthropist his secretary made him out to be.

She steeled her resolve and picked the lock in under a minute. Motion detectors were placed in strategic corners. The control pad for the alarm was by a door in the kitchen she figured led to the garage. The cheery note ready to arm blinked on the screen. She opened the door to an empty garage. Did Parker usually leave his alarm off, or had she lucked out?

What was she here to find? Would someone really keep a kid locked in their basement? Even as she chided herself for being ridiculous, she made a circuit through the house, one floor at a time. Everything was neat and tidy. Nothing out of order in a freakish kind of way.

The refrigerator was organized like a grocery store. All the condiments were in neat plastic boxes on one shelf. Eggs, yogurt, sour cream, and butter were neatly lined up on the top shelf. Another shelf housed cans of LaCroix water and cold-brew coffee. The vegetable tray and meat bins were filled with organic greens, grass-fed beef, and a variety of cheeses in fancy paper packages and handwritten labels.

There were, as Dorothy had told her, bunk beds in the other bedrooms. Neatly folded stacks of towels and travel-sized toiletries filled up a basket in each room. Each closet contained an assortment of clean clothes and shoes in a range of sizes.

Very little of interest jumped out at Karen. Parker's home was a masculine paradise of metal and leather, even in the master bedroom. Garland Parker was an attorney, so Karen expected the suits in the closet. What she didn't expect was the array of color and organization. Even his gym clothes were neatly arranged in his drawers. The hampers along the back wall of the closet were labeled for dry clean, whites and colors.

It would be hard to live with someone who was this organized. Karen ventured into the bathroom and opened the drug cabinet. The expected array of grooming products was neatly arranged inside. Bottles of men's cologne were neatly arranged along the bottom shelf. Karen sniffed a couple of them, trying to get a sense of who he was. They were all a little on the flowery end for her taste. She preferred men to wear scents with musk and citrus overtones.

The top shelf contained the usual NSAIDs and a brown bottle of prescription medicine. This last was turned away so the label was facing the back of the cabinet. Karen grabbed a tissue and lifted it out. It was a bottle of Tenofovir, a prescription drug in his name with two remaining refills. It sounded familiar, but she'd have to do a search on it later. She put the bottle away, leaving it exactly as she had found it.

The bathroom was utilitarian and clean. The toilet and surrounding white tile floor were free of masculine tell-tale yellow splashes. The drawers were neatly organized with extra rolls of toilet paper and unopened boxes of Sensodyne toothpaste. The bottom drawer contained a douching kit complete with lube and injector.

Karen leaned against the counter. Was Parker gay? Or did he have some strange cleaning fetish that went to the anal?

The door to the basement was locked from the top, as if keeping something downstairs within. She double-checked to make sure it wouldn't auto-lock on her when she went down the steps. The dull light she'd seen from the outside guided her way down.

The basement was a deluxe man cave. The stairs opened up into a room housing a ping-pong table, a pool table, and a bar at the far end. It was stocked with non-alcoholic drinks. She could see the kids he brought home having fun here. It was a non-threatening environment. If you lived in chaos, structure might very well be appealing.

At least Parker wasn't supplying booze to minors. A hallway led into two other rooms. One was a home theater with twelve deluxe recliners on built-in risers like a real theater. The third room was storage. Utility shelves lined the space and were filled with plastic storage boxes, all neatly labeled—tax returns, family papers, Christmas decorations, and mementos.

One box was labeled "Carmen." Karen ran her finger along the edge. This box, unlike the one under her bed, had no lock on it. If either Sophie or Brian died, what would she put in such a box? Their bedrooms were filled with the ephemera of their lives, and yet, how would she be able to cull anything and box it away like this?

The sole photo album told a story of a young couple, their only child, and a conventionally happy life—a cherubic baby covered in messy food, a toddler with arms out wide balancing on his first steps, a young boy at bat. There were a few medals and trophies boasting participation, and a few top honors. Carmen's high-school yearbooks were filled with happy greetings and phone numbers inviting summer liaisons, and photos of him in clubs and on the stage. Letters from various colleges offering him space in their classes of 2012 were tied together with a ribbon. It was a heartbreaking chronology of a boy that only lived on in memory.

She closed up the box and made her way through the back door, not sure what she'd learned here. Jamie wasn't here, so why was she? Backtracking through the house, she wiped down anything she might have touched and escaped out the way she had come. As she came around to the front of the house, she stopped short as she saw Garland Parker at the front door.

He wiped at the glass on the front door with a handkerchief as he unlocked it, erasing the forehead mark she must have left when peeking into the house.

Karen pressed her back up against the side of the house until her heart rate returned to normal.

That was way too close.

## 24

---

Karen waited another thirty seconds after Parker
went inside his house before racing across the lawn and
pretending to be a passer-by on the street. The walk to the
bus stop was a slow hot slog. Traffic was already creeping
along when she made it onto the 545 back to the Eastside.

She found a seat and did looked up tenofovir, the drug
she'd found in Garland's drug cabinet. It was commonly
used to help prevent HIV infection in people at high risk.
That along with the douching kit she found in his bathroom
suggesting Garland Parker was gay. Was he closeted and in
denial? Maybe.

Court Pearson interrupted her with a text inviting her to
a community meeting at Meany Hall on the University of
Washington campus. They were expecting a decent turnout
of the youth community. The missing-persons team planned
to put up some photos, including Jamie's, and Court was
hoping she could be an extra set of eyes and ears in the
audience.

She told Court she'd be there and texted Sophie that she would be staying late in Seattle. If Court had texted five minutes later, it would have been more difficult to get back into town. As it was, she hopped off the bus before it hit the bridge at the stop closest to the UW campus.

Karen arrived at the University Heights building fifteen minutes ahead of the meeting. The room was filled with a couple hundred people, about a quarter of them kids. Many of the adults were ones she'd met the last couple of days as volunteers or workers at the shelters.

Donna was settling into a seat as Karen caught her eye and waved at her. The other woman smiled broadly and returned the wave before turning her attention toward the front of the room. A few of the kitchen ladies from Harbor House were sitting next to Donna. Adin from Rainbow Landing was sitting next to Garland Parker. At least she'd hidden her break-in well enough that he wasn't still at home filing a police report. She looked for Marcus Jolly in the sea of faces but didn't see him.

Court motioned Karen over to him before she had a chance to take her seat. "We're going to put up photos of the victims and some missing teens and stationing officers around the room for people to come forward. You're welcome to hang out near Jamie's photo when the time comes."

The press was segregated in a back corner, with one local television crew in attendance. She was pretty sure Camille Poulin, the reporter Bernice had introduced her to the day before, was in the small group. Her back was to Karen, but the spiky blond hair was unmistakable. If she was going to go undercover, she'd need to work on blending in.

Court stepped up onto the stage. He was wearing a suit jacket, and his shirt was open at the neck, exposing blond fuzz. He wasn't the dark Italian stallion she normally found attractive. He was handsome in a Nordic kind of way. Strong, clean-cut jaw, broad shoulders, but she'd never found herself fantasizing about a guy without a scruffy face and dark curly hair.

She closed her eyes and focused on the missing and murdered teens instead of her annoying attraction to Court Pearson.

Court opened with statistics. What was he thinking? That putting the crowd to sleep with numbers would lull them into comfort? He moved onto the basics of staying safe. Teens needed to stay together, not go off with any strangers. Not to get into cars with anyone they didn't trust, and even not to go off alone with people they knew.

He showed photos of all the dead boys—old school photos, not crime-scene shots—and pleaded for anyone who had contact with the boys to come forward. "We're trying to piece together what they might have had in common. Anything you know, no matter how irrelevant you might think it is, might actually help us create a full picture."

He waved toward a group of police officers. "We've got plenty of officers here to take down information. Additionally, we have a list of fifteen young men who have been reported missing over the last two weeks. While it's unlikely that any of them are in the hands of the serial killer, it *is* possible that one, or more, of them is."

The odds favoring Jamie's safety plummeted even

further. *One in fifteen. Crap.*

"We are hoping the killer has entered another dormant phase and we can capture him before he claims another victim," Court continued. "However, we do know that the killer holds his victim for at least two weeks, possibly longer. We want to find all of these people to ensure they are safe."

Two weeks or *longer?* Karen relaxed. Jamie had only been gone a week. Even if he were being tortured or beaten or God knew what else, there was still time to save him.

Court identified each of the missing teens by their known street aliases and legal names. When he talked about Jamie, Karen closed her eyes and breathed in deeply. Bursting in tears in public would do no good at all. Every one of the boys they featured was similar to the boys who had been murdered. Blond. Wispy thin gay teens. Guitar players. Jamie.

*Marcus Jolly* knew all of them. He had the means. He had the opportunity. But why? Why would he kill his moneymakers?

When Court called for questions, most people stared at him in stunned silence. The press crew were faster to raise their hands than anyone else.

He pointed to Camille Poulin. "Cami?"

"Have you invited in the FBI to help solve these murders? If not, why not, and if so, what are they doing to help?"

Court spread his hands wide. "You've been watching television, haven't you?"

Court's smile spread slowly, turning his serious face into that of a Norse god. It was his use of the name *Cami* that reminded Karen of where she had met Camille, aka Cami before. She'd been one of the three women Court introduced her to at the Indigo Girls concert in the spring. Cami had been wearing full leathers top to bottom and presented as super-butch, nothing like the professional she had appeared in Bernice's office or now.

At the concert, Cami's arm was draped casually over a very feminine black woman with a locked collar around her neck. Karen hadn't paid as much attention to them as she did to the woman Court was with that night, but it had struck her as interesting that Court was hanging with people from the kink community. Maybe he wasn't entirely closed-minded about a little kink.

She focused on Cami. Some people really transformed themselves, and Cami was one of them. Why hadn't she said something at Bernice's office the other day? *Weird.*

"Actually, the FBI is helping," Court said. "We have two FBI agents on our task force. They have been very instrumental in helping us develop a profile of the killer."

Court continued: "We are looking for a white male, twenty-five to fifty years old. He fits in with society. He's got a job, may even be a professional. He might be married. It's possible he even has children and comes across as entirely normal. He's focused on young men, so he might be confused about his own sexuality. We think he's punishing these young men for being homosexual as a way to punish himself. He is at odds with his religion and his sexual identity."

Karen wanted to jump up and point at Garland Parker, but held herself still. Having been accused of murder simply because of her profession, she was loath to do the same without more proof. All she had on Garland was his closeted homosexuality, his proximity to youth, and his history with his son.

The timing between each killing was getting shorter and shorter. If she continued drawing the line on the graph, the next death was still three weeks away.

"And how long were each of these boys missing before they were found dead?" another reporter asked.

Karen leaned forward in her seat to get a better view of who asked the question. It was another reporter, this one from a local television studio. Cindy Ryan. It would be a long time before she forgot that face. Ryan had camped on her front yard and accused her of murder for days. Exposed her to the world, and her neighbors, as a pro-domme.

Karen sat back and hoped the woman hadn't noticed her presence. She didn't want to end up as a sidebar on Ryan's next news report. *"Remember the dominatrix who had Berkeley Drummond on his knees? She might be snooping on your street sometime soon… she's now a P.I. What happens when a pro-domme changes careers? Exclusive interview at eleven."*

*No thank you. No fucking way.* Hopefully, the other woman was much more interested in chasing a killer.

"Unfortunately, the victims all had a history of living on the street before their capture," Court said. "They were all out of contact with their families for weeks to months before they were found, so we don't know how long they might have been held by the killer."

*Weeks to months.* Jamie had been missing only a few days. Karen let out a long release of breath. Maybe the question wasn't *if*, so much as how much time did they have? The last body was found nine weeks ago. At the rate of escalation, it could be five or six weeks before he killed again. Or less.

Court called on a teen next. Her long turquoise-colored hair was braided into a work of art, and it appeared she'd been elected by a group of friends who clustered around her to speak for them. "The City Council has been paying people in hazmat suits to clean up Seattle. They pay people money to come by and destroy all our stuff, ripping apart our tents and sh… Trashing it all. Taking away everything we have."

Court's face remained attentive. "I'm sorry to hear that. My understanding is that people are given a chance to collect their belongings and escorted to shelters and minors are given transportation home."

"Yeah, but, what I'm saying is, some people are disappearing. They go off and never show up again."

"Are you suggesting that some of these missing teens might have gone back home?" Court asked.

"Yeah. That, and some of them people that come do the work are mean sons of… Well… they are really, really mean. They hang around as we regroup. Taunting us with telling us we have five minutes to grab everything—like *everything* we own—you know? We gotta run before the department shows up to throw us in juvie. Like it's fun to watch us scurry around gathering up the bits and pieces of our lives, you know? One of them creepers might be the dude that's, like, you know, the killer."

She sat down. The group she was with leaned in close to her. They exuded a powerful defiant energy. Karen guessed they were all under eighteen. She wondered how long it would be before she was standing on her lawn waving a cane.

**25**

———

As things wrapped up, Court asked Karen to wait for him a few more minutes while he gathered things to take back to the office.

Donna Richards emerged from the bathrooms and made a beeline for Karen, her eyes red from crying. She pressed at her cheeks with the palms of her hands. "Seeing everything laid out like this is so draining. I can't believe how many of those boys I knew."

"Did most of them stay at Harbor House?"

"All of them. It's awful."

"I'm really worried about Jamie," Karen said. "Thinking he could be somewhere… now. With…"

"You don't really think that monster has him, do you? It's so close to when they found the last one."

"I don't know what to think. I go back and forth between being convinced he's trapped somewhere, and thinking he's off doing something scary on his own."

"Scary on his own?" Donna asked, a small apologetic smile on her face. "What do you mean?"

Karen shook her head. "It's hard being a homeless youth. People prey on them in a variety of ways. But not all predators are killers."

Donna's mouth opened slowly and she let out a long slow, very Southern-sounding "Ooooooohhhh" of understanding. "It's so sad when they have to earn money that way. Breaks my heart. Bless their little souls."

"Yeah, well, I'd rather he be off somewhere like that than off with the crazy lunatic who's doing this to innocent kids."

Donna tilted her head. "You know, I heard once that the villain is the hero of their own story. Maybe he thinks he's doing something good."

"What? That's… what possible good could come of these murders?" Karen shook her head in disbelief.

"They might be thinking they're getting rid of an abomination. I can't tell you how many times I've heard people say we should 'round them up' in regards to any manner of people. *Gays. Blacks. Mexicans.* Didn't that officer just say there might be a religious motivation behind all of them?"

"That's pretty twisted."

"Exactly. Everything is twisted inside and out these days," Donna said, squeezing a hand gently on Karen's shoulder. "Well, enough of that for now. I'm heading over to the sausage place down the Ave for dinner, want to join me?"

"Thanks, but I'm waiting for Detective Pearson. I want to go over some things with him."

"Really? About finding Jamie?"

"I need to tell him about my encounter with Morena Parker."

"Oh my goodness. Maybe I'm right about the abomination thing. I was kidding, but now that you mention her… she is rather fanatical. But the cops say it's a man."

"Maybe she and her ex are working together. Maybe she has a boyfriend?" Karen shrugged. "I don't have all the pieces."

"It is very complicated, I'm sure," Donna said. "Well, sorry you can't join me for dinner. I do so enjoy your company. That detective in charge is very good-looking. I can see why you wouldn't turn down an opportunity to talk to him. You'd make a cute couple."

"What? Oh, no. We're… no… he's taken Jamie's disappearance very seriously. He's helping me work things through."

Donna gave her the universal *yeah, right* look. The heat of a blush crept up her cheeks as Court turned toward them, as if on cue.

Donna reached out a hand to Court. "You did a splendid job in there tonight. And I wish you all the best luck."

He shuffled a box he was holding to under his arm to shake her hand. "Thanks. You work at Harbor House, right?"

"Wow. Good memory, Detective. Technically, I'm just a volunteer. And, now I must be off. Have a good evening, you two." She smiled with a teasing, knowing smile and sauntered away.

Court tilted his head toward the door. "I'll dump this in

my car and we can get some food over on The Ave. If you're hungry, that is."

"Where's Detective Langston today?"

"She's taking a personal day." Court didn't elaborate. "My car is in the main garage under the library."

They crossed Red Square and took the elevator down to the parking lot. Karen had never liked parking there late at night. Even when classes were in session, the parking lot was empty and felt desolate.

"You like shwarma? There's a place on the Ave I used to like. I'm pretty sure it's still there."

"Love it," he said. "What'd you think of the presentation?"

"Do you really think the killer is dormant right now?"

"We don't have any reason to believe he's going to kill again anytime soon. There were nine weeks between the last two victims."

"That was a carefully worded response. I'm not the press."

"You're not a cop, either."

Karen tried a different tack. "I saw Jolly again today."

"That guy is a piece of work. Get anything new?"

The restaurant was packed with people, but they managed to find a cramped table for two near the front window.

"When I casually brought up the rumors about him paying for more than music, he got pretty angry. Tossed me out."

The waitress interrupted them to take their order. Court ordered the lamb and a soda. Karen ordered beef shwarma and a beer.

"It sounds like your interviewing technique might need some improving," Court said. "Exactly how did you ask Jolly about him paying kids for sex?"

Karen rolled her eyes. "I told him there was a rumor going around that he was paying kids for more than music."

"Subtle, Hunter. Very subtle." Court shook his head and laughed.

"I ran a background check on him, didn't find anything that showed him as a sexual predator. He's clean that way. He moved here two years ago, and he's building a legit business with a lot of the local software companies. Did you know there's something like fifty companies in the area that make games for the consoles? You know Sony, Nintendo, Xbox."

"I didn't. I'm not much into games, but I know there are a lot of software geeks around here. We got the same on Jolly. *Nothing.*"

"Here's the thing, Court. Before things went south today? I had him give me a tour of his studio, and there's a fake back wall in his office."

Their food and drinks came.

"Hmmm. That is weird, but it could be a closet. A storage room."

"Why no visible door? I swear that man is hiding something. And with all that soundproofing, it could be a person. No one would hear them screaming in the room next door."

Court shoved a bite of food in his mouth and chewed it slowly.

*Was he stalling for time? Thinking about what she'd said?* She stabbed at her pile of meat for a good-sized bite then swirled it in the yogurt sauce before shoving it into her mouth.

"Not enough for a warrant. No judge is going to buy that."

"He knew all the kids. They all played guitar. They all worked for him, Court."

"Sure. *And* they *all* stayed at Harbor House and Rainbow Landing. They had a lot in common."

"He had unique access to them. One on one time without witnesses."

"I see what you're trying to do, but I don't have a problem telling you we've cleared him. He does a lot of traveling, and he was out of town during one of the murders."

"Really?" she asked. "You're sure about that?"

"He showed us train ticket stubs. We followed up on them. Both were used. He took the train down to Portland two days before the death. Then he was back in town, on the train from Portland the next day. Given the timing of the death and when the body was found, there was no way he could be in both places at once."

Karen deflated at the news. She took a break to shovel hot fragrant bits of meat into her mouth, closing her eyes as she savored their garlic yumminess. "Man, this place knows how to do it right."

"Thanks for pointing it out. I'll come back here when I can," Court said. "Sorry to bust your bubble about Jolly. Did you get any leads on Jamie?"

"I can't believe I forgot to tell you what I found out about the Parkers," Karen said.

"What'd you learn?"

There was no way she could tell Court she'd broken into Garland Parker's home. A P.I. license did not give her permission to commit crimes.

"Well, you probably know as much as I do, but I got some new snippets from his secretary. The newspapers incorrectly reported that Carmen was kicked out because he was gay. It was because…" Karen stopped, suddenly realizing she could be putting her foot into a giant sinkhole. She had no idea what Court's upbringing was like, what kind of trauma she might be ripping open.

"Karen?" Court prompted.

Karen shifted from her excited voice to a little more sympathetic one. "Garland and Morena Parker kicked Carmen out because she came out to them. She wanted to transition. And on top of that, she was a lesbian, too, and her parents lost their shit."

Court's eyes narrowed slightly, and she heard his teeth snap against each other. The angle of his jawline drew into sharp focus and then he relaxed.

"I can never get used to people throwing their kids away," he said at last, giving her no indication about his own personal experience.

"According to his secretary, Carmen's death really threw Garland over the edge. He fell apart and was taken to a mental-health facility to be put back together. When he got out, he was reformed. Still believes in God, but is doing 'loving work' now."

"Making amends."

"Yeah, I know, but the salient point is coming."

"Do tell, Miss P.I.," Court said.

She sipped at her beer. "Morena Parker. She's a piece of work."

"In what way?"

"She's bat-shit crazy, like brimstone and fire crazy. She has this gigantic wooden cross around her neck, talks about abominations. Nuts beyond nuts."

She recounted the conversation she'd had with Morena. When she was done, Court was staring at her, fork mid-bite.

"Can you repeat that last bit?"

"Which one?" Karen asked.

"The soul-cleansing bit," Court said.

She repeated it. "*Cleansing by the fires of hell will be all that is left for your immortal soul.* Weird, isn't it? Like she was cursing me or something."

"She actually said that?"

"Yep. Warning me that I was heading straight to hell. For wearing perfume? Crazy."

Court was looking through the window with a blank gaze. She could almost hear the gears whirring around inside his head.

"Court? Yoo-hoo?"

He smiled tightly and shook his head, as if to clear it. "Sorry. I'm trying to think through some things. I'm not smelling anything except garlic, by the way."

"I'm going to be smelling like garlic for days," she said, laughing.

"Did you talk to Garland Parker directly?"

"No. He was at the community meeting, though."

"Really? How'd you recognize him?"

*I saw him entering his house as I was leaving it—after I was done breaking in.*

"All those newspaper articles." She would have recognized him from that too. Maybe. Karen sat back, suddenly chilled. "Court, you're using Jamie's missing-persons case as a way to find the killer, aren't you? You think he's already been kidnapped."

Court laced his fingers together and rested his chin on them. This brought his eyes level with hers across the tiny table. "The kids who've been killed? They were missing and no one cared. Donald Marsh? He was kicked out of his home a year and a half before he died. His family never filed a report. No one ever asked about him.

"Jeremy White ran away after his father hit him with a baseball bat. He moved from shelter to shelter. His mother reported him missing after he'd been out of touch for eight weeks. She's the only other mom we know about who hired a P.I. to look for her kid. He was found a couple weeks after that."

Karen shivered. "You think the killer is keeping them prisoner for weeks, or longer?"

Court shrugged. "It's hard to know. Marshall Haller was in touch with his family a week before he died."

"In what way, in touch?"

"A text."

"So it could have been sent by the killer."

"Possibly, or he was caught shortly after sending the text, or the day he was killed." Court sat back in his seat. "We can't tell if some of the signs of starvation are from living on the street or from food being withheld from them."

He was holding something back. The quick glimpse she had gotten of the photos had shown slender bodies. None of the victims had started out fat, so they didn't have much to lose.

Court waved his hands over their plates. "Let's get out of here. I can walk you to your car, if you'd like."

"I took the bus."

Court glanced at his watch. "You want me to give you a ride home?"

"I don't need one all the way home. If you could drop me off at the bridge, that's good enough. There's a convenient stop there."

"You got it."

———

As THEY WALKED to his car, Karen filled Court in on Maria's activities over the last year since the Berkeley Drummond Incident.

"So, the career switch? Would that have happened anyway? Or do you think you'd still be a pro-dominatrix if that hadn't happened?"

"I was ready for a change. My being outed on TV like that was the final impetus I needed. It killed my business completely."

Court shook his head. "I'm so sorry that happened."

"Yeah, well. I don't get as much money being a P.I., but I'm certainly more respectable."

They reached a boring white car that, for all its attempts to blend in with things, screamed *police* even though it was unmarked and had no lights. There was something about it that made it obvious.

"I thought you didn't drive," Karen said.

"I don't own a car. This is from the motor pool."

The dashboard was modified from a standard-issue whatever model it was. Karen's general lack of enthusiasm around cars made it hard for her to care much, but the radio and computer screens were kind of cool.

"And you all worry about people texting and driving?"

"Police don't have to worry about that."

"Oooh. Isn't that special?" Karen said pulling out her best Dana Carvey Church Lady impersonation.

Court laughed. "So, so special."

Traffic had picked up on the Ave, and people spilled out the entrances of some of the clubs. Women in short skirts and teetering heels gathered in small packs. Most of the restaurants were hole-in-the-wall joints with few or no seats. Court slowed as they approached the light at 43rd. He leaned over the wheel, focusing on one of the thirty or so people crossing the street in front of them. "Motherfucker."

Court hit a whoop-whoop signal on the car and almost everyone turned to look. A short person with a hoodie took off down the street at top speed.

"Well, shit. Stay with the car. I've been looking for this guy for weeks, and he has to show up right now?" He slammed his hand against the emergency flasher and parked the car at a funky angle to the street on a yellow line. He jumped out of the car and disappeared into the crowd heading west at a run while yelling into a radio.

Court could move. And in such a delicious way, too. Karen sighed and reminded herself again of the thousand reasons dating a cop would be a bad, bad, idea.

Court had left the keys in the car, and the angle he'd parked at had the tail end sticking out into traffic. Karen couldn't slide over to the driver's seat with all the electronics in the way. She got the stinky eye from people driving by as she walked around to the driver's side and maneuvered the car into a better position. It was still in a no-parking zone, but at least it was parallel to the curb and no longer snarling traffic.

Sirens blared in the distance. After about three minutes, two cars whooped by her from different directions.

Rather than stay in the car, she leaned against the hood and waited for Court. He had disappeared down one of the side streets. This could take a while, particularly if he ended up making an arrest. It was also kind of exciting.

"Is this your car, ma'am?"

"Meter maid" did not come close to describing the parking-enforcement officer standing in front of her. The woman was at least six-foot-four and weighed over two hundred and fifty pounds. A Viking of a woman, her coppery hair was pulled back in a bun so tight it made Karen's head ache.

"Nope. I'm babysitting it for a cop friend. He's chasing down a suspect."

Brunhilda raised an eyebrow. "Credentials?"

"Don't cops get to park anywhere they need to?"

The woman shielded her eyes from the light and pressed her face close to the window. She flipped her book closed, and, looking disappointed, walked away. The last time Karen had tried talking someone out of a ticket, she'd been told she should learn to read. Was it her fault that the sign declaring that side of the street verboten was hidden behind tree branches when she parked?

The ice cream shop across the corner had a lull in business. On a warm summer evening like this, she would have expected lines around the corner. It was one of those local all-organic places that used local ingredients. Seattle could compete with Portland for hipsterdom.

Karen saw flashing lights on a corner, but didn't see Court anywhere. It wouldn't take long to grab a couple of scoops. She locked the car and pocketed the keys. The daily special featured white pepper, so she opted for the Nutella brittle and got a cup of pistachio cardamom for Court.

He was visible halfway down the block, returning to the car, when she emerged from the cool interior of the shop.

"You said you liked cardamom," she said, handing him his cup.

They leaned against his car as they ate. Karen took her first bite of the hazelnut and chocolate and closed her eyes to focus on the cool creamy richness, holding the hazelnut brittle in her mouth for a finishing crunch.

"Wow," Court said. "You really like ice cream, don't you?"

Karen licked her spoon and waggled her eyes. "So, what was the big chase about? You catch your guy?"

"It's a different case. Has to do with the thing I was working on when I got taken down in the spring."

"I read about that in the papers—Chinese mob, right?" She pointed her spoon at his face. "Sounds like you got off easy with that scar."

"Yeah." Court touched the scar and his hand dropped to over his chest. "It's not the scariest wound I got."

"Isn't the bigger threat coming from Native American gangs these days?"

"It depends on what you mean by *threat.* The Chinese

mob is old-school, very focused on bringing in meth from North Korea. Big-scale operations. The main difference from both the Hispanic and Native gangs is they don't use their kids so much to distract cops. The scary violence you hear about are gang-bangers going around creating havoc as a way to keep eyes on them instead of the bigger shit going on behind the scenes. The Chinese just skip that part and keep things better hidden."

Karen had almost zero knowledge about gangs. She'd heard things about them growing in the area, but she lived in the white-bread suburbia of Redmond. "So, did you catch the guy you ran after?"

"They're taking him in for me. I'll head there next. It's not exactly the highest priority at the moment." Court stabbed his spoon into his ice cream. "Ivy is not going to be thrilled with me interrogating him without her. I might let him stew overnight."

"I'm glad you didn't let me stew overnight," Karen said. "Is that because you believed I was innocent right away or because I'm white?"

"Really? You know SPD has a female POC chief, right?"

"She's new. There hasn't been time for the culture to shift down the ranks."

"I'm tired of defending police all the time. Believe what you want."

They ate their ice cream in silence for a while.

"Oh," Karen said, happy to find another topic. "I can't believe I forgot to tell you. I talked to a girl whose street name is Ozzie today. She sometimes works for someone she calls Mama Gong. She said that Jamie works for her too."

Court's face shifted from annoyance to interest, and the

bad moment between them disappeared. "Jamie works for Mama Gong? Any details?"

"She puts together parties. Mostly on the Eastside. Apparently they occasionally take a vanload of kids down to beach resorts on the coast in Washington and Oregon for week-long parties."

"You think Jamie could be off at a party?"

"It's happened before."

"This Ozzie girl, any chance you get her real name? Contact info?"

"No. I gave her mine. Asked her to text me if Mama Gong tries to get in touch."

"You think Mama Gong is going to admit to having Jamie at a party?"

Karen stuck her spoon in the remaining lump of ice cream. "You know, I don't know what I was thinking. Maybe there would be some nugget of information that might point us in one direction over another."

Court squeezed her elbow, his forearm pressing upward against hers. "I know you're upset, but you're working scattershot here. Since we started dinner, you've accused Jolly, the Parkers, and now Mama Gong of all being involved in Jamie's disappearance."

"They're all possible suspects. Of something. I'm not saying they're all killers, but any one of them could have something to do with his being gone."

"I agree. But you're tossing out theories without rationales. Without the supporting evidence we need. Imagining someone has a hidden room that he keeps captives in doesn't make it true."

"If you can't imagine it, how do you find it?"

"You follow evidence. Make connections. I'm not saying you aren't picking up important clues, Karen. Instead of fanning out from one starting point, you're playing hopscotch all over the playing field."

He was right. Karen's head ached from the possibilities swirling around inside. "How do you keep it all straight when you're doing an investigation?"

"You saw our boards. We make a chart. Try to figure out the next logical step after we get a piece of solid evidence."

"What about hunches? Don't you ever follow up on a hunch?"

"Sometimes. My hunches, such as they are, are usually informed by evidence."

"Okay. Fine. Maybe I'll go home and fill in my board. I have a great map. And an excellent cork board."

"How do you like being a P.I.?"

"You mean as compared to being a pro-domme? Both let me set my own hours, do things my own way. I'd never be good with a boss. I don't take directions very well."

"So I noticed," he said.

"Money's not as good. I've focused mainly on background checks and some skip traces. This last surveillance gig I did made me realize how much I hate sitting in my car." Karen shrugged. There were pros and cons to every job. "I don't get to tie people up anymore."

"Do you miss it?" Court asked.

"Tying people up? Yeah. I never was much of a sadist. I got off on the bondage part. The power… being in complete control." Karen grasped the lapel of his jacket and dropped her voice to the one she used on subs after they did something that pleased her. "I have my outlets."

Court laughed and colored at the same time, a nice pink from his neck up along his cheeks. "Once a domme, always a domme?"

It was her turn to laugh. Karen lifted her spoon to her lips, wrapping them around it as salaciously as possible. She wasn't usually one for crude gestures, but there was something refreshingly fun about teasing this man.

"Keep that up and I might have to arrest you for indecency."

"I'd be interested in seeing how you use your handcuffs, Detective. I've never been one to wear them. For you? I might make an exception."

"I get the impression you wouldn't stay in them for long."

A sticky drip of ice cream trickled down Karen's thumb. She licked the dribble off with a practiced swipe of her tongue all while maintaining eye contact with Court. "You're distracting me from my ice cream, Detective," she said in her best naughty-boy-scolding voice.

"Oh my god, you sound like you're about to pull out a paddle and spank me."

"You'd like that, wouldn't you?" It was an automatic response from her, a teasing banter that she'd done thousands of times with clients. How had they gone from talking about missing teens to this? Karen welcomed the warm glow it was giving her, even though flirting with this man could lead to absolutely no good.

Court's lips twisted and he opened and closed his mouth, biting back some response. The Amazon reappeared as if on cue and stood in front of them with her hands on her hips. "You said he was chasing down a subject when he was actually inside getting ice cream?"

Karen shrugged. "Parking around here sucks."

"Using pool cars for dates goes against regs, Detective. Can I see your ID?" She was already writing down the license plate number.

"We're leaving now." Court's cheeks turned crimson.

Karen couldn't tell if it was because of their flirtation or if it was because the meter maid had assumed they were on a date. Court was quiet, obviously over-focusing on the road as they crept along the Ave. As they neared the bridge, Karen pointed to a corner. "I can walk to the bus from there."

Instead, Court drove onto the freeway heading east toward Redmond. "I hope you're okay with me taking you all the way home."

"Don't you have a suspect you need to get to?"

"He'll keep."

## 26

---

Court parked in Karen's driveway and kept the engine running. He didn't make a move to get out of the car. It was clear that their playful little tête-à-tête was over. As she opened the car door, he placed a hand on her shoulder.

"Karen, let me do the step-by-step work we need to do to document and build a case. Okay?"

Karen put a hand on top of his and squeezed. "I'm not going to stop trying to find Jamie. I'll try not to get in your way too much."

Court sighed and shook his head. "You're playing with fire."

"No. I'm finding someone I care about."

She released his hand and jumped out of the car. She turned around at the door and watched him drive off.

Inside, all the niggly aches kicked in. Her back, her feet, her legs screamed at her for overusing them. Walking for so many hours a day was doing a number on them. She took some pain-killers and headed toward her bedroom. A long hot bath was exactly what her body needed.

Sophie's tinkling laugh drew Karen down the hall. Karen knocked on the door and opened it at the same time. Sophie was on her phone.

Karen flopped onto the bed next to Sophie. She was talking to Poe over one of those online chat programs. She couldn't see anything behind Poe other than a blank white wall.

"Hey, are you back home?" Karen asked.

Poe nodded. "Yeah. My mom is trying to be cool about things. Saying I have a girlfriend really helped."

"Anytime, my friend," Sophie said.

"Is it too much for a little show-and-tell? Having you hang out sometime will really sell it."

"You want me to come visit?"

"I'm sorry, Sophie. If you feel too much like I'm using you…"

"No. I'm teasing. Can't you take a joke?"

He blinked and smiled awkwardly. The kid was awkward and clumsy. And clueless. "Oh. Okay. Thanks. I'm so bad at all of this."

"Yeah, you suck at peopling."

"Thanks, Sophie. How are you, Mrs. H? Any news on Jamie?"

"Nope. Hey, Poe, I'm sorry I have to ask you this, but did you ever go with him to one of Mama Gong's parties?"

Poe's jaw dropped down a bit. "I know he did them. But they're not my gig."

"So you don't know anything about where they took place or how to get in touch with Mama Gong?"

Poe shook his head. "Sorry. Jamie didn't talk about that much. He knew I didn't approve."

Karen left the two to their idle chatter. Poe was filling the friend void left by Jamie's absence. Sophie being his beard was a little weird in this day and age, but Karen's heart warmed at her daughter's generosity of spirit. She could be out there dating for real, and she chose to do this instead? *Sweet, sweet girl.*

She knocked softly on the door to Robbie's room. There was no answer. He must have finally gone back to his apart-ment. It was probably a good thing. Karen's brief flirtation with Court left her wanting more, and she would have ended up using him as a stand-in for Court.

*Don't go there, he's a cop. And yet…*

Karen went to her office so that she could clear her head. Her cork board and white board reflected the scatter-shot method Court had called her on. She spent half an hour organizing all her facts, separating them from supposi-tions, before calling Maggie to talk things through.

"Girl, you seem to be covering all the bases," Maggie said after she'd told her about her day. "Except for all your questionable activities, anyway. You're getting a little reck-less and cavalier with things. Stretching the law is one thing, but you're breaking it left and right. I sure as hell hope you didn't leave any prints in Parker's house."

"No, I didn't," Karen said, somewhat annoyed at being called on things.

"Next time you do a B&E, you better wear gloves. It's better to not do any of that shit."

"Sometimes information is more important than the law."

"Court was right, you know. He gave you some excellent advice. Back up and connect the dots. Go slow and steady. Take things one step at a time so you don't get caught up in the whirlwind of possibilities."

"I know, I know. I'm going back into Seattle tomorrow. I want to talk to Parker directly."

"Are you sure you should go alone?" Maggie asked. "I could pop down and hang out with you."

"I don't want you to go to any trouble."

"It'd be fun to see you in person."

"We could do lunch after."

"Okay. I'll meet you at Cal Anderson Park around ten."

Karen spent the rest of the evening doing a dozen background checks for Bernice's clients and writing up reports on each. They were all men applying to be clients to various dommes, and it was her job to make sure none of them had prior violent histories.

*Not that past behavior was an indicator of future performance, yada yada yada.*

In her room, she found Robbie asleep in her bed. His gentle snoring was hard to miss. She sneaked across to the bathroom so she could brush her teeth. She considered sleeping on the couch, but her king-size bed provided plenty of safe space between them. As she settled into her side of the bed, he rolled over toward her, his eyes sleepy and dreamy.

"How you doing?" he asked.

"Go back to sleep."

"You sure? I can rev myself up. You smell like you need sex."

And the inevitable thing between them popped right up just as she knew it would. Maybe sex with Robbie would take Court off her mind.

## 27

KAREN BOUGHT A LATTÉ FOR MAGGIE AND WAITED FOR her at the northern edge of the sculptural fountain at Cal Anderson Park. The end of summer was near, and families were out in full force enjoying one of the few remaining Saturday mornings of freedom.

It was an easy place to meet, and close to the light rail Maggie would have taken from her home down in Tacoma.

"Ah, you didn't have to do that," Maggie said as she accepted the latté.

"What's our game plan?" Karen asked as they made their way through the park. She always felt like an Amazon when walking next to the older woman. Even in flats, Karen was a good foot taller. It was a good thing in the P.I. biz, though, as people rarely saw Maggie as a threat as she knocked on their door.

"So, you going to put on your domme mask, use a little vocal intimidation?"

"Hard to say. Everyone is different. It's better for me to

play it safe and assume he wouldn't react to a power play on my part. I'd need to get a sense of him first. He's either bi or gay, and I have a harder time figuring out how to control gay men. They aren't as susceptible to my womanly charms."

"Well then, let's go for simple honesty. Probably our best bet. We're out to do good in the world by finding our missing boy. That kind of thing."

"Sounds like a plan," Karen said.

"It would be great if we could get him ranting about his ex. Or to fess up they're in on these killings together."

"Right. Just a crazy couple in love." Karen tossed the remnants of her coffee into a trash bin as they headed out of the park.

"Wow. Nice digs," Maggie said as they approached Parker's house.

"Yeah. He paid two million for it two years ago."

"Some people."

Karen looked through the glass on the door before knocking on it. The living room was filled with teen boys in various lounging positions, each with a Bible on their laps.

"He had one of his sleepovers last night," Karen said. She knocked and stood back. "We might be able to get something good out of those kids."

Parker answered the door, his lips pressed together. "The sign says no solicitors."

Karen held up a card. "I'm a private investigator. We're trying to locate a missing youth. I'd like to ask you a few questions, if you don't mind, Mr. Parker."

Parker eyed them through narrowed lids before opening the door wide enough for them to pass.

"Mr. Parker, maybe you and I could talk in the kitchen while my associate speaks to the boys in the living room?"

His eyes slid toward the teens and he shrugged. "Yeah. Sure. Boys, answer the questions this lady asks."

Maggie waved and smiled at the boys. Parker led Karen into the kitchen. Dishes were piled in the sink and bits of food covered the immaculate granite counter top of the day before.

"So, who's the missing kid?" Parker asked. "There're so many these days."

She held up the photo of Jamie. "He goes by Strings. He's been known to hang around Harbor House and Rainbow Landing, the park. Really, the usual. What do you know about him?"

"Strings. Yeah. He's never stayed here, though. The only thing I know about him is he has no respect for authority or for God."

"So you have talked to him," Karen said.

"I've seen him play his music. I've chatted with him a couple of times, hoping to bring him into the fold. But he steadfastly refuses to allow Jesus into his heart."

Parker's tone was not accusatory so much as pained. He came across as genuinely hurt that Jamie hadn't accepted his guilt-love.

"Maybe he didn't think you were genuine. His parents kicked him out of his house for being gay based on their Christian teachings, Mr. Parker."

"My goal is to teach these boys that there are loving Christians out there. People like me who will love them without conditions and help them overcome their sinful yearnings."

"So, being open to Christianity is required to stay here overnight?"

"Not exactly. I don't bring those who are openly antagonistic to the Bible. And that Strings kid? He is extremely unwilling to engage with me on any level."

"So you do know him."

"Only by sight and reputation."

"Have you seen him at Rainbow Landing or the park the last few days?"

Parker closed his eyes for a moment before answering. "No. I haven't seen him in a couple weeks. I think he prefers Harbor House to Rainbow Landing."

"Isn't Harbor House affiliated with a church? Why don't you volunteer there instead of Rainbow Landing?"

Parker shrugged. "Rainbow Landing is specifically set up to service LGBTQ youth."

"So you have a pool of kids to help."

"It's also closer to my house."

"Why do you bring them over in a van when they could walk? It's not very far."

"I don't want them coming here on their own."

"There's nothing to stop them from doing that."

"So far, they have obeyed my rules."

"The Bible thing out front. One of your requirements?"

"I ask everyone who sleeps here to spend an hour in the morning in earnest contemplation of the Bible. They can read any section they want. I strive to bring them into the fold slowly and of their own volition."

"You're trying to convert them?"

"Absolutely. To bring them to God's path."

"And that is?"

Parker's lips twisted into a smile. "If you don't know that by your age…"

"Is it the same path Morena has chosen?"

Garland's face hardened. "Morena is haunted by our decisions as much as I am. Carmen's death tore us apart."

"Have you had any contact with her recently?"

"No." Parker sighed. "You know, she was joyous in the hospital. Carmen was all hooked up to machines. Tubes everywhere. She'd go in there, get on her knees and pray, thanking God for the trial. For the chance to bring Carmen back to his good graces."

"And you? What did you do while she was praying?" Karen asked.

Parker continued as if he hadn't heard her. "And then, as the days wore on, she got this rapturous notion. Forty days of tribulation and cleansing. She asked our pastor to re-baptize him and declare him innocent from all past sin. A re-birth. When he died, she praised God for taking him before he could continue his sinful ways."

"Sinful ways?"

"My son was an abomination, Ms. Hunter. We are taught to love the sinner, not the sin. I didn't love my son enough to save him. All I can do now is to find that pure love whenever I can." He tilted his head toward the living room. "I'm sure some of these young men will find their salvation through Jesus. I have only to present them the opportunity. You know the old saying: ask and you shall receive."

Maggie had managed to get the teens to open up to her and was chatting happily away. No surprise there. She offered all the kids high-fives as she said goodbye to them.

As they emerged into the bright summer sunshine, Karen said, "You sure know how to get people talking."

"I've been doing this a long time. Besides, you find the right subject with teens and you can't shut them up."

"Did you get anything useful from them?"

"Not much. Parker has been all hands-off with them. It's all about the Bible in the morning and love, love, love. He insists they shower and wash their clothes or replace them from his overflowing closets. He provides them dinner, usually something gourmet and different from what they get at the shelters. He makes waffles or pancakes for breakfast. Sends them off with a sack lunch."

"Wow. Like Dorothy said—Saint Garland. Are any of them really into the Bible study?"

"Only two seem genuinely interested. The rest admitted they were there for the clean sheets and three squares."

They walked over to Broadway and found a place that served an out-of-this-world Tex-Mex brunch buffet. After three rounds, Karen sat, back full of tamales and churros.

"Was visiting Parker all a waste of time?" Karen asked.

"Nope. You got a better sense of who Garland Parker is. I don't have the gaydar you do, but even I picked up on that part of him."

"None of this is helping us find Jamie."

Maggie dipped her last churro into a pot of melted chocolate. "It's information. It's like a puzzle piece out of place, and once you find the hole it fits in, it will pop into place."

"It's like I've opened one of those thousand-piece puzzles that are all shaped the same and are all one color."

"You'll figure it out." Maggie licked the sugar crystals

off her fingers before wiping them on her napkin. "Thanks for having me along, but I need to get to some of my own work."

"I've got breakfast. You go ahead and get on with your day."

Karen watched as Maggie made her way through the crowd, grateful the other woman was so willing to help her. She paid the bill and walked back through the park without any set course in mind.

She stapled a few more flyers to a few more poles as she walked and showed Jamie's picture to as many people she could. Same old story. A lot of people knew him but hadn't seen him lately. After an hour of meandering she found herself standing in front of the Seattle Police Department. It was as if she'd been drawn there like a magnet.

**28**

———————

Technically, Maria Wells was her boss. Because there was no money or contract involved, Karen didn't feel compelled to call her. She'd much rather talk to Court.

When she got off the elevator, there were dozens of people flowing out of a room at the far end of the hallway. She must have shown up as their morning briefing ended. Court and Ivy were the last two to file out.

Court hadn't appeared to notice Karen yet, so she headed to his desk and leaned against the cubicle partition between Court and Ivy's desks.

Ivy saw her first. "Hunter. What are you here for?"

"I talked to Garland Parker today. I stopped by to give you the deets and see if there's anything I can do to help."

Ivy rolled her eyes. "You're not a cop. Can't really help you there."

"I've given you good solid leads. The Parkers?"

"And you went and talked to him anyway?" Ivy asked. "That's not helping, that's interfering."

"How's she interfering now?" Court asked as he joined them.

"I spoke to Garland Parker today."

Court and Ivy exchanged a glance. Karen was either stepping on toes or bringing them new information.

"Anything pertinent?" Court asked.

"He comes across as a guy making amends. Nothing surprising. Kids love him. Or his cooking, anyway. Doesn't appear to be a perv. My gaydar is dinging fully, though. And he pretty much admitted he was gay when I mentioned it. But the kids say he's hands-off."

"Well, thanks for reporting in," Court said. "But we've got a long list of things to do today."

"I was kind of hoping you could give me something else concrete to work on. Some guidance."

"You can go home, Hunter," Ivy said, though not unkindly. "You've exhausted your resources at this point. You've talked to everyone you could talk to."

"I can't keep wandering the streets asking everyone I see if they've run into Jamie. It's not doing any good. I've posted flyers everywhere and talked to hundreds of people," Karen said. "I have to do something. Please. Anything?"

Court frowned and then sighed. "I suppose you could go through the missing-persons book again. Mark off anyone you saw yesterday or today. That would help us some. We are following all leads we can. Every possibility we chop off gets us closer to the reality."

Before Karen could answer, a frumpy older detective lumbered up to them. There was something very Columbo-like in his appearance. She expected him to pull out a half-used cigar and chomp on it. He thrust a paper at Court while bobbing his head toward Karen and Ivy, but his eyes were on Court the whole time. "Good morning, *lad-ies*." He drew the last syllable out.

Karen gave him the stink-eye. Court either didn't notice or was used to this kind of bullshit. "Thanks, Fergy," he said.

The other detective huffed a little and shuffled off. Karen peeked over Court's shoulder. It was a report from the State Patrol Crime Lab.

Court pointed to his chair. "I better keep you close this time around so you don't accidentally end up in the wrong room again. Stay there while I grab the binders from Cook."

Court disappeared down the hall as Karen dropped into his chair. Ivy leaned over the partition from her side of it. "You know, you really don't want your kid to be with this lunatic."

"The odds are one in fifteen, according to Court's song and dance routine last night. It's that whole *almost* thing that fueled my nightmares last night."

Ivy shook her head. "No, the odds are better than that. He put up fifteen *known* missing boys. There are dozens or more out there that we can't put a name or face to. People no one loves enough to report them missing."

"It's been a week. Today," Karen said. "We're running low on time."

Ivy's eyes clouded over, indicating the information flow was over. "Let's hope we find him. Soon." She disappeared as she dropped into her chair.

Court returned with the binders Karen had gone through once before. "Here you go. Make notes of people you have seen and know are safe. I know you did this the other day, but you've been out there for hours since then. I'll be working in the incident room."

Ivy popped up. "If you need anything, ask me." She looked pointedly at Court. "We don't need her going anywhere near the incident room again." Then she focused on Karen again. "Got that?"

Karen nodded. She flipped through the records Court had brought her. No matter how hard she tried, her mind kept wandering back to what might be in that room. She'd seen the most gruesome of the photos already, hadn't she? What else was in there? Police only give out so much information to the press, and they'd certainly only told part of the story yesterday. If she could only get the details they were keeping to themselves, she might be able to put the whole picture together.

Breaking into that room would be a bad idea on so many levels. She could hardly pretend it was an accident a second time. Karen forced herself to get to the task at hand and push aside the impulse to rush down the hall and thrust the door open.

As she went through the photos, Karen wrote down the last known location on a Post-it note and stuck it to the page. She considered adding street names when she knew them, but it felt like a violation to the kid. Whether they were kicked out or voluntarily left their families, their street names were their new identity. Sometimes it was all that was their own.

When she found Ozzie's report, she sucked in her breath. Her parents had reported her missing two years ago. Her report listed a monthly call from her parents to the police. Karen's heart clenched with pain for Ozzie's parents. They had been waiting two years for any word on their daughter, and there was nothing. The case notes said that the girl had never been seen.

How could that be? Ozzie's distinctive spikes were hard to miss. Maybe Ozzie had left her family with good reason. She would need to find out the backstory before blithely pointing a possible abuser straight toward their victim. She wrote that she'd seen Ozzie near Pike Place Market and an approximate time. Karen wasn't sure how much information to put on the sticky. Eventually, she added *has connections to Mama Gong*. That was just too important to leave out.

By the time she finished with the first binder, she'd used up what was left of her Post-it pad. With each kid she recognized, she felt a little lighter. At least their parents would learn they'd been seen alive recently. The ones that reported their kids missing deserved to know that much at least.

She needed more sticky notes. Karen stood and stretched. She had somehow managed to block out everything around her for the last hour and a half. Court and Ivy had disappeared, and the squad room had gone quiet.

At least the lights were still on.

After a fruitless search for a supply closet, she paused at the incident room and put her ear to the door. Who was she kidding? She'd been drawn to that room like a magnet pointing to the North Pole. She needed to know what else was inside. Karen was certain that if she could learn everything they knew, all those puzzle pieces would fit together.

She turned the door handle slowly and prayed that the door hinges wouldn't squeak.

COURT AND IVY stood in front of a large smart board, their backs to the door which they hadn't, by some miracle, heard open. Karen closed it and leaned against it, her heart racing while she pretended to be invisible.

"Let's flip through them again," Ivy said.

Court tapped the computer in front of him. The image was outlined in red and had photos of VICTIM 1, Donald Marsh, living, then dead. There were smaller blocks with text in them Karen couldn't read. There was a timeline under the photos, a map showing the location of his body, and a list of items he was known to be carrying when he disappeared.

The next screen was outlined in orange. At first, Karen assumed it was some sort of coding. The image of VICTIM 2, Jeremy White, showed that he wore an orange collar around his neck and nothing else. His body had been placed face down—the way she'd seen priests lying prostrate.

The photos Karen had seen the other day showed the bodies bound in ropes, indelicately tied, as if the killer were trying to make them into a wrapped package. Something easy to move.

"Go back and forth between red and orange," Ivy said.

Both of their backs were covered in thick red welts in the shape of a cross. Multiple marks along their buttocks and legs showed signs of heavy beating. They conveyed a raw brutality, and yet, in the closest photo, she could tell that some of the marks were on top of older, healed-over scars.

Karen didn't move from her spot, mesmerized by the brutal rawness of the slides. Red, orange, yellow, green, blue, indigo… The slides were color-coded, and dependent upon the collar found on each victim.

"This time, I want to concentrate on the foreheads," Ivy said.

Court tapped into the slide show and up came close-ups. The number 31:23 was written on their foreheads, each the same color as the collars around their necks. The numbers flashed by in rainbow order. "It's the same handwriting on all of them. Colors to match the collars."

Karen must have made a noise, because the next thing she knew, Court was at her side. "What the fuck?" He grabbed her gently, but firmly, by the upper arms and ejected her from the room, shutting the door behind them. "I made it clear this room was off limits the last time you were in here."

"I needed more stickies," she said, holding up the empty pad as evidence. The flimsy excuse wasn't going to fly, especially when Karen didn't believe it herself.

"How long were you watching?" Court was looking at her with a hardness she'd never seen in him before. His jaw clenched and tightened.

"Not long. Too long. I don't know."

"I gave you a lot of latitude. Information. And you repay me by doing exactly what I asked you not to do?"

*It was so easy to open that door.*

"I know. I'm sorry. It was too tempting. Knowing you were in here… I want to help."

Court rubbed at his temples and shook his head. "I understand your motivation, Karen, I do. But you can't magically absorb all the facts and have it mesh in your head."

"Why not?"

Court crossed his arms. "I'm going to say this once, and I want you to listen. You are not to tell anyone. *Not anyone*, what you saw in there. Do you understand? We keep certain details from the public for a reason."

She pushed a finger against his chest. "You knew that this psycho is torturing these kids. The marks on the bodies? Some of them are healed up. You knew they're being held longer than a few days."

Court shut his eyes and breathed deeply. "Yeah. Very likely there is some poor kid who is being starved, beaten, raped, and god knows what else, right at this very moment. We're doing our best to find them. And, there's still some chance that the killer doesn't have *anyone* right now."

"Why? Because he's not 'due' for another kill anytime soon? Did you see those marks? Even if he's not killing someone, he's hurting them." She put a hand to her mouth.

"Karen, we are doing everything possible to find this guy. Okay?"

"What makes you so sure it's a guy? What about Mama Gong? Or Morena Parker?"

"Mama Gong is clearly doing illegal shit, and we've got other people working to shut her down. Besides, she doesn't fit the killer profile. And Morena Parker is on our list. *Our* list, Karen."

"Okay, fine. What about the guy who runs Rainbow House? There are rainbows everywhere, Court. Red, orange, yellow, green and blue… There's a nice twist to things, isn't it? He breaks the rules, let's local people take teens home with him."

Court shook his head. "We haven't been able to

clear *every* volunteer at *every* shelter, but they do run their own independent background checks. Besides, we know we're looking for a man, so we're focusing on them."

"How can you be certain? There are creepy women out there."

He leaned in close. "We're certain it's a man. We have proof."

"What kind of proof?"

"I can't tell you that."

There could only be one way for them to know there was a man involved. "You found DNA. Semen?"

Court's lips twitched in a tell that made her pretty sure she'd hit the mark. "Karen, it's time for you to go."

"Not until you tell me."

Court wrapped an arm over her shoulders her to guide her away from the room. "You broke my trust by coming in here, and now you need to leave."

They passed his desk. She pointed at it a little frantically. "I didn't finish the missing-persons binders."

"You're done, Karen." He didn't let go of her until they were at the elevator and he had pushed the down button. "Hit the streets. Keep showing Jamie's picture around. Keep praying, or meditating, or whatever it is you do, that he's not with our killer."

Karen stepped inside. "Court? Even if it's not Jamie, he probably has someone else, doesn't he?"

Court slipped his hands into his pockets. He didn't answer as the doors slid closed between them.

## 29

Karen spent the rest of the day posting the rest of the flyers and flashing Jamie's picture everywhere. By the time she got home, her feet were burning from all the walking.

Robbie had left a note saying he was taking Sophie school-shopping. Karen had been meaning to get all of that done, and it was such a relief that Robbie had taken the initiative. He must have been coming out of whatever slump he had been in recently.

Karen flipped open her GPS app and saw they were at Redmond Town Center. Their blue dots were right on top of each other at one of her favorite restaurants. She texted them both asking if she could pop over and join them if it wasn't too late. They told her they hadn't even ordered yet, so she told them what she wanted and jumped into the car.

She found Robbie and Sophie in the back end of the restaurant. Robbie half stood when she arrived, and she kissed him on the cheek.

"How's it going, Mom?" Sophie asked.

"Meh," she said. "Nothing new. And I got in trouble for snooping around the police station."

"What do you mean by snooping?" Robbie asked.

"I… snuck into the evidence room."

"Mom! You are so badass."

Robbie was less impressed. "Burning bridges?"

"I hope not."

Robbie switched the subject to school prep and plans for Brian's return as their meals were served.

"I haven't really missed him," Sophie said.

"Yeah, right. You know that's not true," Karen said. "His plane comes in pretty late Monday. I want to go to the Seattle City Council meeting and it's late in the day. I'm not sure I'll be out in time to get down to Sea-Tac."

"I'll pick him up. But his plane is *next* Monday, not this one. He has another week away."

"I'm losing track of the days," Karen said. "I guess I'm really caught up with finding Jamie."

"What's the council meeting about?" Sophie asked.

"There's this program to get rid of homeless people in Seattle. It's supposed to be about getting rid of the trash they bring in. The problem is that they also throw away belongings along with the trash. Minors who get caught up in it get taken to juvie. Older young adults get taken to a bus station and told to go home. They lose everything."

"Oh, yeah. Poe was telling me about that. He's totally pissed. Apparently, they took his tent and sleeping bag, even though he left a sign on it saying it wasn't garbage."

"I don't think a sign would sway this crew."

"What good will a meeting do?" Robbie asked.

"Not sure," Karen said. "I'm thinking there might be people there I haven't talked to."

"How does this have anything to do with Jamie, Mom?"

"I'm not sure it does, but there are some kids I've spoken to that think there's a more nefarious thing going on with these cleaners than is obvious."

"I doubt it," Robbie said. "It would be too easy to document and prove. I'm guessing the kids are upset about losing all their possessions and paranoid about people going missing."

Karen was suddenly weary of all the details this case was throwing at her. "Hey, why don't you tell me about your shopping adventures."

They spent the rest of the dinner on lighter topics. As they finished up, they went to the parking lot where Robbie brought all of their purchases over to Karen's car.

"You going to your apartment?" she asked as she slammed the trunk.

"Yeah. No. Sort of. I have a date."

"Oh. Okay."

"We need to cool it for a while," Robbie said.

"After last night?" she asked, after making sure Sophie was in the car and out of earshot.

"*Because* of last night."

"I don't get it. You complain because we don't get it on for two weeks, then when we do, you're ready to move on?"

"You were using me like a sex toy. Your head was with someone else."

"And yours wasn't?" It wasn't all one-sided usage. Robbie was getting as much pleasure out of their benefits package as she was.

"Honey, we know each other super well. Better than most people who are still married. Last night was perfunctory. A simple fuck with no emotion attached to it. You might as well have been using your Hitachi Magic Wand. I deserve more than that."

"And you found someone to go out on a date with in the last fifteen hours?"

"Sajeeda and I work together. She's been after me for months. I finally said yes to a drink. Karen," he said, sweeping up her hands, "I'm needing more than you can give me right now. Or ever. I don't think I'll ever not love you, but we both know it won't work long-term for us. We can move in and out of whatever this is, but I'd like something steady. *Someone* steady."

It was the same old song and dance. When they were both uninterested in anyone else, they never had these kinds of conversations.

"I thought you didn't want another emotional attachment," she said. And yet, why did she care? Was she so selfish she wanted Robbie to wait around for her, to be available whenever she needed?

He kissed the palms of her hands. "Nothing's really changed, Karen. I love you. Always will. You're falling for that cop, and I'm not going to be caught in the middle of that shit."

"I'm not—"

"Stop. I'm going now." He kissed her on the cheek.

As Karen strapped in her seatbelt, Sophie asked, "What's up with Dad?"

"He's going out on a date." *And he accused me of falling for a cop. Really? That was never gonna happen.*

"Oh. I was hoping you guys were maybe trying to get back together again."

"What makes you say that?"

"He spent the night in your room last night. The walls in the house are thin."

"That happens a lot. Honey, you need to know that we're not getting back together in any long term sense." Karen tossed Sophie an apologetic smile. Robbie was right. He did deserve more than what Karen could offer him, more than she had ever been able to offer him. "Sorry. Didn't mean to snap at you like that. Or to be too noisy last night."

"You guys are so weird. None of my friends have to deal with this."

---

"So what do you think?" Sophie asked, spinning around like a model on the runway.

"It's very retro," Karen said. "Did you go shopping or find some of my old clothes in the basement?"

"Mom, are you kidding?"

"Nope. I had those exact pants back in the day. Okay," Karen said, "maybe not in camo, but definitely in white."

"Eew. White pants?"

"It was the eighties. The shirt is fresh. Will school be okay with your midriff showing?" Karen needed to review the latest school emails and updated dress codes. Showing belly buttons had to be pushing the limits even in Redmond.

"They better be," Sophie said. She twisted her finger

around her belly button. "This would be way cuter with a ring in it…"

"Not until you are eighteen. Then you can get all the body piercings and tattoos your heart desires."

Sophie stomped her foot halfheartedly. "Spoilsport."

"You and your dad did a good job."

"He sat in a corner while I shopped," Sophie said. "Next time, I'd rather go with you."

Karen opened her arms to Sophie. For once, the girl didn't hesitate.

"Mom, are you going to find him?"

Karen had spent most of her parenting years following the maxim that children needed reassurance. Now, however, Sophie was at an age where such false reassurances would do more harm than good.

"I hope so, baby," Karen said. "I'm doing my best."

Sophie leaned back, forcing eye contact. "I need you tell me everything's going to be okay. Not the truth. That's too scary right now."

"Oh. Okay," Karen said, her heart shattering yet again. "I'm going to find Jamie. Everything will be fine."

Sophie melted into her for a moment. "Thank you."

Karen held Sophie in her arms, relishing the contact for as long as it lasted.

Sophie pulled herself away. "I'm going to my room. Talk to some friends. You know."

"I know. I'm going to my office to do some more work."

Karen poured herself a glass of wine before going down to her office. The mixtape from her sister sat on her desk, reminding Karen she needed to order a new player. A quick search on Amazon turned up a cassette-to-MP3 converter that was only fifty bucks. She hit 1-Click and ignored all the lovely suggestions that popped up about what she could buy next.

Karen flipped through her notes on Jamie. She needed to cast her net further if she was going to find him. First, she texted Court. *Sorry about being snoopy today. I still think there's something whacked about Jolly.*

He responded right away. *Yeah. But he's not our killer. 99% sure on that.*

Karen didn't like being patronized. *I'm sitting outside Jolly's house watching him.*

A couple minutes went by before Court responded. *No, you're not.*

Court must have checked in with a surveillance team tasked with watching Jolly. *At least you've got eyes on him.*

Court texted back right away. *Smartass. Go to sleep. It's getting late. He's not our guy.*

Karen laughed. *His DNA didn't match?*

Court sent a GIF of giant eyes rolling around.

The numbers on the foreheads were obviously some message from the killer. The Sharpie colors matched the collars, and the deaths were in the order of the rainbow.

Karen Googled "31:23." A bunch of repair how-to's for a video recorder popped up. Partway down the page, a quote from Psalms showed up. *Of course.* She searched "bible 31:23." The first quote that came up was from Psalms— something about pride. The second was one from Deuteronomy, about being faithful. The third made her blood run cold.

It was from Numbers. She read it out loud twice, not quite believing it.

> *Anything else that can withstand fire must be*
> *put through the fire, and then it will be*
> *clean.*

Morena Parker had used similar words. It couldn't be a coincidence that the bodies were turning up with a number written on their forehead for a Bible verse with the exact same concept. No wonder Court had asked her to repeat what she'd said. He'd already seen the Bible quote.

The police were sure the killer was a man. Could Morena and Garland Parker be working on this together?

Maybe Court was sure it wasn't Jolly because of some DNA evidence. If it was Garland Parker, Karen had put Court onto him a couple of days ago. No way they could have a DNA test done by now.

Garland Parker held such obvious antipathy toward his ex, how could they be working together? Or had it all been an act? Garland Parker hadn't struck Karen as particularly capable of such nuances. Morena hadn't quoted this verse directly. She'd said "cleansed by fire." Was that a common Bible-thumper concept?

The other images she'd seen, the ones showing the branding and welts of burning, suddenly made sense. The killer must be torturing the boys with hot metal to fulfill his stated mission of cleansing them. Was it a sick sort of ritual cleansing? Karen shuddered. Was Jamie going through some bizarre torture while she sat in the comfort of her office sipping wine?

She almost texted Court again, but stopped herself short. Morena Parker was a small woman. There was no possible way she could get the victims from wherever she was torturing them to the dog parks without help. And it was unlikely Garland would be helping her, given his homosexuality. Morena's use of the words "cleansed by fire" had to be a coincidence.

Karen fell back, deflated. Jolly remained the best suspect. He was a male. He had multiple contacts with each of the victims. Court almost admitted they had eyes on Jolly earlier. Maybe the train alibi hadn't completely convinced Court either, and he'd lied to Karen to get her to back off. That, and Jolly had a creepster vibe about him. He was a big man and could easily carry around the younger, smaller victims.

Karen headed up to bed. She tossed and turned for a while, thinking about Jolly's train alibi. Was his being in Portland for one of the killings his only alibi? So what about the other five?

Karen sat upright as it came to her. There was at least one way for Jolly to have fooled the system. If he boarded the train at King Street Station, he could have gotten off down in Tacoma. All he'd have to do is walk to the light rail and use cash to buy a light-rail pass to get back to Seattle.

He could have done his killing and gotten back down to Portland to catch his return train. He would need to have gotten to Portland some way other than by train. He could've rented a car, caught a lift with a friend, stolen a car, taken an Uber. It was definitely possible.

But why? Why on earth would Jolly want to kill these boys, especially Jamie? Jamie could be Jolly's ticket out of mediocrity and video-game mixing. Maybe all those rumors about money for sexual favors were true. The victims could be the ones that balked and said they would report him, so he overcame them and killed them.

That wouldn't explain the torture and abuse, unless Jolly was a sadistic, twisted, sociopathic psycho killer. In that case, Karen needed to find out what dirty secret Jolly kept in that hidden room.

30

Karen woke up determined to find out what Jolly was hiding. Sophie was already up and cooking them breakfast.

"Do you mind if I go to Poe's today? His mom has suggested we all go to church together."

Karen almost dropped her coffee. "Church? You want to go to church?"

"Yes. Church. It's for Poe. You know, to show her he's playing along with her rules."

"Which one?"

"Which rules?"

"No. Which church?" Karen said, tossing a napkin at Sophie.

Sophie laughed and rolled a barely cooked omelet onto a plate. "Not sure. Somewhere over in Seattle." Sophie scattered the eggs with chopped chives and stood back to admire her creation. She snapped a picture before cutting it into two pieces and giving Karen half.

"Well, I suppose there are much scarier places for you to

be than at a friend's church on a Sunday morning," Karen said. "I was planning on doing yard work today. Can I drop you at the park-and-ride?"

It would make it easier for Karen to pretend she was home rather than doing something illegal, and Sophie's being gone would make it easier for her to slip into Seattle.

After dropping Sophie off, Karen doubled back to the house and switched cars. She put her phone on the kitchen counter so her GPS would show her at home the entire time she was gone. As she drove across the bridge, her fingers aching from her tight grip on the wheel. She rehearsed her plan, such as it was, as she drove. There were a few details she didn't know the answer to, and prayed she would be lucky.

That what she was about to do was breaking the law weighed heavily on her. Breaking into Garland Parker's house had been impulsive, and the stakes were much lower. Getting caught had barely crossed her mind and she hadn't really believed Parker was holding Jamie in his basement.

Breaking into Jolly's studio required planning and fore-thought. A B&E charge would get her license revoked. If Jamie were inside, she'd get away with it by claiming exigent circumstances, much like saving Bernice's children from the fire. If she were wrong, and there was nothing but piles of paper or CDs in the hidden room behind Jolly's office, and she were caught, she'd not just lose her license. She might go to jail.

What if Jolly captured the boys while they were at the studio, held them there until he could transfer them out? Where to? The bad access and lack of privacy made his condo an unlikely place for him to take them. And, he didn't have any other property. Not in his name, anyway. Maybe he kept them hidden in a sound-proofed space while doing business as usual in the rest of the studio. There might be drugs or handcuffs or rope or whatever to keep them captive and quiet. Any evidence she exposed during her B&E would be "poisoned fruit of the vine" and not admissible in court.

If she could take photos of the evidence and get out before the police were there, she could tell Court what she saw without telling him how she saw it. Then, she remembered she had left her phone at home. The next best thing would be to tell Court about whatever she found and say a scared teen told her about it. She'd have to lie to him about all this anyway so he wouldn't be put in a compromising position.

If Jamie was not there, she'd take a minute to assuage her curiosity before hightailing it out of there. If her gut was wrong and she found nothing of interest inside, there was no way she'd lose her license over it.

Karen drove up the east side of Green Lake. Already, hundreds of people walked and jogged along the path around the lake. She found a parking space a block away from Jolly's building. She remained in her car for a few minutes, going over every step of the operation. It was possible the door to the street was locked. She would have to play that part by ear. Picking the lock on that door, right on the street, would be pretty brazen. When she'd taken the tour the other day, she didn't notice any cameras inside the studio or on the street.

Karen slipped her car key into the zippered lining of her sports top. Over this, she threw on her sweatshirt and pulled the hoodie over her head, tucking her ponytail inside. She tossed her backpack with her electric drill, awl, and picks over her back and jogged away from the car.

First, she jogged casually past the building, trying to find street cameras. She didn't see any pointing at the front door of the building. Good enough. She circled back around and tried the door.

It was unlocked. *So much for building security*. The street was empty. So far so good. She left the door unlocked behind her as she slipped inside.

She listened for movement from within when she reached the top of the stairs. It was possible someone was inside.

A light shone in the psychotherapist's office. She tiptoed to the door and placed her ear against it. She heard no voices from within, but that didn't mean it was empty. The door was locked. Even though the other offices were dark, she stopped at each and put her ear against the door listening for signs of life within. Everything was quiet and dark except for that one office. She crept past it, hoping they'd left the light on by mistake. There were no obvious cameras in the hallway.

She stood in front of Jolly's studio door and breathed deeply, preparing herself for the next seven minutes. That was Seattle Police's average response time. On a Sunday morning, Karen hoped for low staffing and slow police. She'd give herself seven minutes to get in and get out in case she was wrong about her hunch and all Jolly was keeping in the back room was boxes of blank CDs or old tax returns. The place was sure to be alarmed and would alert the police the moment the front door was opened. If that was true, would he keep someone captive in a storage room knowing the police would be there? Or maybe he was one cocky asshole who would flaunt something like that. A psycho who got off on the police not noticing the walled-off space.

Karen dropped to her knees, put on a pair of tight-fitting latex gloves, and drilled a hole in the bottom of the lock. She replaced the drill with her awl. Slipping the thin point inside the hole she'd made, she circled it around until she found the release spring, pushed up, and twisted the little knob on the outside. The door swung open. She tapped her watch on for a seven-minute countdown.

She sprinted down the hall to Jolly's office while switching the awl out for her picks. She dropped her back-pack by the door, and started on the lock. Her hands, sweating inside the gloves, shook as she picked it. The working pick caught on something and it flew out of her hand to the floor behind her.

*Damn.*

She picked it up and started over. By the time she got the door open, she had only five minutes left. The bookshelf serving as a door to the hidden room was pressed up against the left and back walls. The only way it could possibly move was to the right—either on a hinge or on a slider.

She pulled toward her. It didn't budge. Not a hinge, then. She tried again as if it were a slider, and this time she was right.

Jolly was a fairly big guy. Moving a shelf laden with hundreds of books wouldn't be as easy for Karen. The slider that the shelf was attached to was disguised as track lighting in the ceiling. She braced her back and tugged hard. The shelf slid toward her with a lumbering slowness.

She really should be going to the gym more or get back

into karate. She and Sophie had spent five years at a local dojo until Sophie switched to dance. Karen had never been more fit than when she'd been working out and fighting three times a week, but going to the classes without Sophie never appealed to her. Karen lowered herself into a firm stance and pushed the door nearly open with a centered kiai. *Almost like riding a bicycle.*

"Jamie?"

The room stank of latent sweat and sex. There was only darkness and dead silence ahead. She felt around for a light switch and found a panel of them. She flicked on the one closest to her and a torchiere in the opposite corner lit up, casting a low yellow glow across the room.

Her watch beeped another minute gone past.

Directly across from the opening was a bed with only a stained fitted sheet on top. No pillow, no covers. A professional camera set-up faced the bed. Against the wall near the entryway, a computer with multiple monitors and editing equipment crowded together on a desk.

*Shit. No Jamie, but shit. Shit shit.*

Karen turned on the other switches and professional stage lighting lit up the bed. On the wall next to the door, and out of view of the camera, was a shelf with dozens of binders on it—each labeled with names, dates, and ages. She picked one at random—Georgie/May 2018/14— and opened it. Clipped to the top of the binder was a small thumb drive. The outside of the drive was labeled with the same name as on the binder.

The first page was an index. At the top was the name followed by a paragraph description. *Georgio Smirnov. This hot teen twink will blow your mind and your wad…* Karen skipped the rest.

Under that, the header row at the top labeled each column—date, scenario, distribution, and notes. Under the scenario column were various sexual acts. She cautiously turned the page, knowing what she was going to find and unable to stop herself. She needed proof before accusing Jolly of such a heinous crime—one almost as bad as the murders she'd been so certain of barely ten minutes prior.

The first image was of an innocent headshot done for professional modeling. Smiling, eyes bright and grinning, the boy was the perfect model for wholesome America. Georgie's blue eyes twinkled and his blond hair was gelled into thin spikes across his head. He held his chin in his hand like a grinning little cherub. Georgie reminded her of Brian.

The next few pages were a series of the same boy naked, on the bed behind her. Most of the photos showed him alone and masturbating. Several showed him with another boy his own age involved in sexual acts. A couple were with the boy and a much older man in a different setting outside. Some of the photos were taken on site, others elsewhere.

Karen's stomach lurched and twisted. She lunged for the trash bin next to the bed. Inside were several used condoms. *No.* She couldn't ruin evidence by puking all over it. She dropped to her knees and breathed in great gulps of air, gaining control, swallowing the bile, and forcing herself to get a grip. Then it hit her like a slap in the face.

*Sophie. Sophie had been here more than once. Was there any possible way…?*

"No… no… nonononono…" Karen swung back around to the bookshelf and scanned the binders, searching for her daughter's name. Did she have a street name? *Crap.* She opened half a dozen binders at random, going straight to the head shots, dropping them on the floor as she went, not caring about the mess she was making.

Her watch buzzed another warning against her wrist. She was running out of time. She counted the binders. There were thirty-four of them including the ten already open. She went through four more and let them drop to the floor. More boys. None of the names sounded the least bit feminine. None said Jamie or Strings. No Sophie. No girls as far as she could tell.

*Fuck. Fuck. Fuck. Fuck.*

Karen did a quick search of the rest of the room. The cameras and computer set-up were sophisticated. She bet there was a separate router to the computer and specialized hardware for distribution without a trace.

Everything in here pointed to a large-scale porn ring. It was possible the alarm she'd undoubtedly triggered when she broke in was all it would take to get Jolly to run, and that he was packing his bags already.

*Shit. What had she done?*

She wanted Jolly to go down for this without getting herself in trouble. If the police responded to a burglary, and found this—if it happened to be exposed through the burglary, she was pretty sure it could be used as evidence. The door wouldn't close without pushing. All she needed to do was ensure the cops responding to the alarm found the room full of porn.

Her watch buzzed her into action. There was one minute left to lay it all out and get out of there. If she was lucky.

Karen grabbed one of the binders and opened it. Moving backward toward the front door of the office, she left a trail of naked-boy photos—bread crumbs straight from the witch's oven to the front door. She pushed a chair from the reception room to hold it open and dumped the last of the photos on the floor near the front door.

There was no way even the stupidest cop wouldn't figure this out. Her watch alarm went off, signaling her time was up.

Karen raced back to Jolly's office to grab her backpack as the sound of voices coming from the stairwell reached her. She'd been in a soundproof room and hadn't heard the sirens.

---

THE ONLY POSSIBLE hiding place was the reception area. Karen slipped around the desk, pulled the stool out, and scooted underneath. The desk only went partway to the ground. Karen spread her legs to the side walls of the desk and dug the sides of her feet into two narrow support beams, holding her body off the ground in an extreme plank. If she was lucky, the police would see the photos and be distracted before they could find her.

She slowed her breathing. Each inhale and exhale sounded like a crashing wave in her head. Every muscle burned with her effort to hold herself above the gap.

It was only a couple seconds before the police were at the open door. Karen sucked in a big breath of air and went still as a statue.

"This is the place," a woman's voice said, her voice right over Karen's head.

The second cop said. "Left it wide open. Let's clear it."

"Police! If you are inside, drop to your knees with your hands on your head," the woman yelled.

"I don't think anyone is here," the man said after a few seconds.

"We better clear it anyway. Reception's clear." The woman's footsteps came closer, and Karen could see her shadow across the floor as she approached the desk.

Karen's heart rate went wicked crazy. It was as if she were running a marathon even though she wasn't moving. It took all of Karen's remaining strength to hold her in position.

"Whoa. Holy Jesus fuck! Hippolito, you gotta see this shit."

He must have found the photos. The shadow disappeared as the woman, Hippolito, retreated to join the man.

"What the actual fuck? I think I'm gonna be sick," she said.

Karen waited until their voices disappeared, hoping they were deep within Jolly's office, before lowering herself to the floor. She cautiously climbed out from under the reception desk and poked her head around the corner. The hallway toward Jolly's office was clear. She took a deep breath and ran to the window, praying it would open.

The window didn't want to move. She dropped her backpack on the floor and shoved with both hands. It was slow going, as if the window hadn't been opened in a long time. It went up an inch with each tug.

As soon as it was barely wide enough for her to get

through, Karen shimmied through and onto the fire escape. She shut the window, willing it to stay silent, and crawled over to the ladder, swung her legs over, and caught her feet on the rung. She took a deep breath and let her weight fully onto the ladder as it slid downward. A piercing metallic shriek accompanied her achingly slow ride down and sent her running at top speed.

She slowed down as she rounded the corner toward the front of the building. There were only two police cars, parked askew in front of the building, but no police were visible. She pulled her hoodie down tight over her face and casually walked away from the building, pulling off the latex gloves and dropping them in a trash bin.

Her heart pounded heavily, and her hands shook from the adrenaline rush. It was difficult to not cast furtive glances to see if she was being followed, but that would only cause suspicion. As she rounded the corner onto Green Lake, she heard more sirens. She melded into the crowd of joggers and walkers ringing the lake and picked up a steady run. It would take her fifteen minutes or so to make the loop and get back to her car.

Karen drove away without trolling past the studio, even though she wanted to see what was happening.

She was halfway across the bridge when she realized she'd left her backpack on the floor by the window at Jolly's studio.

**31**

———————

ONCE BACK HOME, KAREN CHANGED INTO WORK CLOTHES, and spent a couple hours outside catching up on yard work and pretending she'd been home the entire day. Aspen followed her around, happy to have her close by. The dog was getting old.

Sophie got home from her church date with Poe and suggested they go to a movie. Mom-daughter outings were few and far between the last couple years, and soon Sophie would be gone to college. Karen jumped at the chance to do something with her that was not related to Jamie or this Jolly business. Besides, losing herself in buttery popcorn and hot superheroes sounded like a good way to take her mind off everything.

As they settled into their seats, Karen asked Sophie about her day with Poe.

"It was okay."

Karen waited for Sophie to elaborate, but it took her a couple handfuls of popcorn to get around to it.

"Poe's mom is like Mrs. Wells on steroids."

"In what way?"

"Super helicopter-y. She kept watching us. Poe held my hand for a while, and it felt more like he was hanging onto me as much as he was trying to convince her we were a couple."

"Did she buy it?"

"I don't know how *anyone* could really buy us as a couple," Sophie said, laughing. "I tried, Mom, but I got this strange feeling his mom was trying to trip us up. I dunno. Poor Poe. She made us a nice lunch. They have a nice house. It was okay that way. But … I really don't like her. There's something about her that makes me twitchy."

"Your instincts are telling you something, then."

"What? Am I overreacting to her super-conservative dress and the cross around her neck?"

The huge wooden cross around Morena Parker's neck came to mind. Compared to the little one around Donna Richards' neck, it was a little freaky. "Unless she's trying to stab you with it, you're probably safe," Karen said.

"I guess I'm not used to it. Poe's room is empty, too. Like, nothing on the walls. No posters, I mean *nothing*. The desk was empty. The only book in the room was a Bible next to the bed. It's like she erased him when she kicked him out."

"You were in his room?"

"For like, ten seconds. He was giving me a tour of the house. I swear, his room was like a hotel room. His mom's room was a whole other thing. It was like a little girl's paradise. All flowers and flounce. Princess-y. Maybe that's what creeped me out."

Karen's own personal style verged on minimalist. Her bedroom was simple without any ruffles. "What about church? How was that?"

"Oh, sooooo not my thing. The sermon was all fire and brimstone without any of the love. I told Poe I wasn't going with him again. Hanging at his house? That'll be okay. The church? Nope."

"It's up to you, sweetie," Karen said. "What you're doing for him is nice, but I doubt it will work long-term."

"It only has to work long enough for Poe to get stable. He has a part-time job, but it's hard to live on the street and have a full-time job. His plan is to get a place of his own as soon as possible."

The movie interrupted their discussion. They followed up the movie with dinner at the Pho place next door. As they got back home, Court texted Karen, asking her to call him.

"Oooh… Mom's in trouble now," Sophie said. "People never want to talk unless it's serious, you know that, right?"

The possibilities rushed through Karen. Could they have found Jamie? Was he dead? Did Court find out about the break-in at Jolly's studio and figure out she was behind it? She'd worn gloves. Left no proof she was aware of. Except for the backpack.

"I hope it's not bad news," Karen said. She asked him to give her five minutes; she needed to hide herself safely behind her closed door and far from Sophie. After a couple minutes in a good yoga pose, she called him.

"What've you been up to today?" he asked.

His voice *sounded* casual. Did he suspect her? Or was he calling because they clicked the other night while eating shwarma and ice cream? "Yard work. Movie with Sophie. What about you?"

"Working."

"Do you ever get any time off?" she asked. It was a Sunday evening.

"Of course we do," Court said. "Long hours are part of the job when a case is hot."

"Is this call work or social?"

"Both."

Karen sat back in her chair, the tension easing a little out of her shoulders. If he were ready to lambast her, he wouldn't have admitted to the social part of the call. "What will your work friends say about you hanging with me?"

Court laughed. "Cops love gossip more than anything. I'm constant fodder for them."

"I bet," Karen said. "You've been in the news a lot lately."

"I ignore most of it."

"At least it's mostly positive."

Court laughed. "Well, there is that. Hey, you know how you were really sure about Jolly being the killer?"

*Here it is.* The sudden switch of topics and tone in his voice told her he was about to get down to business.

"Yeah?" she asked, adding in quickly, hoping to turn the conversation, "Did you catch him? Wait, was Jamie with him? Is Jamie okay?"

She had spoken too quickly. And with too much fake excitement.

Court was silent for a long moment. "Uhm. No. Jamie wasn't with Jolly, but you were right about him having something to hide."

"Oh? Really?" She tried to sound interested and yet casual. "Like what?"

"Where were you this morning? Around ten thirty?"

Karen had left her phone at home, hoping the GPS on it would back her up if it ever came to that. "At home. Why?"

"At home? You've been there all day?" The skepticism in his voice was unmistakable. "You with anyone who could verify that?"

"What's going on? Sophie was gone from around eight thirty until one or so. So no. I was home. Alone. Why?"

"Someone broke into Jolly's studio. You know that hidden room you were talking about?"

Karen sucked in her breath. "Yeah? What was in there?"

"Whoever broke in left a trail of pedo-porn from the front door all the way back to his office."

"Pedo-porn? Is that what he was doing? I knew he was a creeper. I told you there was something off about that guy," Karen said, hoping she sounded surprised enough. "Wow. That's kind of convenient, isn't it? I mean, for someone to break into his office right now and reveal all that?"

"It is. *Very* convenient."

Karen sucked in some air. "I knew there was something freaky about Jolly. I knew it. I told you, didn't I?"

"You did."

"You think the burglar was so disgusted by what they found they ended up leaving it so that there was no way the police could miss it?" she asked, hoping she wasn't tipping her hand.

"Anything is possible. Is that what you would have done?"

*He must know. Crap.* How could he have linked her to the backpack? She couldn't admit that she'd broken in.

"I don't know whether or not to be relieved, Court. I mean, you found something horrible, but nothing to help find Jamie?"

"No. All we found was porn—massive quantities of kid porn—the routers to link him to a massive online ring, and a bunch of helpful data to arrest a lot of people." Court paused. "The good news is, we had eyes on Jolly anyway. About ten minutes after the alarm went off, he was in his car heading out of town. He was being tailed when the word about the porn came through, so it was easy to arrest him. Got him at a rest stop heading toward Idaho."

"I'm glad you were able to get him," Karen said. She couldn't even begin to emphasize how lucky she felt about that. If she'd triggered the alarm and Jolly's escape, she would have felt guilty about him getting away.

"We did a thorough search of his home. Nothing there. No links to the porn or the murders."

"Nothing new on Jamie at all?" Karen asked.

"No. Jolly's house was totally clean. He kept his business in his office."

It was Karen's turn to go quiet. She let out a sigh and then asked, "So, did you recognize any of the victims? In the photos?"

"No Jamie, if that's what you're asking."

Karen fell silent once more. *Only boys.* Guilty relief that Sophie couldn't have been part of it even if she'd been at the studio multiple times flooded over her once again. "I can't stomach the idea that there are people out there buying it."

"Lots of money in the dark web. It's pretty heavy, that's for sure. And, he might have been paying kids for sex favors he never recorded. We'll probably never know the full extent of it."

"Hey, Court?" Karen asked. "You'll let me know if Jamie is in any of the photos, too?"

"I'll let you know if I see either of them. Better prepare his mom for that possibility. Jolly shuffled hundreds of kids through his office for the music scene. I didn't count how many binders there were. Aside from what was on the floor, it was pretty well organized and chronicled for a digital porn ring."

*Thirty-four.* There were thirty-four binders, presumably one for each kid he'd exploited. Karen should forget everything she saw in Marcus Jolly's studio that morning. All she needed was to slip up with a detail that only the police should know. "Thanks for calling, Court," she said.

Again, Court went silent. "Karen, you didn't happen to lose a black backpack recently, did you?"

Karen's heart thumped loudly *Busted*. "Uhm… no?" It wasn't lying because she hadn't *lost it*. She knew exactly where she'd left it. "Why do you ask?"

"You know what's really interesting? Nothing was taken from the studio. Expensive equipment? Guitars? All the rooms holding the goods were left locked. The only door that was open inside was Jolly's office. Oh, and the person who broke in left their tools behind."

*Busted.*

"Kind of sloppy-sounding to me," Karen said.

"It was as if they were heading straight to that hidden space you were so concerned about the other day."

"Very Interesting. What would have happened if the burglar was still there when the police arrived?"

"They would have been arrested."

"And the porn? Would that all be in evidence now?"

"Yes."

"But the burglar would be in trouble for breaking and entering?"

"Definitely."

"But you can still use the porn as evidence against Jolly?"

"Absolutely."

"So, is there really a problem here? Sounds like that burglar did you a solid—breaking in and laying out all that juicy evidence like a feast on a platter."

"Cheeky burglar. Good thing this backpack doesn't appear to have any trace evidence on it. Like long auburn hair stuck in a zipper."

Karen's heart rate ratcheted up to about five hundred beats a second. "Good thing," she said, her voice cracking with the effort. "Theoretically, what happens to that kind of evidence?"

"Well, if it were put into evidence, we could run a DNA match to it."

"I see," Karen said.

"Like I said, it's a really good thing no one found hair on that backpack."

What he was telling her finally got through. There was no doubt now that he not only knew she had broken in but that he'd buried evidence pointing to her. "Yeah. A really good thing."

After they hung up, Karen returned to the back yard, hoping to lose herself in the sunset and heavy-duty yard work. After half an hour of digging out comfrey, Karen was sweaty and tired and no closer to mental clarity. Lying to Court was wrong on a number of levels, but if she had told him she'd broken into Jolly's studio, there would be other legal ramifications. Karen didn't want to mess up the case against Jolly.

And she had to protect Court, too. By not admitting it to him, he'd have plausible deniability. Even though he already suspected her? *What he doesn't know for sure…*

She'd been right about Jolly being a creeper. The hole in her heart widened and deepened. She was no closer to finding Jamie than she had been almost a week ago. And what did she have to show for her efforts?

Karen tossed the pile of weeds into the compost bin and hung up her shovel on the tool hook. She dropped onto her back, ignoring the little prickles of grass burrowing into her skin, and spread her arms wide to soak up the dwindling light. The rays' low angle soothed her with its fleeting, comforting warmth. She fell asleep with Aspen's head on her tummy.

"Mom. Mom? Wake up." Sophie was leaning over her, amusement pouring out of her. "You okay?"

Karen stretched and sat up, pulling Sophie down into her arms.

"Baby, you gotta tell me the truth about something."

32

Starting her week off with an uncomfortable phone call to Maria Wells came unbearably close to a real desk job. While Karen appreciated people who lived a normal nine-to-five kind of life, she would never be one of them. She stumbled out of bed, showered to wash away the remnants of horrible sleep, and drank a pot of coffee before picking up the phone.

Admitting any kind of failure to the other woman was almost as difficult as her failure to find Jamie itself. Karen left out the details of her inadequacies and promised Maria she would continue the search.

"I'm sorry," Karen said. "I'm not giving up, but it's not an easy job."

"Do not apologize, Karen. The police are doing no better. Thank you for what you *are* doing." Maria's voice trembled and clogged with tears as she spoke.

Karen parked her car near Cal Anderson Park and took the bus over to Green Lake, once again retracing Jamie's steps. There was some woo-woo part of her that felt as if she could capture his essence, the answer would come to her.

As she rode the bus, she thought about her most recent conversation with her daughter. Sophie was completely shocked to learn about the pedophile-pornography ring. She swore up and down that Jolly had never asked her to do anything of the sort. Jolly had offered her money only for her singing. Karen believed her, if only because the alternative was too difficult to bear.

Sophie was almost certain Jamie would have told her if he'd been asked or forced to act in a porno movie, but she admitted he didn't tell her about his working for Mama Gong, either.

Dark gray clouds hovered overhead, promising a long-needed rain. Karen pulled her jean jacket tight around her and leaned against a tree near the bus stop. The Starbucks across the street was a nonstop hive of activity.

A young man about Jamie's age set up on the corner of the store outside, their mini-amp plugged in to the wall. The singer was marginal, and the playing even less inspired, but people stopped and put money in the open case anyway. Cash for effort played well in this part of town.

Jamie had told her that he made good money busking and didn't need to do sex work. Karen counted a steady stream of bills dropping into the case and guessed it was maybe fifty bucks. That wasn't bad for a half hour. If Jamie made even just fifty bucks a day busking, why would he need to move into survival sex? What else was he paying for? Karen wanted to believe he wasn't doing drugs, but what else would he need the money for?

Karen crossed the street, dropped a couple of quarters into the open guitar case, pretending to look at the CD for sale while counting the change in the case. Her estimate of fifty bucks was pretty close to the fifty-seven she counted without touching it. Not a bad guess, if she said so herself.

She went into the store and ordered a quadruple macchiato. The tables were full up, and it wasn't exactly a surprise when she found Donna Richards sitting at a corner table with a newspaper. "Mind the company?" Karen asked, interrupting the other woman's reading.

Donna startled and folded the newspaper in half. She fluttered her fingers at the seat opposite her. "Be my guest. Any luck with finding Jamie?"

"Not really."

Donna put her finger on the headline of the newspaper. "Did you see this? In my neighborhood, no less."

Karen hadn't seen the paper. The headlines was enough to know what it was about: Child Pornography Ring Discovered in Green Lake Neighborhood.

"I saw something about it online this morning," Karen said.

"It was that Marcus Jolly fellow. The one who is always paying the kids for their music? Now we know what else he was paying them for. And to think, not a one of these children ever said a word."

"Shocking," Karen said. "It's much worse than the rumors flying about him."

"Those were bad enough. Filthy, evil man. Forcing those children to…" Donna shook her head and hugged herself. "Those poor innocent babies. I suppose it is useless to think too hard on it. It irks me that this was going on right under our noses."

"It's scary, too. As a parent, especially. All those predators out there ready to hurt them makes me want to hold them tight at home."

"Karen, tell me. What is the world coming to? Honestly, it's so I'm almost afraid to do anything."

Karen shrugged. The world had always sucked, and now it sucked a little more, was all. People had always gone missing, died, been taken advantage of. The only thing that was different was the current proximity.

Donna swirled her drink around and sighed heavily. "You know, I'm done with these dark topics for the day. Do tell me, did anything happen with the cute detective the other night? I saw you later on, with the ice cream? That sure seemed like a date to me."

Karen hadn't seen Donna at all after they left the meeting. She brushed aside the prickles that danced along her neck. The streets had been crowded that night and Karen had been focused on Court and the traffic cop. It wasn't that weird that Donna would have seen them as she walked back to campus from the sausage house.

"Definitely not a date thing going on. I couldn't date a cop for about a thousand reasons."

"You know him pretty well, though, right? You seem comfortable with him."

"He saved my life last year."

"Oh, did he, now? How romantic."

"Not really. I definitely crushed hard on him right after that, but he… well. His being a cop was an issue then, and an issue now. He's the only cop I know or feel comfortable talking to. So when I was asked to find Jamie, he was my only resource."

"It's an issue because cops usually hate private investigators?" Donna asked. "Is that a real thing?"

"Some things on TV are pretty accurate. In general, cops don't like us because we're usually trying to prove the cops failed or did something wrong. It's a delicate dance."

"I had no idea. If you hate cops so much, why did you pick a profession where you have to deal with them?"

"I was going to keep my P.I. work simple. Background checks, real estate reviews, occasional genealogical research projects."

"Okay. Fair enough. Did you talk much about the whole Dog Park Killer thing? You were with him right after that meeting."

"Not really."

"Oh. I find the whole business kind of creepy. And intriguing. Like watching something on TV, but real. Some guy taking these kids off the streets? If it is a guy. Not all women are completely sane, you know?"

Karen shrugged. "Oh, they know it was a guy. At least they've got that part right."

"Really?" Donna asked. "How can they be so sure of that?"

"Apparently they have some DNA evidence that proves it's a guy."

"DNA evidence?" Donna leaned forward. "Don't they have some database then? You know, something that will link it up to someone specific?"

"Only if the killer is already in the system."

"I'm amazed at what they can find out from something like a hair follicle or a single drop of blood these days."

"Or semen." Every so often, the image of a dead Berkeley Drummond popped up bright and clear as a Kodachrome picture, hitting Karen by surprise. She shut her eyes against it to clear the vision.

Donna stiffened. "Semen? Are you saying they are finding semen on these boys?"

*Shit. Fuck. How the hell had she let that slip out?*

"I was actually thinking about another case, one I was involved in last year," Karen backpedaled the best she could.

"Are you okay, Karen? You're downright pale."

"Someone really close to me was murdered last year. They found semen on him as evidence. It's still raw, I guess."

"I *see*. Semen would make it obvious a man was involved. If they're sure a man is involved, I mean." Donna held up her hands and shook her head. "And we are back on darkness again. It's hard to stay away from when we're living so close to it, isn't it? I need another couple shots, what can I get you?"

"I'm good," Karen said, lifting her venti cup as evidence. It was still half full.

Karen conjured a livelier image of Berkeley and focused on it. If she tried hard enough, she could hear his rumbling laugh bouncing around her studio. It was getting fainter each time she tried for it. She played it over and over again until Donna was back in her seat.

"You're still lookin' sad as a cucumber," Donna said, her Southern twang kicking in again.

"I'll be fine. What's really strange is how I can go days, weeks maybe, without thinking about Berkeley. And then, poof. I see him again."

Donna cocked her head at Karen, her eyes narrowing at her. "Berkeley? As in Berkeley Drummond?"

Karen sucked in her lower lip and breathed out. "Yeah, that Berkeley."

Donna snapped her fingers as her eyes widened. "Wait a minute. Last fall. You said that cop saved you last fall?"

Karen knew what was coming. Why had she said anything?

"Goodness gracious. Hold on one hot minute." Donna leaned in close to Karen, her jaw dropping open. "*Oh.* Now I'm remembering."

Donna's eyes narrowed, and her lips compressed themselves into a hard line. Her eyes flashed with something new Karen hadn't seen in her before. "You are that dominatrix all over the news when he died."

Karen held up a hand, ready to ward off whatever Donna was about to say. "What you saw on the news? It was grossly exaggerated."

Something in Donna's demeanor shifted. At first, Karen was sure Donna was going to get up and leave. Excoriate her. Instead, she blinked rapidly a few times before a mask fell across her face, replacing the momentary anger.

"Well, bless your heart, it must have been a trying time for you," Donna said after what felt like a full minute. Her smile did not completely reach her eyes, but at least she was trying for kindness.

"I take it my last profession doesn't gel with your values?"

Donna opened her mouth and closed it, sucking in her lips. She intertwined her fingers around the outside of her coffee cup and leaned over the table to lower her voice. "I'm taken aback, that's all. I've never met a dominatrix before. Everything I thought I knew about you shifted, and I admit, I am recalibrating."

"Ex. Ex-dominatrix," Karen said. Although, there were days where she was reconsidering her decision to switch professions. At least as a domme, she was in charge and in control of every moment.

"Well, you're doing good work now, and that's all that really matters, right?"

Karen didn't like the subtle meaning behind Donna's words, but she wasn't about to jump into a diatribe of pro-sex worker propaganda. That was Bernice's job.

Karen maneuvered the conversation into safer territory. They chatted for a bit more about mundane things. Eventually, Donna got up, smoothed out her cotton dress and excused herself. By the time she left, Donna was back to her composed sweet self.

## 33

KAREN RETURNED TO THE BUS STOP AND STOOD WITH HER back against a tree and her eyes closed. While not into the woo-woo side of life, she hoped for some miraculous inspiration to come to her. There was a new busker at the corner of the store now. She sang a folk tune Karen vaguely recognized. It was something else from the soundtrack of her childhood—one of those nebulous Simon and Garfunkel songs her mother played endlessly.

Karen tuned it out as best she could and made out bits and pieces of conversation from people passing by. A group of guys were talking geek-speak. A couple of women were talking about diaper rash. The screech of car tires, engines whirring, laughter, dogs barking… sounds of the city whooshed past her in their vague generalities. Nothing new occurred to her or felt important.

Karen walked to Garland Parker's office. She stood across the street from it for about half an hour, hoping for something to occur to her. She doubted Jamie would have been interested in a sleepover that required Bible study. She could find no concrete link between Jamie and Garland Parker.

It took her ten minutes to walk from Parker's office to Jolly's studio. The police cars were gone, and, from the outside, everything was back to normal. She imagined there might be crime-scene tape marking the door. Going inside would be pushing her luck.

Karen needed another look at Morena Parker's house. Her only encounter with the other woman had shaken her up. Such rabid evangelism was a rare thing in Seattle. Fringe Christian crazy didn't get along with educated liberal for the most part. There were pockets of all kinds of hateful crazies crawling out into the sunlight lately.

She passed the house, crossed the street and passed it a second time. Karen hid in the shadow of a tree, considering the simple landscaping, the singular cross on the ground. Then Garland Parker's van glided around the corner and backed into the driveway.

Garland had told Karen that he hadn't talked to Morena lately, and now, two days after asking him about it, he was at her house?

He opened the trunk of the van, walked casually to the front door, and rang the bell. Morena answered it, said something, and led him inside. Karen was too far away to hear their words. So the two were talking, but Parker wasn't entering uninvited. They were closer than either had admitted to her without being exactly chummy.

While they were inside, Karen ran across the street and hid in the next door neighbor's driveway, behind large box hedges. She crouched down low, hoping the neighbor wasn't paying any attention. She had a peek-a-boo view of the van through the bushes.

She turned her camera on and snapped a photo of Morena and Garland Parker carrying boxes out to his van.

"Honestly, you are overreacting, Morena," Garland said.

"She has to know *something*."

"What could she know?"

"We should make them *all* call home so their parents stop sending private investigators…" Morena's voice broke off as they went back inside, continuing their conversation. They returned with another, large box.

"Morena, you need to chill. What we're doing is saving souls. We're serving God in all that we do."

Morena climbed into the passenger front seat as Garland closed up the van. He climbed behind the wheel and pulled out of the driveway.

*Crap.*

Karen watched in dismay as the van made its way down the street. Traffic snarled to a stop at the cross street. Maybe she could catch up to them if she ran. The van stayed out of reach. Every time she got close, the van leapt ahead. As the van finally turned north onto the major through-street, Karen noticed someone climbing out of a Lyft on the corner—the little pink sign was visible from quite a distance. She caught up before the car left.

"Can you follow that van? I've got the app, but I don't know where they are going."

The driver twisted around in her seat and gave Karen a hard once-over. "Fifty bucks cash. Nothing on the record."

"Okay, I've got it. Just don't lose that van."

The driver rubbed her fingers together and eyed Karen over the top of her sunglasses. Karen fished out the money and thrust it into the driver's greedy little hand. "Now go."

In spite of the driver taking her sweet time getting into traffic, the van was only six cars ahead of them when they reached the next light. Karen slumped back into her seat. She called Court. He didn't answer. What would she have told him, anyway?

How could she not have believed her instinct from the other day? The Parkers were definitely into something shady. There was no reason for Garland Parker to lie to her about never seeing or speaking to Morena—other than that he was hiding something. And what else could he be hiding besides some twisted dark secret?

They had been talking about her, she was sure of it. What was it she didn't suspect?

Being so sure about Jolly had made her blind to the Parkers' working together. Maybe they were on their way to their secret lair right now—some out of the way place where they held their captives while doing unspeakably horrible things to them?

After a tense ten minutes of swerving in and out of traffic, the van turned off Ninety-nine and headed west. They wound through residential streets and Karen told the Lyft driver to back off a bit lest they be noticed. As they got close to the water, the van turned onto a road marked private drive.

"Let me out here, and wait for me. I'll need a ride back," Karen said.

"That'll be another fifty off the record. Now, before you go."

Karen handed the driver the last of her cash. "I have your license plate, so make sure you're still here when I get back."

"You have fifteen minutes."

The driveway was a private road serving six houses off it. The first house was gated, and there were twelve cars packed inside. There was no way Garland's van would have made it past the mini-parking lot. The other gates were closed and not another car to be seen. Garland's van had disappeared inside one of them somewhere.

Karen's background on the Parkers hadn't shown any properties in this part of town. As far as she could remember, none of their family members lived over here, either.

Movement at a window in one of the houses drew Karen's attention. Had she been spotted by the neighborhood busybody? Karen ducked between the brick fence of the house and a lush rhododendron, and peeked around the corner. All she saw were closed curtains and a dark interior. The garage door opened, and Garland's van, with him at the wheel, emerged from within. Karen dropped to her knees as the gate swung slowly open. She held her breath as the van passed her. Morena was not in the van.

Karen crawled as quickly as she could around the column of the gate and into the yard. The gate closed behind her with an ominous *thwang*. She caught her breath hidden in another rhododendron bush and scoped out her options. The grass was freshly cut. No remnants of cut-up dog poop stink told her that there were no dogs ready to defend the property.

The garage side of the house was a big wall of fake brick. She sprinted to the corner and edged her way around to the back of the house. She had eight minutes left before the driver left, if she was even still there.

A seven-foot tall wooden fence barred her way into the back yard. The gate was locked with a combination padlock —something she couldn't pick. Karen stepped onto a rock to get a glimpse of the yard and back of the house.

The house angled away from the garage so that she had a perfect view inside. The sliding door from the kitchen opened out onto a generous patio. Off that was a large, almost Olympic-sized pool. Six teens swam back and forth in straight lines. There was no horseplay or calls of "Marco Polo." No splashing or rambunctious play. Their faces were down in the water. None of them was Jamie. Unless his head had been shaved, for all the boys in the pool had short hair, almost bald.

Inside the kitchen, five other teens stood at counters, quietly chopping vegetables or stirring things in pots and bowls. No Jamie. She shuddered at the notion of his long flowing blond hair being shaved off. The boys in the kitchen wore blue jeans and yellow shirts with print she couldn't read.

The kitchen was open to what must have been a living room at one time. Tables and chairs filled the space, cafeteria-style. There were twenty-four places set on the tables, complete with napkins and regular dishes.

Two more boys were moving the boxes Morena and Garland Parker had brought from near the interior garage door and out of the room. Karen snapped photos of the boys in the pool and kitchen. A boy at the kitchen sink looked directly at her.

Karen's stance on the rock wobbled as she tried to get a

better view. She dropped down and caught her breath. She found a second rock and stacked it on top of the first. She grabbed onto the top of the wooden fence and little pieces of wood jabbed into her hands. She balanced on top of the rocks and steadied herself.

The boy at the sink was focused on washing dishes.

Almost out of her field of vision, Morena Parker and another woman stood off in a corner. Morena's arms waved emphatically as she spoke. The other woman glanced at the teens in the kitchen over her shoulder and turned back to Morena, putting calming hands on her shoulders.

Karen counted heads. Thirteen boys visible. Twenty-four places at the table. Karen searched the upstairs windows for any signs of life. Could Jamie be inside, hidden from the world?

Karen's foot slipped and she slid from her precarious perch. Her fingers instinctively closed around the fence, swinging her in against it. Pain burst across her face as she hit the wood, nose first. She let go and dropped, twisting her ankle. She rolled off to the side and onto her back, one hand feeling for her nose, the other grabbing at her ankle. She breathed in and out, forcing calm through her body. Her short stint with yoga came in handy occasionally. She tasted blood in her mouth and her lip buzzed.

This was all too much to deal with on her own. Karen limped to the front gate and found a space wide enough to squeeze through. She cast an anxious glance back toward the house as she freed herself. It took her another few minutes to hobble back up the street to where she'd left her ride. The car was gone.

"Wait a second," Court said. "Let me get somewhere I can talk."

Karen sat on a bench at a small neighborhood park a couple blocks away from where she'd been abandoned by the Lyft driver. Calling 911, she realized, would have been excessive and overblown. In spite of the thick chain and heavy lock on the back gate, none of the kids in the house appeared to be imprisoned or injured. Not physically, anyway.

Court came back on the line. "Okay, I'm alone and can hear you. What's this about Garland and Morena Parker?"

"I overhead them talking. They didn't like there being a private investigator around asking questions. Morena told Garland that they *should have all the kids call home.* Then I followed them to this house up in Shoreline. It's a commune or something." Karen took a deep breath. She was practically ranting and made little sense even to herself.

"You followed them?"

"Yes. And you know what? I got photos. I'll text them to you."

"Hold up a second," he said. "Slow down and tell me exactly what you saw. From the very beginning."

Karen went through it all again, slowing down and putting everything out there in a more cohesive way, and as she did, it came to her. "Hey, Court? It might be some sort of conversion therapy thing they're doing. That could explain everything."

"That's illegal in Washington," he said. "The police

can't run over there and bust into the building without some proof. And you're in Shoreline."

"What if Jamie *is* there?"

"You said they look like they are there voluntarily."

"Come on, Court, if they're all brainwashed, how voluntary can it be?"

"Send me the photos. The address. I can forward the information to the local authorities. What else do you have on them?"

"The Bible verse fits, too."

"Bible verse?"

"Come on, Court. I saw more than enough when I snuck into that room. The numbers in Sharpie on the foreheads? The other day, when I was interviewing Morena Parker, she got all rant-y about cleansing by fire. You know, crazy preachy rant-y, with wide eyes and spittle flying. I told you about all that, and you didn't mention the Bible verse on their foreheads."

"Privileged information. Which, by the way, you were not supposed to have access to."

"Garland Parker told me on Saturday that he hadn't had any contact with Morena. That was an outright lie."

"I'm hearing you. I'll send this info over to Shoreline PD," Court said. "It's too bad you didn't actually see something bad happening to a kid. Like, if *someone thought* they saw a kid being injured, they *could call 911 or CPS.*"

The impact of Court's suggestion hit her. "Or, maybe a snoopy neighbor might call in with concerns," she said.

"That would be convenient."

*Somewhat like a recent break-in.* Maybe Court wasn't a total straight-arrow when it came to his job. Maybe there were unplumbed depths to this man after all. "Here's hoping."

"We are looking into Garland Parker, but these things take time."

"We don't have time."

"We do. Now, will you stop snooping around and go home? There's nothing left for you to do."

"I'll be in Seattle for the rest of the day passing out flyers and stapling them all over town. I can't give up. I can't sit at home doing nothing."

"Okay, okay. Promise me you'll stay away from the Parkers. That includes their homes and his office. And this new place. You got that?"

"You're not my boss, Court. I'll do what I need to. Something doesn't feel right, and I'm worried."

She hung up, her hands shaking with excitement and energy and no small amount of annoyance. How could she not have believed her instinct from the other night? Being so sure about Jolly had made her blind to the Parkers working together. She'd been right about Jolly for all the wrong reasons. What about the Parkers?

Karen opened her Lyft app and ordered a car. The Toyota that pulled into the parking lot was not the same one that had abandoned her less than half an hour before. It was probably a good thing. She had the driver stop at the closest 7-Eleven so she could use the payphone.

After dialing CPS and giving an exaggerated report of the boys in captivity, she went inside the store and bought some painkillers and an Ace bandage. The split on her lip hadn't dripped blood, and the swelling of her nose was minimal for now. She wrapped the tape around her ankle as her new Lyft took her back into town. She would continue canvassing the area near Cal Anderson Park for anyone willing to talk to her about Jamie. She needed to do something besides sit at home twiddling her thumbs.

After a fruitless pass through the park, she went into Harbor House. The older woman behind the desk hadn't seen Jamie for a couple weeks, either. No surprise there. As Karen turned to go, the woman, who identified herself as Lucinda, reached for Karen's hands and grasped them between her gnarled fingers.

"Please find him. I don't know him well, but I know in my heart he's a good boy. He has talent that should be released to the world."

There was something about this woman's demeanor that screamed authenticity. It was more than the casual unconscious way she carried herself. There was a depth to her bright warmth, something that flowed from within. Her hands were comforting, reminding Karen of the grandmother she barely knew. Even her scent was familiar—spicy and musky, with a hint of weed.

"You and Donna couldn't be more different," Karen said.

"Donna? Oooh, Donna Richards. That woman drives me nuts," Lucinda said. "Absolutely batty."

Karen tilted her head to the side. "Really?"

"Yeah. Well, she acts a good game for the sake of the kids here. She was fine with me until I told her I was a lesbian. If her face could have gone any more white, it would have, poor thing. As if I'd be interested in *her*." Lucinda rolled her eyes in emphasis.

"She came across as pretty authentic when it came to

her grief over Blake. Her son."

"Well, people have their boxes, now don't they? Donna has one she's comfy with, and if you push her she gets a little wiggy."

"She's pretty friendly with me, but it was pretty obvious she was uncomfortable when I told her I used to be a dominatrix." For some reason, Karen didn't have any qualms sharing this detail with Lucinda. There wasn't a judgmental bone in this woman's body. She was all love and light. Karen wanted to fall into her arms and listen to her honeyed voice.

"Welcome to the club. It took Donna six months to talk to me again without looking at me like I was a creature from another planet."

Karen dragged herself away from Harbor House and turned toward Rainbow Landing. The blatant rainbow painted across the building, the rainbow colors assigned to each victim, Parker's picking up kids there—these things must be connected.

She texted Court with her latest theories. Maybe the Parkers tried to convert kids and kill the ones that are incapable of being "fixed." Morena Parker had said that her son was saved in the final days of his life. She stressed the forty days of redemption when they spoke. Maybe the Parkers kept the kids for forty days and killed them once they had converted. Was killing them a way of preserving their cleansed souls?

Karen dropped into Molly Moon's and got a double scoop of salted caramel ice cream with hot fudge sauce. She sat in the window watching people walk by as she enjoyed every sweet bite. When Bernice texted, asking her to come to her office, Karen welcomed the diversion.

## 34

Cami was seated across from Bernice when she arrived.

"Oh, hell no. I thought you wanted to talk about other business," Karen said, ready to turn around and leave.

"Please, Karen, hear us out," Bernice said, jumping up and pointing to the chair next to Cami. On the desk in front of them was a tray with fresh coffee and some cookies. She leaned over her desk, eyes narrowing on Karen. "You've got quite a bruise forming there. Did you get punched in the face?"

Karen poured herself a cup. "I'll stay. For the coffee." She winced as the hot brew stung her cut lip with the first swig.

Bernice settled back into her chair, eyebrows creasing together. "I'm worried. Karen. Were you in a fight, or what?"

"I'm fine. And I don't want to talk about it." A fight would have made for a better story than her clumsy fall against a fence. She turned to Cami. "I didn't recognize you the other day, but figured out where I knew you from when I saw you at the community meeting Friday night."

Cami cocked her head to the side. "Oh, I thought you recognized me."

Karen's bullshit meter dinged. *Move on, Hunter. Move on.* "I told you I wasn't interested in this gig. What makes you think I will change my mind?"

Cami pulled out a binder thick with statistics on sex slavery. "Interview almost anyone in this country and they will say they've heard of kids getting kidnapped or sold outright in Asia. They are always shocked to hear that the majority of sex slavery in the country comes from within the U.S. Add in that a huge number of native and POC girls are targeted, it goes underground even deeper."

Karen hadn't quite recovered from seeing the photos in Jolly's studio yet, and investigating girls being forcibly sold to men sounded dark and depressing. "I'm all for turning this around and shining a light on the difference. This kind of gig is too out there for me."

Cami leaned forward. "I want to work with a P.I. who can do some solid background checks. The guys who get involved use aliases, but they're not always the greatest at covering their tracks. They might log in with a proxy server, then they accidentally reconnect with their regular IP. Or, they text using their regular phone. You're uniquely qualified in that you also know the sex trade. How to keep things underground. How it all works. Not all P.I.s have that kind of experience. And, you're a woman."

"And the FBI, or whoever is in charge, isn't already doing this?"

"I believe that I will be turning over some new names and faces. Following leads in the moment, acting very locally. I'm planning some sting-style gigs that will help catch some of the leaders, and then we have to prove what they are really up to. Break open the scale of it all. Show how far they move the girls within the country."

"And the police? How do they come into this?" Karen asked.

"I want to have a solid case and story ready to go when I hand everything over to them. I'll hand over all my evidence and the story goes up live at the same time. No cover-ups that way."

"Do you suspect law enforcement of being complicit?"

"Some turn their heads—in good ways and bad," Cami said. "I don't know if anyone in our local SPD is actively engaged in the slave trade or not."

"Are you in this for the fame and glory or for putting an end to this kind of slavery?" Karen asked.

Bernice lifted an eyebrow, her lip twitching. "Does it really matter? Her motivation *can* be two-fold, Karen."

"I'm sick of seeing kids getting exploited," Cami said. "And, yes, it would be awesome to get professional recognition. I can't deny that part of it."

Karen's resolve melted away as she opened her heart to the possibilities. Maybe she could make a small difference here. "Tell me more," she said.

They talked some more about the logistics. The most disturbing part about the whole project was they would have to do it over time, knowing all the while that some girls would be repeatedly abused.

Court's words about building a case on solid evidence

that would stand up at a trial resonated more fully now. She wrapped her arms around herself as she wondered what was happening at the house in Shoreline. She doubted it was a child-sex-slave ring. Her theory about conversion therapy fit more closely with the Parkers' religious convictions.

Bernice asked Karen to stay after Cami left so they could talk about their own business.

"Thad has decided to not pursue custody at this time," she said. "He knows how his leaving the kids home alone will affect his chances. I got CPS to drop their case against him in return for one weekend a month. He has to stay with the kids the whole time, no babysitters allowed, and no extracurricular trips."

"That's good news, right? Isn't that what you wanted?"

"It is. I considered counter-suing for full custody, but am holding off for now. I'll play it by ear." Bernice paused. "Karen, I'm hoping you'd be a backup guardian for my kids. If anything happens to me, I can't have them going full time back to Thad."

"Who's the primary guardian?"

"My mom. She turned seventy-five a couple months ago. My dad is dead. My brother is dead. She's all I have left, really."

"No cousins? Aunts? Uncles?"

"No one I would trust to raise my kids." Bernice turned back to face her. "They're all… very much not on board with my personal agenda. My aunt told me I should have stayed with Thad. Let him have his secrets."

"Really? You told her the whole story?"

"Really. Even after hearing how he'd lied to me about

being gay for so long. Sleeping around behind my back. She said marriage is forever—for better or worse."

"Different world, same planet. Jeesh."

"Is this a yes? I'll have the papers drawn up this week."

"Bernice? I don't want to get into a custody battle with Thad. Not that I want anything to happen to you either, but… make sure that's taken care of somehow before you put my name on the paperwork."

"That'll be tricky. But, yeah, I know a legal way around that." Bernice laughed. "The things we do for things that we never want to happen, right? Thank you, Karen. It eases my mind knowing they'll have a good, safe place to stay if anything happens to me."

They spent another hour going over the client list and background checks Karen would be doing in the next couple weeks.

"One more thing, Karen," Bernice said as she opened the door to leave.

"Yes?"

"I've got another attorney friend who needs a P.I. to do some investigation for a couple of his cases. You interested in criminal defense at all?"

Karen considered it. Part of her wanted to run from criminal work as much as she'd wanted to run from helpless girls. It was the hard part. The difficult work. "I'd like to do some of that work, yes."

"Great. I'll send her your info."

---

KAREN LEFT Bernice's office with time to kill before the city council meeting started. Instead of returning to Cal Anderson Park, she headed to Westlake. After a thorough circuit of the area, she moved on to Pike Place Market.

For about the ten thousandth time, she checked her messages, hoping for something from Jamie. Her heart about stopped when she looked at her phone. A text from Jamie's phone number lit up her screen.

She stared at her phone in shocked silence, holding back tears of relief. *She had a text from Jamie.* Was it finally over? Had he been freed from the Parkers' house by CPS? She swiped at her phone, eagerness making her fingers shaky.

Jamie: *Sorry, battery died, couldn't find charger. All is good.*
Karen: *Please check in with your mom, she's worried silly.*
Jamie: *I will. Sorry. Am with friends.*

Karen texted Sophie: *Did you hear from Jamie? I got a text from him! Says he's with friends, but his syntax is weird.* Sophie texted back with an emoji showing her excited delight. A few moments later: *Find My Friends shows him in Seattle now. Yay!xx*

Karen asked her to screen-shot the FMF.

As she waited, Karen's momentary sense of relief was short-lived. There was something off about his text. Jamie usually wrote in complete sentences. It was an odd thing for a teen, but he rarely left off pronouns and verbs like that. And, if he'd been with friends this whole time, why hadn't he borrowed one of their phones to let someone know he was safe? Especially Sophie.

The screenshot showed up. It showed Jamie's little dot

right at the edge of Cal Anderson Park, right across from Molly Moon's. Where Karen had been less than two hours before.

Sophie called, her voice near panic. "Do you think he's there right now?"

"I'm not far from there. I have time to do a quick run-through the park before the city council meeting."

"Mom, something is not right here. Jamie almost always adds an emoji on his text. There wasn't one on this last text. And he's not answering me. That's not like him."

"It's about time for people to check in for beds and dinner. So maybe he is in the park and not wanting to be bothered?"

"Let me know if you see him. Mom, I don't think that text was from Jamie."

Karen agreed to call or text Sophie later before logging into Maria's Starbucks account and checked the usage. Jamie hadn't purchased anything in ten days. She caught the light rail from downtown back up to the park. She wormed her way through the throngs of people, waving at people she'd met the last couple of days.

Tink bobbed over to her. "Any luck finding Strings?"

"You haven't seen him today?"

"Sorry, Mrs. H. I've asked, too. No one knows anything about where he is."

Same old story.

Karen did a full circuit of the park. No sign of Jamie. Where did he go? Granted, it had taken her fifteen minutes to get from downtown to the park, but if he were hanging out waiting for a bed, he'd still be here. The shelter line wasn't long. The weather was warm and a lot of kids liked sleeping outside in their makeshift homes, where they could keep their pets.

She waited until the line disappeared and went inside where Lucinda was finishing up with the last two kids signing in.

"Back so soon?" she asked, full of eager friendliness.

"I got a text from Strings. Any chance he's checked in for the night?"

Lucinda shook her head. "I've been here since you left. I would definitely have told him to call home. Hell, if he were signing in for the night, we'd have to call his mom."

"Have you seen anyone odd hanging around the shelter? Strangers?"

The woman laughed. "Have you ever walked through the park? This is the odd part of town. Though, I guess it depends on how you define odd."

Karen went back to the park and dialed Jamie's phone. It rang and rang. She continued redialing, hoping she'd hear his familiar ringtone. She texted Sophie asking if her app was still giving her Jamie's location.

Apparently, the phone hadn't moved. Karen made smaller and smaller circles around the area, hitting redial over and over. When Diana Ross's "I'm Coming Out" finally sang out at it her, it almost didn't register. Karen spun around looking for Jamie. He had to be close. Strangers pressed to get by her as she stood still, head cocked, listening for the music. She called two more times before she finally pinpointed the source.

Karen texted Court: *Someone put Jamie's phone in the trash can after texting me.* She gave Court directions and stood over the can until he got there, making sure no one threw anything else inside.

Court and Ivy appeared with a couple of other officers carrying black plastic tackle boxes. The technicians set to work. Karen hung off to the side, protective of her find and curious about how this would all go down.

Two uniformed officers appeared as if out of nowhere.

"Hang on a minute," Court said. "I'll give you instructions when we've got the phone out of the garbage."

The techs worked quickly, moving the trash from the top of the heap. One photographed each element while the other bagged and tagged items, placing them in the box. When they found the phone, it appeared to be by itself, though it could have slid out of some sort of wrapping.

The tech dropped it into an evidence bag and Court held it up for her inspection. "Is this it?"

Karen nodded. "I'm pretty sure." She dialed Jamie's number again and the front screen lit up with a photo of Jamie and Sophie—a selfie Jamie had taken at the fair the previous year.

Ivy and Court exchanged a meaningful glance and turned away to talk quietly to each other. Karen inched closer and butted in on their conversation. "You told me another victim had texted someone? Did you ever find their phone?"

"No. We never found the phone," Court said.

Ivy crossed her arms. "Was there anything unusual about his text?"

"He always sends her emojis at the end of his texts to Sophie. She didn't get one this time. The text he sent me was off, too. It took me a minute to figure out why. He always uses full sentences when he texts me. He calls me Mrs. Hunter, not Mrs. H, not Karen. This text was full of fragments and abbreviations."

A cloud crossed over Court's face and he motioned for her to continue.

"You once said only one of the other victims texted after they might have been captured already. There were syntax errors in that text, too. How long before you found him?"

"It was about a week."

"We have a week to find him?"

"Or less," Court said.

"Why today?" Karen asked. "Why would they text today?"

"The other text was from Jeremy White. His phone, anyway."

"Jamie and Jeremy... both letter J's starting their name?" Karen said. "Wait. Didn't you tell me that Jeremy's mom also hired a P.I.?"

"Yes."

"And how far did they get?"

"Similar to you. They interviewed people at the shelter. Spent time at the obvious locations—the park, Westlake, Pike Place."

"You think that getting a P.I. involved makes the killer rush?" Karen asked. "That just my asking questions has prompted the timeline forward?"

"I don't know that for sure. It's just a theory."

Karen found a bench and dropped her head into her hands. How many ways had she fucked everything up?

## 35

IF YOU WANT TO TRY TO MAKE IT TO THE COUNCIL MEETING, we could give you a lift over there," Court said. "It's not too far from the station."

Karen accepted their offer and walked with them as they returned to the car they'd parked cattywampus at the edge of the park, close to where a game of bike polo was gearing up. Players were warming up, riding in circles and practicing their shots with multiple balls. Just watching made her dizzy.

Ivy opened the back door of the car for Karen. At least it was a motor-pool car and not a regular squad car. Karen could still open the door from the inside. Ivy drove like a maniac even though traffic was stop and go. Court appeared not to notice, but his grip on the safety handle turned his fingers white.

"Hey, did you get any response from the Shoreline police?" Karen asked. In light of everything else she had going on, she'd almost forgotten about the Parkers and their commune.

"They said they were looking into it," Court said. "Honestly? I haven't followed up with them. Sorry about that."

Had he not taken her seriously after all? Had CPS? Karen searched her phone for breaking news. Surely, if CPS had found teens being held hostage in Shoreline, it would have been huge. But she found nothing.

The crowd of people leaving City Hall blocked the entrance. Police formed a phalanx around council members as they were surrounded by the press.

"Looks like I missed it," Karen said.

"Sorry about that." Court turned around in his seat. "I'm betting you didn't miss much."

Instead of dropping her off, Ivy drove past and drove on to the motor-pool garage across the street from police headquarters. "I'm starved," she said. "Let's hit Barrolli's for happy hour before we get back to work."

Court turned to Karen. "Want to join us?"

"Isn't Barrolli's the place cops tend to hang out?"

"Yep. You scared?" Ivy asked, her lip quirking into a smile.

"Of course not. It's not a place I'd typically choose to go. You guys aren't known for your love of P.I.s."

"You're with us, you'll be fine. Besides, they have good food at good prices this time of day," Court said.

Karen's stomach overruled her head. She'd had only coffee and ice cream all day long, and pasta sounded perfect. They walked the three blocks to the bar that managed to survive in its pristine 1950s state as Seattle in general went hipster block by block. Brown leather chairs and dark tables managed to still stink of cigarettes even though indoor smoking hadn't been legal for more than a dozen years. The long wooden bar was filled with off-duty cops, shoulder to shoulder. Most were paying attention to the preseason Seahawks game on the giant screens above the bar.

They found a booth and ordered. Karen's iced tea was surprisingly fresh. Her chicken parmesan was crisp and covered with the perfect amount of cheese. The garlicky tomato sauce covered up the staleness of the room, and she'd be smelling of garlic from the aglio e olio spaghetti for days.

Shortly after they were served their food, Camille Poulin entered the bar, scanned the restaurant, and came straight toward their table.

"Heya," she said, pushing herself into the seat next to Court's. Ivy and Karen adjusted so that Ivy was sandwiched between Court and Karen. Cami helped herself to one of Court's bruschettas without asking. "That was some crazy-ass meeting."

"Anyone get egged?" Ivy asked.

"It was pretty exciting. That asshat Reed was in his usual dickish form."

"He won because he promised people in Seattle that he would make sweeping changes. Clean up the streets of homeless scum, enforce ordinances, and make Seattle livable again." The bitterness in Ivy's voice made Karen like her a little more.

At least they were on the same side of this particular issue.

"Well, I tell you, he's not going to last more than one

cycle. People are fed up with him, and this next election will have him out on his ear."

"Is your husband going to run again?" Court asked Ivy.

"No way. He's done with politics."

Her husband must have a different name than Langston, because Karen would have remembered it if he'd run for Seattle City Council. "Who's your husband?"

"Ely Kratzenberg. He ran against Reed in the last election." Ivy was focused on twirling the optimal layer of spaghetti around her fork.

Kratzenberg and Ivy were married? The guy came across as sincere and milquetoast. It didn't help that he could have been a younger Richard Nixon's twin brother.

Karen suppressed a shudder, imagining the gorgeous Ivy with Kratzenberg—definitely not a matched pair. He was at least fifteen years older than Ivy, too. She managed to catch Court's eye, and she could tell he knew exactly what she was thinking. She widened her eyes in a *what the hell?* question, and he smiled his gorgeous bright smile and winked an *I know, right?* wink. She melted a little at the mind-reading moment. *Damn it.*

Cami gave them a broad outline of the meeting.

"By the time it was over, the council members were running tail and the police were holding people back." Cami held up her fork, pointing it at Karen. "Hey, I thought you were going to be there. What happened?"

"I ended up delayed elsewhere."

Cami waved the fork around the table, encompassing them all. "Hey now, this other case? I've seen you at all these meetings and shit. You're working on the Dog Park Killer? As a P.I.?"

Karen shook her head. "Nah. I'm looking for a missing teen, so it only vaguely dovetails in." Karen was pretty sure telling a member of the press exactly what she'd been up to would not go over well.

Court burst in. "So, how did you know Karen was heading to the council meeting?"

Cami waved her hand back and forth between her and Karen. "Bernice set me up with Karen as a P.I. to help me with a story. We had a meeting earlier today."

Court gave Cami a look that Karen couldn't quite place, and it was more than a little awkward for everyone at the table. Cami leaned across the table. "How about we get together next week on the project. I want to go deep by the end of next month."

"What's this all about, anyway?" Court asked.

"We're working on a story together. I'll fill you in on the details sometime, but not here. Not now," Cami said.

Court turned toward Cami, his jaw clenched. "You're serious, aren't you? That's some nerve."

The tension between Court and Cami was suddenly very thick. Cami pursed her lips and growled. "It's all going to be cool, okay?"

"Don't you think you should fess up before getting her to work with you? Does she even know what you did?"

Cami's face flushed a bright splotchy pink. "I was going to tell her." She glanced briefly at Karen. "Eventually."

Court crossed his arms. "Go ahead." Cami tossed her napkin onto the table and glared at Court.

"What the hell are you two talking about?" Karen asked.

Cami turned to face Karen full on. "Soooooo… Karen,

I'm really, really, really, sorry, but, I… uhm… I was the one who leaked those photos of Drummond and doxxed you to the press last year."

The words came out so fast Karen had to replay them in her head a couple of times on slow-mo to understand them and put all the pieces together.

Cami took a deep breath and continued, her words flowing with a speed and force that made her hard to understand. "I stole some photos from Court's phone by texting them to myself while his phone was in his jacket at a party. He didn't know—I swear, it's not Court's fault. Then I saw you at the police station one day, and I followed you home. I was dating Cindy Ryan at Channel 8 News at the time, and I was doing it for her. To help her career. I'm really sorry."

Ivy's jaw was practically on her chest, and she was staring at Court wide-eyed. Karen wasn't the only one blindsided by this information.

Karen turned to Court. "You knew about this?"

She jumped out of the booth and escaped the restaurant.

## 36

KAREN WALKED AS FAST AS HER BANDAGED ANKLE WOULD
allow, straight down the hill toward the waterfront. She
needed a bit of cool, salty-sweet air on her face. The sky
had cleared without any hint of rain. The reflection of the
low sun streamed across the sound in bright shades of pinks
and oranges.

Court had known all along that Cami had been the one
who'd doxxed her. And he hadn't mentioned this to her. Or
apologized for his part in it.

His best friend had turned against him and yet here they
were all chummy and pally. And then, Cami had somehow
talked Bernice into getting Karen involved in her trafficking
story. Karen wanted to hit something. *Hard.*

Cami should have told Bernice they couldn't work
together and asked for help from a different P.I. Or had
Cami sought Bernice out because she knew Karen and
Bernice were tight? There was no way Bernice knew Cami's

part in last fall's craziness. It had to be all on Cami. And Court *knew*.

All those reporters with cameras camped out on her front lawn—filling the cul-de-sac and generally being in her face for days, accusing her of being a killer in front of her family, her neighbors and her friends? There was nothing worse than being trapped in your own home, unable to go anywhere without being confronted.

If it hadn't been for the doxxing, Karen would have never been outed so publicly on camera. It would have taken more time for people to find out her role in Berkeley's life and death. Her neighbors wouldn't have come after her with virtual pitchforks. Jamie wouldn't have been defending her with his warped sense of honor, and he wouldn't have been kicked out. Jamie would probably still be home. Safe. Not with a psycho killer.

Karen found a spot at the pier and leaned against the railing. The rainbow oil slicks around the pilings bobbed up and down, a black miasma ringed in flotsam and jetsam. She closed her eyes and breathed in the briny air, counting to four. She released it on a long slow count of seven. She did this five times before her heart rate slowed and her desire to hit something lessened.

She would call Bernice and tell her she wasn't going anywhere near Cami or her project. She didn't get why or how Court could continue to be friends with her. That had been a whopper of a secret. How could she trust him?

The waves on the sound were choppy, splashing up the sides of the ferries. The salty air had a freshness to it that Karen equated with freedom. The closeness of land she'd been raised in had always been claustrophobic. The first time she'd seen an ocean, she'd been on a trip with her father. It was the first time she'd ever been outside Montana. He'd demanded a two-week visit, and her mother had been all too happy to send her.

He'd driven straight from Montana to Oregon. She'd slept in the back of the car and woke to this terrifying sound crashing in around her. He'd parked the car at the edge of the ocean in a park to rest. He'd dropped his seat as far back as he could go and slept, his head lolling off to one side, his jaw open and snores roaring out.

She couldn't hear him breathing over the sound of the crashing waves. She had slipped out of the car without waking him. He'd come to find her, ankles deep in the slurping swallowing sand, yelling and red in the face for scaring the shit out of him. She'd been mesmerized by the waves and their rhythmic coming and going, and clueless about the fear her father faced when finding her gone.

The vastness of the ocean, the way it spread out forever without anything getting in the way, called to her. Redmond, Washington wasn't exactly on the ocean, but it was close enough for when she needed to dig her feet into the icy cold sand. Not off the pier in downtown, however. Here, she was above the water by a dozen feet.

The smell of the ocean was tempered by the burnt-oil smell on the wood of the piers. Several ferries made their way across the sound as various barges and container ships headed to the port. It was amazing that they managed the intricate ballet without ever crashing into each other.

Court appeared at her side, his shoulder pressing against hers.

"You followed me?"

"Of course. I didn't want to leave it like that."

"Like your best friend being the one who outed me to the planet?"

"She was… she still feels…" He let out a sigh. "I can't really explain her to you. I have forgiven her because she has always been a good friend—except for that one thing. She's been a rock. I don't expect you to forgive her. Or me for my part in what happened. I want you to know that I felt really bad for letting her have access to my phone. Nothing on my phone had anything to do with you. Cami followed me, then she followed you."

"And yet, you said nothing to me until it came out in the open."

Court's proximity was a little unnerving. The warmth of his arm against hers had a burgeoning familiarity to it. He was close enough that she could smell his musky blend of aftershave and sweat that came only at the end of a long day. A part of her wanted to bury her aching nose against his neck and breathe him in. It had been a long time since she'd been attracted to anyone in such a personal way. Her own white-knighting him last year wasn't an anomaly. If anything, the current revelation about Cami should have her wanting to slap him, not kiss him.

She turned toward him to open some space. "Why didn't you say anything?"

"I'm sorry. I won't let it happen again. I've learned my lesson."

"You knew about this when it was happening?"

"No. Not until it was all over. If I hadn't walked you out of the station that day I questioned you, she wouldn't have had such an easy time of it. Still, she's actually a pretty good investigative journalist. She could easily have figured out the legal ownership on the lease of yours. It would have wrapped back around to you eventually."

Karen knew all about documentation and how it could eventually bite you in the ass. One of the biggest lessons she learned as a budding P.I. was about the digital trails everyone leaves all over the place.

"How did you get over that kind of betrayal?"

Court shrugged. "I'm a forgiving kind of guy. Plus, she hounded me for months and broke up with her girlfriend as proof she was earnest."

"She broke up with her girlfriend to prove her loyalty to you?"

"Yep."

Karen considered that for a minute. "Is Cami into you?"

He laughed. "No way. Cami is not into me in any way, shape, or form."

Karen couldn't understand that. She used all her willpower to not reach out and caress his cheek.

"I hope you'll find it in your heart to forgive me for hiding my part of that from you," Court said. "When it was all happening, I didn't expect to see you again. Mending fences with Cami took priorities. We've got a history."

"I made the switch to being a P.I. to make life easier," Karen said. "My plan was to focus on background checks from the privacy of my own home. I have a beautiful cave of an office I haven't spent much time in."

"You're not exactly good at staying secluded, are you?"

"You did a background check on me last year, didn't you?"

"Can't deny it. We had to consider you a suspect. You were there. His body was in your office."

"Berkeley. Berkeley was… not a body." *Body* sounded so cold. So distancing.

"You loved him?"

"Love? It was complicated. There are so many kinds of love. His death tore me apart."

"How does your ex fit into all this?"

*All of what, exactly?* Telling Court about Robbie's mental-health issues would break a confidence. She wasn't willing to go there with Court, not yet anyway. "My ex and I have an unusual arrangement. We share the house with the kids. He has his room, I have mine, and we each have our own separate apartments. Usually I go to mine when he's on duty, and he goes to his when I'm on duty."

"Ah, that explains that," Court said.

"You saw my lease on the background check?"

"I assumed it might be another… erm… workplace. We never got around to checking it out."

"Yeah, so he sometimes stays in his room even when he's not on parent duty. He gets lonely. Likes to be around us. Around me. You could call it a friends-with-benefits sort of thing—an ex-with-benefits. We really are best friends, and that will never change. He's the father of my children. He will be in my life forever."

"Do you stop the benefits thing when you date other people?"

"Depends on the other people."

Karen turned her back to the railing hooking her arms over it. "Last year, you said you didn't date sex workers."

"I'm capable of being a huge asshole. I shouldn't have said that."

"So, you're no longer an asshole?"

"I watched *Pretty Woman* over the summer."

"Except I'm the rich one in this scenario."

"You definitely took in more money as a domme than I ever will as a cop. Do you remember that kiss from last fall?"

*Duh. Yeah?* Nine long months ago. "You were my big white knight. Waltzing into my house and saving me like that."

"I was seeing someone. We broke up a couple months ago."

"Why?"

"She was more attracted to the danger of my job than to me."

Karen turned to face him, but he was leaning over the rail, focused on the water again. "How does that work?"

"Her husband died in Iraq. I should have seen some signs, I guess. Like the night at your place, I got a little cut on my shoulder and she was over at my house to 'nurse' me. To 'be with me.' I didn't really see how bad it was until I was in the hospital after I got beaten to shit."

Karen ran a finger along the silver ridge of a scar along the side of his face. "The scar is pretty hot, you know."

He shook his head. "It's really weird, but I've had a bunch of women come onto me since I got it."

"It gives you an edgy, dangerous *je ne c'est quoi*."

"Huh. Weird. Anyway, while I was in the hospital… She was always into the medical details. She wanted to look at my chart and ask about the medicines I was on. She got off on my being injured and worrying over me. She got all excited over the scars on my body. Tending to them."

"Now I'm really glad I just caressed your scar."

He laughed. "The way you did it wasn't so… erm… mother-like."

"Whoa. I'm definitely not into any kind of incest scenes."

"Not that it was like that, either. I can't quite explain it. Maddie wasn't actually wanting a relationship as much as someone to take care of. Like she needed to be needed. It wasn't that she sent me out to hurt myself, but there was always this feeling she was a little too happy when I was in pain."

"You realize you said that to an ex-domme, right?"

He laughed. "So…"

"So. You're a cop. I'm a PI. And we've both started off with some lies. That can't possibly be a good omen."

Court returned his gaze to the water. "Which lies are you talking about?"

"Yours. Mine. And, what if… If Jamie… If he dies? I'll never get over that. I can't deal with anything else at the moment."

"Gotcha. Bad timing all around. Can I walk you back to your car?"

"It's over by the park. I'll take light rail to get over there." They turned uphill toward the station.

Karen's phone buzzed several times. A number of texts had piled up on her. She must have been in a dead spot for cell phone coverage on the pier. The first two were from Sophie. *Damned dead zones.*

The first asked if she could go out with Poe. He wanted

to go to a local bookstore for an author reading on Capitol Hill. They could have passed on the sidewalk. The bookstore was half a block south of Cal Anderson Park.

The second text was Robbie giving Sophie the go-ahead as long as she was home by 10:30. *Great.* Karen was pretty sure that Robbie had no idea Poe was using Sophie as a beard, but that didn't really matter, did it? They were friends and she guessed there was no harm in Sophie going with him.

The last text was from a number she didn't recognize, and it came with an attachment. The text said: *Mama Gong talking in the car on our way to tonight's party.*

She held it up for Court to see, and his eyes lit up. She played it, but it was in Chinese and Karen didn't understand any of it.

Court tilted his head as he listened. "Shit. Can I take this?" he asked, holding up her phone.

"You understand Chinese?" Nothing could have surprised Karen more.

"Yeah. I had a Chinese nanny when I was a kid and lived in China for a year before I went to college. This is Mandarin."

"Wow, okay. But, I'm not sure I want to hand that over. I can forward the message to you. I want you to tell me what it says first."

"Actually," Court said, still holding her phone, "I might be able to get the tech genius to get locations off the phone. It won't work if you just forward the message for me. I promise, I'll take good care of it and get it back to you as soon as possible."

"Fine. Let me text my daughter to let her know I won't be on my phone."

"Can you unlock it for me while you're at it? So we can access it at the station?"

Karen considered the information to be found on her phone. She'd wiped all her ex-clients' contact info, but she deleted her contacts anyway. She logged out of her social-media applications and deleted her email accounts. Everything was backed up in the cloud. She'd learned her lesson about sloppy email maintenance the hard way and had cleaned up her act since last year. When she handed Court her phone back, there was practically nothing left on it. She'd re-install everything when she got it back.

"Okay. Now tell me. What was the message about?"

"It's a woman talking in Chinese. She's taking an order about an outright purchase to be brokered at a party soon. She's claiming she has the right boy for it in mind."

"Jamie?"

Court nodded. "Chinese isn't very precise with tenses, and I got the sense she doesn't actually have him right now. I think she's being cagey with the guy she was talking to."

Karen blanched as his words sunk in. *A long-term buy.* "Shit. How does this tie in to his fake text and the phone in the trash can?"

"Well, it could have been Mama Gong trying to throw doubt on things. Dumping the phone makes it untraceable, and his last known shows up at a place where he spends a lot of time."

"It's kind of pathetic that I'm hoping he's with a sex trafficker, isn't it?"

"Considering the alternative…" Court's voice trailed off with implication.

Karen felt a twinge of excitement. This could help with Cami's investigation. Damn. She wasn't going to let herself be dragged back into that.

Court listened to the message again. "Yeah. This is definitely an outright buy. And that voice is one I've heard before. Unfortunately, I've only heard it on some voice recordings. She's remarkably good at not being seen."

"Did she actually mention Jamie by name?" Karen asked.

"No, there is that. Frankly, it's a tossup between a serial killer and the sex trade… between the two of them, you might never see Jamie again."

## 37

Karen grabbed a pillow from the couch and hugged it against her. She was relieved to be home. Her face hurt, her ankle hurt, and she was exhausted. Ozzie had come through with information on Madam Gong, and the police were doing what they could to find her. But Court had said he was pretty sure Madam Gong didn't have Jamie. So where was he?

She kept coming back to him being with the killer.

The short light-rail ride from downtown to Capitol Hill had been uncomfortable without her phone. Without being able to hide behind her screen, she found herself watching the people around her.

Making up stories about these strangers' lives only provided so much entertainment. The bored faces, the eyes glued to screens, the lack of human interaction was almost too much for her. Was she normally so shut off from the world? A parking ticket waved cheerily at her from under her windshield wiper when she got back to her car. At least the rush-hour traffic had calmed down and the trip back to the Eastside was short.

More unsettling had been her latest conversation with Court. Her finger still tingled from where she'd touched his scar. It had been as intimate as the kiss they'd shared last fall.

Two times now, she'd been alone with him and they'd gone to the personal. There was something growing between them, whether or not it was a good idea. Court was a cop, she used to be a sex worker, and now she was a P.I. who had broken the law. Given how easily it came to her, she had absolutely no doubt there was more law-breaking coming her way.

Add in that future work with other attorneys on criminal-defense cases would have her questioning cops about their busts. Delving into their cases and mistakes was not going to endear her to anyone, including Court.

Karen found an open bottle of chardonnay and poured herself a glass. On the counter was a note from Robbie, along with his phone. He must have been home when she texted.

*Heading to Chicago for work. Back on Thursday. I have work phone with me. Use this 'til I'm back.*
XOXO R

He left a copy of his itinerary on the counter. His flight was departing in less than half an hour. Karen couldn't remember him mentioning this trip. He went on so many.

Karen opened the phone and saw a text from him from his other phone checking in. He really could be a sweet guy.

The last text from Sophie was confirming that the reading should end around nine. Karen let Sophie know that she was on her dad's phone and to text her there, and that she'd be happy to pick her up from the transit center if the connecting bus closer to their home was going to take forever.

Sophie texted back a big smiley kissy face and a photo of the pallid poet she had gone to hear. There was a bigger audience than Karen expected, though everyone appeared to be dressed in black, with dyed hair.

"Okay, girl," Karen said to Aspen, "wanna go for a walk? It's gonna have to be short. Mama's ankle isn't happy right now."

Aspen's tail thumped against the floor a couple of times before she rose slowly to her feet. She hobbled over to the front door. They'd make a pretty pair together. Karen found the adjustable leash and attached it to Aspen's collar. She flipped the tags so they all lay in the same direction and ran her fingers around the inside of the collar along the dog's neck, checking for new lumps or bumps and smoothing the fur underneath.

"Good girl," she said as she led the dog outside.

The summer heat had dissipated and the night air had taken on a welcome coolness. The last edges of sunlight peeked through the trees along the horizon across the street. Aspen limped alongside her, tail wagging as she explored the smells on the sidewalk.

For a while after Maria had launched her campaign against her, Karen had taught Aspen to shit in Maria's front yard. It was one of the nastiest, passive-aggressive things she could do without getting physically violent. She didn't regret

Aspen's big dumps, but now she held her back from the Wells' yard.

Maria came out of the front door with an awkward glance back inside. "I'm making sure she's not letting that dog crap on our yard again."

She hustled out to Karen and dropped her voice. "I only have a minute. Is there any news?" Then, in a shout toward the house, "I know you've let her poop here plenty of times. We're sick of it."

"I can't control where she poops," Karen said, matching Maria's volume. Then, she lowered her voice. "Sorry, I am really just walking Aspen. What's Mitch doing home so early? I thought he was bowling on Monday nights."

"You damn well can." The look of crushed hope transformed Maria's face into a wrinkled mess. "Bowling was canceled tonight."

"I am sorry, but there's nothing new for you, Maria. Jamie's picture is up all over town. All his friends know to call me." She wasn't about to tell her that Jamie was probably still alive but someone was trying to hide where he was —a killer, a sex trafficker, a conversion therapist? She didn't think any of those would be a comfort to Maria.

"That's right. Get that dog away from my azaleas." Maria turned back toward the house. "I need to go in. Mitch is in a really foul mood tonight."

"Maria, wait. Do you know anything about Morena and Garland Paker?"

Maria stopped in her tracks, stiffening and came back close to Karen. "What do you know about them?" She cast a glance back at the house.

"I've met them both recently. Their son Carmen was killed eight years ago. They're… housing teens…"

Maria put a hand up to her mouth. "Could Jamie be with them?" She cast a glance back to her house, and her face changed into a hardened mask. "He said he was bowling."

"Maria?"

"Maria?" Mitch Wells bellowed from the front door. "Get back in here. Now."

Maria grasped Karen by the shoulders, shaking her hard. "Do you think Jamie is with the Parkers?"

Aspen barked at her, and Karen ordered her to sit. "What would that mean? What are they doing with those kids?" Karen shook Maria off. "Maria?"

Maria's mouth opened and closed as if she were about to say something when Mitch suddenly reappeared with a shovel in his hand, charging toward them. He raised it, swinging for Aspen's head.

Karen yanked Aspen away and shortened the leash tight as she backed off the driveway into the street. "You son of a bitch. How dare you come at my dog? Big man with a shovel. You think you're hot shit because you can beat your kid and your wife and get away with it? Not gonna happen with me, buddy. You don't scare me."

Maria retreated to the front door, hands crossed over her chest, mouth hanging open. Mitch glared at Karen. "You keep that animal away from my yard, or there will be hell to pay, you lousy whore."

Aspen barked a deep warning growl, and her hips wiggled in preparation to attack. "Sit. Sit, Aspen. Stay. He's not worth it," Karen said. "And he'd taste bad."

Karen held her ground with Aspen tethered close, sitting unhappily and growling. By this time a few neighbors had come out of their homes and hung along the edges of their driveways.

"Get out of here," Mitch said, swinging his shovel in her general direction.

Karen spread her feet shoulder-width apart and into a relaxed ready stance. She smiled her most indulgent domme-y smile and dropped her voice into a sultry alto. "Make me, you little man-child."

Mitch rushed at her, swinging high with the shovel, his face flushed red, his lips parted and his teeth showing. Karen sucked in her breath, certain she'd read him right. She was ready with a solid block and counterstrike to end this deadly game of chicken if she had to.

Mitch brought the shovel down hard right next to her, hitting the pavement with a loud *thwang*. "Fucking cunt."

"Sticks and stones."

Mitch stepped up into her face. "Watch it, you stupid bitch. I will show you what a man can do to little cunts like you."

Karen held her ground. "I give about zero fucks, Mitch," she said, her voice still low and calm. She poked a finger against his chest. "Don't you dare threaten me or my dog ever again. I don't put up with that shit."

Mitch raised himself up to his full height, his fingers gripping more tightly around the shovel still in his hand. A handful of neighbors had moved closer, forming a circle behind Karen.

Mitch's lips twisted and he stepped back a pace, then two. He spun around and stomped back to his house, throwing the shovel angrily onto the front lawn. He slammed the front door.

Karen turned to the magical support group behind her. "Can someone get Maria out of there? I'm worried he might kill her. She's his easiest target."

Tommy and Craig Summerville stepped forward. "We'll take care of her, Karen. We'll call the police and bring her to our house."

Karen dropped down beside her dog, smoothing down her fur, calming her. "Good girl. Big ugly man was very rude, wasn't he?"

Karen tugged at the leash to get Aspen moving again. As they got to their yard, Aspen tensed, focusing on something Karen couldn't see. She pulled hard to the right, running toward the back yard, barking. Her collar broke open and she was off. Karen caught up with Aspen at the closed gate as the dog barked and dug at the ground.

All Karen could see was a pair of gray squirrels chasing each other in an elongated spiral up the trunk of a fir tree. She grabbed Aspen gently by the fur on her neck.

"Poor girl. There's nothing there. Let's go inside now."

Karen led Aspen back into the house and examined the leather of the collar. The side against Aspen's neck had taken on a smooth sheen from rubbing up against her fur. The rivets had come apart at the buckle end. She'd need to buy a replacement. She looped the collar over a coat hook by the front door and headed down to her office, Aspen close at her heel.

She went online to search for dog collars. The first image that popped up contained a rainbow of dog collars. She shuddered as the images of the dead boys in their collars filled her mind. Had the killer ordered the collars with 1-Click?

All the colors of the rainbow were there. She counted the colors off on her fingers again, singing the children's tune in her head. *"Red, orange, yellow, green and blue, indigo and violet, too."* The song might not be scientifically accurate, but the colors were lining up just right.

Karen clicked on the darkest purple in the selection. That would be the next one on the killer's list if he was actually following the rainbow.

Karen's insides twisted as she stared at the collar. Everything around her went dark except the image on the computer screen. It was the exact color she'd seen at Donna's house in the Amazon box. A purple cat collar had no connection to dog collars and dead boys.

Karen closed her eyes and went through the things she'd picked up. Everything put together in context went to creepy really fast. A collar. Latex gloves. The cleaning brushes and the collar were both purple. Violet was the next and last color of the rainbow. Violet, purple—same color. Hell, Donna's hair had a purple stripe in it. Karen hadn't looked at the shipping label, but she was willing to bet there was a dog collar listed.

Donna was a woman. She couldn't have anything to do with the killings. Could she? Was she coordinating her cat's collars with the boys' as she held them in her basement? No way.

Court was right. Karen was casting about wildly for explanation anywhere she could. *And yet.* And yet, Donna knew all the victims. She admitted to giving them rides. She was showing up *everywhere*.

Karen opened her best database, the one that cost her a fortune in monthly subscription fees, and plugged in Donna's name.

———

Karen developed a chronology of Donna's life. She approached it in an orderly fashion, one step at a time, trying to prove her latest crazy theory wrong.

Donna was only thirty-four years old. Karen would have guessed she was a youthful fifty. She was born Donna Jean Calhoun in July 1984, and she became Donna Richards when she married Billy Joe Richards in February 1998. Her son, Blake Calhoun Richards, was born at the end of September 1999.

She married at fourteen and gave birth to a son at barely fifteen. One of Donna's cousins, a Peggy Sue Calhoun, had a penchant for family history and had put up a comprehensive family tree on a genealogy website. She'd posted a thorough family tree for Donna's side of the family. Donna had eight brothers and no sisters.

Karen found a dozen articles in various papers about Donna's father, a traveling tent preacher. He spent his life making a circuit all around Southern Appalachia. He died at the same time as three of Donna's brothers—all from botulism from a "spoiled can of green beans"– according to one article, when Donna was fourteen, a month after she was married.

At the time, she and her husband were living in the family home. When questioned why she hadn't eaten the green beans, she claimed she had nausea from her pregnancy and wasn't eating much of anything. Her husband had been out on the road during the accident.

Billy Joe was also a mobile preacher. Karen found a newspaper article on her husband's death, except it wasn't a car accident like Donna had told her. She had made that up. Her husband had been murdered during a break-in. The news reported that the family was asleep when three men broke into the home. One of the men tied Donna up while the other two killed her husband. They had used the wood-pile ax to chop off his head.

Blake, aged six at the time, slept through the entire thing. He woke in the morning to find his mother tied to a chair with his father's head on her lap. He untied her and they called the police together.

Karen pictured the little boy waking up and walking into a scene like that. It could totally mess him up, especially if he hadn't received specific trauma care after the event. Given the fact they were living in rural Appalachia, she doubted he'd been given any counseling.

Could Donna be covering for her son? That kind of made sense. Donna had said Blake was dead. And yet, there was no death certificate anywhere for a Blake Richards.

The sensation of *knowing* she was right flooded through Karen. She rushed upstairs to call Court, tell him she was absolutely certain this time. She stopped halfway up. Did she have the evidence she needed? Was she rushing things again?

What was she going to say? *"I saw a purple cat collar at Donna's house. Donna is color coordinating her hair and her cat's collars with that of the victims."* Karen bet that would fly well.

Well, add in that she admitted to giving kids rides to

Harbor House, and that she knew them all. Every single one of them. And she had been asking all sorts of questions about the investigation. Wasn't that what killers did? Insert themselves into investigations?

But she'd been wrong about Jolly. And the Parkers. She had to be certain about Donna before bringing anything to Court or else she'd appear like the P.I. who cried wolf.

Instead of calling Court, she called Maggie. She had to get this right.

"I'm coming over," Maggie said after Karen filled her in on what she already knew and suspected. "We can work on her history together and get it all straight. You're right in wanting to have all the pieces together before going to your cop friend."

"We could go over there, demand to see what's in that basement of hers."

"You know she's not doing this alone. Some man is involved. We can't barge in there without knowing what we're facing."

"I feel like we're running out of time."

"I know, I know. But Court is right. Let's do it the right way and then take it to the police."

"They'll waste even more time confirming our work."

"It's only been a little over a week. There is still time."

"Every day that we let slip by is a day he's being hurt. Starved."

While she waited for Maggie to get there, Karen checked on Sophie. Her little blue dot showed up at Molly Moon's. It was nine fifteen. Karen did the mental math in her head. If the reading had ended at nine, and they were getting ice cream now, she'd be on a bus by nine thirty or so.

That would mean her getting home around ten thirty, depending on the bus.

Sophie accounted for, Karen dived back into her efforts to trace Donna. If Blake were alive, and they were doing this together, then she could start by proving he hadn't died. At least death records were easy to come by.

By the time Maggie arrived, half an hour later, she had traced Donna and her son's path from western Kentucky to Seattle, a meandering northwesterly route across the country. The two didn't stay anywhere for more than a couple of years. It was an odd path for someone who had grown up so fast and young in a place like Kentucky.

Karen didn't feel so good about the stereotype, but Donna had been raised in a poor Southern town, married to a much older man with theology degree from one of those Bible-thumping colleges. Donna had not finished high school. She came across as a smart, educated woman now, though, so how did she go from super-poor to owning a house in Green Lake?

Maggie set up her laptop across from Karen's. They worked on various parts of the puzzle, checking in with each other.

"It's weird. Donna owns the house in Green Lake without a mortgage," Karen said. "She bought and sold homes at a profit every time she moved."

"How'd she get started?" Maggie asked. "You don't go from poverty to home ownership anywhere very easily."

"I don't know. Seed money?"

Maggie pumped her fist in the air. "Found it. There's a lawsuit with the manufacturer of the green beans. They settled with Donna and her remaining siblings. The newspaper described it as an 'undisclosed substantial sum.'"

"Okay, so Donna got the settlement," Karen said.

"And… she sold the house her husband was murdered in for a loss. I'm guessing no one wanted to live in it after the murder."

Karen jumped up and stretched then leaned in to look over Maggie's shoulder to read the rest. Donna paid cash for a house in Dallas for three hundred thousand dollars, turned around and sold it two years later for four hundred thousand. She made money on real estate everywhere she went.

"None of this is illegal. Lucky. But not illegal," Karen said.

"And smart."

"Okay, after Dallas. She had a place in Phoenix. Then Salt Lake. Las Vegas, Sacramento, Portland. Finally, Seattle."

Karen tapped on the screen. She had been in the house, stood in the kitchen over the basement. Was Jamie being held right underneath where she'd so casually had iced tea?

**38**

———————

Karen stretched and stood up on tingling legs and feet. Her back was sore and her legs were half-asleep. She shook them out and moved into a yoga pose she hoped would counterbalance the rounded back she'd maintained while hunched over her computer screen.

"The weird thing is, I was getting along with this woman really well," Karen said.

"I hear Ted Bundy was a nice guy, too."

"That's comforting."

"Yeah, well," Maggie said. "Deep down, there was some part of you picking up on the odd things."

"I feel like a fool, though. I trusted her, and I spoke out of turn. I told Donna the cops were sure a male was involved. Mentioned semen. That means it has to be her and someone else. Blake? He's only what, eighteen?"

"Could be she has another man in her life. Hard to know since we don't know anything about Blake. Except he's not dead."

Karen sat back down at her computer. "Where do we go next? Do we have enough to take to the police?"

Maggie shook her head. "Almost. We are damn close. I started searching on news events around the dates they moved out of each state. Some very interesting shit is popping up."

Karen hadn't even thought of that angle.

"I've got a good start on Dallas," Maggie said. "Why don't you get into Salt Lake. See what you can find."

Karen logged into the database that linked every newspaper that had been digitized into one amazing search engine. They spent the next hour reviewing news articles about local deaths in each town Donna had lived in. Maggie sent Karen links to new information as fast as Karen could log it and put it on a spreadsheet.

A pattern emerged that put every fiber of her being on edge. Everywhere Blake and Donna moved, there were stories about one or two young gay boys being found dead. As she logged in the names and dates of all the deaths, it became clear that Blake could not possibly have been responsible for all the murders. He was way too young when the first occurred.

"You think Donna groomed Blake from a young age?" Karen asked.

"Well, if there is definitely male DNA on the current victims, it would point to that. Unless Donna has some other man helping her."

"Mother-and-son killing team?" Karen asked.

Karen felt a deep sense of sadness as they delved into the cross-country carnage. The first murder appeared shortly after they moved to Dallas. Donna's husband died only a year before that. Did having her husband's head chopped off in front of her turn Donna Richards into a killer?

Maggie stood and paced around the office. "Let's put it all together. Donna gets married at fourteen. That's a trauma in itself. Then her father and brothers die of botulism, from a meal she served them. Soon after that, her husband is murdered. Hell, I might lose it if all that happened to me, too."

Karen leaned back in her chair, shaking her head, her stomach lurching and spasming. "No. You know what? I think she was a psychopathic serial killer all along."

Maggie motioned for her to keep talking.

"It started with her getting married at fourteen. Being married to a thirty-eight-year-old preacher would make any fourteen-year-old snap, right?"

"It's pretty gross, sure."

"What if she was forced to marry him?" Karen opened the marriage certificate she'd copied and then Blake's birth record. "Yeah. Blake was born five months after they got married."

"Oh shit."

"Assuming he was full term, Donna is four months pregnant when she is forced to marry an older preacher by Papa. What if there's something more nefarious going on? Maybe she killed her brothers and her dad. As payback for the shotgun wedding?"

"This is pretty far down the rabbit hole, Karen," Maggie said with the same voice Court had used to caution her about jumping the gun.

"Okay. Okay. Fine. What we do know is that her father

and brothers died, but she didn't. Maybe she poisoned them, maybe she didn't. Not long after that her husband is murdered in cold blood. Maybe she did that, too."

"What reason would she have for killing him?"

"Maybe he was a jerk. Maybe she's a psychopath?"

Maggie rolled her eyes.

"Okay. Okay. Let's say Donna didn't do in her family or husband. Let's start with the husband's head on her lap. That's going to mess someone up, right?"

"Probably, yes."

"Even if they weren't in love, there would be some major shit going on inside Donna's head. Maybe she only felt responsible for his death by wishing him dead, and then along come the burglars."

"Okay."

"Imagine being a mom with a head on your lap, and your kid walks into the room. Anyone would be messed up from that alone."

"Start there. With what we know. Stop the speculating."

"Head on lap. Goes a little bonkers. Moves to Dallas. She suddenly starts killing teen boys."

"It doesn't actually follow all that well," Maggie said.

Karen deflated. "Okay. Let's go back to the deaths. Are there any indications they are similar to the ones happening here?"

"We need to figure out what happened with Blake. Does he have a record?"

"But Blake would have been too young for the first few years."

"Still," Maggie said. "Let's set Donna aside for bit and see what this new avenue can bring us."

Getting access to records on a juvenile was exceedingly tricky. Maggie helped her navigate through some of the harder bits. It didn't hurt that her mentor had years of experience and contacts that got her information Karen wouldn't have access to. Soon, they had Blake's documented history displayed across her screen. The story that emerged was one of multiple CPS visits based on reports of abuse and neglect.

"I can't believe you got this," Karen said.

"Technically, we don't have this." Maggie waggled her fingers at the screen. "You don't see anything."

"Got it."

"This is all extremely circumstantial. Lots of people move around to places where there have been murders."

"All locations? And the kinds of murders and disappearances?"

"Yeah. It's not coincidence, but proving that Blake or his mom were involved in them might be impossible. It could be that they moved every time CPS opened a case against Donna—they coincide with the killings in each case."

"What happens when a kid grows up with a mom who's a serial killer? Was he indoctrinated from a young age? Brought in later? Something had to explain the semen on the bodies."

"Is there a way to find out if the earlier victims had semen on them?" When do boys even start being able to ejaculate? Karen had no idea. Even though she had a son, boys were still a mystery to her. It wasn't until they became men that she understood them.

"Let me make some phone calls. See if I can get someone from Salt Lake or Dallas to talk to me. These cases were all left as cold and unsolved. There's going to be a few cops out there who are still looking for answers."

"And they probably aren't working this late at night."

"Nope. But, honestly, I think we have enough to be handing over to your friend."

Karen hesitated before calling Court. She'd been as sure about Jolly and the Parkers as she was about Donna. Was she the girl who cried wolf?

She didn't have his cell number memorized, so she called the station directly. His desk phone went to voicemail. He had told her he'd be working late.

"I'll drive over with everything we've got."

"So far. You take it, and I'll stay here to keep building this up."

Karen paused. "I can't go. Sophie's heading home soon. I don't want her walking from the park-and-ride in the dark."

"I can pick her up. She knows me, right?" Maggie asked.

The blue dot on the GPS app was on I-5, well north of the bridge to the Eastside. "This is weird."

She texted Sophie: *When will you be home? I have to go to police station ASAP. It's important.*

Sophie: *Heading to Poe's house now. He has a book I want to borrow by the poet we saw tonight. His mom said she'd give me a ride home from there. No bus!*

Relief flooded through Karen. She could leave and not worry about Sophie. Even though it meant Sophie would get home later than her curfew, she was getting a ride straight home and not walking from the transit center or the bus stop. Redmond was safe, but Karen didn't like the idea of her daughter walking that last mile and a half from downtown in the dark. Karen could go into Seattle without having to worry about Sophie.

TRAFFIC across the bridge was surprisingly heavy given the lateness of the hour. Where was everybody going this time of night? It had been a long time since she'd been part of the night scene in Seattle.

Karen parked in one of the many open spaces near the police building. Being inside wasn't the uncomfortable head trip it had been a few days earlier. The squad room was nearly empty by the time they got there, but Court was leaning over his cubby talking to Ivy.

"Karen, what are you doing back here?" Court asked.

"I left a voicemail. Told you I was coming."

Court glanced at his phone. "Sorry. Didn't get it."

"I know I'm right this time," she said.

Ivy and Court shared a look. *Crap*. Were they likely to believe anything she said? She took a deep breath and held up the shiny silver thumb drive.

"I have lots of evidence, and there's more to come."

Court logged into his computer and held out his hand for the thumb drive.

The file with all the links popped up. Karen laid out the chronology one step at a time. A widow and her son traveling around the country, the mom making amazingly lucky real-estate investments along the way, with various murders in each of their locals.

"So, you're telling me Blake Richards, who is barely eighteen now, is responsible for these killings? Dating back twelve years?" Court asked leaning back in his chair.

"Not alone. It's the mom and son. Together."

"Have you seen this Blake kid at Donna Richards' house?" Ivy asked Karen. "Didn't you say you've spent some time with her this week?"

"I haven't seen him. I was only there twice, and for a short time. Donna talks about him like he's dead, but she's used the word *gone*. Not dead or died. There are a couple of pictures of him around aged two, but nothing recent."

"You saw a purple *cat* collar? This is what made you jump to the conclusion that you were hanging out with a serial killer?" Ivy asked. "Really?"

"If Blake is involved, we can get a DNA match from the mom even if we can't find the boy himself," Court said quietly.

"Why not go over there and search her basement? Right now?"

Court and Ivy shook their heads in unison. "We have to tear this apart, step by step. I can't go tell a judge that this woman having a purple collar as proof."

"It's brand new."

"Karen, people buy collars for their cats all the time. Mostly, they're not serial killers. But the timeline you've come up with and Donna Richards' proximity to the victims does make sense."

The detectives took the conversation into a new realm, questioning Karen over and over about her methods and assumptions. The experience was completely different than when she'd been questioned about Berkeley Drummond's death in one of the little rooms down the hall. This was more like colleagues working through a puzzle.

As they picked apart every little detail, Karen felt more and more a part of the whole thing. Like she was really helping to solve this huge case. And that she'd helped bring these other murders to their attention, linking the trail of bodies across the entire country for the very first time.

Their conversation focused on the legalities. How to proceed so as to make sure every bit of evidence they gathered didn't get tossed out of court based on a technicality.

Karen appreciated that, but had a sense of urgency she didn't think they did. "If they're the killers, and they're holding Jamie, don't you think this is a little more urgent? She could be killing him right now. That fake text I got had to be her panicking or something."

Court motioned for her and Maggie to follow him into the hallway. "We've gone over the timeline. It's highly unlikely that they've escalated to the point where they're ready to kill again."

"Court, come on, we found his phone. In the garbage."

Court squeezed her shoulders. "I believe you. But we have to verify everything ourselves, double-check things before we can move on this."

"How much time, Court?"

"Hours. Go home."

"Isn't there some sort of thing where you can bust in if you think someone is in danger?"

"And how would we think anyone is in danger? Your gut feeling isn't enough to justify that kind of move. The urgency isn't there. We know they take weeks with their victims. Even if Jamie is with them, we need to get the legal side down."

"Even if he's with them? What are they doing to him? I saw those photos in there. It's not like they're having a tea-party. They're torturing him." Karen sounded a little hyster-ical even to herself.

"We don't have any reason to believe they've escalated their timeline."

"But you do. The text. She's panicking. They're panicking."

Court's grip on her shoulders tightened. "Karen? What exactly did you tell her? Why would she be panicking now?"

Karen met his eyes. "I… it… slipped out when we were talking. She asked me whether or not you were sure it was a man doing the killings."

His fingers dug even deeper into her. "What did you tell her?"

"That you found semen on the bodies."

"Are you fucking kidding me?"

Karen shook him off before he could leave bruises and met his eyes. "It was an honest mistake."

Court sighed and dropped his hands to his hips. "Go home, Karen. Let us take it from here."

"Let me help."

"You've helped plenty. Thank you. Really. You've done the groundwork here, and we need to take it to the next step with all the right paperwork and legal procedure. Karen, please go home." He pointed at the elevator. "I'll call you tomorrow."

Karen left, the sense of accomplishment fading with

each mile. Once home, Maggie greeted her from the kitchen. "I was grabbing a quick something before heading home." She sat at the counter with three bites left on a PB&J and a nearly empty glass of milk.

"No worries, find anything new?"

"I made a list of people to call tomorrow if your guy doesn't come through with a warrant on what you gave him. If we're lucky, some of the more recent deaths will have DNA evidence waiting for a match."

"He says it will be a few hours to get the warrant. Maybe tomorrow even."

Maggie wiped her fingers on a napkin and balled it up. "You should get some sleep. Let them do their work."

"You want to stay in Robbie's room? He's off for a few days."

"Nah. I have to take the dogs out. I would have brought them with me if I'd planned on being gone this long, but I need to get back."

After Maggie left, Karen opened the door to Sophie's room, not wanting to disturb her. Her room was dark, but the light from the hallway shone a beam on Sophie's bed.

She wasn't there.

It was way past Sophie's curfew. What happened to the ride home that Poe's mother had promised? Karen breathed in to calm herself. Sophie and Poe were really into this poet. Maybe they had gotten to talking and lost track of time.

Worry and anger vied against each other as she opened the Find My Friends app on Robbie's phone. A little dot showed Karen at the police station, reminding her that the device and the person were not always the same. Sophie's dot popped up next. Karen widened the map to help her pinpoint the exact location. *No. No way.*

Karen's feet went out from under her and she slid along the refrigerator to the floor. Sophie was at Donna Richards' house.

**39**

———

IF KAREN WAS RIGHT ABOUT DONNA RICHARDS, THEN THAT meant that Poe was Blake Richards. And a killer. Or an accomplice.

Poe had been to her house half a dozen times over the summer. He was weird and super quiet. But a killer? Wouldn't she have picked up on that? She'd read him completely wrong if this was true. And she had liked Donna Richards, too.

Maybe she'd been wrong about the Donna-and-Blake-as-killers theory. She texted Sophie again: *Where are you? You are out way past your curfew.*

She started to text Court, but realized she didn't have his number memorized and she'd left her phone with him at the police station. Instead, she called Court through the police department's switchboard to his desk for the second time that evening.

He didn't answer. His voicemail picked up again, and she left a message. "Sophie is at Donna Richards' house. I am going over there now. Donna's son, Blake, goes by Poe on the street. He's been here several times over the summer, and Sophie is *over there now*."

She jumped in the car. None of this made any sense. She wasn't close to Poe, but he knew her. He knew Sophie. And they had gotten particularly close over the last couple of days. Poe and Jamie were friends, too.

She must be wrong about Donna and Blake being killers. It was another unsubstantiated witch hunt she had sent Court on. She had twisted their history into something sordid. They moved around a lot for whatever reason, but they weren't serial killers. They couldn't be.

Sophie could not be with a killer. *This isn't happening. I've gone bonkers.*

She pushed the gas down to the floor as she hit the bridge. All the evidence she and Maggie had put together still fit the scenario. How the hell did Sophie fit into it?

The Dog Park Killer was interested only in boys. Homeless gay boys. Sophie was not remotely part of that scene. Karen had to be wrong about everything, just like she'd been wrong about Jolly and the Parkers. Except, she wasn't entirely wrong about either.

Karen made the curve onto I-5 north at a screech and blasted past the first exit to the University District at about ninety. Flashing lights came up behind her, and she hit the steering wheel hard with the palm of her hand as she pulled over onto the widest section of the shoulder she could find.

She lunged for her wallet and registration, rolled down the window and held the documents out for the officer.

"In a bit of a hurry, ma'am?" He took the documents and flashed his light into the car, over her and across the other seats. "Do you have any idea how fast you were going?"

Why do cops always ask that question? Their stupid little laser guns would tell them exactly how fast people are going.

"Sorry. I lost track of the speed. This car is kind of like that."

She wasn't about to tell him that her daughter was in the clutches of a serial killer. They'd think she was nuts. She'd laid out the whole story to Court and Ivy and neither of them saw the urgency she saw. Sounding paranoid was a sure-fire way of elongating this encounter.

"Stay in the car, I'll be back in a minute." The officer took his sweet time. She watched him in her rearview mirror as he sat in his car. As far as she could tell, he was doing nothing but killing time to annoy her.

She called Court's desk again. Yet another voicemail. "I got stopped by a cop for speeding. Can you get to the Richards' house? I'm afr—"

"Ma'am, put down the phone."

The cop had come back to the car, startling her. She lost the grip on the phone and it landed on the floor close to the passenger door.

As she lunged for it, the cop put a hand on her shoulder. "Leave it, and now please step out of the car."

"What for? Can't you just give me the ticket?"

Another cop car pulled up, and a female officer got out and approached them. This was all a waste of time. Why did they want her out of the car?

"Oh, you can't possibly think I was drinking," she said, suddenly conscious of the glass of chardonnay she'd had. It was only one glass. And she didn't feel tipsy. Besides, that was hours ago. "I'm in a hurry to get my daughter from a date gone wrong."

There, that sounded better than the truth.

"We'll let you go as soon as we can, ma'am."

She held her arms out to her side and touched her nose one hand at a time. She did this. She did that. She did all the things. She wobbled on her hurt ankle, but forced her body to submit. She was not going to let them win at this. It took every ounce of willpower she had to remain calm and not flip out. Every second they delayed her was putting her daughter in danger.

Her old hatred and mistrust for uniformed officers rose to the surface. They had never been helpful in the past, and now, here they were, playing this game to punish her for speeding. Karen leaned against her car, arms crossed, waiting for them to give her the ticket she deserved for speeding.

The female officer got in her car and drove away while the original officer wrote out a ticket. He took his time about it, making sure to write as slowly as possible.

He handed it to her in slow motion, and withdrew it from her as she reached for it, holding it high and out of reach. "You need to slow down. Nowhere is so important to get to as safety. You endangered yourself and others by driving ninety-three miles an hour."

She snatched the ticket out of his hands without comment. The cop followed her all the way to the exit at Green Lake making sure she didn't speed the whole way. Karen watched in her rearview mirror as she took the exit, relieved he hadn't followed her off the exit. As soon as she was sure he couldn't see her, she floored the gas again.

KAREN PARKED her car across the street from Donna's house. For the first time since she'd become a P.I., she wished she'd gone for the armed license. A gun might give her an advantage here.

Karen leaned across the front seat of her car to pick up Robbie's phone as the text notification dinged. Court was on his way to Donna's house. *ETA 20 minutes. Do not go in.* The fact that he hadn't sent squad cars ahead meant he didn't entirely believe her theory.

Sophie's GPS showed up in the center of Donna's house.

A light from the basement window was barely visible through a slit in the curtains. It flickered like a movie or television show might. Karen didn't recall seeing a television in the main floor of the house, so maybe they were downstairs watching a movie like normal people. But if nothing was wrong, why didn't Sophie answer her texts?

There were a couple of different scenarios here.

*Option one.* Karen would knock on the door, Donna would apologize profusely for keeping Sophie longer than intended and call Sophie up from the basement, and all would be well. They would all have a laugh over the coincidence that the P.I. who was looking for Jamie had a daughter that her son was dating. *Wouldn't that be nice? Ha.*

*Option two.* Karen would knock on the door, Donna would know the gig was up immediately and plunge a dagger into Karen's chest. If the woman had actually killed her father, husband, brothers, and all those other boys across the country, what would stop her at from killing Karen when backed into a corner?

*Also not likely.*

The reality was likely to be somewhere between the two extremes. Karen couldn't sit in the car and wait for Court to show up. She hadn't promised Court that she wouldn't go in, either. The very least she could do is scope the place out and see what she could from the outside.

Karen took a moment to tighten up the Ace bandage around her ankle to keep the swelling down and give her some stability. Her face had stopped hurting, at least as long as she didn't touch it. She dug around in her purse and found the bottle of pills and took two more and shoved the purse under the passenger seat. She moved her lock picks to her front jeans pocket.

After crossing the street, Karen tiptoed onto the porch, not wanting to alarm Donna to her presence. Karen pressed her forehead against the front window. A light above an armchair was on in the front room, but it gave enough illumination to see inside.

There was nothing on the mantle. The singular photo that had been there was gone. The room had been spare before, and now only furniture remained.

The stairway leading up was dark. The kitchen light shone brightly. On the table, a platter of cheese and crackers sat next to three glasses and a pitcher of lemonade. The family cruet set was nowhere in sight. Sophie's new bomber jacket was draped, inside out, over one of the chairs as if she'd sat down and shrugged it off.

Karen backed away and crept along the perimeter of

the house, looking in each window as she went. Donna was nowhere to be seen. Neither were Sophie or Poe.

The carport held the one car she'd ridden in a few days before. Karen used the phone to cast light on the dark interior. A row of suitcases covered with open cardboard boxes crowded the back seat. A cat carrier sat in the middle of it all. The flash of curious green eyes pushed her into action.

The cat was already in the car. You didn't put the cat in the carrier until you were ready to go. If Donna and Blake were about to get away, what were their plans for Sophie? There were only two seats available in the car.

*Crap.* She couldn't wait for Court to get here. Karen texted Court: *Can't wait. I'm at Donna's house. I'm going in.*

Karen limped her way back to the front door and rang the bell. She turned her phone's memo device to on and shoved it into her bra with the microphone up.

There was no movement from inside. Karen rang the bell again. This time, she saw Donna's head pop around the kitchen door frame. She smiled and came out of the kitchen, her hands working at a towel.

"Karen, what a surprise. I wasn't sure I'd actually heard a doorbell. I was listening to some music and thought I was hearing things."

Karen's mouth had gone dry and speaking was suddenly very difficult. "I saw Sophie was here, so I came over to get her."

"And I had no idea Sophie was your daughter until an hour or so ago. Isn't that amazing? Our two darlings becoming such close friends."

"You told me Blake was dead."

Donna smiled. "Oh, you misunderstood. That's all. I said he was gone, for he had sorely disappointed me. But that is all past now. Knowing he has your sweet girl in his life has changed everything. They're both welcome in my home."

"You were going to bring her home?"

"Oh, yes, but they decided to watch a show on television. They're in the basement."

"I texted Sophie, but she's not answering."

Donna turned and walked toward the kitchen. "That's because she left her phone up here. There's no reception in the basement anyway, and she needed a charge." Donna picked up the phone from the kitchen counter and held it out to Karen. "See? Technology is amazing and frustrating at the same time."

"Would you call her for me?"

Donna opened the door next to the refrigerator. "Sophie? Blake? Time to come up. Sophie, sweetie, your mama is here to pick you up."

Karen remained at the edge of the kitchen, not trusting her senses.

Donna stood at the top of the stairs, her hands on her hips. "Well, they must be very engrossed in that movie." She raised her hands and yelled down for them again.

A faint laugh track floated up from below, but neither teen answered.

"We might have to drag them off that sofa. Let's go down together, shall we?" Donna swept her arm in invitation.

Karen didn't know what to believe anymore. "Sophie?" She called out from the top of the stairs, not wanting to go down. "Sophie, it's time to go."

"Oh, my gracious, bless your heart. I'll go down first, you silly scaredy cat. It's just a basement."

Karen's phone buzzed in her bra. She ignored it.

Donna stepped ahead of her and disappeared down the steps into the flickering half-light. Karen followed, feeling each step as she went. Billowing white curtains lining the staircase created a dramatic airy effect. Her fingers trailed along the bannister loosely as a point of reference so she wouldn't lose her footing as she half-stepped, half-limped down the stairs. Her damn ankle throbbed with the exertion. She willed the drugs to kick in.

Karen's eyes were not yet adjusted to the darkness as she reached the bottom step. There was a flash of something coming directly at her face.

Instinct kicked in. She dropped into a forward fighting stance as she raised her arm in an upright block. A baseball bat landed hard against the middle of her forearm instead of her head. The crunching sound was muted and loud at the same time. Pain burst bright, and Karen dropped to her knees.

Donna's face twisted in anger and then amusement. "Oh, bless her heart. Bitch knows some moves, don't she?"

**40**

———

KAREN CRADLED HER INJURED ARM AGAINST HER CHEST, tucking her hand in her bra strap to hold it close. She rolled away from Donna, onto her knees, and jumped up onto her feet. She swayed as she caught her balance.

Donna swung the baseball bat casually, as if she were warming up for a friendly game.

"I wish you hadn't gotten involved, Karen. I really liked you." Donna's voice shifted into a soothing, cooing tone, like one used on a child. "I missed that your daughter has a different last name. I should have thought of that, maybe. You modern West Coast people and your modern ways."

"You won't get away with whatever it is you think you're doing here."

Karen's eyes adjusted to the gloomy interior. Donna stood between her and the stairs. To her left was a wall. To her right, Sophie and Poe were taped to chairs. They faced the opposite wall, so she couldn't see their faces.

Directly in front of them was a table covered in brocade

cloth, several candles, an ornate Bible, and a large curved knife. Off to the side, a laptop played some inane television show with a laugh track.

The same billowing curtains that lined the stairway covered all the walls, their bottoms pooling along the cheap linoleum floor. A rusty drain sat dead center in the room directly under Sophie and Poe. Karen hoped it was rust. The pure whiteness of the curtains contrasted starkly against the dingy creepiness of the rest of the room.

"What did you give them?" Karen asked, tilting her head toward the kids.

Donna kept her distance, but she continued a slow gentle teasing swing of the bat. "A little ketamine. They're almost awake."

Karen had heard of ketamine. The only thing she knew about it was that it was used on animals and that it was a popular date-rape drug. Karen inched away from Donna.

The other woman seemed too relaxed for Karen's comfort. Karen's foot connected with something behind her, but she didn't dare tear her eyes away from Donna again.

She reached behind her with her good arm, trying to map out the room in her head. Her fingers ran into the familiar contours of a metal cage.

Cold fingers wrapped around hers. "Mrs. H? Oh, God, not you too."

*Jamie.* The remnants of her dinner lurched upward. She choked it back down. Being right never felt so wrong.

"Jamie, it's okay. It's okay. The police will be here soon."

Donna swung the bat toward her again in a criss-cross pattern. She jumped forward with a forceful swing.

Karen ducked. The clang of wood against metal jarred

her into action. She wrenched her hand free from Jamie's and jumped into a forward stance. She smashed the heel of her palm of her good hand up into Donna's chin.

Donna dropped the bat, arms in a wild crawl stroke as she fought for balance. Karen dropped back onto her injured foot into a back stance as her other foot lifted into a front kick, square on Donna's chest. The other woman stumbled backward but remained upright. She came back at Karen with an angry roar, long-nailed fingers spread wide like weapons.

Karen pushed past the searing pain in her ankle as she shot her leg out once more for a stronger, more forceful kick. She followed it by landing on her front foot and punching with her free hand straight at Donna's nose. She heard a satisfying *thwak* that was followed by a gush of blood.

Donna stumbled backward onto her butt, her hand flying to her nose. She examined the blood on her hand, a smile creeping across her face.

"Didn't think you had that in you, Karen." Donna crab-walked backward toward the stairs. She scurried upward and out of sight.

The door at the top of the stairs slammed with an ominous thud, followed by the clunk of the deadbolt snapping into place. Being locked in a basement with a crazy woman upstairs was probably better than being locked in the basement *with* the crazy woman.

Court was on his way, and even if they were locked in the basement and Donna had fled, they would only be down here for a few more minutes. Karen let out a breath and focused on freeing the kids. By the time help arrived, they'd be ready.

"BABY? SOPHIE, HONEY." Karen hobbled over to release Sophie from her bonds.

Sophie blinked with droopy eyelids, obviously working hard to open them at all, her unfocused eyes moving back and forth in their sockets. Karen took hold of the duct tape across Sophie's mouth. "This is gonna hurt a little." She ripped hard and fast without any countdown.

"Mom? WhyreyouhereWhashappening?"

"Don't you worry, baby. It's over," Karen said, tugging at the tape. "Donna's gone. She was all packed and ready to go. She just left us here."

Donna must have used an entire roll to wrap Sophie like a mummy. Karen grabbed the large curved knife from the altar. She wedged the sharp tip into a space in the duct tape close to the arm of the chair. She didn't want to slip and cut Sophie. Duct tape was strong, but it didn't hold up to a knife.

When she'd freed Sophie, she turned to Poe. She almost left him, but he looked so young and innocent. His mother was the obvious force behind all these murders. He was as much a victim as anyone else. She freed him.

Sophie leaned forward and stretched out her arms, wiggled her legs and toes. "I'm so confused. We were having lemonade. Why am I down here?"

Poe groaned and dropped to his knees. He crawled to the altar and laid his torso across the Bible, weeping.

"Mrs. H? Any chance you could get me out of here?"

How had she forgotten Jamie? He sat, huddled against the cage, a purple collar around his neck his only clothing.

Karen hugged Sophie. "I'm going to help Jamie. I'll be right back."

"Jamie?" Sophie turned in her seat. "Oh my god. Jamie?" She stood, teetered with her arms flying out for balance and sank back into her chair.

The lock on the cage was a simple padlock. Karen fished her picks out of her pocket.

Jamie hugged his legs tight against his chest. "Poe said he'd work things out for us."

Karen set the tension bar and slid the pick in, finding all the pins on her first attempt and opening it in less than thirty seconds. "What do you mean?" she asked as she helped Jamie out of the cage.

He launched himself into her arms. "Poe. He didn't want to do any of this. His mom made him. He knew that you would come for Sophie and find me."

Poe was still draped across the Bible, sobbing. Sophie stood with a hand on her chair to steady herself and lurched toward them. Karen gathered both children into her arms. "It's okay. It's all over now. The police will be here soon to help."

Sophie wiped at her tears. "I think we could find Jamie some clothes, okay, Mom?"

Jamie pointed to a shelf in the corner on the back wall. "Over there. My clothes are on the top."

Underneath were three more shelves. Folded clothes, shoes, books and other belongings were neatly arranged around photographs of all the victims. She grabbed Jamie's clothes without touching anything else. The police would want it all for evidence. Next to the shelf was a stack of seven guitar cases. A large backpack leaned against the wall, next to piles of rope.

Jamie's clothes hung on him. He tucked in his shirt and pulled his belt to its last notch. "They tried to make me eat. I just couldn't most of the time."

Whatever adrenaline that had gotten her through this was wearing off. The pain in her arm and ankle was hitting her hard now. She stumbled over to one of the chairs and sat down. "I think my arm might be broken."

Karen had no cell service in the basement, so she couldn't call 911 or ask Court when he'd get there.

"Okay, kids. I think we have another ten minutes before help arrives."

Jamie and Sophie dropped onto the floor in front of her. "You'll be okay, Mom, won't you?"

Karen nodded and swallowed the rising pain-induced nausea. "We're going to all be fine. I know a really nice cop who's on his way over. He'll get us out, no problem." Karen cradled her injured arm.

Poe turned from the altar and fell onto the floor, flat, in front of them. "I'm so sorry. So so sorry. I tried so hard to make things right. But she wouldn't let me." He put his hand on Jamie's leg. "I love you so much, I couldn't let her do what she did to the others to you. Blake is evil. I'm not Blake. I'm Poe, okay? Just Poe. Poe's a good boy."

Jamie moved over so that Poe's head was cradled in his lap. "Be quiet, Poe. We'll work this all out later, okay?"

How had Karen not seen how fucked up Poe was? He had come across as weird, not… whatever the hell this was. What had been the plan? Their car was packed, and Donna and Blake were leaving.

Karen had interrupted their plan. Why had Donna drugged Poe if she intended to take him with her? Maybe that had changed, too. That would all have to be figured out later. She relaxed into the chair. Pain she'd managed to ignore or hold at bay flared through her. That baseball bat had done some damage. Karen breathed in and told herself it was only a matter of time. Court would be here soon. She'd get to a hospital and suck down some sort of opioid and all would be well.

When the door at the top of the basement finally screeched open, Karen breathed out a deep sigh of relief. She was more than ready to get the hell out of there.

"Come on, kids. Let's get the hell out of here." Sophie helped her up. Poe clung to Jamie.

"Court? We're down here."

Karen hobbled over toward the stairs leaning on Sophie for support, the others close behind.

Donna stood at the top of the stairs, a blowtorch in her hand.

**41**

———

Donna had a smile on her face, but it was one of those fake fixed smiles Karen associated with psychopaths. "You forced my hand. There is no way any of us are getting out of here." She slammed the door shut and locked it. She threw her keys past them and into the far corner of the basement. They skidded across the top of the shelf holding the victims' belongings and fell behind it.

"Quick, Jamie, get the keys," Karen said. Jamie spun away after them.

"You realize the police will be here soon. They'll rescue us," Karen said. She reached her good arm out and around, herding Sophie and Poe behind her. They might still be able to get past Donna and out the door.

Donna laughed as she held a light up to the torch and flicked the dial. A bright flame burst to life and cast a strange blue glow over Donna's face. "By then, it will be too late. Did you know certain fabrics burn faster than others?" Donna tossed the lighter on the ground and adjusted the flame on the torch to high. Her eyes fixed on the small bright flame. "I chose these curtains because they would act as tinder for the whole house."

"You were planning to burn the house down all along?"

The smell of gasoline wafted down the stairs as Donna descended, slowly dragging the blowtorch along the curtains. The fabric caught and licked its way upward.

"You messed up my plans by coming here. To get your brat."

"Were you really going to kill your own son?"

Donna pointed her flame at Poe. "That… that abomination." Her face twisted as she spat out the words. The blowtorch died, but she appeared to not notice. She continued to hold it toward the curtains as if it were working. Not that it mattered much, as it had already done its job.

"There's no getting out of here, Karen. None of us are leaving here alive. It's over. And I'm tired."

The flames from the top of the stairs were gaining traction. Smoke moved upward, so they had a while. The rest of the curtains surrounding the room would soon be ablaze and the wood studs that were probably behind them would catch all too easily.

Donna finally noticed the torch had gone out and dropped it. It rolled down the stairs and off to the side.

"I've got the keys," Jamie rushed back to Karen, putting them in her good hand.

Donna snarled. "It's too late. I layered gasoline throughout the kitchen and lit that first."

"Jamie, the window," Karen called. "Behind the altar. Get the curtains away from the altar and go out the window. All of you. Now."

"Mom?" Sophie asked.

Karen shrugged her off. "Get the window open. Get out. I'll follow you."

Donna picked up the bat from the floor. Karen had overlooked it in her haste to free the children. "And now for some fun, eh? I might as well enjoy the few minutes I have left. Go down in a blaze of glory." She shouted it out like a preacher calling to his congregants.

Karen finally put two and two together. "You were going to kill Blake and Sophie as stand-ins for you and Blake. You were going to leave Jamie in the cage and let that be the answer to the whole serial-killing question. The authorities would think you and Blake were in on it together, killed Jamie and then had a suicide pact."

"Good for you, Karen. Of course, I didn't know that this little Sophie belonged to you."

"You knew I was looking for Jamie."

"Oh, yes. You were getting close, weren't you? I thought my text this afternoon would have sent you off the rails for a bit longer than it did. Little did I know your girl was so close to my boy. That you were that oh-so-cool lady Blake has been going on and on about. But he knew, didn't you, Blake?"

Blake stood close to Karen, immobile.

Karen put a gentle hand on Blake's shoulder and squeezed it. "Blake turned against you. You had to end things and get rid of him because he was a liability."

"You. You're the one who turned him against me. With all those calming words. Reassuring him it was *fine* to be homosexual."

"You sent him hunting," Karen said. "That's how it all

worked, isn't it? You sent him out as Poe to find boys to target."

"Blake wanted to save other boys. To help them find the peace he found in salvation and Jesus. Until you came along."

"You don't believe that. Not for a minute."

Donna swung the bat hard against the ground. "You don't know what I believe." Her face turned beet red with the exertion. She turned and slammed the bat against the wall four more times, yelling with each crash.

Karen had backed up until she was even with the altar. Jamie had shoved everything off it and stood on top of the table. He ripped the curtains down, and Sophie balled them up and threw them away from the growing fire.

"No one would have known until I was far away."

"But I could prove it was Sophie, not you. Why bother using a substitute?"

"Yes. That's the rub, isn't it? I only needed three hours to get to Canada, but your meddling has messed that all up. Now… well, we'll have to make do with a final little party here."

Donna's eyes lost their focus. It was as if she had shifted into another world all on her own. Her eyes were fixed on the altar, a calm smile on her face.

Karen didn't trust the serenity. "You're pretty proud of yourself, aren't you?"

Donna tipped her head to the side, as if considering the question. "Proud? Well, this is certainly not my proudest moment. Getting caught is nothing to be proud of."

"How many people have you murdered?"

"Murder is such a harsh word. I like to think of it as taking out the trash. Cleaning up the world."

"Was killing your husband part of that cleanup?"

Donna laughed. "Oh, nice one. I knew I liked you, Karen. How did you figure that one out?"

"You're sick. Putting your son through that?"

Donna's eyes glazed over even more. "Oh, that was one of the best moments of my life. When he walked into the room and saw all the blood, his precious daddy's head on my lap… It was perfectly staged."

She glanced at Blake with a fondness that Karen hadn't seen her display toward him before now.

"His anguish was exquisite to behold. He loved his father so much. When he saw his dead daddy… oh… It was beautiful." Donna's lips pinched into a tight line. "He was too much like his father. Abominations, both of them."

Sirens blared in the distance. *Finally*. Even so, they were not close enough.

Karen stood between Donna and the three teens. Jamie struggled with the window.

"And your brothers? Your dad? It wasn't botulism, was it?"

Donna's brow came together, and she shook her head. "Oh, no, no. That was botulism. I just happened to know a bad can of green beans when I saw it. I lucked into that one. Though, to tell you the truth, it was hard to savor their individual agonies when they were all so close together like that."

"And yet you fed it to your brothers? Your father?"

"Who's going to think a little mite of a fourteen-year-old

girl is going to lie about a thing like that? It was easy. They weren't the first, though. Or my second. Or third."

Karen stifled her rising nausea at this confession. If Donna had already killed so many people by the age of fourteen, when had she started? Earlier even?

"No." Donna's eyes following the line of fire as it spread through the fabric. "There were others before that. Plenty. Too many to keep track of."

"You're sick."

"Who's sick, Karen? People who put up with misery or people who do something about the misery? The way I see it, I am removing pain. Those children were in withdrawal from their crack-whore mother. My brothers beat their wives and fucked me raw. My husband was a sodomite who brought disease upon us. They all deserved what they got."

"But these kids? They didn't deserve to be tortured. Murdered. For being gay?"

"The first was a surprise," Donna said. "He came to a prayer meeting and the pastor helped him find God's blessing. As he left, he turned to me and said 'If only this would last forever. I am so weak, I fear I shall be overcome with my base desire and ruin everything.' That was such a brilliant moment. All I had to do was convince him that there was a way for his purity to last forever." Donna listed off ten names. "Then Blake could help me. That's when we were able to do so much more." Another six names rattled off her lips. Sixteen kids, not including the most recent six found in Seattle.

"Why did you change things here?" Karen asked. "Why the dog parks? The collars? You drew attention to yourself by making yourself obvious."

Donna turned on her. "Do you have any idea what it's like to go about your life's work and have zero acknowledgement?"

"Attention? This is about getting attention?"

"All the others, they died cleansed of their sins. Their souls were released pure and simple into heaven, away from the temptations of this world. And *no one even noticed.*"

"Their loved ones did. Their parents. Their families."

"And yet, no one got the point. The whole reason for it."

"You're delusional."

"And you're not?"

"You're a killer. Plain and simple. You do it because you like it. Admit it. You killed because you wanted to. It felt good. It's an excuse you told yourself."

"Have you never wanted power? Control?" Donna laughed. "Oh, but of course you have, Miss Dominatrix. You know exactly what I'm talking about. You don't want to admit it, but we are cut from the same cloth, you and I."

"No," Karen said. "We are nothing alike."

Donna waved her hand in the air. "Deny it all you want. We found our power in different ways. I found it in the way their eyes widen as the truth of what is happening to them seeps in. The very awareness of death fills them up, terror overcomes them, and they look at you like you are God. Because, you know what? Right in that moment, when you drain them of their last heartbeat? That's exactly what you are. God."

She needed to keep the woman talking until the kids were free.

"Why bring your son into it?" Karen asked.

Donna was breathing heavily, her face flushed and her

eyes shining with an ecstasy worthy of an old-time hellfire-and-damnation preacher. Keeping her talking was the only thing Karen could do for the moment.

"Blake was a good little helper until someone told him it was all right to be gay. Some little do-gooder who loves the sin as much as the sinner." She pointed an accusatory finger at Karen. Donna's mouth dropped open for a second before spreading into a wholly disconcerting grin.

"And to think, you never told me you were Sophie's mother."

All those street names and double identities had made it hard for Karen to see the truth about Poe. Blake.

"You used your own child for… for…"

Donna cackled. "You're the one who told me they found semen on the bodies. How else would it have gotten there? Believe me, there's only one way to really get semen out of a man, isn't there?"

Tears streamed down Poe's face. He dropped to his knees on the floor next to Karen, facing his mother. "I can't believe you killed Papa."

Donna jutted her chin out. "Of course I did, you idiot. You think a real intruder would have spared me? Or you? You have always been such a disappointment."

Jamie called out from the window. "I can't get it open. It's totally jammed. Painted shut."

Karen edged her way to the altar. Jamie stood on the table, the window bottom at his chest height.

Karen scooped up the largest metal candlestick from the ground and handed it to him. "Break the glass. Get as much of the glass out of the frame as possible so we can climb out."

It was going to be a tight fit for any of them, but they could get through.

"No," Donna screamed as Jamie smashed the glass. "No, you don't." She rushed at them all, her baseball bat in front of her like a sword.

Blake lunged for her from where he knelt, grabbing her by the knees. The two of them tumbled to the ground. "Go. Get them out."

Donna shrieked. She swung the bat around, but he was on top of her and too close for it to be effective. She tossed it aside and lashed out at him with her fingers, scratching him anywhere she could. Blake held firm.

Sophie climbed on the table next to Jamie. Jamie and Sophie helped Karen up. The metal shrieked and the table collapsed under their weight, sending them sprawling. Without the table to hold them up, the window was above their heads.

Blake and his mother rolled on the ground, battling each other. Blake tore out great swaths of Donna's hair. She shrieked and cursed. The firestorm grew all around them, the ceiling now engulfed in flames.

Donna had wholly dissolved into a foaming-at-the-mouth lunatic. All pretense at humanity had evaporated, had gone up in flames just as quickly as the fabric along the walls.

Karen grabbed the chair that Sophie had been taped to, put a foot on it, and patted her knee as a step for Sophie. Jamie helped push her upward into the casement from below. Sophie cried out as shards of glass cut into her. Karen and Jamie propelled Sophie upward and out of the window, and she scrambled onto the front lawn.

With the window broken, Karen could finally hear the oncoming sirens. So close, yet nothing was visible on the street outside. Sophie knelt on her hands and knees on the front lawn, breathing in fresh air.

Karen turned to Jamie. "You next."

"Mrs. H. I can lift myself, you go next."

"We're not going to argue. You go, now."

"My guitar." He turned toward the pile of guitars in the opposite corner.

She shoved him against the wall under the window. "Jamie, I will buy you a new guitar. Leave it. Get out of here. Now." She braced her knee on the chair again, and he reluctantly put his foot on top and lurched upward.

He wriggled his way up onto the lawn. He turned around to reach down and pull her up. He couldn't do much from that angle in his weakened state.

"Go, make sure Sophie is clear. I'll be out as soon as I can."

She couldn't abandon Poe to a fiery death with his crazy mother. How guilty could he be? Blake had gained control of Donna and straddled her chest. His fingers closed around her neck. She pummeled him with ever-weakening punches.

"Poe, leave her. You need to get out of here, now." Karen was pretty sure she said the words, yelled them, even. The stairs had caught fire, and the dry wood—easy kindling —snapped and crackled loudly. Smoke filled the room; thick dark clouds filled the corners and roiled across the ceiling. They did not have much time before the smoke killed them.

Poe shook his head. "It's too late. You go. Leave us."

Donna's face was an unnatural blue and her arms fell

loosely to the side. Poe's grip around her neck remained firm. Her eyes grew wide one last time, and Donna's mouth gaped in a wild grin. Blake lifted his gaze to Karen's and all she saw there was a power-filled ecstasy—and a sense of accomplishment. He leaned back, dropping his hands and tilted his head toward the ceiling, his arms spread wide as if in supplication and prayer.

Karen turned her back on them and grasped the edge of the window. But the pain in her arm was too much. She didn't have the strength to get herself free.

**42**

———

KAREN TRIED TWICE MORE TO WORK THROUGH THE PAIN IN
her arm and pull herself through the window. Each attempt
left her weaker. Her lungs ached from the smoke and her
eyes stung. Karen dropped to her knees. Help should be
here soon. Jamie and Sophie would tell Court where she
was and he could save her again.

Karen dropped to her stomach, hoping for a bit of fresh
air, found it and filled her lungs.

The table! The tall end of it would be enough to get a
hold of, wouldn't it? Karen lifted the broken table onto its
side and leaned it against the wall, the unbroken metal legs
on top. She put the chair against the table and stepped onto
the chair. Pushing with her good foot, she used the metal
legs and table edge as the second and third rungs of a
makeshift ladder to launch herself upward.

Karen's palms shot through with new pain as she
grasped the broken glass around the casement to haul
herself up and out. She flopped out onto the grass, dragging

herself on her belly until her legs were free and once again on solid ground.

She pulled her knees under her and puked into the grass. Then turned back to the window, reaching down into the room, screaming for Poe.

She could barely see him through the smoke. He still straddled his mother's chest arms out wide in supplication, face heavenward. Flames licked at Donna's jeans, and coursed up her legs to meet Blake's pants.

Karen was barely aware of the activity taking place behind her. The bright flashes of emergency lights, screeching of tires, radios blaring, men shouting—none of it could make her tear her eyes away from the tableau inside the basement.

Poe's clothing was fully engulfed in flame. He didn't move or scream or do anything to save himself. The two bodies melded into one giant conflagration, a misshapen cross of human flesh.

Karen was vaguely aware of arms wrapping around her waist and lifting her away from the burning building. Cool air brushed across her face. A cool cloth. Warm lips against her ear.

It was Court. He shifted her into his arms. "Is there anyone else inside?"

Karen shook her head. "Not alive. It's too late."

The fire crew surrounded the house with hoses. Sophie and Jamie sat on the tailgate of an ambulance waiting in the street. They already had blankets draped over their shoulders and oxygen masks over their faces.

Karen wrenched herself free from Court, and engulfed

Sophie and Jamie in a group hug. They were both okay. They were both alive.

After a while, she turned back to watch the conflagration. Flames shot out of the roof of the house. Cracking booming sounds filled the air and the house collapsed inward into the basement. Dark plumes of smoke roiled upward into the pre-dawn sky.

The firefighters moved in, surrounding the house with hoses and squelched the flames, keeping them from spreading to the neighbors.

"We better get you guys checked out at the hospital," Court said.

Court pointed to the other waiting ambulances, but Karen refused to let go of either Jamie or Sophie.

"We all stay together."

---

THE ER TRIAGE at Harborview was fast and efficient. They put Jamie and Sophie in separate beds with a curtain between them. Karen opened the curtain so the two could still see each other.

The cuts from the shards of glass on Karen's hands and along her arms from the window were many but shallow. Only one required a couple of stitches near her elbow. She had a hairline fracture from her fight with the baseball bat, a sprained ankle, and a bruised face from earlier in the day.

Sophie had fifteen small cuts from the glass, requiring one or two stitches each, and one long prominent slash along her tummy that called for sixteen stitches. One team tended to Jamie while another tended to Sophie.

"I guess bikinis are out for a while," Sophie said as the doctor stitched her up.

"Depends on what kind of tattoo you get to cover it up," the doctor said. Karen was sure he was only half joking.

Karen perched on the side of Sophie's bed and held her hand as the team surrounding Jamie did their work. He had multiple injuries from his time in the basement. Only half of which, probably, were physical.

By the time they were done with the cuts and bruises, Jamie had dozens of little white plasters all over him, but his general mood was one of relief and happiness.

Maria Wells showed up an hour later by herself. She dissolved into an incoherent blubber as soon she saw Jamie. He looked ten times worse in the bright hospital light than he had in the basement. The cuts from climbing out the window were minor in comparison to the marks on his back and torso.

After all the bleeding wounds were tended to, Sophie and Jamie were placed in rooms for an overnight stay. Karen refused to be admitted; she would not leave Sophie. Maria grasped Jamie's hand with all the ferocity of a mama bear, not willing to lose him a second time. It was early morning by the time Sophie was settled in and sleeping soundly.

Robbie was still in Chicago. Karen called him to fill him in on the events of the previous night. He didn't say much while on the phone, but this particular kind of quiet unsettled her more than a screaming match would have. They would have a very difficult confrontation once he was home.

Court dropped by at noon to check in on Sophie. Sophie

was sleeping soundly. Karen played the memo she'd recorded to Court.

"Wow. Can't believe you got a full confession out of her like that," he said.

"Will you ever be able to know for sure? All the people she killed?"

"She left a trail. I wonder at the ones she killed when she was a child, though. That could be boasting. Or it could be true. We'll probably never know the full extent."

Karen blinked the weariness away the best she could. "There were so many."

"The more recent ones will be easier to prove if Blake left his DNA on them. He could have started helping her as early as age ten or eleven, maybe younger. He wouldn't have been disposing of the bodies until he got older. Or dumping semen on them. It took some strength to get these last few to their locations."

With Donna and Blake both dead in the fire, there wouldn't be a need for evidence for a trial, but the recording would be useful to survivors of other crimes. Maybe the families of all those boys she'd killed while traversing the country would have some closure.

Karen wasn't sure if she would want that kind of closure. Was it better knowing your child had been tortured and mutilated, or thinking your kid was a victim of a more random hate crime?

When Robbie returned home a few days later, the worst of their bumps and scrapes had healed. He brought them dinner from the Thai place down the hill and kept the topic of conversation to things like the upcoming school year and Brian's return home.

Robbie waited until Sophie had retreated to her room before lighting into Karen. "You almost got Sophie killed. Again. You have to find something else to do with your life."

"You can't blame me for everything that went wrong here. You were as encouraging about bringing strays into the house as I was."

"You are a fucking P.I., Karen. Why didn't you background these kids who were coming here?"

"It's not like they handed me their IDs as they walked into the house."

"You let him take our daughter to his house. You let her go."

"No. You were the one who said it would be fine for them to go to the bookstore together. We thought Poe was an okay kid with a messed-up family. We had no way of knowing he and his mother were a pair of psycho killers."

"Well, it has to stop. You can't keep working with all these dangerous people."

"All these…" Karen stopped short. She hadn't even told him about the case she had almost taken with Cami. He'd blow his gasket over that one. "I'll do better at keeping Sophie out of it. She's going to start school again, anyway. She'll be focused on that. Now that Jamie is home, she won't have as much reason to go into Seattle."

"You can't keep putting this family in danger."

"None of this has been my fault. I did what I could to keep her safe. I saved Jamie, too."

Robbie stood in front of her, puffed up and red-faced. "I can't take this anymore."

Their arguments often led to a hot session in bed to

smooth things over. This was not going to be one of those times.

"I'm serious, Karen. You have some sick need to get yourself into weird and crazy situations. And two times in one year, one of our kids has been almost killed." Robbie looked up at the ceiling, his usual sign of being done with it. Instead of reaching for her to make up, he squared his shoulders and left.

Karen watched from the window as he pulled out of the driveway and out of the neighborhood. Something fundamental had changed between the two of them.

# EPILOGUE

The last notes of the song hung in the air over the crowd filling Karen's back yard. After a couple of heartbeats, applause erupted, washing over Jamie, Mullet, and Sage. They stood at the epicenter of the gathering, bowing and blushing.

Karen had rented a small stage and put it against the back fence. She'd asked everyone to bring extra lawn chairs, and they'd set up a makeshift theater around the stage.

Everyone in the neighborhood had shown up except Mitch Wells. He had been arrested for his part in the conversion center in Shoreline. His bowling nights were a cover for volunteering there on Monday nights.

Jamie's stay in the hospital had started the healing process, but he faced months, if not years, of counseling ahead. Living on the street had forced him to grow up faster than any teen should.

The money he had earned through busking and survival sex had been used to help other kids eat and otherwise endure their life on the street. Jamie had agreed to work with the police to find Mama Gong and shut down that avenue of trafficking. Maria decided to go through the foster parent certification program specifically to foster teens in situations similar to Jamie's.

This was a day for celebration, and Karen focused on what was happening on the stage. For the first time in nearly a year, the entire neighborhood was partying.

"Thank you everyone," Jamie said. "I can't say I'm completely recovered yet, but I think I will be. Thanks to all of you. So, we're going to play a little cover song here…"

The trio counted off and launched into a Beatles tune, "All Right." A couple of people got up and danced off to the side.

Karen made her way inside to grab a couple more bags of chips to fill out the bowls on the serving table under the porch.

Brian followed her in. "Mom, can I give you a hand?"

She tossed him the tortilla chips and nodded to the fridge. "We also need a new tub of guac out there. And take the mango salsa, too."

Brian had been amazingly easy since his return from camp. He'd taken the news of his sister's abduction with a mature stoicism. The new rules about the house? Not so much. Robbie had decided that he would no longer spend time at the house if Karen was there. She was to leave the house on her weeks off and stay at her apartment, something she had ignored for the last six months or more.

Karen opened a fresh beer for herself and stood at the kitchen sink, wishing Robbie had come. They'd spoken only twice since she'd found Jamie. Sophie swore that his anger had subsided, and that he was keeping his distance to make sure he didn't end up saying something he regretted later.

Still, she had hoped Robbie would come to the party that she and Maria were throwing together. They were celebrating Jamie's safe return. Maria had gone to everyone in the cul-de-sac and apologized for her behavior to Karen and invited them to the party and concert.

Karen grabbed a fresh six-pack to add to the cooler. As she passed the door, the bell rang. Court Pearson stood on the other side, holding out a bouquet of peonies.

"I didn't think you were going to make it."

"Turned out to be a super-easy case."

"I thought you got it yesterday," Karen said as she took the flowers from him and inhaled their sweet scent. "I love peonies. How did you know?"

"I'm a detective, remember?"

"Come on in and we'll get these in some water."

She filled a vase and plopped the flowers in, arranging them so they could spread into a large pink mound.

A raucous laughter from outside drew them both to the window. Brian was up on the stage and waving his hands around.

"Brian's taken up magic?" Court asked.

"He got hooked at camp." He had gotten the patter down, as well as some pretty sly tricky movements. Even the adults were watching him. Their backs were to Karen, so she couldn't see their faces, but she imagined they were either rapt or amused. Brian's sense of humor was unusual, and he had a rather sardonic wit about him.

"Can I have one of those?" Court asked, pointing at the beer.

"Are you upset you didn't get to make an arrest?" Karen popped one open and handing it to him.

Court caught the overflow of beer at the top of the neck. "Nah. That's not so much as the why of it. And the how. We still don't get exactly how they managed the bodies. Blake wasn't a big guy. They hauled them to pretty remote locations. It's not like they drove up and rolled them out of the trunk."

Karen was hyper-focused on getting Sophie and Jamie out before the house burned down around them, and hadn't taken a full inventory of Donna's basement. She closed her eyes, trying to remember the details. White billowy walls. Guitars piled next to a shelf. Drain in the middle of the room. The altar. She opened her eyes wide as it came to her.

"The backpack! There was a ginormous backpack in the basement."

Court bobbed his head back and forth as he considered it. "Might have worked. The way they were wrapped in rope…"

More laughter and lots of clapping interrupted their conversation. Brian bowed to the crowd and Jamie stepped back up to the front. "I'd like to dedicate this song to Mrs. H. Where are you?"

Karen yelled from the window. "I'll be right down." She sprinted out of the kitchen and down the stairs, Court following her.

The crowd parted to let them through.

Jamie tinkered with the tuning on his guitar and nodded to Sage. She plucked out a bass line for a couple of measures before he and Mullet picked up on the guitar. It was a new tune, something Jamie had written over the last couple weeks.

He sang of being alone while not being alone. Throughout his captivity, he had believed strongly that his mother would find him. He sang of the hope he held throughout, the sadness around being betrayed by the man he thought he might love, the anger over what Blake's mother had done to him.

The sweet lamenting ballad was moving without being maudlin. It ended on a positive hopeful message. By the time they were done with the song, more than half the neighbors had tears streaking their faces.

Karen retreated from the limelight as the trio did another cover to lighten the mood, Court following her along.

"That answers some more of it," Court said. "Blake was fine going along with his mother, but he fell for Jamie."

"And Blake was smart enough to know that I was a P.I. with a different last name than Sophie, so he chose Sophie as the girl to stand in for his mother. He knew I'd keep close tabs on her."

"That was a huge gamble on his part."

"He couldn't go on living. Not with what he had done. His final act was to hold his mother down in the fire. And make sure we got out." It would be a long time, if ever, before she could forget the look in Blake's eyes as he held Donna by the throat. Determination. Anger. Relief.

"Still not exactly a hero, but maybe he redeemed himself at the end."

"I'd like to think so," Karen said. "I'm glad the house in Shoreline got busted."

Court snorted in disgust. "It's unlikely anyone will see jail time, though. The Parkers already have a deal signed and delivered. The church will likely close. Most of the kids are so brainwashed they think they wanted to be there."

Karen couldn't tell Court about the HIV meds she'd found at Parker's house. "Did you ever link Parker to Adin over at Rainbow Landing? That's how I picked up on Parker. I saw Adin talking to him outside the shelter."

"That's totally fucked up, as far as I can tell. Adin screened kids for Parker. He'd funnel the kids he thought were ripe for conversion therapy to Parker for one of his sleep-overs. Then, Parker would take the kids who were willing over to the conversion center." Court tilted his head toward Maria Wells. "That's Jamie's mom, right?"

"Yeah. I feel like I owe her an apology. She was right all along about Jamie being in danger, but I didn't want to believe it. More like I didn't want to believe *her*."

"Moms always go to the worst-case scenario. It's natural."

"I know. I do that more than I'd like to."

"Yeah, well, I'll tell you one thing, Jamie is a trooper," he said. "He's given us some pretty solid information on Mama Gong and her parties."

"He told me he did the parties to earn money for an apartment. He, Sage, Mullet, and a couple of other kids were pooling their funds."

"What these kids have been through…" Court shook his head.

Their shoulders touched as they leaned against the house.

Court stayed late to help pick up after everyone had left. They sat on the edge of the stage under the clear night sky.

"How much longer before the rain kicks in?" Court asked.

"Any day now. Enjoy it while it lasts."

"Now that everyone is gone, I was hoping we could chat." He pressed his shoulders against hers meaningfully.

"I didn't like lying to you about breaking into Jolly's place."

"Then don't do it again," Court said.

"You know it will happen again." Karen still hadn't told him about breaking into Garland Parker's home. No reason to, really. "I'll be breaking some law or other every now and again. It's the nature of the job."

"How about we just go out on a date or two, and see where things go. It's not like I'm proposing marriage here."

She leaned her head against his shoulder. "It could get really complicated."

"I thought you like complicated. Is it really about my being a cop? Or is it really about me being trans?"

Karen jerked her head up so she could look at him straight. "No, Court. Seriously? You think that would be a problem for me?"

"It is for a lot of people."

She considered his question seriously. Imagined the possibilities. "No. That is definitely not an issue for me. It's all about our jobs. What I do. What you do. I don't see them meshing long-term."

"Give it three months? We can go out on a few dates, and you can practice not breaking the law. Try it on."

"It's tempting, Detective Pearson. And what happens after those three months are up?"

"We talk. See how things are going."

Karen traced the scar on his face and rubbed her nose against his. "Okay, Detective. You get three months."

# ALSO BY LAURIE ROCKENBECK

When a prominent Seattle businessman is found hanging naked in a dominatrix's studio, lead Detective Court Pearson is pressured to find a fast, quiet solution to the man's death. Court's investigation uncovers secrets within his own department and raises the ghosts that linger from the suicide of his wife.

*I absolutely enjoyed this novel. Plenty of twists and turns. Rockenbeck does a wonderful job creating complex characters with nuance.*

— Dharma Kelleher, author Jinx Ballou Bounty Hunter series

*Rockenbeck deftly manages a very real crime story while still keeping you on the edge of your seat.*

— AJ Scudiere, author The NightShade Forensic Files

# ACKNOWLEDGMENTS

Thank you for reading *Cleansed by Fire*. If you first heard of me by reading *Bound to Die*, I appreciate you following the story onto the next stage.

I'd like to thank family and friends who continue to support me in this writing life. I'd like to thank my writing group for your attention to detail, your inspiration, and your unfailing honesty--Sandy Esene, Heidi Hostetter, Bridget Norquist, Ann Reckner, Emma Rockenbeck, Heather Stewart McCurdy, and Elizabeth Visser. Your insights, questions, and willingness to thwap me upside the head have helped make this a better book than I could possibly have done on my own.

My editors Jason Black at Plot to Punctuation, Jim Thomsen Creative, Meg Cooper at Pair of Nines Publishing, and Margy and Bill Rockenbeck have helped me plug plot holes and repair structural damage. Without them, this book would have been a complete mess and full of typos.

Thank you for your fine attention to detail! More thanks to authors Dharma Kelleher and AJ Scudiere for your support.

Many thanks to Scott Driscoll, Kathleen Alcala, and Pam Binder for their teaching and mentoring. My craft would be crap without your coaching and support.

Finally, my family gets the biggest hugs. Margy and Dave, my in-laws have donated their time-share many times to provide me a space for mini writing retreats. They've been there for my kids while I was away—feeding them, driving them, and doing whatever I wasn't doing because I was writing. Bill, Emma, and Eli—my husband and children--have supported me through this journey and put up with many night classes and my being away for days at a time. I love you all.

# ABOUT THE AUTHOR

Laurie Rockenbeck was raised a Navy brat and moved around a lot as a kid. She lives near Seattle with her family, two cats and four chickens. She graduated with a degree in journalism and quickly learned that writing fiction was a lot more fun. With a grandmother who started every story with *This is a true lie...*, there is no doubt that story-telling and exaggeration are part of her genetic make-up. She is creating a mystery series set in Seattle featuring a transmale detective and a professional dominatrix turned private investigator. Rockenbeck has her private investigation license but prefers writing about made up cases to investigating real ones.

Sign up for her newsletter by CLICKING HERE.

*For more information:*
www.laurierockenbeck.com

9 781947 234161